HORRORS

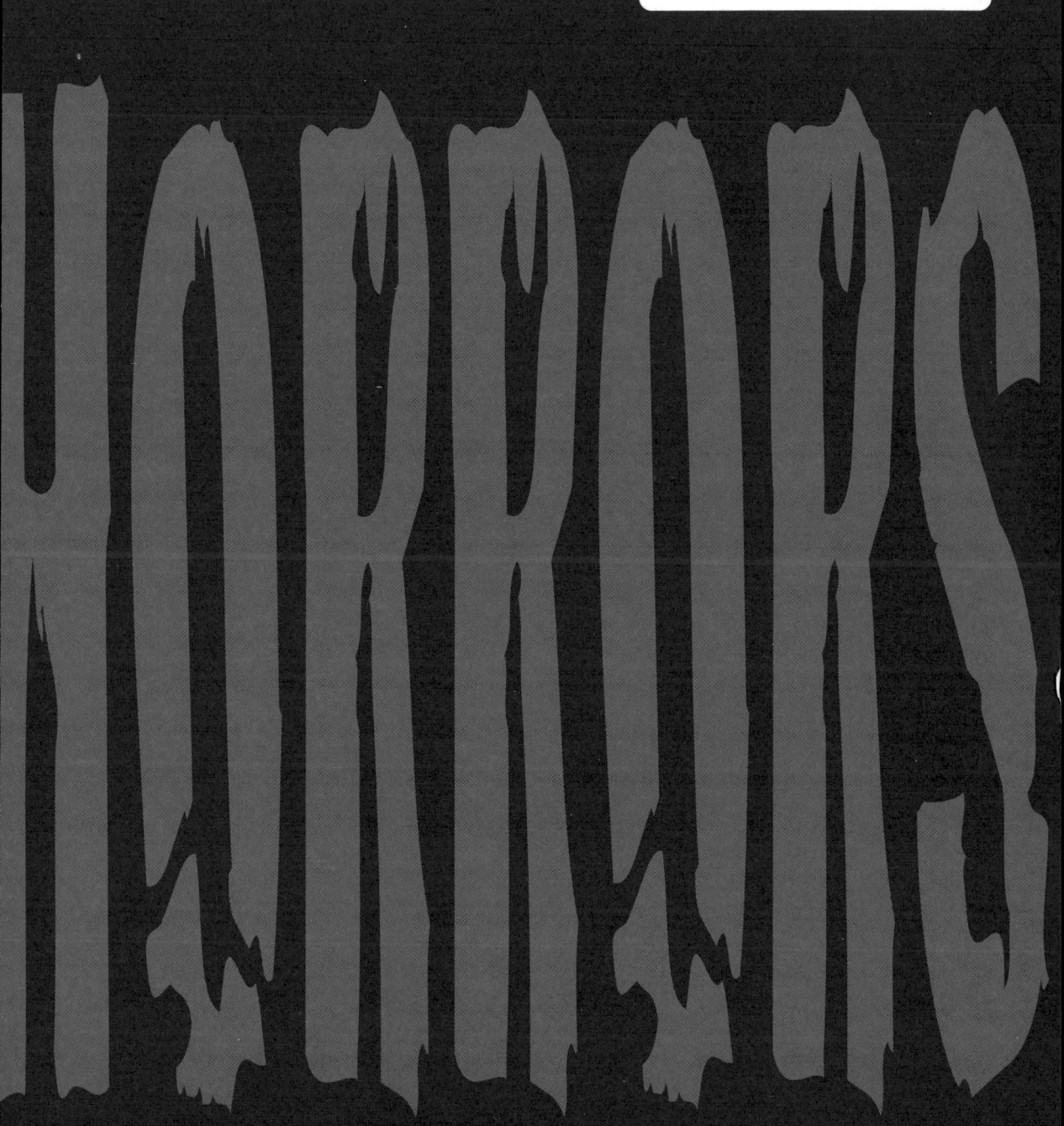

TALES OF TERROR AND SUSPENSE

CHAMBER OF CHILLS

HARVEY HORRORS
COLLECTED WORKS
CHAMBER OF CHILLS
VOLUME FOUR

November 1953 - December 1954

Issues 20 - 26

Foreword by

Kim Newman

PS Artbooks

HARVEY HORRORS
Collected Works
CHAMBER OF CHILLS
Volume Four

FIRST EDITION
2012

Bookshop ISBN 978-1-84863-465-7
Slipcase ISBN 978-1-84863-466-4
Traycase ISBN 978-1-84863-467-1

Published by
PS Artbooks Ltd.

A subsidiary of PS Publishing Ltd.,
www.pspublishing.co.uk
award-winning, UK-based, independent publisher of SF, fantasy, horror, crime & more...

Copyright © PS Artbooks 2012

Originally published in magazine form by Harvey Publications, Inc.

Foreword © Kim Newman 2012
Painting of Kim Newman © Martin McKenna 2012
Article on Vic Donahue © Peter Normanton 2012

Printed in China

design communique

Conditions of Sale:
This book is sold subject to the condition that it shall not, by way of Trade or otherwise, be lent, re-sold, hired out or otherwise circulated without the publisher's prior consent in any form of binding or cover other that in which it is published and without a similar condition including this condition being imposed on the subsequent purchaser.
PS Artbooks Ltd., PS Publishing Ltd., Grosvenor House, 1 New Road, Hornsea, East Yorkshire, HU18 1PG, England

All stories in this volume are public domain but the specific restored images and overall book design are © PS Artbooks Ltd. 2011.
All rights are reserved.
Permission to quote from or reproduce material for reviews or notices must be obtained from the publishers, PS Artbooks Ltd.

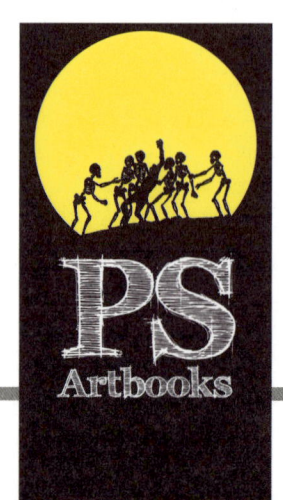

ACKNOWLEDGEMENTS

The Publishers would like to thank the following,
without whose help this project would have been
considerably more difficult than it ended up . . .
and it was pretty difficult to begin with:

Kim Newman
http://www.johnnyalucard.com/

Martin McKenna
http://www.martinmckenna.net/

Peter Normanton
http://fromthetomb.blogspot.com/

Heritage Auction Galleries
http://www.ha.com/c/index.zx

The Lewis Wayne Gallery
http://www.lewiswaynegallery.com/

Take a bow, folks!

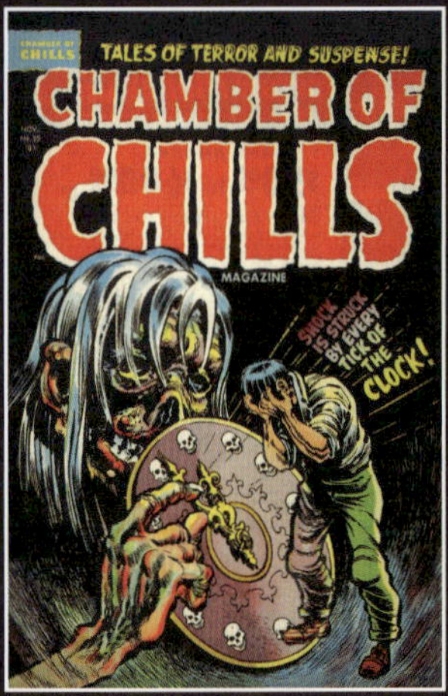
TALES OF TERROR AND SUSPENSE!
CHAMBER OF CHILLS
MAGAZINE
SHOCK IS STRUCK BY EVERY TICK OF THE CLOCK!

TALES OF TERROR AND SUSPENSE!
CHAMBER OF CHILLS
THE SHOCK OF YOUR LIFE AWAITS YOU IN...
NOSE FOR NEWS!

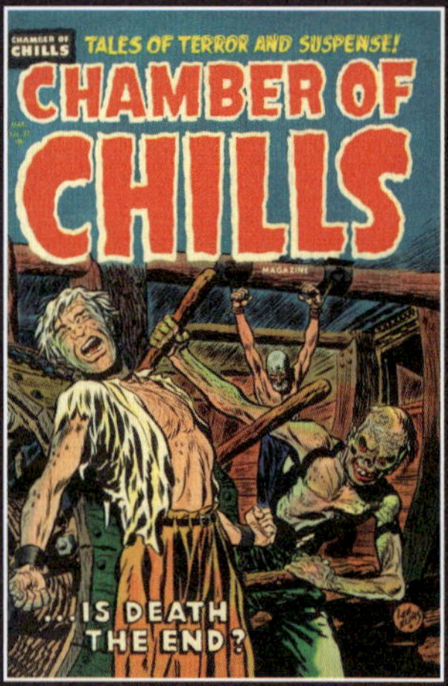
TALES OF TERROR AND SUSPENSE!
CHAMBER OF CHILLS
IS DEATH THE END?

TALES OF TERROR AND SUSPENSE!
CHAMBER OF CHILLS
A STRAIGHT LINE TO HORROR IS....
HEARTLINE!

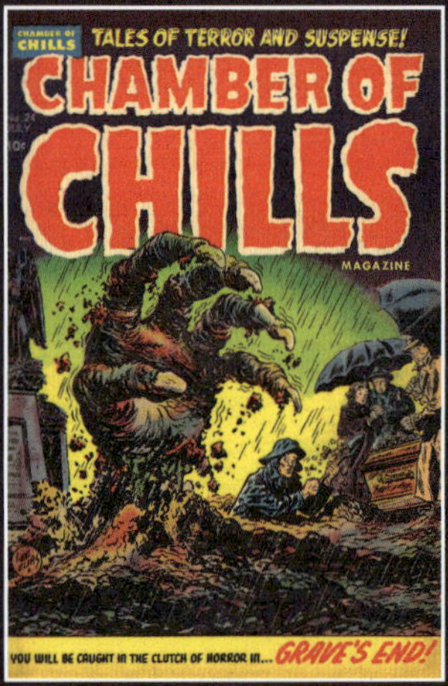
TALES OF TERROR AND SUSPENSE!
CHAMBER OF CHILLS
MAGAZINE
YOU WILL BE CAUGHT IN THE CLUTCH OF HORROR IN... GRAVE'S END!

TALES OF CHILLS AND SUSPENSE!
CHAMBER OF CHILLS

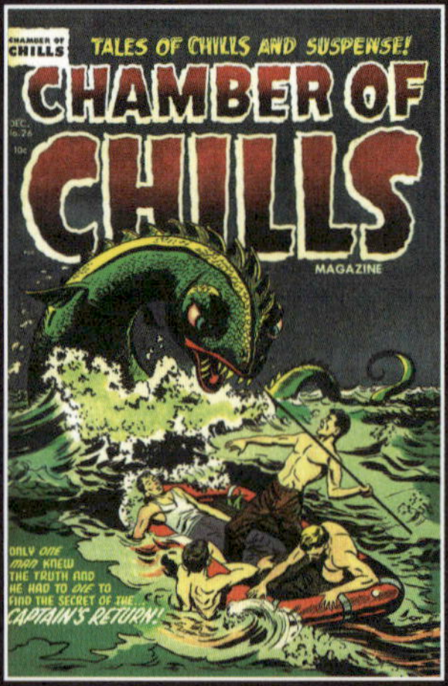
TALES OF CHILLS AND SUSPENSE!
CHAMBER OF CHILLS
MAGAZINE
ONLY ONE MAN KNEW THE TRUTH AND HE HAD TO DIE TO FIND THE SECRET OF THE CAPTAIN'S RETURN!

8
A foreword by
Kim Newman

12
Macabre Maestros - featuring artist
Vic Donahue

18
Chamber of Chills
November 1953 Issue #20

56
Chamber of Chills
January 1954 Issue #21

94
Chamber of Chills
March 1954 Issue #22

132
Chamber of Chills
May 1954 Issue #23

170
Chamber of Chills
July 1954 Issue #24

208
Chamber of Chills
October 1954 Issue #25

246
Chamber of Chills
December 1954 Issue #26

Kim Newman - Original illustration by Martin McKenna

Chamber of Chills

A foreword by
Kim Newman

In 1972, I went on a school trip to France. Having caught the monster bug from late-night TV screenings of Universal and Hammer Films, I was well along the road I've taken in life. At the ferry port, some kids joked that I was likely to be hauled aside by customs – which puzzled me, until I saw the list of items travellers were not permitted to bring into the United Kingdom. There, alongside drugs, guns, weapons-grade plutonium, disease-spreading French cheeses and slaves were horror comics.

Horror comics?

I was well aware that things which interested me were disapproved of in some official circles, but didn't know they were prohibited. Illegal? Horror films were on television and at cinemas – though I wouldn't be old enough to get past that laxly-enforced X certificate for a year or two, and going to a cinema underage would have the frisson of law-breaking – and there was a horror section in W.H. Smith's, even if it barely stretched to the **Pan Book of Horror Stories** and Dennis Wheatley. If horror comics existed, it was odd that I hadn't heard of them – though, as that customs notice suggested, not odd that I'd never seen them. I'd had a craze for comics a little before and overlapping with my craze for monsters, and remembered odd things that only now began to add up.

At the time when I was pretty much exclusively reading Marvel superhero comics, there was a fuss around **Amazing Spider-Man** #101 – not because Peter Parker was stuck with six arms, but because the new villain was a bleached-white, noseless longhair called Morbius, the Living Vampire (when Sam Raimi was directing Spider-Movies, it was suggested Michael Jackson would be ideal casting for Michael Morbius). I didn't get why Morbius was a big deal. Plenty of Marvel villains were monsters (eg: the Lizard, who also showed up in **ASM**#101). The X-Men had fought Frankenstein's Monster (well, an alien who looked like the Monster and supposedly inspired Mary Shelley, only to become a troubling continuity glitch when Marvel started issuing **Monster of Frankenstein**) and Thor, Daredevil and others had tangled with Mr Hyde (well, Marvel's version of same). So, Morbius was a vampire. So what?

Dean Skilton, my friend who read DC, was collecting Jack Kirby's run on **Jimmy Olsen**, and so I saw #142, which shouted 'it's the vampire bit! but like you've never seen it before!' on the cover and introduced Count Dragorin 'the Man From Transilvane' to give Superman's freckle-faced sidekick a hard time. **ASM**#101 and **Superman's Pal the New Jimmy Olsen** #142 were both cover-dated October 1971, though they'd have taken months to get to Somerset and into the hands of me and Dean. Only later did I realise that Marvel and DC rushed to get vampires into their comics because of a modification of the guidelines of the mysterious body which issued those puzzling 'approved by the Comics Code A Authority' stamps. Hitherto, as a result of Something Which Happened in the 1950s, vampires were a no-no. Now, apparently, they were allowed, if presented in a tasteful manner. Roy Thomas and Jack Kirby both hedged bets by making Morbius (a *Living* Vampire) and Dragorin (refugee from a Universal Monsters pocket universe) not quite proper vampires.

After the world didn't end when vampires featured in Marvel and DC Comics, there was a rush of monster-themed titles which (perhaps oddly) I didn't take to heart until much later. With a snobbery only possible in a thirteen-year-old monster/horror fan, I decided that the likes of Marvel's **Tomb of Dracula** and **Werewolf by Night** were beneath me. I was reading Lovecraft and Machen in those great Granada paperback editions by then. I could finally get into X films, which meant changing out of school uniform and genuinely believing that the ticket clerk thought we were eighteen, beginning with a cool double bill of **The Wild Angels** and **Dr Phibes Rises Again** at the Palace, Bridgwater, in 1973. A few weeks after that life-changing experience, me and Dean – he shared another of my enthusiasms, **MAD Magazine**, in the UK monthly edition and paperback collections – saw another great double bill, **The Fiend** and Amicus's **Tales From the Crypt**. Ralph Richardson as the Crypt Keeper! Peter Cushing coming back from the grave as a heart-ripping zombie! Joan Collins throttled by Santa! Nigel Patrick chased through a thin corridor lined with razor blades by his starving attack dog!

According to the novelisation of **Tales From the Crypt** – by Jack Oleck, a mainstay of the horror lite DC titles **House of Secrets** and **House of Mystery** which had survived under the Comics Code by never remotely offering anything scary – the film was based on a comic book published by William M. Gaines, the man behind **MAD Magazine**. Being well up on the **MAD** catalogue, I remembered how often horror strayed into the paperback collections – especially in the thicker-lined, more comic booky ones I recognised as drawing on the 1950s (Wally Wood's parody of 'the Heap' in Outer Sanctum, the punchline of the 'Batboy and Rubin' parody in which vampire Batboy drinks Rubin's blood through a straw) as opposed to the more sophisticated, magaziney material from the '60s (full of digs at Madison Avenue and suburban life). A kid at school had a strange mutant paperback animal: it looked like a MAD collection, but was called **Tales From the Crypt** and contained black and white reprints from Gaines's EC horror titles, including 'Poetic Justice' – the original of that Cushing episode from the Amicus film. Thanks to this, I had a sense of a horror/monster culture that was Before My Time and which had been erased from history, like those disgraceful pharaohs whose names were chipped out of hieroglphs for some unnameable crime.

In 1974, the **Radio Times**, of all publications, ran an interview with Milton Subotsky, the producer of **Tales From the Crypt**, in connection with a **Film Night** special about the company (which would be worth digging out of the archive, if it exists – I remember footage of Vincent Price on the set of **Madhouse**). In the accompanying picture, Subotsky was shown hugging an oversize hardback book, **The EC Horror Library of the 1950s** – which I realised I had to own. Smith's in Bridgwater stocked many books which were crucial to me – Denis Gifford's books on horror and science fiction films, Richard J. Anobile's photonovel-type preservations of key films (**Frankenstein**, **Psycho**, **The Maltese Falcon**, etc), those Granada classic pulp horrors (after Lovecraft, they moved on to Clark Ashton Smith, August Derleth, Frank Belknap Long and others). But they didn't have that **EC Horror Library**, a pricey item issued by Nostalgia Press, and so I had to ask a friend of my parents, the cartoonist Glen Baxter, who lived in London, to get it for me. It took Glen a while to track the thing down and post it to me. As compensation for the delay, he slipped in a press sheet for **The Abominable Dr Phibes**.

Besides reprinting key stories from **Tales From the Crypt**, **The Vault of Horror**, **The Haunt of Fear**, **Shock SuspenStories** and others, **The EC Horror Library** had introductory material (you know, like this is) setting the work in the context of the times and chronicling the horror comic boom and bust of 1950-54. Glen, old enough to have been a comics buyer in the 1950s, recounted first-hand the months when the heavy hand of official disapproval came down, certain that horror comics were more responsible for rising juvenile crime than rock 'n' roll or the communists. Martin Barker's little book **A Haunt of Fears** digs up the fascinating story of the **British** campaign against horror comics – in parallel with the American Old Witch Hunt – and the strange alliance of churchy do-gooders and the UK Communist Party (they hated horror comics because they were a pernicious **American** influence) which formed to combat the pulp paper ghouls you'll find in this volume. The **EC Horror Library** reprints a desperate ad Gaines ran as his business was circling the drain which alleges that anti-comics activists were 'red dupes', embodying sneaky Soviet policies. It was a sad, ridiculous assertion – the types of congressional bullies who wanted Gaines out of business were just as keen on stamping out commies – but in Britain it would have been true. Glen remembered he was made to burn his own precious stash of horror comics after a radio broadcast by Edgar Lustgarten, known for his lurid true crime books and perhaps itchy about the competition from crime comics, alleged that American crime and horror comics were toxic and evil.

An air of zeitgeisty desperation and neurosis which throbs throughout the final issues of Harvey's **Chamber of Chills** – in the ads, with their unbelievable money-making schemes (buy stuff to sell to your friends, if you have any friends after you've pestered and nagged them to take your shit shoes or suits) or 'bay window'-concealing male corsets or offers to 'borrow money by mail' almost as much as the stories, with their many monsters, murderers, creeps and crawlies. That cover image of 'shock is struck by every tick of the clock' illustrates a weird fable about an obsessed clockmaker, but it also evokes the Council of Nuclear Scientists' 'minutes to midnight' Armageddon clock, which suggests the likelihood of atomic annihilation. Reading these comics, you get a sense of anxiety, of a fast-changing world, of the possibility that any new house purchase or surgical procedure will result in hideous death. Even the title's most distinctive, **MAD**-ish feature, the 'chilly chamber music songs from the spook box' half-page song parody gags, are often more desperate than funny; and will now send you to lists of pre-Bill Haley hit parades for the mostly forgotten numbers being riffed on by the likes of 'Ghoul Train' and 'How Are Things in Dannemora?'. Time is running out, not just for the Affluent Society, but for the besieged horror comic book industry.

In **CoC**#21, January 1954, the unsigned editorial boasts that as of the next issue, 'you'll be in for a big surprise … all that can be said now is that this surprise has been worked on for months. And that it will be the most important development in terrror magazines! Read it and see it in action in next month's issue.' What could it be? 3-D? Hallucinogenic ink? A free severed head with each issue? In the event, **CoC**#22 weakly announces that 'the four greatest weird books, in announcing a new policy, have pulled one of the most terrifying coup d'etats in the sanctified realm of horror' and that Harvey's four bimonthly books will arrive on newsstands in a cycle so that a new issue shows up every two weeks. This at a time when newsstands were returning bundles of horror comics unsold (and undisplayed, even) to avoid being smashed up by angry mobs of comics burners (who were seldom comics buyers) or picketed by concerned mothers and clergymen. By the end of the year and December's **CoC**#26, it would all be over for horror comics … the Comics Code would wipe them out, though the victorious forces of censorship seemed not to notice their own success and kept harping on about the now-extinct beasts for decades thereafter …

This hardback edition, from Pulsatin' Peter Crowther and Pernicious PS Artbooks, lovingly assembles the once-despised – hell, **still**-despised, even by many comics fans who see Harvey horrors as sub-standard EC ripoffs – materials. Like Nostalgia Press's **EC Horror Library** – a seminal tome in the history of **reprinting** archive comics material – the paper, reproduction and general loving attitude to the content far exceeds that of the original issues, which seemed tatty even when new. These comics will warp your mind, stunt your growth and turn you into a seat-slashing, greasy-haired, pimple-faced delinquent – and, frankly, we could do with a few more of those around these days.

Kim Newman
London, June 2012

Macabre 💀 Maestros

Featuring artist
Vic Donahue
(August 28th 1918 - 2008, USA)

When, in 1948, Vic Donahue was invited to join the studio of those Golden Age giants, *Jack Kirby* and *Joe Simon*; he would have been considered by many to be something of a late comer. However, his credentials had already garnered their respect, which was echoed amongst his aspiring colleagues in the studio's employ.

Vic Donahue was born in Croydon, Pennsylvania, a town very close to the city of Philadelphia shortly before his family made the move to Omaha, where he would spend the rest of his formative years. As a boy, he showed an aptitude for art and in his mid-teens caught the eye of the local newspaper leading to him being accepted by the Omaha World Herald. There he remained working as an artist and touching up the Herald's pages prior to their going to press, until he enlisted for active service as the war in the Pacific became increasingly more intense. During these years, he was also known to have spent some time as a newspaper illustrator in Chicago and freelanced for several book publishers where he was asked to embellish the pages for a series of books. Vic was also a musician with a forte for the drums, which he played for a local dance band.

While Jack and Joe were boosting the moral of America's youth with the exploits of Captain America and his allies, Vic was on the front line in the Pacific serving as a combat artist in the US Marine Corps at Guadalcanal. In the Pacific Theatre of Operations, he was distinguished in being one of the first men to be officially recognised as a combat artist. In these hostile environs, he experienced the brutal nature of war as he captured the day-to-day lives of his compatriots, akin to a modern day Goya. Several years later, he would refer back to these encounters as he created some of the grittiest war comics of the day. Following the surrender of Japan in the wake of the cataclysmic events of August 1945, Vic returned to civilian life along with tens of thousands of former GIs. Soon after he set off to find work and discovered his wealth of experience placed him in an exceptional

Chamber of Chills #24 Dec 1951

Image kindly supplied by Heritage Auctions (HA.com)

Chamber of Chills #23 October 1951

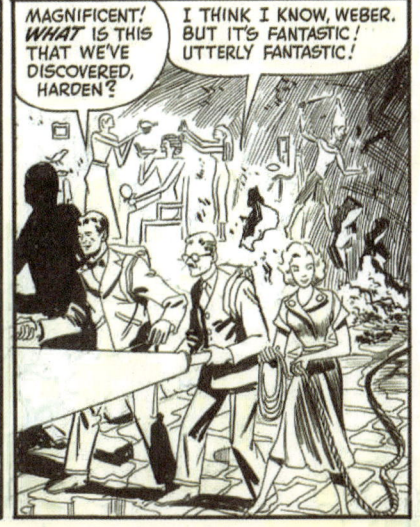

CHILLS #24-3

IN THE STEAMING, CRAWLING DARKNESS OF THE FLORIDA SWAMP COUNTRY, THE GHASTLY SPECTERS OF HORROR PLAN A MURDER... SHOWING THAT THERE ARE...

TWO WAYS TO DIE!

JAMES, THERE'S NO WAY OUT... OUR MONEY IS GONE! WE MUST DO SOMETHING TO GET MONEY! I'D EVEN KILL FOR IT!..

I'VE BEEN THINKING, LESLIE! OLD AUNT LENORE IS OUR ONLY LIVING RELATIVE... AND SHE'S VERY RICH! SUPPOSE WE LURED HER DOWN HERE...!

JAMES, ARE YOU THINKING THE SAME THING I AM...?

EXACTLY! GET HER DOWN HERE – AND IF ANYTHING WERE TO HAPPEN TO HER... AS HER ONLY RELATIVES, WE'D GET HER MONEY!!

Chamber of Chills #24 Dec 1951

Black Cat Mystery #33 Feb 1952

Chamber of Chills #10 July 1952

position. When a meeting was arranged with representatives from the Scripps-Howard newspaper syndicate in Cleveland, Ohio, Vic was summarily appointed as a feature artist. Here amongst his many duties he was assigned to illustrate articles on scientific subjects scribed by the eminent scientists of the day, including Henry Erikson, David Dietz and Charles Tracy. This was a remarkable period in his life, which resulted in his being twice nominated for the prestigious Pulitzer Prize for Best Newspaper Feature of the Year. His work also made its way north of the border to the Quebec based newspaper Le Petit Journal in 1947.

The year 1948 saw Vic begin to freelance in New York, while continuing to illustrate the interior pages of books and paint an assemblage of covers. These endeavours brought him to the attention of Simon and Kirby and, under their tutelage, his first comic art appeared in the pages of **Headline Comics** Vol. 4 #2 (October-November 1948) in a tale entitled "The Mystery Of Room 712". This wasn't the polished Donahue of a few years later, but it was a start and led to further appearances in **Headline** before he expanded his remit in Prize's companion titles **Justice Traps the Guilty**, **Real West Romances**, **Western Love**, **Young Love and Young Romance** between 1949 and 1950. His finale for the company came in the pages of their venture into terror, **Black Magic**. The sixth issue cover dated August 1951 was his inauguration as a horror artist in the five-page "A Wolf That Hummed A Nursery Rhyme". The style on show in this tale witnessed a departure from the crossing hatching and the close attention to detail that was so characteristic of his tales of romance; here he strived for a far darker appreciation of the medium. With Bill Draut, Mort Meskin and John Prentice now assuming their place as the lead artists in the Simon and Kirby studio, Vic now looked elsewhere for other comic related work.

Just as **Black Magic** #6 was about to hit the newsstands, Harvey Comics chose their moment to darken this already tenebrous domain having previously unveiled **Witches Tales** in the January of 1951. Vic's artistry was to make it to the debut issues of two comics that were to become paramount in Harvey's reign of terror, **Black Cat Mystery** #30 and **Chamber of Chills** #22. These latest additions to the boom in horror comics would appear almost inauspicious when compared to the depravity he set loose in the pages of **Chamber of Chills** #6 (March 1952). The tale "Dungeon of Doom" has been mentioned on many occasions, for no other reason than it rates as one of the most torturous tales of this unhallowed era. The scenes of an innocent woman being melted alive by a collective of deranged mutants below the streets of New

15

Chamber of Chills #14 November 1952

York City would have disturbed even the most hardened aficionado of horror. He later proved himself to be a zombie artist of repute in **Chamber of Chills** #14's (November 1952) poignant telling of "It". These tales disclosed an artist with a consummate ability for comic book narration, using ingeniously staged layouts contained within an uncomplicated panel structure, symptomatic of a highly accomplished draughtsman. Vic would continue to produce more than a score of subversive entries to Harvey's line of horror comics before the Comics Code summoned an end to this wholesale depravity. While he was terrorising the horror devotees of North America, Vic was also making a name for himself in Alfred Harvey's war comics **War Battles** and **Warfront**, producing several stories whose realism captured the uncompromising terror of the battlefield. He was able to draw upon so much of that which he had seen in the Pacific to create some of the most accurately depicted tales of war to see publication during the period.

The introduction of the Comics Code meant an end to his time in comic books and although he did find work with **Treasure Chest**, Vic resumed a lucrative career as an illustrator of books. He also turned his talent to the all too often neglected field of men's 'sweat magazines', providing interior renditions and covers for titles such as **Double-Action Detective Stories** and **Mike Shayne Mystery Magazine** between 1956 and 1959. These magazine covers contained more than a suggestion of Vic's affinity for fine art and his move to Vermont introduced him to a new friend and neighbour Norman Rockwell. He would move to Tuscon in 1962 before eventually returning to Omaha where he devoted his time to watercolour illustration and painting. These pursuits would earn him a reputation as one of the United States' most renowned western artists and acclaimed showings ensued at the Museum of Modern Art in New York, the National Gallery in Washington D.C. and the Whitney Gallery and Joslyn Museum in Omaha. His portrait of Pope John XXIII remains one of his most remembered works, being reproduced across the globe on both calendars and prayer cards.

Vic Donahue passed away having returned to his childhood home of Omaha. His time as a comic book artist was all too short; remembered only by Harvey Comics' most dedicated fans. His life as an artist however saw him acquire acceptance amongst a far wider and more appreciative audience, one that may have been quite appalled at his mastery of the darkest of genres.

Peter Normanton
2012

Chamber of Chills #14 November 1952

Chamber of Chills #14 November 1952

Chamber of Chills
November 1953 - Issue #20

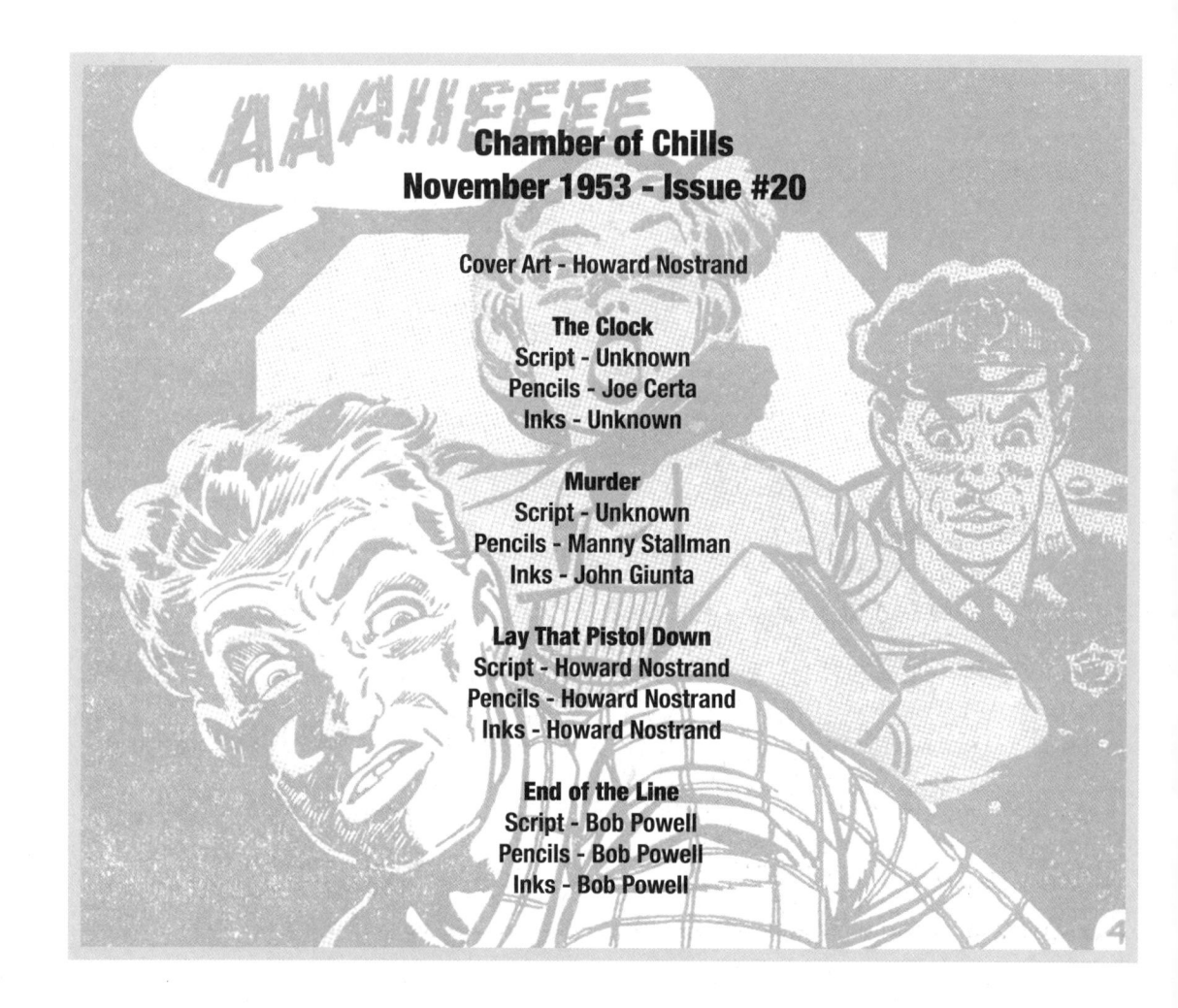

Cover Art - Howard Nostrand

The Clock
Script - Unknown
Pencils - Joe Certa
Inks - Unknown

Murder
Script - Unknown
Pencils - Manny Stallman
Inks - John Giunta

Lay That Pistol Down
Script - Howard Nostrand
Pencils - Howard Nostrand
Inks - Howard Nostrand

End of the Line
Script - Bob Powell
Pencils - Bob Powell
Inks - Bob Powell

Information Source: Grand Comics Database!
A nonprofit, Internet-based organization of international volunteers dedicated to building a database covering all printed comics throughout the world.
If you believe any of this data to be incorrect or can add valuable additional information, please let us know www.comics.org
All rights to images reserved by the respective copyright holders. All original advertisement features remain the copyright of the respective trading company.

Privacy Policy
All portions of the Grand Comics Database that are subject to copyright are licensed under a Creative Commons Attribution 3.0 Unported License.
This includes but is not necessarily limited to our database schema and data distribution format.
The GCD Web Site code is licensed under the GNU General Public License.

CHAMBER OF CHILLS

TALES OF TERROR AND SUSPENSE!

MAGAZINE

NOV. No. 20 10c

SHOCK IS STRUCK BY EVERY TICK OF THE CLOCK!

Borrow Money BY MAIL!
ON YOUR OWN SIGNATURE

PAY DOCTOR BILLS

PAY OLD DEBTS

PAY INSURANCE

HOME REPAIRS

ANY AMOUNT
$50.00 to $600.00

Our Guarantee If for any reason you return the money within 10 days after the loan is made there will be no charge or cost to you.

Quick – Easy – Private – Confidential

No Matter Where You Live in the U. S. — You Can Borrow from State Finance
No Endorsers or Co-Signers Needed — Complete Privacy Assured!

So much easier than calling on friends and relatives... so much more business-like... to borrow the money you need BY MAIL from fifty-year old State Finance Company. No matter where you live in the U. S., you can borrow any amount from $50.00 to $600.00 *entirely by mail in complete privacy* without asking anyone to co-sign or endorse your loan. Friends, neighbors, employer... will NOT know you are applying for a loan. Convenient monthly budget payments. If loan is repaid ahead of time, you pay ONLY for the time you actually use the money! If you are over 25 years of age and steadily employed, simply mail the coupon below for your FREE Loan Application and Loan Papers. State amount you want to borrow. *Everything you need to make a loan by return mail will be sent to you in a plain envelope!* So mail the coupon below today!

Thousands of Men and Women Like Yourself Use Our
Confidential By-Mail Loan Service
Repay in Convenient Monthly Installments

Monthly payments are made to fit your budget best. You can start paying six weeks after the loan is made, and repay in convenient monthly payments out of your future earnings. The cost of the loan is regulated by the laws of the State of Nebraska. For example, if the loan is repaid ahead of time, you pay only for the time you use the money... not one day longer! One out of three applicants get cash on their signature only. Furniture and auto loans are also made. No matter in which state you live, you can borrow from State Finance Company in complete confidence.

Clip and Mail Coupon Below for Fast Action

FREE LOAN PAPERS
NO OBLIGATION

If you are over 25 years of age and steadily employed, simply mail the coupon below for your Loan Application, sent to you in a plain envelope. There is no obligation, and you'll get fast action. You can get the money you need to help pay bills, to buy furniture, to repair your home or car, to pay doctor or hospital bills, to pay for a vacation, a trip, or for schooling, or for any other purpose. This money is here, waiting for you, so rush this coupon today!

CONFIDENTIAL
Complete privacy is assured. No one knows you are applying for a loan. All details are handled in the privacy of your own home, and entirely by mail. ONLY YOU AND WE KNOW ABOUT IT!

IMPORTANT
You must be at least 25 years old to borrow by mail from State Finance.

Old Reliable Company —
MORE THAN 50 YEARS OF SERVICE

STATE FINANCE COMPANY was organized in 1897. During the past 54 years, we have helped over 1,000,000 men and women in all walks of life. Confidential loans are made all over America, in all 48 states. We are licensed by the Banking Department of the State of Nebraska to do business under the Small Loan Law.

You'll enjoy borrowing this easy, confidential, convenient way from this old, responsible company in whom you can place the greatest confidence.

STATE FINANCE COMPANY
Dept. F-143, 323 Securities Bldg.
Omaha 2, Nebraska

STATE FINANCE COMPANY   MAIL COUPON TODAY!
Dept. F-143, 323 Securities Bldg., Omaha 2, Nebr.

Without obligation rush full details in plain envelope, with FREE Loan Application and Loan Papers for my signature, if I decide to borrow.

Name..

Address..

City........................State....................

Occupation......................Age................

Amount you want to borrow $..........

CHAMBER OF CHILLS MAGAZINE, NOVEMBER, 1953, Vol. 1, No. 20, IS PUBLISHED BI-MONTHLY by WITCHES TALES, INC., 1860 Broadway, New York 23, N.Y. Entered as second class matter at the Post Office at New York, N.Y under the Act of March 3, 1879. Single copies 10c. Subscription rates, 10 issues for $1.00 in the U. S. and possessions, elsewhere $1.50. All names in this periodical are entirely fictitious and no identification with actual persons is intended. Contents copyrighted, 1953, by Witches Tales, Inc., New York City. Printed in the U.S.A. Title Registered in U. S. Patent Office.

WELCOME

CHAMBER OF CHILLS *Contents* NO. 20

THE CLOCK

MURDER

LAY THAT PISTOL DOWN

END OF THE LINE

The tops in horror brings you once again a trail of endless suspense! CHAMBER OF CHILLS, a terror mag with the shock touch, opens its doors to the newest treat in terror!

Here we have an assortment of stories designed for electrifying impact. Every one has been built on the geometric plane of horror, well-calculated to keep you in suspense from start to the shocking finish!

Every tick of THE CLOCK runs off an experience in clashing, mind-searing thoughts... where every cog wheel meshes with evil!

An attempt at MURDER fills the package for death. It is the frantic account of a man possessed with evil, but caught in its web!

A recluse, caught in the web of the shadows he calls home, suddenly is confronted with a Martian. This is the meat of LAY THAT PISTOL DOWN, a science-fiction saga that rocks the heavens!

You'll be trapped in a horror unlimited that rocks with frantic fury till you reach the END OF THE LINE!

But now is the time for the unknown, the time to face shocking suspense that waits in the CHAMBER OF CHILLS!

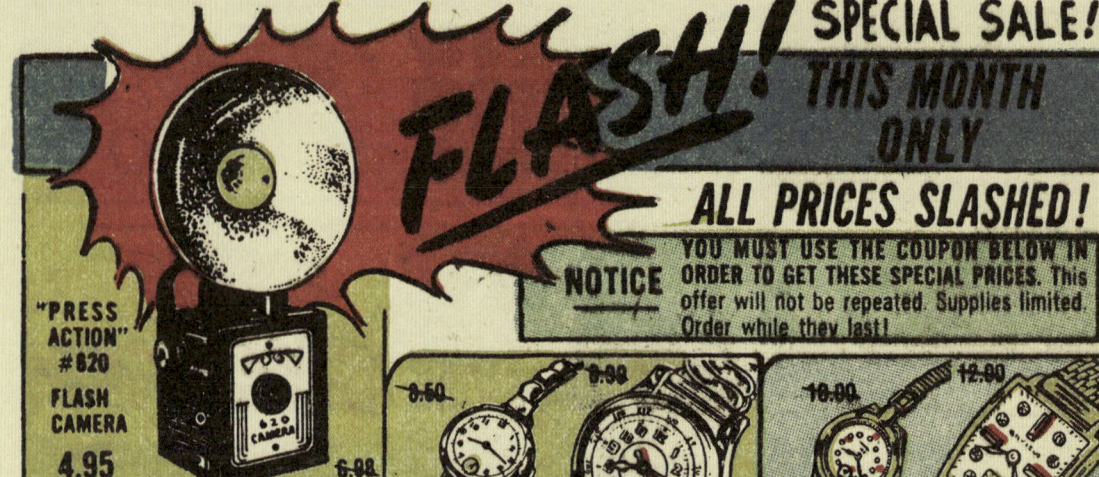

FLASH! SPECIAL SALE!
THIS MONTH ONLY
ALL PRICES SLASHED!

NOTICE — YOU MUST USE THE COUPON BELOW IN ORDER TO GET THESE SPECIAL PRICES. This offer will not be repeated. Supplies limited. Order while they last!

"PRESS ACTION" #620 FLASH CAMERA
~~6.98~~ **4.95**

INDOORS! OUTDOORS! BLACK & WHITE! FULL COLOR! PARTIES! NEWS SHOTS!

An AMAZING Camera. Takes pictures DAY or NIGHT, indoors or outdoors. Sharp BLACK and WHITE snapshots or FULL COLOR photos, using Kodacolor film. 12 Big pictures on 1 Roll of film. Flash attachment snaps on or off in seconds. Catch valuable news photos. Win admiration at parties, dances. NOW $4.95

CHECK FOR FILM ☐ Special #620 Orthochromatic, 3 ROLLS for $1.00

~~8.50~~ **NOW 6.98**
PERFECT for active women and girls. Fine JEWELLED movement in dainty case. GILT hands and numbers. Smart Link Expansion Bracelet. NOW $6.98

~~9.98~~ **NOW 6.99**
BEST for active men and boys. SHOCK-RESISTANT and ANTI-MAGNETIC! Luminous Dial! Jewelled Movement! Red Sweep-Second! Expansion Bracelet. NOW $6.99

~~10.00~~ **NOW 8.49**
Ladies' Jewelled Watch in a smart Gold finish case. Dial has 12 Flashing imitation DIAMONDS and RUBIES. Glamorous Snake Bracelet. NOW $8.49

~~12.00~~ **NOW 9.95**
Rich, Flashing Men's Jewelled Watch with 11 Sparkling imitation DIAMONDS and RUBIES. Smart Gold finish case. DeLuxe Basket-weave Bracelet. NOW $9.95

INITIAL RING — 3.79
A Handsome, Masculine Ring with your own INITIAL set in Raised GOLD effect on a BRILLIANT RUBY-RED color stone with 2 SPARKLING imitation DIAMONDS on the sides. Rich 14K R G P. ~~4.95~~ NOW $3.79

FREE NO-RISK HOME TRIAL
SEND NO MONEY! We want you to inspect and enjoy this fine quality merchandise — right in your own home. You risk nothing! If not delighted, return for FULL PRICE REFUND. Every article we sell is GUARANTEED! Order from this famous company and be convinced.
IDEAL CO. BOX 232, MAD. SQ. STA., N.Y. 10, N.Y.
GUARANTEED SAVINGS

POWERFUL Private Line WALL PHONES
BATTERY-OPERATED
Inter-Office • Room-to-Room • House-to-Garage • Shop-to-Storeroom

~~7.50~~ **NOW 5.49** COMPLETE SET
for HOME or OFFICE USE

NOW!! Your own PRIVATE-LINE "PHONE SYSTEM" that sets up in minutes—easily—anywhere you want it. Powerful BATTERY-OPERATED circuit carries two-way conversations loud and clear. Signal buttons and buzzers on each phone. SAVE TIME, SAVE STEPS—just pick up the receiver, buzz your party and make the call! A thousand uses for this amazing instrument. All-steel construction in handsome Hammertone Enamel finish. Complete set of 2 Phones, 50 feet of Wire, Instructions and Guarantee. NOW $5.49

NOTE: When ordering this item, enclose $1.00 Deposit.

BRILLIANT MEN'S WATCH
15 JEWELS — ~~20.00~~ **12.95**

A MAGNIFICENT Men's Watch that you'll be real proud of! GUARANTEED 15 JEWEL MOVEMENT in a Handsome GENUINE 10K R.G.P case. Rich, brilliant GOLDEN-SPRINKLED Dial with flashing GILT-NUGGET hour dots. Contrasting Jet-Black center. Genuine Alligator-grain leather strap. TERRIFIC VALUE. NOW $12.95

"PRINCE" RING — NOW $3.49
Here's a Rich, Massive Ring for you. With a Huge Flashing imitation DIAMOND and 6 Fiery Red imitation RUBIES. 14K R G P. NOW $3.49

CLUSTER RING — NOW $3.49
with your OWN RAISED GOLD-COLOR INITIAL on a Rich RUBY-RED color stone set in a circle of Blazing imitation DIAMONDS. 14K R G P. NOW $3.49

ROMANCE SET — ~~4.95~~ **3.74**
Real Sparkling, Shining BEAUTY! Engagement Ring has 4 Flashing Brilliants and a BEAUTIFUL imitation DIAMOND SOLITAIRE. 7 Twinkling Brilliants in the Wedding Ring. 12K GOLD Filled. Both rings NOW $3.74

DIAMOND RING — NOW $4.98
for Men 14K R.G.P. REAL DIAMOND CHIP on Gen. MOTHER OF PEARL face. 2 RUBY color side SPARKLERS. NOW $4.98

BIRTHMONTH RING — NOW $2.98
for Men. BRILLIANT STERLING SILVER with your PERSONAL BIRTHMONTH STONE. Choose Ruby, Emerald, or Sapphire colors. NOW $2.98

MAIL THIS COUPON
IDEAL CO., Dept. CS-1S
Box 232 Mad. Sq. Sta., New York 10, N.Y.

SEND NO MONEY! Just cut out pictures of articles desired and attach to this coupon. Pay postman plus few cents postage and excise tax on delivery. THEN EXAMINE IN YOUR OWN HOME. SATISFACTION IS GUARANTEED OR YOUR MONEY BACK.

PLEASE PRINT

NAME _____
ADDRESS _____
TOWN _____ STATE _____

(Send RING SIZES, INITIAL WANTED and your BIRTH-MONTH. If you need more room attach a sheet of paper.)

Home Sweet Home
Home Sweet Home

THE CLOCK

THE CLOCK IS COMPLETE! IT'S FINISHED. I'VE MADE IT! BUT-- BUT RACHEL IS DEAD!
Home Sweet Home
1

THAT'S THE CLOCK, ALL RIGHT! THE CLOCK THAT STARTED IT ALL...THAT TOOK RACHEL'S LIFE!
TICK TOCK
I'M A CLOCKMAKER...ONE OF THE BEST IN TOWN! BUT I WAS ALSO A HUSBAND WHO WAS VERY MUCH IN LOVE. RACHEL THERE--WAS MY WIFE!
SHE'S NOT PRETTY TO LOOK AT NOW... LIKE MY CLOCK.. BUT SHE USED TO BE! RACHEL WAS THE WORLD TO ME! GUESS NO HARM IN TELLING YOU--WHAT WITH THE CLOCK ALL FINISHED NOW... I LOVED HER WITH MY HEART AND SOUL!
TICK TOCK TOCK TICK TOCK
RACHEL AND I SHARED THE LOVE OF OUR CLOCK SHOP. HOW WE LOVED IT!
JUST THINK, DARLING! AFTER FIFTEEN YEARS, WE'RE STILL NOT BORED WITH OUR LIVES! YOU LOVE ME--DON'T YOU?
OF COURSE I DO, HONEY! THAT'S WHY I SPEND ALL DAY IN MY WORK-SHOP HERE! EVERY-THING I MAKE--I MAKE FOR YOU! I JUST ATTACHED THE TIME-SPRING! LISTEN!
TICK..TOCK.. TICK..TOCK.. TICK!
2

Panel 1:
Then one day, I came up with the idea of making this clock... a new, *different* clock...

"Cal, dear... your supper is getting cold! Please put down your work for a moment and come inside!"

"Wait-- just a few more minutes... this coil-spring belongs here-- and I can put another small rod there..."

Panel 2:
I started on it, getting the pieces together, designing it-- thinking it out-- *forming* it! It took up most of my time...

"Will you *please* come to bed? It's almost four in the morning! How can you work so much?"

"Shh-- don't bother me now! This is very *important*! Go back to bed, Rachel!"

Panel 3:
At first, Rachel didn't mind. She went along with it. But as my time got to be taken up with the clock, my attention towards Rachel became so much the less...

"It's going to be the *best* clock in town! Everyone will point to it and say that *Cal Stevens* made it!"

"Yes-- at the *expense* of his *wife*!"

Panel 4:
It began to affect her. She got mad. Her attitude began to change. Despite this, I still paid more attention to the clock...

"You never help me around the house anymore! You never fix things that *need* fixing! Nobody gave you an order for that clock! Where's our money going to come from?"

"Yup... nearly finished with this thing, huh? What's that, Rachel?"

Panel 5:
Things got worse! The more I progressed toward the completion of the clock, the less I showed any outward signs of love towards Rachel...

"We could go to that movie in town if we hurry, Cal. *Please*-- just for *tonight*! Stop working on that horrible clock! *Please*!"

"*Can't*, Rachel-- I'm almost through! *Wait* till you *hear* it *chime*! Right pretty it is! Right pretty!"

Panel 6:
"That's the last straw! I'm not putting up with your stubborness any longer! You're *not* going to work on that clock!"

"Please, dear... temper... temper... you'll feel better in the morning! Wait till you see it! I just painted it and, I--"

I THINK I'LL SEE IT RIGHT NOW-- THIS VERY INSTANT!
WHERE ARE YOU GOING, DEAR? IT'S NOT LIKE YOU TO LOOK SO STRANGE--!
IT'S NOT LIKE YOU TO IGNORE ME FOR WEEKS FOR A MISERABLE CUCKOO CLOCK THAT DOESN'T BRING IN ANY MONEY!
IT'S NOT A MISERABLE-- RACHEL! WHAT ARE YOU DOING?
I'M GOING TO SMASH THAT THING TO BITS! I'M GOING TO BEAT IT TO A PULP! I'LL TEACH YOU NOT TO PAY ANY ATTENTION TO ME!
NO--RACHEL --NO!!
NO, DEAR --NO!
CAL--Y-YOU'RE CHOKING ME! CAL!
PLEASE STOP, HONEY! YOU MUSTN'T TOUCH THE CLOCK! PLEASE--DEAR-- STOP! PLEASE!
LET-- GO-- CAN'T BREATHE! CAL... CAL...
TICK TICK TICK TOCK
CAAAL...
--MY PRETTY CLOCK, DARLING-- YOU WANT TO HURT IT! YOU WANT TO SMASH IT! YOU MUSTN'T, HONEY! I LOVE YOU--BUT I CAN'T LET YOU DO IT!
ARR-R-RGHH.
4

I DIDN'T WANT RACHEL **TO DIE.** I JUST WANTED TO STOP HER -- THAT'S ALL! BUT RACHEL DOESN'T BREATHE ANYMORE. SHE DOESN'T KISS ME ANYMORE! SHE DOESN'T GET ANGRY AT ME! SO I HAD TO MAKE SOME **CHANGES** ON THE CLOCK...

THERE IT IS -- THE CLOCK THAT STARTED IT ALL! MY *PRETTY CLOCK!*

TICK TICK TOCK

IF RACHEL COULD SEE THE CLOCK -- IN ITS PERFECTION! IF SHE COULD SEE IT WORK AS ONLY *I* COULD MAKE IT WORK!

HEAR IT? IT'S SO PRECISE! THAT'S *MY* WORK! BUT RACHEL WAS JEALOUS OF IT, POOR DEAR! ONLY-- SHE'S DEAD NOW -- SO IT DOESN'T MATTER! THE CHANGES WILL TAKE CARE OF EVERYTHING... YES I'VE *REALLY* MADE A CLOCK!

TICKTOCK TICKTOCK

POOR RACHEL... I ONLY *MEANT* TO *STOP* HER! SHE'LL HAVE TO *KNOW* THAT! HEAR IT? THREE SECONDS...

TICKTOCK TICK TOCK

TICK

...ONE SECOND... I'M COMING, RACHEL!

TOCK

BLLAAAAAMMM!!

Murderer AT LARGE

"Don't worry, Mom. Everything will be all right. I'll be through in another few minutes anyhow." Eloise smiled into the phone, as if her mother could see her calmness.

"Please don't worry, Mom," she continued. "The murderer isn't going to strike here. Besides Mr. Stewart will protect me."

She winked at Mr. Stewart, the building's janitor as he swept the office.

Mr. Stewart whispered back: "Don't know how much help I could be."

"OK, Mom," said Eloise into the phone, "see you soon."

She hung up the phone then and said to Mr. Stewart, "Gads, that murderer is getting everyone excited. How many times have I had to stay late at the office, and no one would even call. Now, my mother calls three times!"

"Maybe she's got a reason," said Mr. Stewart still sweeping away.

"Don't tell me you're worried about that murderer?" Eloise laughed.

"Five murders ain't to be sneezed at," said Mr. Stewart. "But it's you who should be worried . . . only likes girls, you know."

"Oh, Mr. Stewart, don't you pay any attention to those scare headlines in the papers. It doesn't mean a thing."

Mr. Stewart stopped his sweeping. "Young lady," he said. "I don't make myself out to be a brainy man — else I wouldn't be working here — but if I was your mother I don't think I'd be allowing you to be working late at the office!"

"Mr. Stew —"

Eloise was interrupted by a . . . SWOOSHH! at the window.

"What's that?" shouted Mr. Stewart.

They turned around and saw . . .

"Just a piece of paper," smiled Eloise. "Gosh, Mr. Stewart, you're all bumped up with goose-pimples. Like you said, you have no reason to be afraid. The big, bad murderer only kills women!"

"I guess I'm afraid . . . for you."

Eloise had to laugh. "You're awfully sweet," she said. "I believe you really are afraid for me. But you don't have to. I don't even give this murderer a second thought."

Mr. Stewart looked at her with a strong steady stare. "You know," he said, "you can never tell who this murderer might be . . . it might even be me!"

Eloise was startled for a second. Then she chuckled. "But you really aren't," she said, "are you?"

"I don't know," he answered casually.

Still Eloise didn't seem excited. "You know," she said, "it could even be me!"

Mr. Stewart didn't say another word. He finished his sweeping and strolled silently from the room.

A few minutes later, Eloise cleaned off her desk, gathered her things together and walked out of the office. She walked down the stairs and passed Mr. Stewart in the lobby.

Then there were screams!

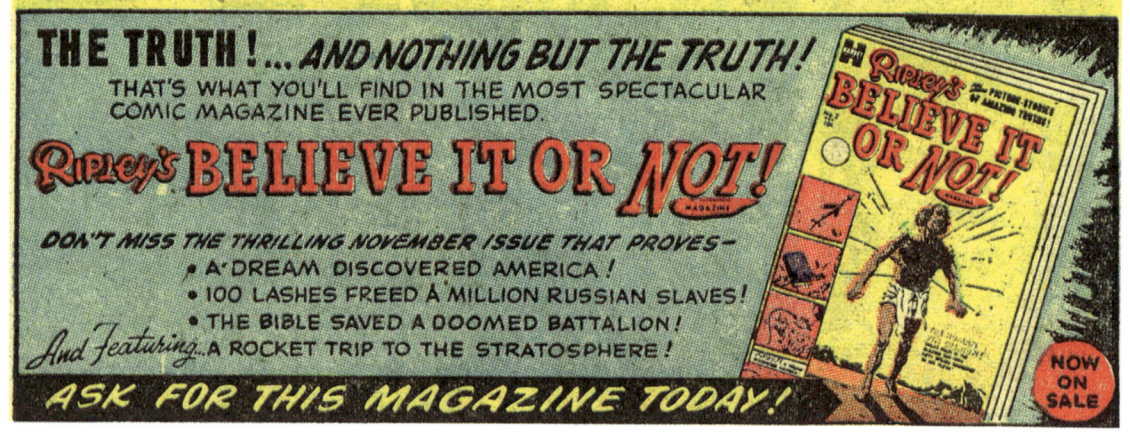

THE TRUTH! ... AND NOTHING BUT THE TRUTH!
THAT'S WHAT YOU'LL FIND IN THE MOST SPECTACULAR COMIC MAGAZINE EVER PUBLISHED.

Ripley's BELIEVE IT OR NOT!

DON'T MISS THE THRILLING NOVEMBER ISSUE THAT PROVES —
- A DREAM DISCOVERED AMERICA!
- 100 LASHES FREED A MILLION RUSSIAN SLAVES!
- THE BIBLE SAVED A DOOMED BATTALION!

And Featuring...A ROCKET TRIP TO THE STRATOSPHERE!

ASK FOR THIS MAGAZINE TODAY!

NOW ON SALE

CHILLY CHAMBER MUSIC
SONGS FROM THE SPOOK BOX!

COME ON-A-MY HOUSE... TO MY HOUSE-A-COME ON...

CLICK!

I'M-A-GONNA GIVE YOU PLENTY OF *LOVIN'* WHEN THE LIGHT'S ALL GONE!

BUT YOU'RE GONNA SCREAM AND HOLLER... AND NOBODY'S GONNA CALL YOU *"LIAR"*...

'CAUSE WHEN YOU COME ON-A-MY HOUSE YOU'RE GONNA LOOK AT A REAL *VAMPIRE!*

CHILLY CHAMBER MUSIC
SONGS FROM THE SPOOK BOX!

CRACK!

MUUU-UU-LE TRAIN... YAAAAAAA!

CRACK!

GIT ALONG THERE... YOU SON OF A BOW-LEGGED COW...

CRACK!

C'MON...YOU RUBBER-HIDE, CROSS-EYED SOW... THIS AIN'T A *MULE TRAIN*...

CRACK!

YAAAAAAA! IT'S A... *GHOUL TRAIN!*

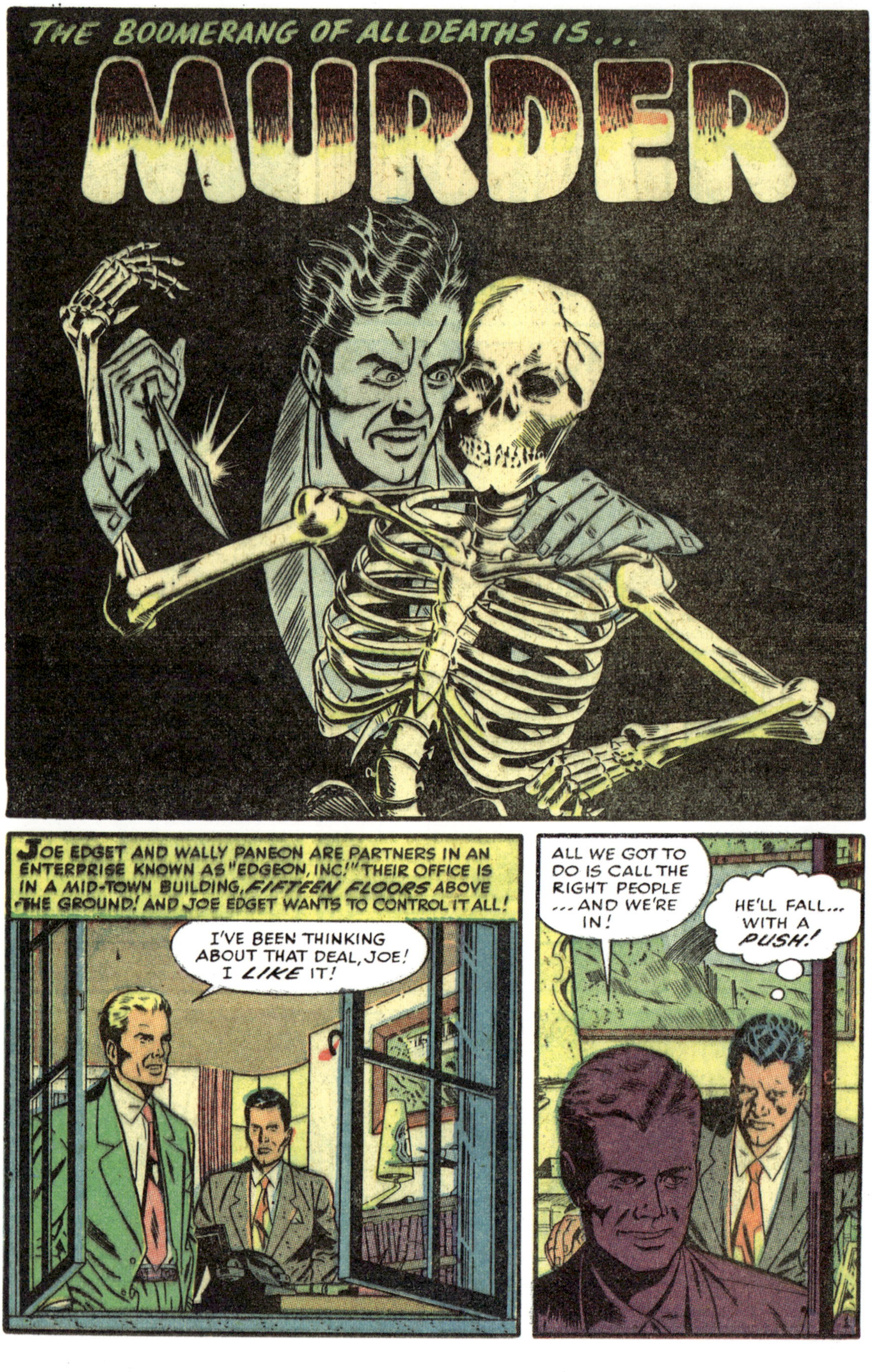
THE BOOMERANG OF ALL DEATHS IS...
MURDER
JOE EDGET AND WALLY PANEON ARE PARTNERS IN AN ENTERPRISE KNOWN AS "EDGEON, INC!" THEIR OFFICE IS IN A MID-TOWN BUILDING, FIFTEEN FLOORS ABOVE THE GROUND! AND JOE EDGET WANTS TO CONTROL IT ALL!
I'VE BEEN THINKING ABOUT THAT DEAL, JOE! I LIKE IT!
ALL WE GOT TO DO IS CALL THE RIGHT PEOPLE ...AND WE'RE IN!
HE'LL FALL... WITH A PUSH!

JUST... A LITTLE CLOSER!
YEP, JOE... EVERYTHING IS FINE!
WE'LL BE RICH SOMEDAY, JOE! I'VE GOT NO DOUBTS ABOUT IT!
BUT, IT'LL ALL BE MINE, WALLY!
BBRRING
JOE EDGET'S ATTEMPT AT MURDER WAS HALTED BY THE PHONE! HIS ONCE-CALM CRIMINAL ATTITUDE WAS SHOCKED INTO NERVOUSNESS!
EXCUSE ME, JOE!
YEAH--YEAH, SURE! GO AHEAD, WALLY!
HEY, JOE... WHAT ABOUT A WEEK-END AT FISHING! I GOT THE SPORTING GOODS STORE ON THE LINE! WE COULD MAKE IT A REAL VACATION! WHAT ABOUT IT, JOE?
SOUNDS GOOD TO ME, WALLY! I--I'M FOR IT!
USUALLY, SATURDAY BEGINS A WEEK-END. JOE EDGET THINKS THAT IT WAS LATE FRIDAY NIGHT OR EARLY THE NEXT MORNING THAT HE THOUGHT OF MURDERING WALLY PANEON AGAIN! ANYHOW, BOTH WERE IN THE WOODS!
THE TROUT'S FINE AROUND HERE! WE'LL TAKE A CANOE ...AND TRY THE STREAM JUST BY THE NEXT BEND!
YEAH! A CANOE'LL BE GREAT!
IT'S DEAD IN THIS NECK OF THE WOODS! I CAN KILL HIM AND NOBODY WOULD KNOW! A SIMPLE "ACCIDENT"!..
2

WALLY AND JOE RENTED A CANOE. WALLY SAID THE FISHING MIGHT BE BETTER UPSTREAM AND THEY PADDLED THERE. THE CANOE CUT THROUGH THE WATER LIKE A RAZOR...
TAKE IT EASY, JOE! I CAN'T SWIM, YOU KNOW!
I KNOW IT, WALLY! BUT... YOU'LL NEVER LEARN HOW TO!
AND... YOU'LL NEVER KNOW WHAT HIT YOU!
HEY, THEAH!
OVEH HEAH, WATER'S CALMER! FISHIN' IS REAL GOOD! HOW YE BEEN DOIN'?
JOE EDGET WAS STOPPED AGAIN. IT WAS A BABBLING GEEZER...SOME GUY WHO SEEMED TO STEP INTO THE PICTURE FROM NOWHERE! HE WAS ENOUGH, THOUGH, ENOUGH TO STOP ANY FURTHER ATTEMPT!
HAVEN'T STARTED YET! WE WERE JUST HEADING UPSTREAM!
PRETTY GOOD UP THERE, TOO! DON'T USE WORMS! AIN'T NO GOOD FOR TROUT! TRY PIECE O' BACON RIND!
3

SATURDAY PASSED INTO SUNDAY! IT WAS TIME TO GO...
IT WAS RESTFUL, JOE! I'M SORRY IT'S OVER, BUT... TONIGHT WE GOT THAT PARTY AT PETE'S HOUSE!
YEAH! ALMOST FORGOT ABOUT THAT! I'LL MEET YOU THERE!
LATER...
THE WHOLE WEEK-END... SHOT! I'LL NEVER GET ANOTHER CHANCE!
NAW! OPPORTUNITY'LL KNOCK AGAIN! MAYBE... AT PETE'S PARTY!
THE PROCESS OF DRESSING WAS OVER. JOE EDGET ARRIVED AT PETE'S HOUSE. THE MUFFLED SOUNDS OF THE PARTY CAME TO HIM BUT HE WAS STILL PONDERING HIS PARTNER'S ONCOMING MURDER!
I'VE GOT TO FIGURE OUT A WAY...
I -- HOLD IT! THIS IS WALLY'S CAR! IF I COULD JUST TINKER WITH THE BRAKES... A SLIGHT ADJUSTMENT COULD SEND IT ROLLING!
AS JOE EDGET WALKED TO THE PARTY, HE WAS IN GOOD SPIRITS. HE WAS STIMULATED BY THE THOUGHT OF MURDER! WALLY PANEON WAS STIMULATED BY SOMETHING ELSE!
HIYA, JOEY BABY! YOU'RE A LITTLE LATE... BUT HERE'S ONE TO CATCH UP!
THANKS, WALLY! I NEED IT!
DOWN THE HATCH, LAD! SIP N' SUP... AND DRINK IT UP! NOTHIN' LIKE A LITTLE HOT CHOCOLATE TO CURL YOUR TOES, EH? HA! HA!
4

SOON AFTERWARDS, JOE EDGET QUIETLY LEFT THE PARTY...OR HE WAS TRYING TO LEAVE IT...
WHERE Y' GOING, JOE?
I'LL BE BACK IN A MINUTE, HONEY! LEFT MY CIGARETTE LIGHTER IN THE CAR!
AT WALLY PANEON'S CAR...
NOW...TO TAMPER WITH THE BRAKE DRUM...
WHEN ...WALLY LEAVES... HE'LL BE FEELING HIGH! HE'LL SPEED...THE BRAKES WON'T HOLD...AND...BIFF! THE END!
JOE EDGET MANIPULATED. EVERYTHING WAS GOING RIGHT. A SPECK DROPPED DOWN FROM THE UNDERCARRIAGE OF THE CAR AND AS HE TURNED HIS HEAD, HE SAW...
WHA?!! SOMEBODY'S... WATCHING ME!
JOE SLID OUT AND CAME FACE-TO-FACE WITH WALLY PANEON!
HELLO, JOE--WHAT D'YA KNOW? THOUGHT I'D COME OUT AND SEE HOW THINGS WERE, JOE! PLEASANT EVENING, ISN'T IT?
YEAH, WALLY... YEAH...
GEE, JOE, YOU SHOULDN'T WORRY YOURSELF ABOUT MY CAR LIKE THAT.
I-I W-WAS JUST FIXING IT, WALLY. THAT'S ALL I WAS DOING!
I KNOW, JOE. BUT FORGET IT--FORGET EVERYTHING! YOU AIN'T GOING TO BE WITH US MUCH LONGER! THERE WAS A LITTLE POISON IN THAT DRINK OF YOURS...THAT'LL LEAVE OUR BUSINESS JUST TO ME!
NO-- NOOOOO!
THE END

NEW BODIES FOR OLD!

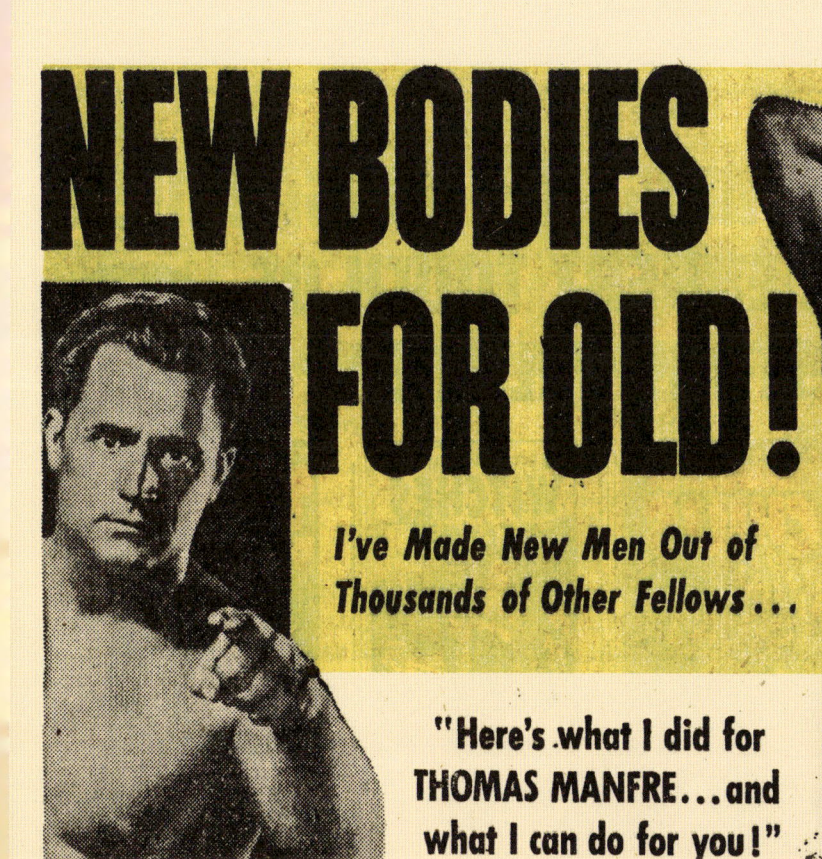

I've Made New Men Out of Thousands of Other Fellows...

"Here's what I did for **THOMAS MANFRE**...and what I can do for you!"
— *Charles Atlas*

GIVE me a skinny, pepless, second-rate body—and I'll cram it so full of handsome, bulging new muscle that your friends will grow bug-eyed ... I'll wake up that sleeping energy of yours and make it hum like a high-powered motor! Man, you'll *feel* and *look* different! You'll begin to LIVE!

Let Me Make YOU a NEW MAN— IN JUST 15 MINUTES A DAY

You wouldn't believe it, but I myself used to be a 97-lb. weakling Fellows called me "Skinny." Girls snickered and made fun of me behind my back I was a flop. THEN I discovered my marvelous new muscle-building system – "Dynamic Tension." – And it turned me into such a *complete* specimen of MANHOOD that today I hold the title of "THE WORLD'S MOST PERFECTLY DEVELOPEN MAN."

What Is "Dynamic Tension"?... How Does It Work?

When you look in the mirror and see a healthy, husky, strapping fellow smiling back at you—then you'll realize how fast "Dynamic Tension" GETS RESULTS! And *you'll* be using the method which many great athletes use for keeping in condition— prize fighters, wrestlers, baseball and football players, etc

"Dynamic Tension" is the easy, NATURAL method you can practice in the privacy of your own room — JUST 15 MINUTES EACH DAY—while your scrawny chest and shoulder muscles begin to swell, ripple ... those spindly arms and legs of yours bulge ... and your whole body starts to feel "alive," full of zip and go!

One Postage Stamp May Change Your Whole Life!

Sure, I gave Thomas Manfre (shown above) a NEW BODY But he's just one of thousands. I'm steadily building powerful, broad-shouldered, dynamic MEN—day by day—the country over.

3,000,000 fellows, young and old, have already gambled a postage stamp to ask for my FREE book. They wanted to read and see for themselves how I build up scrawny bodies, and how I pare down fat, flabby ones - how I turn them into human dynamos of pure MANPOWER.

ARE YOU
Skinny and run down?
Always tired?
Nervous?
Lacking in Confidence?
Constipated?
Suffering from bad breath?
What to Do About It Is told in my free book!

Atlas Championship Cup won by Thomas Manfre, one of Charles Atlas' pupils.

FREE MY 32-PAGE ILLUSTRATED BOOK YOURS —Not For $1.00 or 10c—BUT FREE

Send for my famous book "Everlasting Health and Strength." 32 pages crammed with photographs and advice. Shows what "Dynamic Tension" can do for YOU.

This book is a *real* prize for any fellow who wants a better build. Yet I'll send you a copy absolutely FREE. Just glancing through it may mean the turning point in your whole life! Rush coupon to me personally: Charles Atlas, Dept. 30311 115 East 23rd St., New York 10, N. Y.

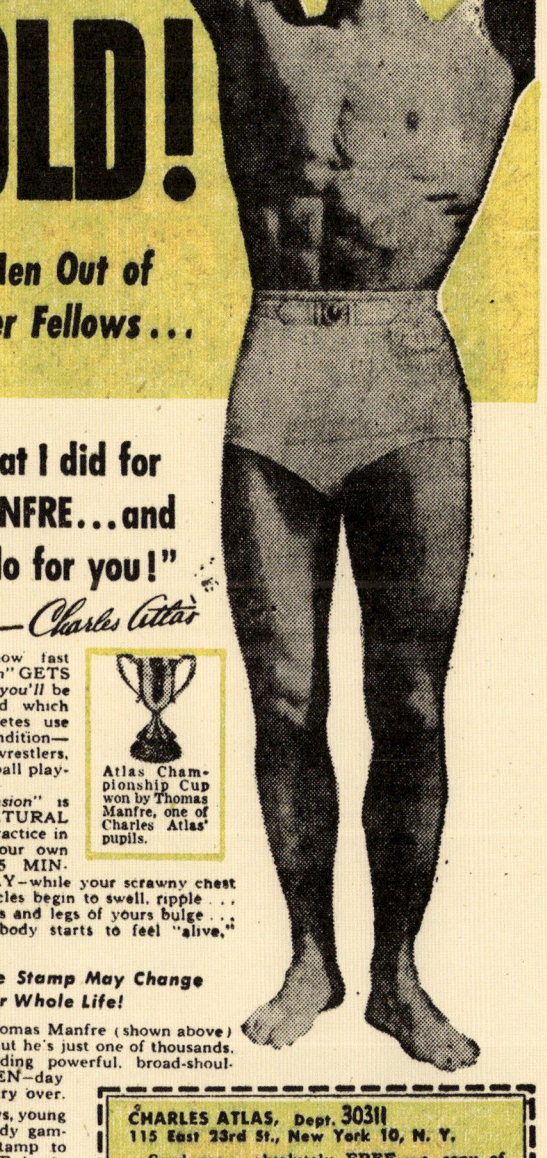

CHARLES ATLAS, Dept. 30311
115 East 23rd St., New York 10, N. Y.

Send me — absolutely FREE — a copy of your famous book, "Everlasting Health and Strength" – 32 pages, crammed with actual photographs, answers to vital health questions, and valuable advice to every man who wants a better build. I understand this book is mine to keep, and sending for it does not obligate me in any way.

Name.. Age......
(Please print or write plainly)

Address ....

City......................... State...................
☐ If under 14 years of age check here for Booklet A.

Read these DIFFERENT MYSTERY MAGAZINES WITH THE EXPERT TOUCH OF MASTER STORY TELLING!

NOW ON SALE

ACCLAIMED THE BEST IN SHOCK MYSTERY, THE BLACK CAT MYSTERY OPENS A TRAIL TO SUSPENSE! DON'T MISS AN ISSUE!

THRILLS AND CHILLS WITH EVER-BUILDING TENSION... YOU'LL GASP AS YOU READ EACH ISSUE OF THE EXCITING CHAMBER OF CHILLS!

A FLIGHT INTO FANTASTIC FRENZY... EXPLORE THE FORBIDDEN IN EACH ISSUE OF THE WITCHES TALES!

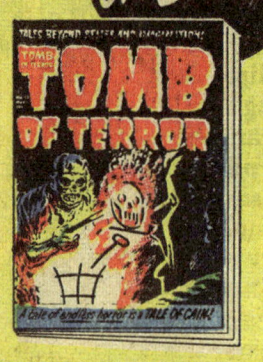

FOR ADVENTURES INTO THE UNKNOWN, FOR INCREDIBLE TREKS TO OTHER WORLDS, READ THE TOMB OF TERROR!

---

80 MILLION FANS FOLLOW BELIEVE IT OR NOT!

IN NEWSPAPERS, RADIO AND TV

NOW IN A NEW **H** HARVEY FAMOUS NAME COMIC

NOW ON SALE

GET YOUR COPY TODAY

CHEW IMPROVED FORMULA
CHEWING GUM!
REDUCE

Up to 5 lbs. a Week With Dr. Phillips Plan

Reduce to a slimmer more graceful figure the way Dr. Phillips recommends—without starving—without missing a single meal! Here for you *Now*—a scientific way which guarantees you can lose as much weight as you wish—or *you pay nothing*! No Drugs, No Starvation, No Exercises or Laxatives. The Amazing thing is that it is so easy to follow —simple and safe to lose those ugly, fatty bulges. Each and every week you lose pounds safely until you reach the weight that most becomes you. Now at last you have the doctors' new modern way to reduce—To acquire that dreamed about silhouette, an improved slimmer, exciting more graceful figure. Simply chew delicious improved Formula Dr. Phillips Kelpidine Chewing Gum and follow Dr. Phillips Plan. This wholesome, tasty delicious Kelpidine Chewing Gum contains Hexitol, *reduces* appetite and is sugar free. Hexitol is a new discovery and contains no fat and no available carbohydrates. Enjoy chewing this delicious gum and reduce with Dr. Phillips Plan. Try it for 12 days, then step on the scale. You'll hardly believe your eyes. Good for men too.

Money-Back Guarantee! 10 Day Free Trial!

Mail the coupon now! Test the amazing Dr. Phillips KELPIDINE CHEWING GUM REDUCING PLAN for 10 days at our expense. If after 10 days your friends, your mirror and your scale do not tell you that you have lost weight and look slimmer you pay nothing.

SENT ON APPROVAL MAIL COUPON NOW!

$1 — 12 DAY SUPPLY ONLY

AMERICAN HEALTHAIDS CO. 15TH FLOOR
1860 BROADWAY, NEW YORK 23, N.Y.

Just mail us your name and address, and $1.00 cash, check or money-order. You will receive a 12 day supply of KELPIDINE CHEWING GUM (improved formula), and Dr. Phillips Reducing Plan postage prepaid.

Name _____

Address _____

City _____ State _____

☐ Send me Special 24 day supply and FREE 12 day package for $2.00. I understand that if I am not delighted with KELPIDINE CHEWING GUM and Dr. Phillips Reducing Plan, I can return it in 10 days for full purchase price refund.

An Amazing NEW HEALTH SUPPORTER BELT

For men in their 30's, 40's, 50's who want to LOOK SLIMMER and FEEL YOUNGER

POSTURE BAD? Got a 'Bay Window'?

DO YOU ENVY MEN who can 'KEEP ON THEIR FEET'?

and then he got a "CHEVALIER"...

YOU NEED A "CHEVALIER"!

DOES a bulging "bay window" make you look and feel years older than you really are? Then here, at last, is the answer to your problem! "Chevalier", the wonderful new adjustable health supporter belt is scientifically constructed to help you look and feel years younger!

The CHEVALIER
LIFTS AND FLATTENS YOUR BULGING "BAY WINDOW"

Why go on day after day with an "old-man's" mid-section bulge ... or with a tired back that needs posture support? Just see how "Chevalier" brings you vital control where you need it most! "Chevalier" has a built-in strap. You adjust the belt the way you want. Presto! Your "bay-window" bulge is lifted in ... flattened out—yet you feel wonderfully comfortable!

FRONT ADJUSTMENT
Works quick as a flash! Simply adjust the strap and presto! The belt is perfectly adjusted to your greatest comfort!

TWO-WAY S-T-R-E-T-C-H WONDER CLOTH
Firmly holds in your flabby abdomen; yet it s-t-r-e-t-c-h-e-s as you breathe, bend, stoop, after meals, etc.

DETACHABLE POUCH
Air-cooled! Scientifically designed and made to give wonderful support and protection!

Healthful, Enjoyable Abdominal Control

It's great! You can wear "Chevalier" all day long. Will not bind or make you feel constricted. That's because the two-way s-t-r-e-t-c-h cloth plus the front adjustment bring you *personalized* fit. The "Chevalier" is designed according to scientific facts of healthful posture control. It's made by experts to give you the comfort and healthful "lift" you want. Just see all the wonderful features below. And remember—you can get the "Chevalier" on FREE TRIAL. Mail the coupon right now!

Rear View FITS SNUG AT SMALL of BACK Firm, comfortable support. Feels good!

FREE Extra Pouch. The Chevalier has a removable pouch made of a soft, comfortable fabric that absorbs perspiration. So that you can change it regularly we include an extra pouch. Limited offer. Order yours today.

FREE TRIAL OFFER

1. You risk nothing! Just mail coupon—be sure to give name and address, also waist measure, etc. — and mail TODAY!

2. Try on the "Chevalier". Adjust belt the way you want. See how your bulging 'bay window' looks streamlined ... how comfortable you feel. How good it is!

3. Wear the "Chevalier" for 10 whole days if you want to! Wear it to work, evenings, while bowling, etc. The "Chevalier" must help you look and feel "like a million" or you can send it back! See offer in coupon!

RONNIE SALES, INC., Dept. 35A11-E 487 Broadway, N. Y. 13, N. Y.

SEND NO MONEY: JUST MAIL COUPON

RONNIE SALES, INC. Dept. 35A11-E
487 Broadway, New York 13, N. Y.

Send me for 10 days' FREE TRIAL a CHEVALIER HEALTH-SUPPORTER BELT. I will pay postman $3.98 (plus postage) with the understanding that includes my FREE pouch. In 10 days, I will either return CHEVALIER to you and you will return my money, or otherwise my payment will be a full and final purchase price.

My waist measure is..................
(Send string the size of your waist if no tape measure is handy)

Name ....
Address ....
City and Zone.......................State..........
☐ Save 65c postage. We pay postage if you enclose payment now. Same Free Trial and refund privilege.

It didn't shout or scream when it said...
LAY THAT PISTOL DOWN

Teddy Cummins lived at 11 Vandernook Avenue. A very exclusive *address*... and a very exclusive *house*... even if the architecture was rather *grim* and *old fashioned*!

To *"normal"* people, Teddy Cummins was slightly eccentric. To Teddy, himself, he was a man who just liked to be *alone*, away from the hum-drum activities of everyday life! Polite society called him a *recluse!*

AND IN THE VAST CONFINES OF HIS CELLAR, TEDDY ACCUMULATED IN MUSTY ABUNDANCE... EVEN *OVERABUNDANCE*... WHAT HE CONSIDERED *IMPORTANT!* THERE WAS NO RHYME OR REASON TO THE STORAGE! IT BEGAN WITH *EVERYTHING*... AND STOPPED AT *NOTHING!*

LOVELY OLD NEWSPAPERS... TO BE PUT AWAY! HEE... HEE!

THERE WERE BROKEN TOYS, WHEELS, SCRAPS OF IRON AND STEEL... AND RUBBER AND CARDBOARD! IN SHORT, ANYTHING HE COULD SALVAGE FROM THE CITY'S MOST ARISTOCRATIC GARBAGE CANS!

IT'S *SO NICE* TO *SAVE!*

AT NIGHT WHEN THE CITY SLEPT TEDDY WOULD TRAVEL FROM HOUSE TO HOUSE, PICKING THE BONES OF THE CITY'S REFUSE! HE WAS *INDUSTRIOUS* AS WELL AS ODD!

AH--THIS WILL DO! IT WILL DO, INDEED!

BUT PEOPLE GOT USED TO THE ECCENTRIC RECLUSE, AS HE BLENDED QUIETLY INTO THE BACKGROUND OF THE BUSY CITY, TROUBLING NO ONE, UNTROUBLED HIMSELF...

HE'S QUEER, ALL RIGHT! BUT *HARMLESS*. EVERYONE'S GOT HIS FUNNY POINTS! I LIKE POTATO CHIPS WITH ICE CREAM... HE LIKES TO *LIVE* IN A *CELLAR* FULL OF *JUNK!*

THAT'S WHAT I SAY! *LIVE AN' LET LIVE!*

TEDDY, HOWEVER, WAS NOT SO TOLERANT. THE *SLIGHTEST* SOUND, THE *FAINTEST FINGER* OF PROBING LIGHT WAS ENOUGH TO SEND HIM SCURRYING INTO A *DARK CORNER!*

HOW I... *DETEST* THE DAYTIME!

FOR... IT WAS AT NIGHT THAT TEDDY CUMMINS DID HIS BEST WORK! AND IT WAS AT NIGHT WHEN *SOMEONE* CALLED... SOMEONE WHO DROPPED FROM *NOWHERE!*

MAGAZINES OVER HERE...

TOYS OVER HERE. HAVE TO KEEP EVERYTHING ORDERLY!
SUDDENLY...
STAY WHERE YOU ARE! DON'T MAKE A MOVE!
WH- WHO ARE YOU? WH-- WHAT ARE YOU DOING HERE?
YOU WOULDN'T BELIEVE ME IF I TOLD YOU... BUT I'LL TELL YOU ANYWAY. MY NAME IS GODRYLL. I CAME BY SPACE SHIP FROM MARS! WE'VE DECIDED THAT EARTH HAS POSSIBILITIES, AND I'VE BEEN SENT AS ... AH... AN OBSERVOR!
TEDDY'S EQUILIBRIUM WAS UPSET! HIS APPLE CART OF PRIVACY WAS OVERTURNED BY THIS UNWANTED, UN-EARTHLY INTRUDER! HE WAS NOT GOING TO STAND FOR IT!
YOU...YOU'RE CRAZY! GET OUT! I--I DON'T LIKE PEOPLE HERE!
PUT THAT DOWN, YOU FOOL! I'M NOT READY TO KILL YOU!
LUX
BUT...
BUT I'M READY TO... HA-HA-HA! HAVE A LIGHT!
KLIKK!
YOU...YOU IMBECILE! NO MORE STUNTS LIKE THAT! THERE ARE IMPORTANT ISSUES AT STAKE AND RIGHT NOW YOU ARE VALUABLE TO ME ALIVE!
3

HOW EASY IT WILL BE TO HIDE IN THIS CELLAR, UNOBSERVED AND UNSUSPECTED. THEN AFTER I HAVE LEARNED YOUR WAYS, WHO WILL TELL THE DIFFERENCE BETWEEN TWO MEN WHO LIVE IN THE SHADOWS?
BUT, TEDDY COULD TELL THE DIFFERENCE! THAT WAS ENOUGH FOR HIM!
YOU...YOU THING! I WON'T LET YOU KILL ME!
GET OUT ...OR I SHOOT!
YOU IMBECILE! IF YOU FORCE MY HAND, I'LL HAVE TO KILL YOU NOW!
HEEE-HEEE-HEEE!
WH-WHAT? WATER? ENOUGH OF YOUR GAMES!
IF IT WAS A GAME, TEDDY HAD TO PLAY, HE HAD NO CHOICE! HE KNEW THAT THERE WERE NO TIES IN THE GAME OF LIFE OR DEATH... AND THERE'S ONLY ONE WINNER!
HA-HA! SCARED YOU, DIDN'T I?
BOIING!
WATER PISTOLS...GUNS THAT SHOOT SPARKS AND FLAGS! THE MAN IS DEMENTED!
RAT-A-TAT
TAT TAT
4

CRAZY, AM I? I'LL SHOW YOU!
HA-HA! YOU BEGIN TO AMUSE ME! THE IDIOTIC MAN WHO PLAYS WITH TOY INSTRUMENTS OF DEATH! DEMENTED BUT HARMLESS! I WAS A FOOL TO LOSE MY TEMPER!
PUT THE TOY AWAY, OLD MAN! DO YOU EXPECT TO KILL ME WITH THAT BARGAIN BASEMENT ATOMIC PISTOL?!!
YES, GODRYLL-- I DO!
THE GUN FIT SNUGGLY IN TEDDY'S PALM. HE WRAPPED HIS FINGER AROUND THE TRIGGER, AND PULLED EVER SO LIGHTLY! THE TRIGGER CLICKED SMOOTHLY... THE FLUID SHOT INTO THE CHAMBER... WAS IGNITED, AND SHOT OUT OF THE NOZZLE IN A STREAM OF RED-HOT FIRE!
AAAGHHH
I PLAYED MY ROLE WELL, EH, GODRYLL?
AFTER ALL, IT IS A GOOD IDEA TO USE THE CHARACTER OF AN ECCENTRIC RECLUSE AS A MASK TO CONDUCT SPYING ACTIVITIES!
BUT... THIS MARTIAN DOG DIDN'T KNOW THAT WE VENUSIANS THOUGHT OF IT FIRST! THEIR AGENTS WILL HAVE TO BE A LOT QUICKER ON THE DRAW... TO BEAT THE VENUS SPY SYSTEM! EARTH IS TOO GOOD A PRIZE TO GIVE UP!
THE END
5

The TALKER

"Stop your idiotic blabbering! What do you know about politics?" Larz Thomas' booming voice burst forth with venom at his son, William.

"I guess I don't know much," said William. His eyes stared coldly at the man who was his father.

The guests in the Thomas' living room looked on with wild-eyed interest. They had seen similar scenes to this before. But they were always fascinated by the hate that lived in Larz Thomas.

"I guess I shouldn't talk unless I'm spoken to," said William calmly.

"You can say that again!" said Larz. "You're twenty now, yet you've still got a mind of a four-year-old! You don't know politics... you don't know people... you don't know life! You'd do a favor for the whole world if you just shut up!"

"You've never liked anything I've said, have you, Dad?"

"No! I can't remember a single instance when I liked to hear your voice! I can't even stand the way it sounds!"

The guests were becoming wary. But no one was sure what to do. Finally, someone said:

"OK, you two. Let's forget it for now. This is a party, so let's make like one!"

Larz Thomas walked away with his guests. He pasted a smile on his face and was already telling a funny story.

William Thomas stayed behind. His eyes followed his father and the guests as they walked out of the room. Then he stared down at the plushy carpet and his mind moved back over the years.

He remembered his days as a child. He remembered how his father would stop his normal child questionings. Then he remembered the sound-proof room his father had built for him, the room he'd be locked into if he spoke too much, the room where he'd cry endlessly and no one could hear!

William recalled his later days. William growing up, yet a father who refused to listen to anything he said. For Larz Thomas only wanted to hear his own voice... his own words!

William Thomas came back to the present. His eyes were now staring out with calm decision. He went into the next room and called his father.

"What do you want?" roared Larz.

"I'd like to see you for a moment," said William.

"The fool won't keep me long," said Larz bitterly as he went to meet his son.

"We'll go upstairs," said William simply, and he marched up the stairs to the room that was sound-proof. Larz Thomas followed him blindly.

They went into the room and William closed the door. Then no one could hear what was happening... no one could hear the talk... or the screams!

Then William opened the door and walked out. Still no sound could be heard. For William was silent, and in his right hand he held Larz Thomas' bloody tongue!

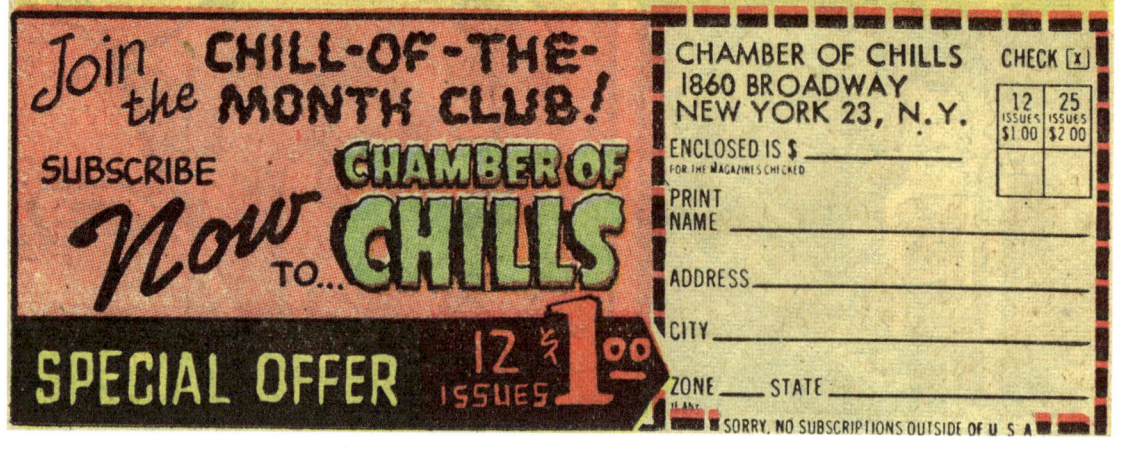

Join CHILL-OF-THE-MONTH CLUB!
SUBSCRIBE *Now* TO... **CHAMBER OF CHILLS**
SPECIAL OFFER — 12 ISSUES $1.00

CHAMBER OF CHILLS
1860 BROADWAY
NEW YORK 23, N.Y.

CHECK [x]
12 ISSUES $1.00 — 25 ISSUES $2.00

ENCLOSED IS $ _____
FOR THE MAGAZINES CHECKED

PRINT NAME _____
ADDRESS _____
CITY _____
ZONE ___ STATE _____

SORRY, NO SUBSCRIPTIONS OUTSIDE OF U.S.A.

CHILLY
CHAMBER MUSIC
SONGS FROM THE SPOOK BOX!

ROW...ROW...ROW...YOUR BOAT GENTLY DOWN THE STREAM!

ROW...ROW...ROW...YOUR BOAT LAY YOUR HEAD DOWN TO DREAM!

ROW...ROW...ROW...YOUR BOAT BETTER GET ON THE BEAM!

ROW...ROW...ROW...YOUR BOAT LIFE IS BUT A *SCREAM*.!!!

CHILLY
CHAMBER MUSIC
SONGS FROM THE SPOOK BOX!

ALL ALONE... I'M SO ALL ALONE!

ALL ALONE BY THE TELEPHONE...

TRIED TO CALL... BUT NOW I *GROAN*!!

DOESN'T MATTER 'CAUSE I'M *ALL ALONE*!!

END OF THE LINE
JUST IMAGINE SEEING EMILY AGAIN, GEORGE!
DO NOT EXIT
SHE'S MARRIED NOW! I WONDER WHAT HER HUSBAND'S LIKE!
IT DOESN'T REALLY MATTER, THOUGH! THERE'S SO MUCH TO TALK OVER WITH EMILY!
NORTH AVE
OH, GEORGE... EMILY AND I WILL CACKLE LIKE OLD HENS! ABOUT THIS...
WHY DON'T YOU SIT DOWN, CLARA? YOU'LL USE UP ALL YOUR WORDS BEFORE YOU EVEN *GET* TO EMILY'S HOUSE!
SNAKE OIL
1

BUT, GEORGE, I DON'T SEE...
BE QUIET, CLARA! PLEASE!
NEW LOTS
IS THAT MAN TRYING TO...?!!
GATE
GEORGE...THAT MAN IS TRYING TO FLIRT WITH ME!
WHERE? WHAT MAN?!
THAT MAN... THERE!
HE IS, IS HE? FLIRT WITH MY WIFE, EH?
WHAT DO YOU THINK YOU'RE TRYING TO DO? KEEP YOUR LOOKS TO YOURSELF, BUDDY! UNDERSTAND!!!
WHA?!!!
2

GET YOUR HANDS OFF ME! WHO DO YOU THINK YOU'RE PUSHING AROUND?!
A TOUGH GUY! WHY, I'LL MASH YOUR FACE IN!
OH, DON'T FIGHT, GEORGE... PLEASE! DON'T FIGHT!
I'VE HAD... ENOUGH! SO... START SMASHING!
UGH...
OH!
GEORGE... IT'S NOTHING TO FIGHT OVER! STOP IT! FORGET ABOUT IT! PLEASE, GEORGE...
GET AWAY, CLARA! I'LL KNOCK HIS HEAD OFF!
I SAID... GET AWAY! AS FOR YOU...
GEORGE, PLEASE STOP! HERE'S OUR STATION!
GET YOUR PAWS OFF ME!
OKAY! LET'S SETTLE THIS OUTSIDE!
OH-- LET HIM GO! LET HIM GO!
3

OKAY, TOUGH GUY! LET'S SEE... IF YOU CAN TAKE IT!
OOF...
I... CAN! CAN YOU?
OH! HELP! POLICE! POLICE!
I--I'M FALLING-- GRAB ME!
WHA---T! I... I CAN'T...
AAAIIEEEE
4

I HEARD THE SCREAMS FROM THE OTHER END OF THE STATION, JOE. CAME AS FAST AS I COULD. I'LL GO DOWN AND TAKE A LOOK!
PROBABLY DEAD, SAM! I'LL GET THE DETAILS FROM THIS GUY HERE!
OKAY, MR. SUMMERS, I GOT YOUR NAME AND A COUPLE OF THE FACTS. GOOD THING FOR YOU I SAW THE ACCIDENT! BUT BE DOWN AT HEADQUARTERS TOMORROW MORNING FOR A FULL REPORT! NOW GET YOUR WIFE OUT OF HERE!
YES... YES! COME, CLARA... WE'RE GOING!
IT STARTED FROM NOTHING-- NOTHING!
TRY TO FORGET ABOUT IT, CLARA! WE'LL FEEL BETTER ONCE WE'RE AT EMILY'S HOUSE!
CLARA! AFTER ALL THESE YEARS ...WHY, WHAT'S WRONG? YOU LOOK AS WHITE AS A SHEET!
OH, EMILY! WE...GEORGE AND I... JUST WENT THROUGH A TERRIBLE ACCIDENT! OH, IT WAS HORRIBLE!
A MAN TRIED ...OH, I CAN'T EVEN TALK ABOUT IT!
TAKE IT EASY, CLARA.
I'LL GO INTO THE KITCHEN AND BREW A STRONG CUP OF COFFEE! THAT'LL CALM HER DOWN A LITTLE!
CLARA...MY HUSBAND'S NOT HOME YET. BUT...YOU CAN SEE WHAT HE LOOKS LIKE, FROM HIS PICTURE BEHIND YOU! HE'S... OH, THERE'S THE PHONE!
BRRNGGG... BRRNNG!
G-GEORGE! T-THAT MAN--THAT MAN!!
T-THE POLICE?!! NO... NO!! OH, MY LORD... NOOOOO!!
THE END
5

MUSICAL WHIRLING ANGEL-CHIMES

AUTHENTIC REPLICA OF ORIGINAL "SWEDISH SINGING ANGELS" CENTERPIECE

MAGIC-LIKE EFFECT Heat from lighted candles makes angels revolve continuously. When wands strike bells you hear pleasant musical chimes.

10 Day Trial Offer! **LOWEST PRICE EVER** Only $1.98 COMPLETE WITH CANDLES — Beautiful Gift Box

- ANGELS WHIRL
- BELLS RING

Beautiful Tapered-Tip Candles

Overall Height 13 Inches

YOUR SATISFACTION GUARANTEED OR YOUR MONEY BACK

AS CENTERPIECE • ON MANTEL OR SHELF • ON BUFFET

- *Here it is!* That beautiful, whirling, chiming, table Candelabra you've seen and admired at prices up to $5 and $10 in the finest shops. Now, for the first time, you can have this lovely, decorative centerpiece in your home, yours to own and enjoy, for only $1.98 complete with 3 tapered-tip candles. All the authentic styling of famed Swedish craftsmen is faithfully reproduced in this enchanting "Singing Angels" replica.

- You, your family and friends will rejoice in the charm and beauty which this decorative innovation brings to your home. Everyone who comes into your home will be fascinated by the gentle whirling action of the Herald Angels as the heat from the lighted candles cause them to revolve 'round and 'round for hours. Your cares and burdens will vanish under the soothing, relaxing influence of the church-like musical chimes as the angel wands continuously strike golden-toned bells during the revolving action. The effect is truly breathtaking. Lighted candles — revolving angels — soft chiming bells — all combine to provide unequalled beauty, peace and contentment for your home and for all who enter it.

- Made for long-life service of all metal construction with rich, polished brass effect, achieved by special anodizing process, can't tarnish, discolor or rust. Circular tray is designed with three candle holders which adjust to width of any candles you may wish to use. Here is a beautiful, decorative addition for your table, mantel, shelf or buffet that will last and serve you for years to come, yours on this offer for only $1.98 or two for $3.79. Order today. Use your Musical Whirling Angel Chimes for 10 full days. We guarantee that you'll be thrilled with its heavenly beauty and action or you can return in 10 days for full refund.

SEND NO MONEY! RUSH THIS COUPON!

ILLINOIS MERCHANDISE MART, 15th Floor
1860 BROADWAY   NEW YORK 23, N.Y.

Gentlemen:—Rush my order as checked below for Musical Whirling ANGEL CHIMES, complete with 3 beautiful tapered-tip candles. I will pay the postman $1.98 for one or two for $3.79 plus C.O.D. postage charges on your 10 day money back offer.

Check how many:

☐ 1 ANGEL CHIMES @ $1.98   ☐ 2 ANGEL CHIMES @ $3.79

NAME_____

ADDRESS_____

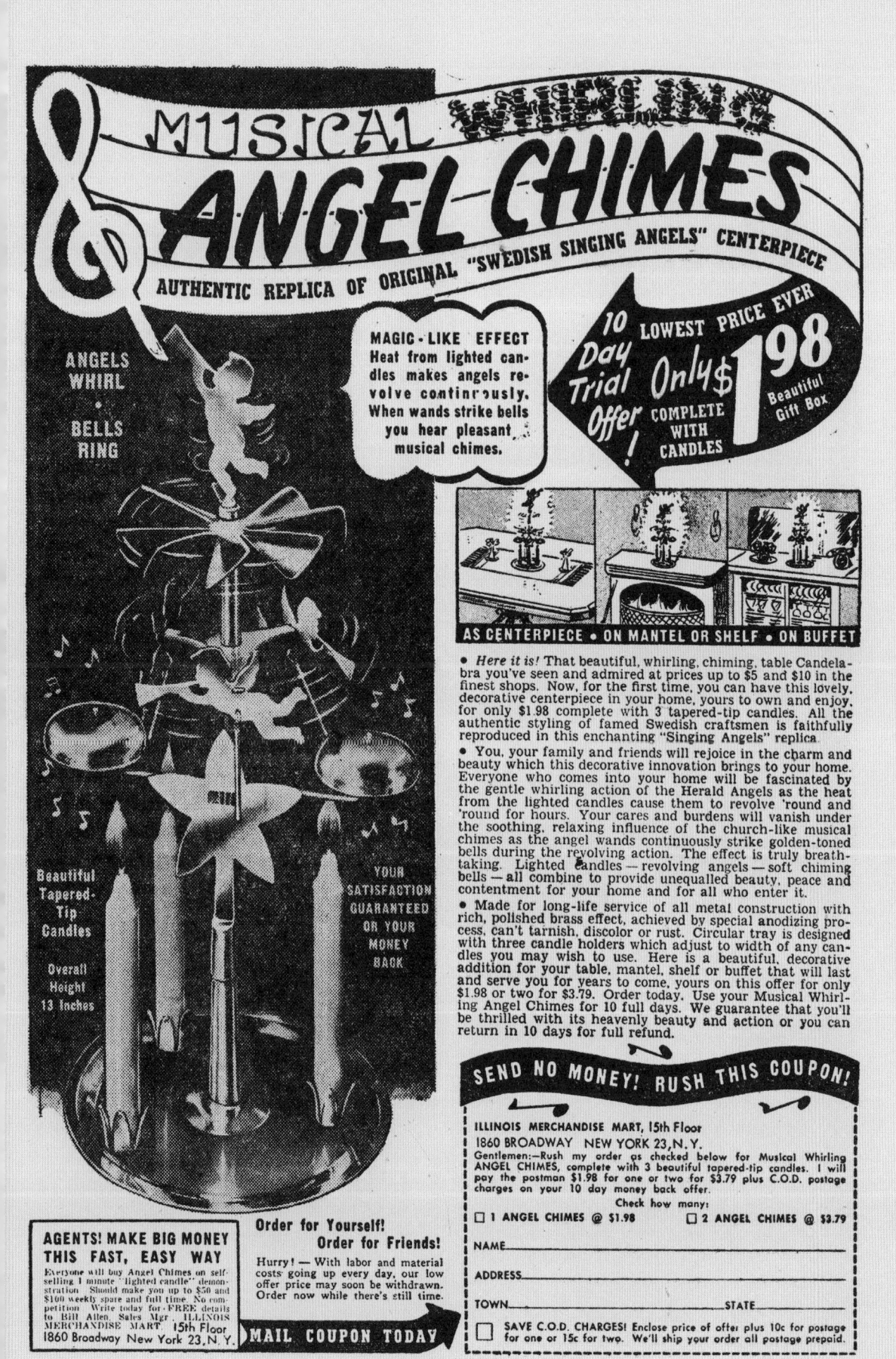

TOWN_____ STATE_____

☐ SAVE C.O.D. CHARGES! Enclose price of offer plus 10c for postage for one or 15c for two. We'll ship your order all postage prepaid.

AGENTS! MAKE BIG MONEY THIS FAST, EASY WAY
Everyone will buy Angel Chimes on self-selling 1 minute "lighted candle" demonstration. Should make you up to $50 and $100 weekly spare and full time. No competition. Write today for FREE details to Bill Allen, Sales Mgr., ILLINOIS MERCHANDISE MART, 15th Floor, 1860 Broadway New York 23, N.Y.

Order for Yourself! Order for Friends!
Hurry! — With labor and material costs going up every day, our low offer price may soon be withdrawn. Order now while there's still time.

➜ MAIL COUPON TODAY

The NEW way to enjoy SPORTS Movies, Plays, Television

NOW GET CLOSE-UP VIEWS ALL DAY WITHOUT FATIGUE

SAVE $8.00

NOW! 1.98 FTI

IMPORTED FROM GERMANY

Here for the first time—Germany's famous **SPEKTOSCOPES**—a revolutionary concept in binoculars. Wear them like ordinary eye glasses—hour after hour—without fatigue. Feather weight—only 1 oz. You'll hardly **FEEL** them! Yet here is a new, truly powerful optical design that gives you greater range than many expensive opera or field glasses and a far greater field of view than some selling for many times more! Has **INDIVIDUAL** eye focusing for clear, sharp viewing, whether you're looking at a play in the first row or a seashore scene miles away! **SPEKTO-SCOPES** are ideal for indoors, outdoors or distant scenes or close-by viewing. Special low price — 1.98, a saving of 8.00 or more!

FAVORABLE EXCHANGE RATE MAKES THIS VALUE POSSIBLE!

This is the first time that this type of optical instrument has ever sold for less than $10.00. The favorable rate of exchange and Germany's need for dollars makes it possible. We have been chosen as the exclusive distributor for SPEKTOSCOPES to the American public. Get yours now at our low, low introductory price of 1.98 tax & post paid!

TRY AT OUR RISK — NO OBLIGATION!

Enjoy at our risk for 5 days. **You must be delighted!** Otherwise your 1.98 will be refunded with no questions asked! Limited supply forces us to place a limit of 2 per customer. Send check or m.o. for prompt, free delivery. COD's sent plus COD Fees. Use convenient coupon below!

INTERNATIONAL BINOCULAR CO., Dept. 125-M-90
53 to 59 East 25th Street, New York 10, N. Y.

INTERNATIONAL BINOCULAR CO., Dept. 125-M-90
53 to 59 East 25th Street, New York 10, N. Y.

RUSH _____ SPEKTOSCOPES at 1.98 each (LIMIT-2) on 5 day home trial. You are to refund my 1.98 if I am not fully delighted.

☐ Payment enclosed. Send post free. ☐ Send COD plus Fees.

Name_____

Address_____

Town_____ State_____

direct from FACTORY to YOU!

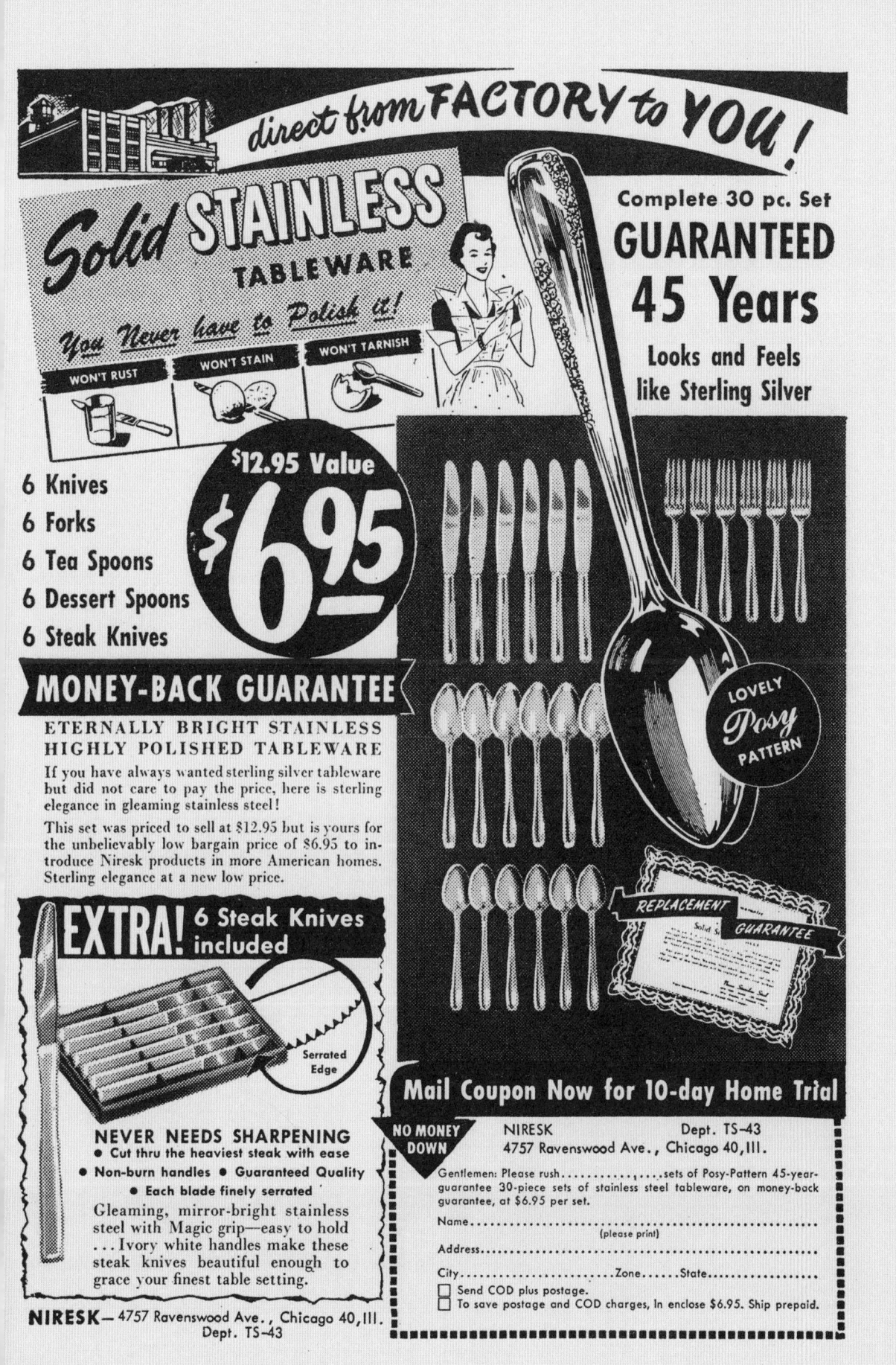

Solid STAINLESS TABLEWARE
You Never have to Polish it!

- WON'T RUST
- WON'T STAIN
- WON'T TARNISH

Complete 30 pc. Set GUARANTEED 45 Years

Looks and Feels like Sterling Silver

$12.95 Value $6.95

- 6 Knives
- 6 Forks
- 6 Tea Spoons
- 6 Dessert Spoons
- 6 Steak Knives

LOVELY *Posy* PATTERN

MONEY-BACK GUARANTEE

ETERNALLY BRIGHT STAINLESS HIGHLY POLISHED TABLEWARE

If you have always wanted sterling silver tableware but did not care to pay the price, here is sterling elegance in gleaming stainless steel!

This set was priced to sell at $12.95 but is yours for the unbelievably low bargain price of $6.95 to introduce Niresk products in more American homes. Sterling elegance at a new low price.

EXTRA! 6 Steak Knives included

Serrated Edge

REPLACEMENT GUARANTEE

NEVER NEEDS SHARPENING
- Cut thru the heaviest steak with ease
- Non-burn handles • Guaranteed Quality
- Each blade finely serrated

Gleaming, mirror-bright stainless steel with Magic grip—easy to hold ...Ivory white handles make these steak knives beautiful enough to grace your finest table setting.

NIRESK— 4757 Ravenswood Ave., Chicago 40, Ill.
Dept. TS-43

Mail Coupon Now for 10-day Home Trial

NO MONEY DOWN

NIRESK   Dept. TS-43
4757 Ravenswood Ave., Chicago 40, Ill.

Gentlemen: Please rush............,......sets of Posy-Pattern 45-year-guarantee 30-piece sets of stainless steel tableware, on money-back guarantee, at $6.95 per set.

Name..
                    (please print)
Address...
City......................Zone......State............
☐ Send COD plus postage.
☐ To save postage and COD charges, In enclose $6.95. Ship prepaid.

If You Like to Draw Sketch or Paint...

Make money with your brush and pen! Take the famous Talent Test. It has already helped thousands toward art careers. No fee. No obligation. Mail this coupon TODAY!

ART INSTRUCTION, INC.
DEPT. 9183-2 • 500 S. 4th St., Minneapolis 15, Minn.
● Please send me your Talent Test (no fee).

Name_____

Address_____

City_____ Zone_____

County_____ State_____

Occupation_____

Age_____ Phone_____

STRANGEST TALES OF FEAR AND TERROR!
BLACK CAT MYSTERY

Collect all 4 Volumes of Black Cat Mystery from PS Artbooks

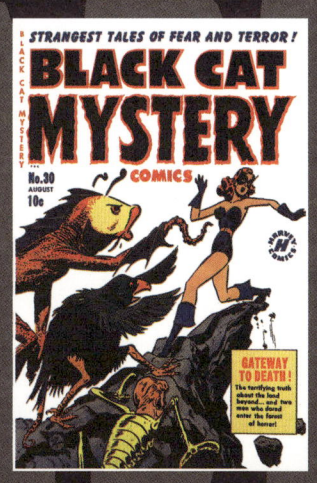

Black Cat Mystery
Volume One

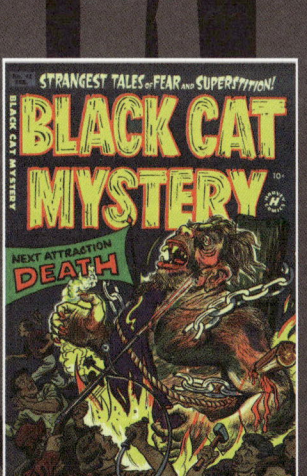

Black Cat Mystery
Volume Two

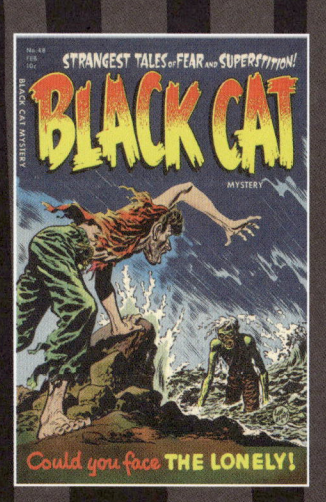

Black Cat Mystery
Volume Three

Black Cat Mystery
Volume Four

Chamber of Chills
January 1954 - Issue #21

Cover Art - Lee Elias

The Choirmaster
Script - Bob Powell
Pencils - Bob Powell
Inks - Unknown

Nose For News
Script - Unknown
Pencils - Manny Stallman
Inks - John Giunta

The Death Mask
Script - Unknown
Pencils - Joe Certa
Inks - Unknown

The Inside Man
Script - Howard Nostrand
Pencils - Howard Nostrand
Inks - Howard Nostrand

Information Source: Grand Comics Database!
A nonprofit, Internet-based organization of international volunteers dedicated to building a database covering all printed comics throughout the world.
If you believe any of this data to be incorrect or can add valuable additional information, please let us know www.comics.org
All rights to images reserved by the respective copyright holders. All original advertisement features remain the copyright of the respective trading company.

Privacy Policy
All portions of the Grand Comics Database that are subject to copyright are licensed under a Creative Commons Attribution 3.0 Unported License.
This includes but is not necessarily limited to our database schema and data distribution format.
The GCD Web Site code is licensed under the GNU General Public License.

CHAMBER OF CHILLS

TALES OF TERROR AND SUSPENSE!

MAGAZINE

THE *SHOCK OF YOUR LIFE* AWAITS YOU IN...
NOSE FOR NEWS!

Draw This Car

Free $295.00 Art Course

6 PRIZES

1st: Complete $295.00 Art Course.

2nd to 6th: Complete Artist's Drawing sets.

Here's your big chance, if you want to become a commercial artist, designer, or illustrator! An easy way to win FREE training from the world's greatest home study art school.

If your drawing shows promise we give you professional comments on it free! Trained illustrators, artists and cartoonists are making big money. Find out now if YOU have profitable art talent. You've nothing to lose—*everything to gain.* Mail your drawing today.

AMATEURS ONLY! Our students not eligible. Make copy of car 8 ins. long. Pencil or pen only. Omit the lettering. All drawings must be received by Jan. 31, 1954. None returned. Winners notified

USE ONLY ONE COUPON... Leave the other coupons so your friends can also enter drawings. Pass this ad on to your friends. Maybe they'll win prizes, TOO!

Art Instruction, Inc., Dept. 11183-1
500 S. 4th., Minneapolis 15, Minn.

Please enter my attached drawing in your contest. (PLEASE PRINT)

Name_____ Age____

Address_____ Apt.____

City_____ Phone____

Zone____ County_____

State_____ Occupation_____

Art Instruction, Inc., Dept. 11183-2
500 S. 4th., Minneapolis 15, Minn.

Please enter my attached drawing in your contest. (PLEASE PRINT)

Name_____ Age____

Address_____ Apt.____

City_____ Phone____

Zone____ County_____

State_____ Occupation_____

Art Instruction, Inc., Dept. 11183-3
500 S. 4th., Minneapolis 15, Minn.

Please enter my attached drawing in your contest. (PLEASE PRINT)

Name_____ Age____

Address_____ Apt.____

City_____ Phone____

Zone____ County_____

State_____ Occupation_____

CHAMBER OF CHILLS MAGAZINE, JANUARY, 1954, Vol. 1, No. 21, IS PUBLISHED BI-MONTHLY by WITCHES TALES, INC., 1860 Broadway, New York 23, N.Y. Entered as second class matter at the Post Office at New York, N.Y. under the Act of March 3, 1879. Single copies 10c. Subscription rates, 10 issues for $1.00 in the U.S. and possessions, elsewhere $1.50. All names in this periodical are entirely fictitious and no identification with actual persons is intended. Contents copyrighted, 1953, by Witches Tales, Inc., New York City. Printed in the U.S.A. Title Registered in U.S. Patent Office.

WON'T YOU COME IN?

IMPORTANT! We want your opinion... we want your letters! For, once again, CHAMBER OF CHILLS has done the something new! Here you will find the story molded within the hard core of realism and ending with a punch that only real life can sock home!

Tell us what you think of this realistic approach to terror, designed for suspense and as strong as your spinal column.

Take, for instance, NOSE FOR NEWS. Against a background of danger, see how it duplicates life in the raw, capturing the whole substance of murder and recording it as only a movie can -- only here, the camera shudders!

And here's something to look for! Starting with the next issue of CHAMBER OF CHILLS, March, No. 22, you'll be in for a big surprise.

All that can be said now is that this surprise has been worked for months. And that it will be the most important development in terror magazines! Read it and see it in action in next month's issue.

Meanwhile, keep those letters pouring in. Write to *Editor*:
CHAMBER OF CHILLS
1860 Broadway
New York 23, N. Y.

CHAMBER OF CHILLS Contents NO. 21

- THE CHOIR MASTER
- Nose for News
- THE DEATH MASK
- THE INSIDE MAN

CAR BURNING OIL?
Engineer's Discovery Stops it Quick
Without A Cent For Mechanical Repairs!

If your car is using too much oil—if it is sluggish, hard to start, slow on pickup, lacks pep and power—you are paying good money for oil that's burning up in your engine instead of providing lubrication. Why? Because your engine is leaking. Friction has worn a gap between pistons and cylinder wall. Oil is pumping up into the combustion chamber, fouling your motor with carbon. Gas is exploding down through this gap, going to waste.

SAVE $50 TO $150 REPAIR BILL

LIKE SQUEEZING TOOTHPASTE OUT OF A TUBE

Before you spend $50.00 to $150.00 for an engine overhaul, read how you can fix that leaky engine yourself, in just a few minutes, without buying a single new part, without even taking your engine down. It's almost as easy as squeezing toothpaste or shaving cream out of a tube, thanks to the discovery of a new miracle substance called Power Seal. This revolutionary, new compound combines the *lubricating* qualities of Moly, the "greasy" wonder metal, with the leak-sealing properties of Vermiculite, the mineral product whose particles *expand* under heat. (Up to 30 times original size.)

Just squeeze Power-Seal out of the tube into your motor's cylinders through the spark plug openings. It will spread over pistons, piston rings and cylinder walls as your engine runs and it will PLATE every surface with a smooth, shiny, metallic film *that won't come off!* No amount of pressure can scrape it off. No amount of heat can break it down. It fills the cracks, scratches and scorings caused by engine wear. It closes the gap between worn piston rings and cylinders with an automatic self-expanding seal that stops oil pumping, stops gas blow-by and restores compression. No more piston slapping, no more engine knocks. You get more power, speed, mileage

This genuine plating is self-lubricating too for Moly, the greasy metal lubricant, reduces friction as nothing else can! It is the only lubricant indestructible enough to be used in U.S. atomic energy plants and jet engines It never drains down, never leaves your engine dry Even after your car has been standing for weeks, even in coldest weather, you can start it in a flash, because the lubrication is in the metal itself That's why you'll need amazingly little oil; you'll get hundreds, even thousands of more miles per quart.

TRY IT FREE!

You don't risk a penny. Prove to yourself that Power-Seal will make your car run like new. Put it in your engine on 30 days' Free Trial If you are not getting better performance out of your car than you thought possible—if you have not stopped oil burning and have not increased gas mileage—return the empty tube and get your money back in full.

Power-Seal is absolutely harmless, it cannot hurt the finest car in any way. It can only preserve and protect your motor.

RUDSON AUTOMOTIVE INDUSTRIES
400 Madison Ave.   Dept. HC-11
New York 17, N.Y.

POWER SEAL MAKES WORN OUT TAXI ENGINE RUN LIKE NEW

Here are the Test Engineer's notarized figures showing the sensational increase in compression obtained in a 1950 De Soto taxi that had run for 93,086 miles. Just one POWER SEAL injection increased pep and power, reduced gas consumption, cut oil burning nearly 50%.

	Cyl. 1	Cyl. 2	Cyl. 3	Cyl. 4	Cyl. 5	Cyl. 6
BEFORE	90 lbs.	90 lbs.	105 lbs.	90 lbs.	80 lbs.	100 lbs.
AFTER	115 lbs.	115 lbs.	117 lbs.	115 lbs.	115 lbs.	115 lbs.

BEST INVESTMENT WE EVER MADE, SAYS DRIVER-OWNER

"We simply inserted the POWER SEAL per instructions and made no other repairs or adjustments. Compression readings were taken before and after and showed a big improvement in both cars. As a result the engine gained a lot more pick-up and power which was especially noticeable on hills. What impressed us most was the sharp reduction in oil consumption. In one cab, we've actually been saving a quart a day and figure we have saved $11.20 on oil alone since the POWER SEAL was applied a month ago. In the other cab, oil consumption was cut practically in half. We have also been getting better gas mileage. All in all, POWER SEAL turned out to be just about the best investment we ever made. It paid for itself in two weeks and has been saving money for us ever since, to say nothing of postponing the cost of major overhauls that would have run into real money." *Town Taxi, Douglaston, N.Y.*

SEND NO MONEY!

Simply send the coupon and your Power-Seal injection will be sent to you at once C.O.D. plus postage and handling charges. Or, to save the postage and handling charges, simply enclose full payment with the coupon. For 6-cylinder cars order the Regular Size, only $4.95. For 8-cylinder cars order the Jumbo Size, $7.95. Power-Seal is now available only by mail from us. Send the coupon at once.

RUDSON AUTOMOTIVE INDUSTRIES, Dept. HC-11
400 Madison Ave., New York 17, N. Y.

Please send me ...... tubes of the amazing new POWER SEAL.
☐ Regular Size, for 6-cyl. cars, $4.95   ☐ Jumbo Size, for 8-cyl. cars, $7.95
On arrival I will pay the postman the price indicated above plus postage and delivery charges. I must see an immediate improvement in the pep and power of my car, less oil consumption, greater gas mileage, reduced engine noise, easier starting, faster pickup, within 30 days, or you will refund my full purchase price.

Name ....
Address ....
City .... Zone ...... State ....
☐ Save More! Send cash, check, or money order with coupon and we pay all postage charges. Same money-back guarantee.

THE CHOIR MASTER

BUT THE PAST WOULD NEVER LIVE AGAIN TO ANYONE BUT THE LITTLE OLD MAN-- FOR THAT NEXT EVENING AT THE THEATRE...
B-BUT.. I AM.. I AM THE GREAT CARLO FURELLI, THE CHOIR-MASTER! YOU SAID YOU WANTED ME TO DIRECT FOR YOU! YOU PROMISED!
LISTEN, POP! ALL I WANTED FROM THE AGENCY WAS... A JANITOR! A SIMPLE JANITOR, THAT'S ALL! COME ON, NOW-- BEAT IT! PLEASE!
THIS IS AN OUTRAGE! I--I WILL GO TO THE MAESTRO HIMSELF FOR THIS! I WILL NOT BE TREATED THIS WAY! Y- YOU CANNOT DO THIS TO ME! YOU CANNOT!
HE WOULD SHOW THEM! HE WOULD GO SEE HIS EX-PUPILS OF TEN--THIRTEEN.. OF MANY YEARS AGO. THEY WOULD LISTEN TO HIM! FIRST... LAWRENCE BROWN...
LAWRENCE... LAWRENCE! LOOK HERE ... CARLO, YOUR... YOUR TEACHER! LAWRENCE-- SEE? I TAUGHT YOU EVERYTHING! PLEASE, LAWRENCE!
ONE SIDE, EVERYONE! MR. BROWN HAS TO MAKE A TRAIN!
TELEVISIO STUDIOS
ZORCH!
THE YOUNG IDOL OF THE BOBBY-SOXERS PASSED UP HIS FRANTIC EX-TEACHER. THERE WERE OTHERS, THOUGH, WHO CLIMBED THE LADDER OF SUCCESS THROUGH CARLO FURELLI, FOR INSTANCE, THE FAMOUS BASSO-PROFUNDO, JOHN RELBA. BUT...
I'M SORRY, MISTER FURELLI --MR. RELBA IS NOT IN AND WON'T BE BACK UNTIL NEXT WEEK. GOOD DAY!
BUT I MUST SPEAK TO HIM! HE WILL UNDERSTAND...
THEN... THERE WAS HENRY NAVARRO... PERFORMING AT THE CONCERT HALL. BUT...
WHY DO YOU TREAT ME LIKE THIS? I MUST TALK WITH HENRY. PLEASE-- YOU--YOU ARE HURTING ME!
LOU--TAKE THIS NUT AWAY-- BEFORE I LOSE MY TEMPER!
OR... MARLA ROYDEN, THE NETWORK'S LEADING SOPRANO. BUT...
GIVE HIM A DOLLAR, WEEMS. I--I FEEL SORRY FOR HIM!
YES, MISS ROYDEN!
B-BUT, MARLA.. I--I DO NOT WANT--CHARITY. YOU MUST ALLOW ME TO DIRECT MY CHORUS! YOU MUST!
2

NOT EVEN MARLA UNDERSTOOD. ALL OF THEM HAD FORGOTTEN. BUT HE WOULD NOT LET THEM! SOMEHOW--HE HAD TO SHOW THEM HOW GREAT HE WAS AS A CHOIR-MASTER. PERHAPS AFTER SEEING THE OPERA ON TV NEXT DAY, HE WOULD THINK OF AN IDEA TO MAKE THEM LISTEN...
BUT THIS IS NOT THE OPERA. THIS IS CRAZY! TWO GROWN MEN FIGHTING! I DEMAND THAT YOU CHANGE THE CHANNEL!
GET LOST!
YOU CANNOT TALK TO THE GREAT CARLO FURELLI LIKE THIS! I DEMAND AN APOLOGY! BAD MANNERS WILL NOT--UGHH--HH...
HA, HA...
SHADDUP, POP! NOW GO STAND IN DA CORNER! GWAN--OR I'LL SEW UP THAT YAP O' YOURS!
HOW--HOW DARE THEY SHOW DISRESPECT FOR ME! IT.. IT IS NOT RIGHT. I--I HAVE WORKED TOO HARD--TOO LONG! I AM OLD--BUT MY BRILLIANCE HAS NOT BEEN FORGOTTEN. NO!
BUT WHAT IF ALL MY FORMER PUPILS WERE TO JOIN ME? WOULD I NOT BE FAMOUS? YES! WHY DIDN'T I THINK OF THIS BEFORE? YES--I WILL ASK THEM!
TWO NIGHTS LATER...
W-WHO IS THAT?
IT'S JUST I, HENRY--YOUR OLD TEACHER!
YOU! WHAT ARE YOU DOING HERE? HOW DID YOU GET IN? YOUR HAND--YOU'RE HOLDING SOMETHING!
OH YES.. IT'S MY INVITATION, HENRY! WON'T YOU JOIN MY CHORUS?
NO--D-DON'T COME CLOSER! NO! NO!
THERE'S NOTHING TO BE AFRAID OF, MY BOY--ABSOLUTE-LY NOTHING!
3

AND TWO NIGHTS LATER, IN THE EXCLUSIVE HOTEL MARLA ROYDEN CALLED HOME...
HELLO, MARLA DEAR. YOU LOOK POSITIVELY LOVELY THIS EVENING!
GOOD HEAVENS! Y-YOU STARTLED ME! W-WHAT DO YOU WANT? WHY ARE YOU STARING AT ME LIKE THAT?
IT'S NOTHING! I JUST REMEMBER WHEN YOU WERE A LITTLE GIRL...
Y-YOU'RE LOOKING STRANGE. I--N-NO! D-DON'T COME NEAR ME! DON'T TOUCH ME!
ONE AFTERNOON AFTERWARDS--ON THE OPEN HIGHWAY...
CALL HEADQUARTERS, JIM. LOOKS LIKE MORE THAN A PLAIN ROBBERY TO ME! YEAH,.THIS IS THE CAR OF SOME BIGWIG SINGER. HERE'S THE GUY'S IDENTIFICATION CARD IN THE GLOVE COMPARTMENT-- JOHN RELBA...
NO GUY--NO CHAUFFER. CAR JUST ABANDONED HERE! THINK THEY LEFT IT FOR SOME OTHER REASON?
NO OTHER REASON, JIM. THERE'S BLOOD IN THIS CAR! LOOKS LIKE--MURDER!
TWO WEEKS LATER, THE CITY WAS SLOWLY HEARING ABOUT HIM...
ALL MY PUPILS ARE WITH ME NOW!
STAR TIMES
MYSTERIOUS KILLER SOUGHT IN SINGER
EVENING
SINGERS DI
DAILY NEWS
NINE STARS DISAPPEAR
POLICE DRAGNET SET FOR KILLER
AT A MAJOR NETWORK STUDIO A FEW DAYS AFTERWARDS...
WHAT'S THE OLD COOT WANT, PETE? THOUGHT NO ONE WAS SUPPOSED TO BE ALLOWED IN HERE!
HE'S FROM MAINTENANCE--SHOWED ME A CARD. HE'S THE COSTUME MAN, HE SAID!
SILENCE
4

AT AN ADJOINING STUDIO ON THE AIR THIRTY MINUTES LATER...
--AND SO TAKE A BOX OF-- A BOX OF...WHERE'S THAT MUSIC COMING FROM? TURN IT OFF!
THE SHOW'S RUINED! WHO'S SINGING OVER THE AIR?
I DON'T KNOW--AND I--I CAN'T TURN IT OFF, SIR.. IT'S NOT COMING FROM OUR STUDIO--PROBABLY FROM ONE OF THE ADJOINING STUDIOS NEARBY!
FIND THE GUY! FIRE HIM! HE'LL WISH HE NEVER TRIED TO PULL ANYTHING LIKE THIS ON ME!
THOSE SOUNDS ARE FROM INSIDE HERE! MUST HAVE A WHOLE ARMY OF PEOPLE INSIDE!
OPEN IT! OPEN IT!
GOOD LORD!
NO! NO! NO!
OH, MY GOD!
AH! MY... A-CAPELLO CHORUS, GENTLEMEN! SWEET...SWEET MUSIC!
AND LITTLE CARLO FURELLI PLAYED ON AND ON--HAPPY AGAIN--FOR HE HAD ONCE MORE WON BACK HIS DREAMS!
THE END.
5

THE MIRROR OF LIFE

"What's the use . . . there's no sense to even going on!" That was Bert Taylor talking. Poor Bert Taylor, a guy with failure for a past, and no hope for a future.

He sat in front of the huge mirror in his living room, and stared at his reflection. He laughed, and so did his reflection. He closed his mouth tight, and so did his reflection. And now he spoke, and so did his reflection.

"Look at us," said Bert. "There are two of us, and we're still worthless. We fall in love, and we lose. We enter business, and we lose. We try to do everything, but we lose right down the line. Neither of us has guts, neither of us knows what to do! It's a crime that we have to belong to each other."

Bert Taylor didn't enjoy talking to his reflection. He couldn't even stand the sight of it. But it was the only thing that understood him, that looked at him, that listened to him.

"What do we do now?" Bert asked the reflection. "Do we look for a job? Do we try and find friends? Do we look for love again? Or do we finally realize that we're going to see the same things again, and fail again and again? Tell me!"

Bert Taylor was quiet now. So was his reflection.

"You're not talking, huh?" Bert angrily said to the mirror. "You're afraid to tell me what you think! You're afraid to say that you agree with me! But you can't fool me — I know what you think, I know every thought that crosses your stupid mind! So don't be afraid — talk!"

Bert Taylor was silent again. So was his reflection.

Then suddenly Bert Taylor smiled. His reflection smiled back at him.

"We've got an idea, don't we?" said Bert Taylor. "And we think it's going to solve all our problems!" Bert Taylor was almost delirious with happiness, his mind was bubbling with a plan for victory!

"You're right," said Bert Taylor as he moved closer to his reflection. "It's going to work." He moved even closer.

"All we have to do is join together! You and me alone are nothing — but if we joined as one, we'd be a mountain of power. We could do anything we want, we'd win, we'd win again!"

Bert Taylor was almost on top of his reflection.

"So what do you say?" he asked. "Is it a deal? Do we? AGREED!"

Bert Taylor smashed into the mirror, he grabbed for his reflection, his reflection grabbed for him. There seemed to be a crash of thunder, and then there was silence.

Bert Taylor had fallen to the ground. He was lying in the midst of broken glass. He looked from piece to piece, and he cried.

"We failed . . . we failed . . . and now, I don't even have you!"

**NOW ON SALE! AT ALL NEWSSTANDS!
AMERICA'S MOST SENSATIONAL COMIC BOOK**

TRUE!

Ripley's Believe It or Not!

FIRST TIME PUBLISHED 10¢

FULL LENGTH STORIES IN FULL COLOR

THE MAGAZINE YOU'VE CLAMORED FOR! DON'T MISS IT!

CHILLY CHAMBER MUSIC
SONGS FROM THE SPOOK BOX!

I'll send him one dozen posies...

I'll put a card in beside them...

I'll smile like a dove...

And send them to the one I love!

For BIG MEN ONLY!

SIZES 10-16 **WIDTHS AAA-EEE**

We SPECIALIZE in large sizes only—sizes 10 to 16; widths AAA to EEE. Loafers, Wing Tips, Moccasins, Dress Oxfords, High and Low Work Shoes, House Slippers, Rubbers, Overshoes, Sox. Extra quality at popular prices. Your satisfaction and FIT are guaranteed. We sell by mail only to thousands of delighted customers. We know they're satisfied because they order year after year. If you wear a large shoe size, send coupon at once for handsome FREE STYLE BOOK in color. Mail your coupon today to KING-SIZE, INC. 337, Brockton, Mass.

CUSTOMERS WRITE LETTERS LIKE THESE:
"I never saw a large shoe look so sleek and trim."
—A. L., Depue, Ill.
"For the first time, I can get shoes that feel right for my feet!"
—R.P., Waterford, Mich.

15 SHOE STYLES IN BIG SIZES: DRESS OXFORDS, WORK SHOES, CORDOVANS, CREPE SOLES, MANY OTHERS plus SLIPPERS, SOX, OVERSHOES, RUBBERS and other specialties for Big Men.

FREE style book for BIG MEN!
KING SIZE, Inc. 337, Brockton, Mass.
I wear shoe size 10 to 16. Please rush your Free Style Book in color showing 15 latest shoe styles, plus sox, overshoes, slippers, etc.

Name_____
Address_____
City_____ Zone____ State____

Nose for News

Death is snooping around with his

The man broke inside the big city editor's office, weaving and unsteady, ignoring the mute whine in the janitor's voice...

"You can't go in THERE! Mister McCombs is busy workin'! I'm sorry, Mister Clayton, stand back!"

"Get outta MY WAY, JERRY! Come on! McCombs'll see anyone when there's a BIG STORY in the making!"

"I--I'm sorry, sir, but I--I couldn't stop him!"

"Okay, Jerry, you can leave him with me now. I won't be needing you until LATER!"

"Make it fast, Clayton--and on your way! EX-REPORTER or not-- DRUNKS aren't welcome here!"

"GLAD to see me ain't ya, McCombs? Mind if I take a chair? I--I'm kinda WEAK on my feet!"

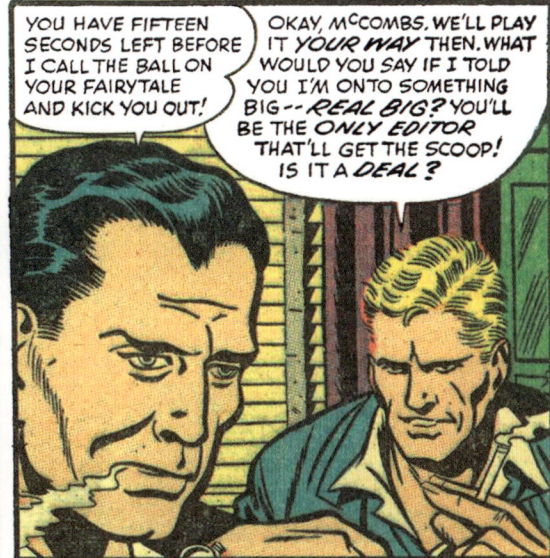

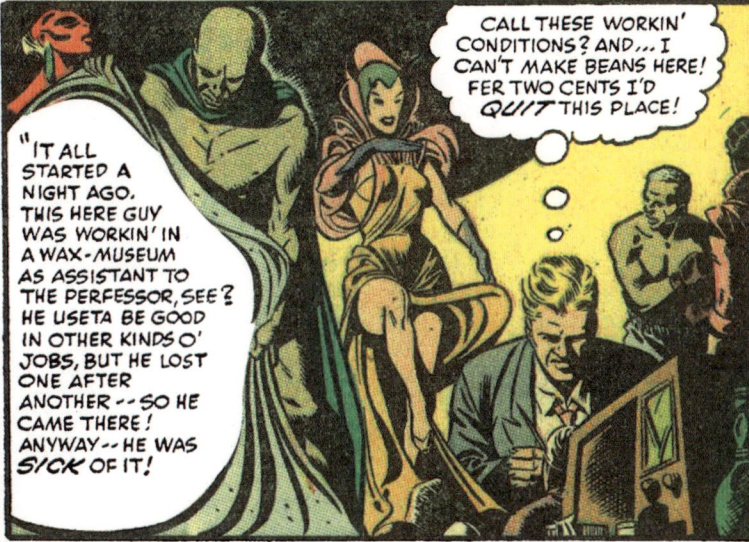

I'LL GIVE YOU EXACTLY *THIRTY SECONDS* TO SAY WHAT YOU HAVE TO SAY--THEN I'M CALLING THE *COPS!* GUESS YOU DIDN'T LEARN YOUR LESSON WHEN I THREW YOU OUT OF THIS OFFICE THREE *YEARS* AGO!

YOU MAKE ME TREMBLE, McCOMBS. YEAH--I'M REALLY SCARED! LISTEN, PALLY! MY ONLY REASON FER COMIN' HERE THIS MORNIN' IS *THIS!* YOU'RE GONNA REINSTATE ME -- WITH FULL PAY-- *RETROACTIVE!*

YOU HAVE FIFTEEN SECONDS LEFT BEFORE I CALL THE BALL ON YOUR FAIRYTALE AND KICK YOU OUT!

OKAY, McCOMBS, WE'LL PLAY IT *YOUR WAY* THEN. WHAT WOULD YOU SAY IF I TOLD YOU I'M ONTO SOMETHING BIG -- *REAL BIG?* YOU'LL BE THE *ONLY EDITOR* THAT'LL GET THE SCOOP! IS IT A *DEAL?*

HMM...IT DEPENDS.. IF IT'S ON THE LEVEL--YOU'LL GET ANOTHER CHANCE. IF NOT--

SIT BACK THEN--'CAUSE WHAT I GOT TO TELL IS ABOUT --*MURDER!*

CALL THESE WORKIN' CONDITIONS? AND... I CAN'T MAKE BEANS HERE! FER TWO CENTS I'D *QUIT* THIS PLACE!

"IT ALL STARTED A NIGHT AGO. THIS HERE GUY WAS WORKIN' IN A WAX-MUSEUM AS ASSISTANT TO THE PERFESSOR, SEE? HE USETA BE GOOD IN OTHER KINDS O' JOBS, BUT HE LOST ONE AFTER ANOTHER -- SO HE CAME THERE! ANYWAY-- HE WAS *SICK* OF IT!"

"BUT HE KEPT IT UP 'CAUSE HE HAD TO HAVE *DOUGH.* ONLY THE PERFESSOR WAS A TOUGH OLD BIRD TO WORK FOR. A REAL SLAVE-DRIVER FROM WAY BACK..."

AND NOW TO CONTINUE WITH OUR HOUR OF MUSICAL INTERLUDES TO SOOTHE YOUR WORKING DAY...

SHUT OFF THAT *INFERNAL RACKET!*

"IT WAS THEN THAT HE DECIDED TO TALK BACK TO THE OLD COOT. THIS WAS THE *LAST STRAW!*"

LOOK, PERFESSOR! IF I WANNA *PLAY* THE RADIO, I *PLAY* IT! MEBBE IF YOU GAVE ME *MORE DOUGH,* I COULD LEARN TO DO WITHOUT ONE!

MAYBE YOU'D LIKE TO BE FIRED, YES? MAYBE I GET MYSELF ANOTHER ASSISTANT WHO TALKS *LITTLE* AND WORKS *MUCH* -- AND WHO DOESN'T GET *DRUNK!*

"SO THE GUY HELD HIS TEMPER. HE HAD NO CHOICE! ONE OF THESE DAYS HE WAS GONNA GET EVEN FOR EVERYTHING! BUT TODAY WASN'T THAT DAY. HE HAD TO HAVE DOUGH TO PACK UP AND GET OUT-- SO HE'D STICK IT OUT. LATER, HE DUCKED OUT TO A BAR FOR A SNORTER...
HELLO, HONEY. LONG TIME NO SEE! WHAT'S BEEN KEEPIN' YOU-- MONEY?
GET LOST, TRUDIE. GO PLAY GAMES WITH SOMEONE ELSE!
I'D RATHER PLAY ALONG WITH YOU, HONEY! GEE, STEVE.. IF ONLY YOU HAD ENOUGH DOUGH TO BLOW THIS BURG. WE COULD GO TO OTHER TOWNS--SEE THINGS-- START A NEW RACKET...
YEAH.. IF I HAD THE DOUGH...
"THE MORE THE GUY THOUGHT ABOUT IT, THE MORE IT ATE INTO HIM. THE DICKENS WITH THE DOUGH, HE THOUGHT. HE WAS GONNA TELL THE PERFESSOR OFF! SO HE WENT BACK TO THE MUSEUM...
HEY, YOU.. COME OUT HERE.. I'M THROUGH-- SEE? THROUGH --DONE FOR!
"AND THEN WHEN HE GOT TO THE DOOR O' THE PERFESSOR'S ROOM, HE SUDDENLY GOT AN IDEA! THIS WAS THE PERFECT SET-UP FOR...
MURDER! I COULD KILL THIS GUY-- AND NO ONE'LL KNOW THE DIFFERENCE!
"HE WAS DRUNK ALL RIGHT... FROM DRINK AND WITH ANGER! HE CREPT UP SLOWLY, SILENTLY...
"AND THEN THE PERFESSOR TURNED AROUND-- AND GOT THE SCARE OF HIS LIFE!
3

"BUT IT WAS A STRUGGLE... RIGHT THERE IN THE DARK--THEY ROLLED OVER AND OVER--EACH TRYIN' TO GET HOLD O' THAT STICKER!
"THEN IT WAS ALL OVER! THE KNIFE WAS COMING DOWN...
YOU'RE GONNA ...DIE...
N-NO.. NO!
"AND THEN...SILENCE AMONG THE WAX DUMMIES...
"THEN--AFTER AWHILE..THE LIVE GUY AROSE. HE WAS TIRED...EXHAUSTED--BUT HE HAD WON!
GOTTA GET OUT OF HERE!
"THEN--MAKING SURE HE WASN'T SPOTTED, THE GUY LEFT BY THE WINDOW INSTEAD O' THE DOOR...
CAN'T TAKE ANY CHANCES. GOT TO BE SILENT!
"TWENTY SECONDS LATER, HE WAS RUNNING THROUGH ONE O' THE ALLEYWAYS--THINKING HE COMMITTED THE PERFECT MURDER...
4

--AND THAT'S YOUR SCOOP! THAT'S THE WHOLE STORY! IT HAPPENED ONLY A FEW HOURS AGO! WELL--IS IT A STORY?
YEAH! IT'S A STORY ALL RIGHT! THERE'S ONLY ONE LITTLE DETAIL YOU'VE OVERLOOKED!
THE COPS!
I THOUGHT YOU'D BE HERE, LIEUTENANT! LEAVING OPEN THAT PRIVATE WIRE TO YOUR OFFICE DID THE TRICK!
OKAY, CLAYTON! YOU HAVEN'T A CHANCE! YOUR ENTIRE TALE IS KIND OF FISHY! HOW COME YOU KNOW THE TIME, PLACE, AND EVENTS IN SUCH DETAIL IF YOU WEREN'T THERE YOURSELF WHEN IT HAPPENED?
THAT'S EASY.. I CAN EXPLAIN--
THEN EXPLAIN THAT BLOOD-STAIN ON YOUR COATSLEEVE, CLAYTON. THE NEXT TIME YOU WANT TO BRING IN A BIG STORY--YOU'D BETTER WASH IT OFF!--IF THERE'LL EVER BE A NEXT TIME!
IT--IT'S COME THROUGH MY CLOTHES...MY OLD JOB--YOU PROMISED!
HOLD IT, BUDDY! MAKE ANY WRONG MOVES AND YOU'LL--HEY! WHAT'S WRONG?
DON'T YOU SEE? I NEVER HELD ON TO THAT KNIFE... I'M NOT...THE KILLER... I--I'M--THE MAN HE...
..MURDERED!
THE END
5

ALL TIME FAVORITES—SMASH VALUES

COULD YOU USE $1,000,000.00?

We'd Like to Hand You the Million — But You Realize That's Impossible

BUT WE CAN MAKE YOU HEALTHY WITH **HIP POCKET GYM** WEIGHS ONLY 1½ lbs.

Put On Muscle — **Take Off Fat**

MR. AMERICA USES HIP POCKET GYM! Among the Mr. Americas of the last three years you'll find a fan of HIP POCKET GYM! In a recent article in a top health and strength magazine he was photographed in 13 poses showing his favorite exercises with HIP POCKET GYM — for developing the biceps, triceps, neck and for adding inches to the back and shoulders.

FREE with every HIP POCKET GYM you get FREE a Complete Book of Health and Strength Exercises! Makes a Wonderful Gift for everyone.

First Time Special Offer $3.95 Postpaid. Sold Nationwide at $5.95.

THERE'S NO MAGIC, NO MIRACLES— HIP POCKET GYM helps both stout and skinny people. Using scientific and medical principles, it helps the body help itself by automatically adjusting to your strength and ability. You do not have to be Mr. America — even children can use it!

SO SIMPLE! SO EASY! No nailing on walls — no crawling on floors—or swinging from ceilings! No lengthy correspondence courses. A few minutes a day in a lazy man's way rids you of that run-down, tired feeling!

- Recommended by Over Half Million People! Hundreds of Thousands of users during past 25 years without one word of advertising!
- Builds Health in Veterans Hospitals! HIP POCKET GYM is used in Veterans Hospitals.
- Scientifically Constructed HIP POCKET GYM is made of pure, natural rubber that actually improves with age! It is so light and compact, you can take it wherever you go!

5 Day Money Back Guarantee

ALL AMERICAN JACKET

Ideal professional style warm-up jacket. Beautifully tailored satin. Contrasting colored sleeve panels, knitted collar, wrists, waistband. Warm lining. Weather-sealed! Great for sport, school, any time or place. Colors: Scarlet & White; Royal Blue & Gold; Royal Blue & White; Maroon & Gold; Kelly & Orange. Boys' sizes 6-20 — $6.95, Men's sizes 34-48 — $8.95 FREE: Your own initials on your jacket!

Play PRO BASEBALL

Newest Sports Game Sensation

VOLUNTARY PITCHING : BATTING BASE RUNNING

SOMETHING DIFFERENT TO DO: Run Your Own World Series at Home—Great Idea for Teen-Ager Parties—Fast Exciting Fun for Adults—

SOMETHING DIFFERENT TO GIVE: Birthday, Hostess, Student Presents, Party Prizes—

Complete with Rule Book, Score Pad, Ball, Base-Runners. Endorsed by members of Organized Baseball.

Action, Exciting Situations Close Decisions as in Big Leagues

A challenge to baseball fans, youth or adult

FORMERLY	$5.00
NOW ONLY	$3.95

TAKING THE COUNTRY BY STORM

"Little Wonder" RADIO SET

Compact in size but big in results. The open type detector permits adjustments to be made to the finest degree. This set includes the Philmore Super-sensitive Crystal which assures quick results when "looking" for a station, because the entire surface of the crystal is sensitive.

- Specially designed hook-up assuring reception within a radius of twenty-five (25) miles from a broadcasting station.
- Under favorable climatic conditions reception may be received as far as one hundred (100) miles from broadcasting station.
- Costs nothing for upkeep.
- No batteries, tubes or expensive accessories required.
- Manufactured in Genuine BAKELITE in various colors. The advantages of bakelite are well-known for its beauty and cleanliness. It will retain its color and can be kept clean for the life of the set which is practically infinite.

LOTS OF FUN FOR YOUNGSTERS AND ADULTS
INTRODUCTORY SPECIAL PRICE **2.98**
NO C.O.D.'s—WE PREPAY ALL PARCEL POST CHARGES

LOOK LIKE A BIG LEAGUER!

Wear This Major League **BASEBALL CAP**

(NOT A CHEAP IMITATION) Real Big League Team colors and insignia. Custom tailored professional all wool with genuine leather sweat-band. Shower-proof. Your choice of any American or National League Team. STATE TEAM & SIZE $2.98

STAR ATHLETE'S T-SHIRT!

Authentic 2-Color insignia of your favorite Big League Team, colored neckband. Best combed yarn, full-cut. Color fast, won't run. Boy's sizes (small, medium, large). State Team and Size ONLY $1.29

DiMAGGIO'S OWN STORY

Lucky to be a Yankee Intimate-Action-Packed Story of His Life in This 244 Pages—$1 Postpaid

---

ALL STAR SALES Dept CB BOX 691
Grand Central Station, N.Y. 17, N.Y.

Gentlemen: Please send me the following:
ENCLOSED find cash, check or money order.
- ☐ Hip Pocket Gym ..$3.95   ☐ Radio Set $2.98
- ☐ Boys Jacket .....$6.95   ☐ Baseball Hat ...$2.98
- ☐ Mens Jacket .....$8.95   ☐ T-Shirt $1.29
- ☐ Pro Baseball ....$3.95   ☐ DiMaggio Book ..$1.00

Name ....
Address ....

IT'S HERE! EXCITING...AMAZING...
HARVEY FAMOUS NAME COMICS
HARVEY 3-D
SO REAL IT
NEVER BEFOR
EFFECTS... AS
READERS FRO
HOW MUCH T
EFFECTS FOU
LOOK FOR T
SIGN THAT IT
OTHER 3-D
LOOK FOR
ON SALE EVERYWHE
FIRST REAL ADVENTURE MAGAZINE IN FULL 3-D TERRIFIC TRUE-STEREO EFFECTS! FIRST ISSUE A SELLOUT! LOOK FOR ISSUE 2.
ADVENTURES IN 3-D
FIRST 3-D HERO! CAPT. 3-D FROM THE WORLD OF THE THIRD DIMENSION BRINGS YOU THRILLS NEVER BEFORE IN A COMIC!
CAPTAIN 3D
TRUE 3D
TRUE STORIES WITH THE NEW PENETRATING THIRD DIMENSION. PULSATING EFFECTS WITH HARVEY'S NEW THREEEEE-D PROCESS
NOW ON SALE
LIMITED QUANTITIES
GET YOUR COPIES NOW
INSIST ON
FOR THE BES

JUMPS OUT OF THE PAGE

YOUR SIGN OF GOOD READING ENTERTAINMENT

HARVEY FAMOUS NAME COMICS

**BEST IN 2D COMICS
BEST IN 3D MAGAZINES**

...WE BEEN ABLE TO BRING YOU SUCH WONDERFUL ... NEW HARVEY 3-D MAGAZINES.
... OVER THE WORLD HAVE WRITTEN AND TOLD US ...E ENJOYED AND MARVELED AT THE TRUE 3-D ...LY IN HARVEY 3-D MAGAZINES.
..."H" IN THE TOP LEFT CORNER, IT'S YOUR ...D 3-D! BETTER THAN YOU'LL SEE IN ANY ...INE!

HARVEY BRINGS YOU THE BEST IN FULL COLOR COMICS --*NOW* IT BRINGS YOU THE BEST IN 3-D COMIC MAGAZINES! LOOK FOR SPECIAL ISSUES OF YOUR ALL TIME FAVORITES IN 3-D!

...ARVEY 3-D MAGAZINES!
...SK FOR THEM BY NAME! INSIST ON HARVEY!

...3-D DOLLY! THE ...MAZING KID WHO CAN ...EE THINGS--YOU *CAN'T* ... UNLESS YOU WEAR THE ...RVEY MAGIC 3-D VIEWERS ...PPLIED IN ANY HARVEY 3-D MAGAZINE.

SHE JUMPS RIGHT OUT OF THE PAGE
3-D DOLLY
...U'LL LOVE 3-D DOLLY.

DON'T MISS THIS!
FUNNY 3-D
JUST LIKE A VISIT TO A 3-D MOVIE! ANIMALS ALMOST JUMP INTO YOUR LAP. WONDERFUL 3-D STORIES FOR ALL AGES!

HARVEY 3-D HITS -- SAD SACK
SO REAL IT JUMPS OUT AT YOU

FREE OF EXTRA COST WHEN YOU BUY ANY HARVEY 3-D MAGAZINE
2 PAIRS OF 3-D VIEWERS

...ARVEY 3-D MAGAZINES
...EAL TRUE THIRD DIMENSION

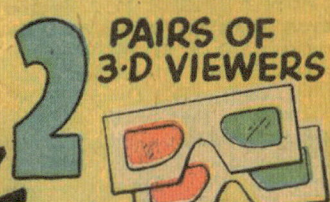

HOW TO FIX ANY PART OF ANY CAR

USED BY U.S. ARMED FORCES

QUICKLY -- EASILY -- RIGHT!

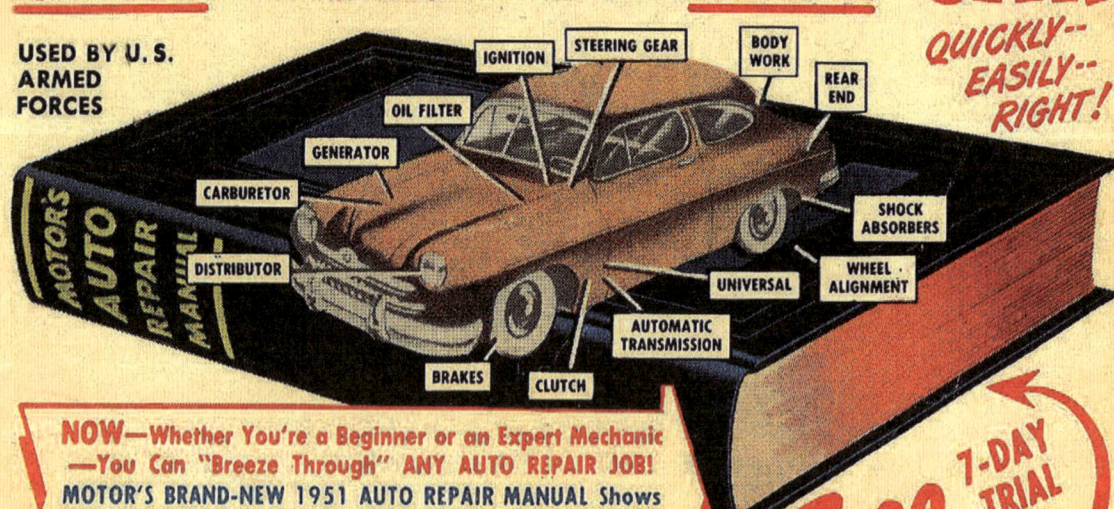

Labels on illustration: IGNITION, STEERING GEAR, BODY WORK, REAR END, OIL FILTER, GENERATOR, CARBURETOR, DISTRIBUTOR, SHOCK ABSORBERS, WHEEL ALIGNMENT, UNIVERSAL, AUTOMATIC TRANSMISSION, BRAKES, CLUTCH

MOTOR'S AUTO REPAIR MANUAL

NOW—Whether You're a Beginner or an Expert Mechanic —You Can "Breeze Through" ANY AUTO REPAIR JOB! MOTOR'S BRAND-NEW 1951 AUTO REPAIR MANUAL Shows You HOW—With 2300 PICTURES AND SIMPLE STEP-BY-STEP INSTRUCTIONS.

Free 7-DAY TRIAL Return and Pay Nothing If Not Satisfied!

COVERS EVERY JOB ON EVERY CAR BUILT FROM 1935 THRU 1951

YES, it's easy as A-B-C to do any "fix-it" job on any car whether it's a simple carburetor adjustment or a complete overhaul. Just look up the job in the index of MOTOR'S New AUTO REPAIR MANUAL. Turn to pages covering job. Follow the clear, illustrated step-by-step instructions. Presto—the job is done!

No guesswork! MOTOR'S Manual takes nothing for granted. Tells you where to start. What tools to use. Then it leads you easily and quickly through the entire operation!

Over TWO THOUSAND Pictures! So Complete, So Simple, You CAN'T Go Wrong!

NEW REVISED 1951 Edition covers everything you need to know to repair 800 car models. 771 giant pages; 2300 "This-Is-How" pictures. Over 200 "Quick-Check" charts—more than 38,000 essential repair specifications. Over 225,000 service and repair facts. Instructions and pictures are so clear you can't go wrong!

Even a green beginner mechanic can do a good job with this giant manual before him. And if you're a top-notch mechanic, you'll find short-cuts that will amaze you. No wonder this guide is used by the U. S. Army and Navy! No wonder hundreds of thousands of men call it the "Auto Repair Mans' Bible"!

Meat of Over 150 Official Shop Manuals

Engineers from every automobile plant in America worked out these time-saving procedures for their own motor car line. Now the editors of MOTOR have gathered together this wealth of "Know-How" from over 150 Official Factory Shop Manuals, "boiled it down" into crystal-clear terms in one handy indexed book!

Try Book FREE 7 Days

SEND NO MONEY! Just mail coupon! When the postman brings book, pay him nothing. First, make it show you what it's got! Unless you agree this is the greatest time-saver and work-saver you've ever seen — return book in 7 days and pay nothing. Mail coupon today! Address: *MOTOR Book Dept., Desk 9011B, 250 West 55th St., N. Y. 19, N. Y.*

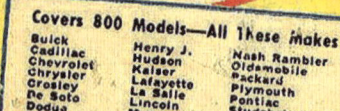

Same FREE Offer On MOTOR'S Truck and Tractor Manual
Covers EVERY job on EVERY popular make gasoline truck, tractor made from 1936 thru 1949. FREE 7-Day Trial. Check proper box in coupon.

Covers 800 Models—All These makes
Buick, Cadillac, Chevrolet, Chrysler, Crosley, De Soto, Dodge, Ford, Frazer, Henry J., Hudson, Kaiser, Lafayette, La Salle, Lincoln, Mercury, Nash, Nash Rambler, Oldsmobile, Packard, Plymouth, Pontiac, Studebaker, Terraplane, Willys
ALSO tune-up adjustments for others

Many Letters of Praise from Users
"MOTOR'S Manual paid for itself on the first 2 jobs, and saved me valuable time by eliminating guesswork."
—W. SCHROP, Ohio.

He Does Job in 30 Min. — Fixed motor another mechanic had worked on half a day. With your Manual I did it in 30 minutes."
—C. AUBERRY, Tenn.

MAIL COUPON NOW FOR 7-DAY FREE TRIAL

MOTOR BOOK DEPT.
Desk 9011B, 250 W. 55th St., New York 19, N. Y.

Rush to me at once (check box opposite book you want):

☐ **MOTOR'S NEW AUTO REPAIR MANUAL.** If O.K., I will remit $1 in 7 days (plus 35c delivery charges), $2 monthly for 2 months and a final payment of 95c one month after that. Otherwise I will return the book postpaid in 7 days. (Foreign price, remit $8 cash with order.)

☐ **MOTOR'S TRUCK & TRACTOR REPAIR MANUAL.** If O.K., I will remit $2 in 7 days, and $2 monthly for 3 months, plus 35c delivery charges with final payment. Otherwise I will return book postpaid in 7 days. (Foreign price, remit $10 cash with order.)

Print Name..Age..........

Address...

City...State.........................

☐ Check box and save 35c shipping charge by enclosing WITH coupon entire payment of $5.95 for Auto Repair Manual (or $8 for Truck and Tractor Repair Manual.) Same 7-day return-refund privilege applies.

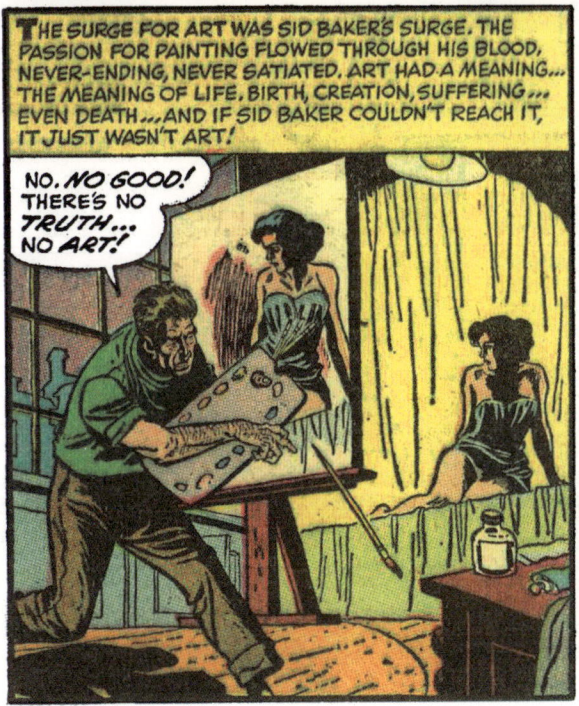

THE DEATH MASK

An artist's soul needs satisfaction. Sid Baker wanted to paint a face worthy of his canvas and oils. And he found...

The surge for art was Sid Baker's surge. The passion for painting flowed through his blood, never-ending, never satiated. Art had a meaning... the meaning of life, birth, creation, suffering... even death... and if Sid Baker couldn't reach it, it just wasn't art!

No. NO GOOD! There's no TRUTH... NO ART!

But Sid Baker knew that an easel, a palette and canvas stretched as tight as skin over a frame don't make a lasting portrait. Those are the ingredients... but the recipe is elusive... the product almost impossible to get.

WEAK! PUERILE! Like all the rest— a face devoid of character—of meaning—of LIFE!

SPLAT!

THE MANY SUBJECTS...THE THOUSANDS OF FACES THAT MARCHED BY SID BAKER IN MYRIADIC VARIETY... WERE NOT ENOUGH FOR HIM. THE BREATH OF LIFE WAS NOT SUFFICIENT--TRUTH IN ART HAD TO COME FROM SOME PLACE ELSE...FROM INSIDE-OUT... FROM WITHIN!
E- ENOUGH OF OTHER PEOPLE...THEY'RE TOO PUNY! MY IMAGINATION WILL GIVE ME A SUBJECT!
AS SID BAKER STRETCHED A NEW CANVAS, ITS VIRGIN SURFACE CLEAN AND BARE...SEEMINGLY SCREAMING FOR THE FIRST CARESSING BRUSH STROKE, HE FELT THE WELL OF INSPIRATION BUBBLE. THE BRUSH DENTED A NEW GLOB OF PAINT...THE SURFACE WAS ADEPTLY STAINED... THE PORTRAIT WAS BEGUN. FEVERISHLY, HE CONTINUED THROUGH THE NIGHT...
THIS IS IT. I--I CAN FEEL IT!
THE HOURS PASSED...FIRST SLOWLY, THEN SWIFTLY...THEN...!
FINISHED! ODD- THERE'S SOMETHING STRANGE ABOUT IT- SOMETHING HORRIBLE ABOUT THE PAINTING...
THERE WAS SOMETHING HORRIBLE ABOUT IT...SOMETHING INDEFINABLY HORRIBLE.. IT WAS THE PORTRAIT OF A MAN...NOTHING GROTESQUE ABOUT HIS FACE...NOTHING UNUSUAL ABOUT HIS SLIGHTLY ROTUNDULAR HEAD... NOTHING...EXCEPT THAT A HEAVY ROPE WAS WRAPPED AROUND HIS NECK! THE MAN IN THE PORTRAIT WAS SCREAMING...HE WAS HANGED!
NO, NO! I SEEM TO HEAR IT SCREAM! THIS IS NOT MY IMAGINATION! SOMEWHERE... SOME PLACE... THIS MAN LIVES!
IF HE LIVES I MUST FIND HIM- WHEREVER HE IS!
AND IN THE STUDIO, THE PORTRAIT REMAINED AMONG THE BRUSHES AND OILS OF SID BAKER-- MUTE! BUT IS IT MUTE? DID NOT THE MOUTH JUST QUIVER WITH PAIN... DID NOT THE EYES JUST BULGE A TRIFLE MORE?
2

Panel 1: SID BAKER RAN OUT INTO THE STREETS...SEEKING THE CONTORTED FACE THAT SPRANG FROM HIS IMAGINATION...BUT THE STREETS WERE CROWDED WITH FACES...ALL KINDS OF FACES...

HOW? WHERE... CAN I SEE... HIM?

Panel 2: HE FOLLOWED THE WINDING STREETS...LEADING INTO ROADS AND DEAD ENDS AND PATHWAYS TEARING INTO THE DREGS OF SOCIETY...AND STILL NOT FINDING THE FACE!

NO. HE'S...NOT HERE! WHERE? *WHERE?*

Panel 3: STILL SEEKING...STILL SEARCHING...

MAYBE?—

HEY, YOU! GET OUT OF HERE!

Panel 4: HOURS...AND I HAVEN'T SEEN HIS FACE YET...

Panel 5: THE MAN IN MY PAINTING MUST BE *SOMEWHERE!*

Panel 6: HIS EYES HURT...HIS BRAIN WHIRLED...HIS BREATH CAME HARD. THEN HE CAME TO A COBBLE-STONED ALLEY DROWNED BY A YELLOW EERINESS THAT CAME FROM A DOORWAY...

OH...(CHOK)...WHERE? *WHERE?*

Panel 7: HE WALKED TOWARDS THE DOORWAY. THE SCENT OF GRANITE AROSE ...AND THE SOUND OF FRAGILE CHIPPING OF STONE GREW LOUDER! HE REACHED IT...AND ENTERED A SMALL SHOP...

HELLO! WHAT CAN I DO FOR YOU?

I...IT'S...IT'S HIM ...*THE FACE IN THE PORTRAIT!*

I-I'M A PAINTER-I-I-SEE YOU'RE A-
YES, I'M A SCULPTOR... PAINTING? BAH! THE ART OF SCULPTURE IS THE NEAREST ART TO LIFE ITSELF!
OH, I'M SORRY... I'VE OFFENDED YOU! PLEASE FORGIVE ME. IT--IT'S JUST THAT I'M VERY... NERVOUS!
THAT'S ALL RIGHT.
I'M SO LONELY. IT'S GOOD TO SPEAK TO SOMEONE... I'M WORKING NOW JUST TO GET THE HORROR OUT OF MY MIND...
LAST NIGHT I HAD A MIND-SEARING DREAM... I FELT A HORRIBLE PAIN...
AND WHEN I AWOKE-THERE WERE ROPE BURNS AROUND MY NECK!
IT WAS TRUE! SID BAKER HAD FOUND THE KEY TO IMAGINATION...THE ONE THING THAT WOULD TRANSPOSE IT INTO REALITY. EVERYTHING WAS CORRECT, EVEN DOWN TO...
THE ROPE!
EVEN DOWN TO THE ROPE!
AGAIN YOU SEEM EXCITED. MY DREAM, PERHAPS? IT PORTENDS NOTHING--A DISORDERED IMAGINATION! I-I DON'T KNOW!
BUT ENOUGH OF IDLENESS... I MUST GO BACK TO MY WORK-I NEVER USE A MODEL, YOU KNOW. I INVENT AS I GO ALONG. THE FACE I AM CARVING IS WITHIN ME-CRYING FOR UTTERANCE IN STONE!
4

THE STONE-MAKER GRIPPED HIS LONG-STEMMED MALLET. HE PLACED THE CHISEL EDGE AGAINST THE GRANITE. THEN... MALLET STRUCK AGAINST CHISEL...A CHIP FLEW CRAZILY IN THE AIR... AND SID BAKER FELT SEARING PAIN!
EEOWWW! MY-- MY FACE!
SOMETHING WRONG? PERHAPS YOU'D BETTER MOVE BACK A LITTLE!
THE MALLET STRUCK AGAIN...
YOU MUST BE CAREFUL. STONE CHIPS CAN BE DANGEROUS!
MY SKIN...FEELS AS IF...BEING TORN...
I--I CAN'T STOP!
THE CHIPPING CONTINUED! BAKER SCREAMED...SCREAMED...
STOP IT! STOP! STOP!
I MUST FINISH! SOMETHING... IMPELS ME!
I--I CAN'T STAND IT. STOP...PLEASE STOP! OH, PLEASE...
BUT THE STONE-MAKER CONTINUED, EACH FLYING CHIP SEEMING TO TEAR A PIECE FROM SID BAKER'S FACE. IT BEGAN TO FALL AWAY LIKE ROTTEN PLASTER ON A WALL... REVEALING THE TAUT MUSCLES BENEATH. FINALLY...
I'VE FINISHED!
WHAT HAPPENED TO ME? WHAT HAPPENED?
THE FACE...THE HORROR ON IT! WHY, IT LOOKS... LIKE... YOU!
THE END

LOVERS

Janet waited for him. She paced the floor of her luxurious living room, and waited.

Will would soon be there. He'd rush in, ready to take her in his arms, ready to soothe her with his kisses. But there could be no more of that. It would have to end tonight.

"Why did I let myself fall in love with him?" Janet asked herself. "Why did I let it go this far?"

She couldn't answer herself. Love had seized her and led her on and on. But now, because of her love, she'd have to tell him it was all over.

The door-bell was ringing now. Janet calmly walked to the door. She opened it, and Will was standing there.

"Hello, Darling," he said. He took her in his arms and kissed her long and hard.

Janet allowed it. This would be the last time ... the farewell kiss. She hung there in his arms, trying to force every second into an eternity.

Then she led him into the living room, onto the spacious armchair.

"What's the matter?" he finally asked. "Why did you call me so suddenly?"

"I have to talk to you," Janet said slowly. "I have to tell you something I should have told you months ago."

"You're married," Will said with a grin.

"Don't be silly," she answered. "And don't joke about it!"

"Then what is it, Darling?" He looked up at her, studying the beauty of her haunting, ashen face.

"I can't see you any more," she said, turning her back to him, holding back her tears.

He didn't move from the chair. All he said was: "Why?"

"Don't ask me," she said. "Please don't ask me."

"Why?" he repeated. He got up now and went to her. He turned her round and looked deeply into her eyes. "Why?" he said again.

"You won't believe me," she said, her voice merely a whisper.

"Tell me," he said.

"Then you must promise you'll leave me, that you'll forget me, that you'll never look for me again."

"Just tell me," he said

She turned her back again, looking out the window at the cold black night.

She spoke deliberately, quietly. "I'm a vampire," she said.

He threw his arms around her. He drew her close to him. "I knew it," he said. "I knew it — and so am I!"

They kissed with a joining of ecstasy as the full moon climbed to the sky.

Join the CHILL-OF-THE-MONTH CLUB!
SUBSCRIBE now TO... CHAMBER OF CHILLS
SPECIAL OFFER 12 ISSUES $1.00

CHAMBER OF CHILLS
1860 BROADWAY
NEW YORK 23, N.Y.

CHECK [X]
12 ISSUES $1.00
25 ISSUES $2.00

ENCLOSED IS $ _____
FOR THE MAGAZINES CHECKED

PRINT NAME _____
ADDRESS _____
CITY _____
ZONE ___ STATE _____

SORRY, NO SUBSCRIPTIONS OUTSIDE OF U.S.A.

CHILLY CHAMBER MUSIC
SONGS FROM THE SPOOK BOX!

HOW ARE THINGS IN DANNE...MORA...

ARE THE STOOLIE-BIRDS STILL SINGING THERE?

ARE THERE FORMER CROOKS...STONEY LOOKS...THAT WANTING-TO-KILL AIR?

ARE THEY STILL HIGH AND DREAMY THERE?

CHILLY CHAMBER MUSIC
SONGS FROM THE SPOOK BOX!

DANCE AROUND THE MAY POLE HOT-PATOOTY PANDER...

DANCE AROUND THE GAY POLE GOOSEY-GOOSEY GANDER!

ALL AROUND WE GO... IN AND OUT...IN AND OUT...

SEE THE TOP...SEE THE HEAD... DRIPPY-DROPPY DANDER!

83

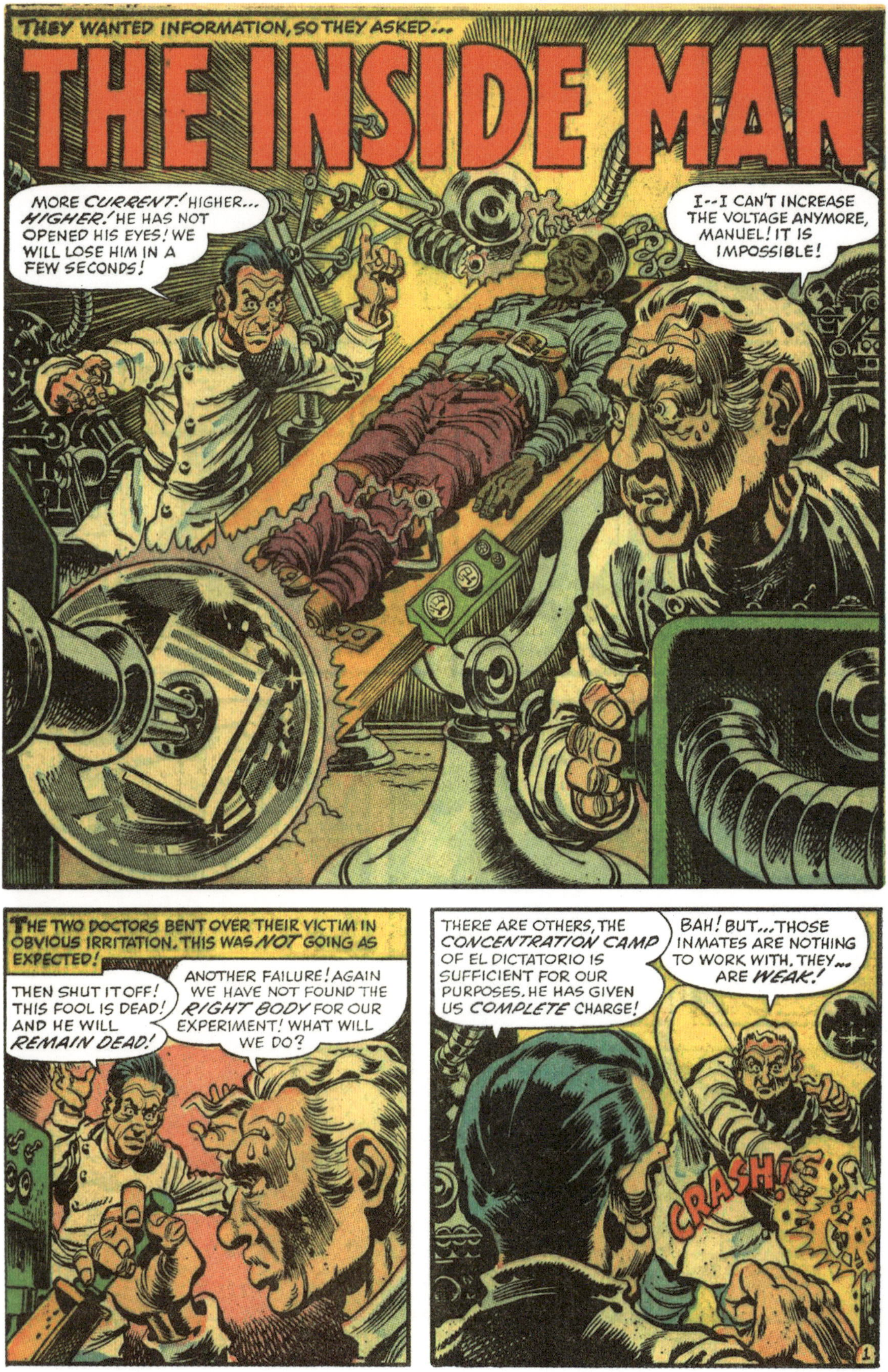
THEY WANTED INFORMATION, SO THEY ASKED...
THE INSIDE MAN
MORE CURRENT! HIGHER... HIGHER! HE HAS NOT OPENED HIS EYES! WE WILL LOSE HIM IN A FEW SECONDS!
I--I CAN'T INCREASE THE VOLTAGE ANYMORE, MANUEL! IT IS IMPOSSIBLE!
THE TWO DOCTORS BENT OVER THEIR VICTIM IN OBVIOUS IRRITATION. THIS WAS NOT GOING AS EXPECTED!
THEN SHUT IT OFF! THIS FOOL IS DEAD! AND HE WILL REMAIN DEAD!
ANOTHER FAILURE! AGAIN WE HAVE NOT FOUND THE RIGHT BODY FOR OUR EXPERIMENT! WHAT WILL WE DO?
THERE ARE OTHERS, THE CONCENTRATION CAMP OF EL DICTATORIO IS SUFFICIENT FOR OUR PURPOSES. HE HAS GIVEN US COMPLETE CHARGE!
BAH! BUT... THOSE INMATES ARE NOTHING TO WORK WITH. THEY... ARE WEAK!
CRASH!
1

COME-- LET US WALK! REMEMBER THAT WE ARE THE PRISON DOCTORS HERE... AND EL DICTATORIO OF THIS COUNTRY IS VERY KIND TO US! WE HAVE AN ENTIRE ARRAY OF HIS POLITICAL HOSTAGES TO CHOOSE FROM!
GIVE ME YOUR WHIP, MANUEL!
AIIEEEEE!
CRACK!
YOU DIRTY DOGS! TOO BAD I CAN'T PUT MY HANDS AROUND YOUR THROATS AND-- SQUEEZE!
AH--! THAT ONE HAS SPIRIT! I THINK HE WILL DO NICELY!
AND ONE HOUR LATER...
W-WHAT IS THIS? WHAT ARE YOU GOING TO DO WITH ME?
AS SCIENTIFIC RESEARCHERS, WE HAVE FOUND A METHOD FOR BRINGING BACK THE DEAD! AND WE WISH TO CHECK OUR FINDINGS!
YOU'RE NOTHING BUT BUTCHERS... BUTCHERS! LET ME GO! YOU HAVE NO RIGHT! HELP! HELP!
QUICKLY! THE CATHODE RAY! QUICKLY!
HE IS DEAD!
NOW...TO WAIT FOR THE NECESSARY TIME LAPSE!
YAAAAA!
2

THE TWO SCIENTISTS ARRANGED THEIR INSTRUMENTS FOR THE RE-AWAKENING, AND MINUTES LATER--OUT OF THE LAB...
TWO HOURS OF COMPLETE DEATH FOR THE BODY ORGANISM WILL MORE THAN PROVE OUR THEORY, CONRAD. WE CAN ALLOW NO POSSIBILITY OF HIS BODY CELLS STILL BEING ALIVE BEFORE WE BRING HIM BACK TO LIFE AGAIN!
YOU ARE RIGHT, MANUEL. LET US HAVE SOME LUNCH!
ONE HOUR AFTERWARDS...
THIS FOOD WAS EXCELLENT! IS IT TIME YET?
COME! WE MUST NOT DELAY!
INSIDE THE LABORATORY MINUTES LATER...
THE VELOCITY HAS INCREASED TO POINT 93675. VOLTAGE HAS BEEN INDUCTED.. OXYGEN AND INERT GASES PUMPING...SWITCH ON THE CURRENT! CAREFULLY!
CURRENT ON!
SNAP!
LUCAS
WHAT IS HAPPENING? IS THE BODY MOVING?
NOTHING--NOTHING YET! TURN ON THE RHEOSTATS--HURRY! WE CAN'T HAVE FAILED AGAIN! HURRY! HURRY!
SUDDENLY--SOMETHING DID MOVE!
LOOK! HIS FACE--!
THE EYES HAVE OPENED!
3

SHUT OFF EVERYTHING! CONTROLS OFF--DYNAMOS CLOSED--SWITCH OUT!
HE IS TRYING TO SIT UP! WE HAVE BROUGHT HIM BACK, MANUEL! WE HAVE BROUGHT HIM BACK FROM THE DEAD!
WHAT WAS IT LIKE--THAT OTHER PLACE? TELL US! QUICKLY! TELL US!
DID YOU HAVE AWARENESS? IS THERE ANOTHER WORLD? WHAT WAS IT LIKE TO BE DEAD?
I--I'VE RETURNED! I'VE BEEN DEAD...AND--I.. I RETURNED BACK TO--HERE!
YES..YES..FOOL! ANSWER US--OR WE'LL RIP THAT SWOLLEN TONGUE OF YOURS OUT BY THE ROOTS! WHAT IS DEATH LIKE?
DEATH IS--ECSTASY! DEATH IS A PARADISE WHERE ALL ENJOY RAPTURES DIVINE! THERE IS--THERE IS NOTHING BUT BLISS!
INCREDIBLE!
Y-YES...YES! DEATH IS A COMPLETE JOY! IT'S...(CHOKE) ...WONDERFUL... MAGNIFICENT! HAPPINESS IS PART OF DEATH!
OUR EXPERIMENT HAS SUCCEEDED!
--BEYOND OUR WILDEST DREAMS!
WHA---T?
BLAM!
4

YOU...YOU HAVE KILLED HIM AGAIN, CONRAD! ARE YOU CRAZY?
NO! WE NEED NOT CONCERN OURSELVES WITH WHAT IS GOOD OR RIGHT! WE CAN LIVE -- LIVE OUR LIVES EXACTLY AS WE WANT ON EARTH -- WITHOUT REMORSE! DON'T YOU UNDERSTAND?
SO MANUEL AND CONRAD QUIETLY MADE PLANS -- UNTIL ONE YEAR LATER, IN THE PALACE OF EL DICTATORIO...
KILL THEM ALL! DO NOT LET ONE ESCAPE! WE SHALL RULE!
BESIDES -- WE ARE DOING THEM A FAVOR! THEY ARE ALL GOING TO PARADISE!
BLAM!
AND AS THE YEARS PASSED BY, MANUEL AND CONRAD LIED, CHEATED, KILLED, BURNED, PILLAGED, MURDERED THEIR WAY INTO EVIL AND AVARICE... THE LIKE OF WHICH HAD NEVER BEEN WITNESSED BY THE WORLD...
THEN -- AS FATE WOULD HAVE IT... BOTH OF THEM DIED ALMOST SIMULTANEOUSLY OF NATURAL CAUSES IN THEIR RESPECTIVE PALACES -- MANUEL THROUGH ONE OF HIS USUAL ANGRY FITS OF TEMPER -- CONRAD BY GORGING HIMSELF WITH FOOD...
...AND WHEN NEXT THEY OPENED THEIR EYES...
WELCOME, FRIENDS!
YOU!!
W-WHY ARE YOU LAUGHING AT US SO STRANGELY?
BECAUSE I'VE MADE YOU LIE AND CHEAT AND MURDER WORSE THAN ANY OTHER SOUL HERE! I'VE LIED TOO -- AND WE'LL ALL PAY -- BUT NOT LIKE YOU -- OH NO! SO WELCOME TO YOUR PARADISE, FRIENDS! WELCOME TO -- HELL!
YAAAAA
THE END

Yours ALMOST AS A Gift!

ONLY 25¢ FOR THIS VALUABLE U.S. COMMEMORATIVE SET OF
30 History IN THE Making STAMPS
Guaranteed to be Worth THREE Times as Much!

GENERALS—Portraits of 3 famous Civil War Generals—U.S. Grant, Sheridan, and Sherman. Color, purple.

COMMEMORATES centenary of first stamps issued by U.S. Pictures Washington and Franklin. Color, blue.

FOUR CHAPLAINS—Honors 4 chaplains who sacrificed lives in sinking of SS Dorchester in World War II. Color, black.

FREEDOM—Pictures Statue of Liberty and Jos. Pulitzer, famous exponent of freedom and press. Color, purple.

FRANCIS SCOTT KEY—Pictures famous author of our national anthem, Star Spangled Banner. Color, red.

CIVIL WAR—Adm. Farragut and his foster-father, Comm. Porter, led opposing forces. Color, purple.

OLD IRONSIDES—Stamp commemorates 150th anniversary of launching of Frigate Constitution. Color, green.

OLDEST U.S. COMMEMORATIVE STAMP (issued 1893) pictures landing of Columbus. Color, purple maroon.

MAIL COUPON TO GET THESE 8 STAMPS
PLUS 22 Other Great U.S. Stamps on this Amazing Offer!

MAIL coupon at once. We'll send you this fascinating set of 30 famous historic U.S. stamps—ALMOST AS A GIFT! All different. Each stamp tells a real, exciting story about an important event in American history. Each stamp is worth REAL MONEY. Our supply is limited. So please don't ask for more than one set.

FREE 32-Page Book

In addition to these 30 commemorative stamps, we'll also include other interesting offers for your inspection—PLUS a FREE copy of our helpful, informative book, "How to Collect Postage Stamps." Contains fascinating and true stories such as the one about the 1¢ stamp (which a schoolboy sold for $1.50) and which was later bought for FORTY THOUSAND DOLLARS.

Free book also contains expert advice on collecting; how to get started; where and how to find rare stamps; how to tell their real value; how to mount them, trade them; how to start a stamp club; exciting stamp games, etc. It has pictures galore! Full pages of pictures showing odd stamps depicting natives from far-away lands; ferocious beasts, etc.

MAIL COUPON NOW

Be the first in your neighborhood to have this valuable set of stamps. Your friends will envy you for it and want to buy the set from you. It will become one of the most prized sets of any stamp collection. But you must hurry. This special offer may have to be withdrawn soon. Rush coupon NOW!

If coupon has already been clipped, send 25¢ DIRECT to:

LITTLETON STAMP COMPANY
Dept. HMG Littleton, N. H.

Free — If you mail coupon AT ONCE, we will send you, free, this fascinating booklet. Supply limited. So rush coupon NOW!

Littleton Stamp Co.,
Dept. HMG Littleton, N. H.

I enclose 25¢. Please send set of 30 historic U.S. Stamps. Also send FREE—while supply lasts—the fascinating booklet, "How to Collect Postage Stamps."

Name_____

Address_____

City_____ Zone____ State_____

The NEW way to enjoy SPORTS Movies, Plays, Television

SAVE $8.00

NOW! 1.98 FTI

IMPORTED FROM GERMANY

NOW GET CLOSE-UP VIEWS ALL DAY WITHOUT FATIGUE

Here for the first time—Germany's famous **SPEKTOSCOPES**—a revolutionary concept in binoculars. Wear them like ordinary eye glasses—hour after hour—without fatigue. Feather weight—**only 1 oz.** You'll hardly **FEEL** them! Yet here is a new, truly powerful optical design that gives you greater range than many expensive opera or field glasses and a far greater field of view than some selling for many times more! Has **INDIVIDUAL** eye focusing for clear, sharp viewing, whether you're looking at a play in the first row or a seashore scene miles away! **SPEKTOSCOPES** are ideal for indoors, outdoors or distant scenes or close-by viewing. Special low price — 1.98, a saving of 8.00 or more!

FAVORABLE EXCHANGE RATE MAKES THIS VALUE POSSIBLE!

This is the first time that this type of optical instrument has ever sold for less than $10.00. The favorable rate of exchange and Germany's need for dollars makes it possible. We have been chosen as the exclusive distributor for SPEKTOSCOPES to the American public. Get yours now at our low, low introductory price of 1.98 tax & post paid!

TRY AT OUR RISK — NO OBLIGATION!

Enjoy at our risk for 5 days. You must be delighted! Otherwise your 1.98 will be refunded with no questions asked! Limited supply forces us to place a limit of 2 per customer. Send check or m.o. for prompt, free delivery. COD's sent plus COD Fees. Use convenient coupon below!

INTERNATIONAL BINOCULAR CO., Dept. 125-M-90
53 to 59 East 25th Street, New York 10, N. Y.

INTERNATIONAL BINOCULAR CO., Dept. 125-M-90
53 to 59 East 25th Street, New York 10, N. Y.

RUSH _____ SPEKTOSCOPES at 1.98 each (LIMIT—2) on 5 day home trial. You are to refund my 1.98 if I am not fully delighted.

☐ Payment enclosed. Send post free. ☐ Send COD plus Fees.

Name_____
Address_____
Town_____ State_____

Men! Send for This Money-Making Outfit FREE!

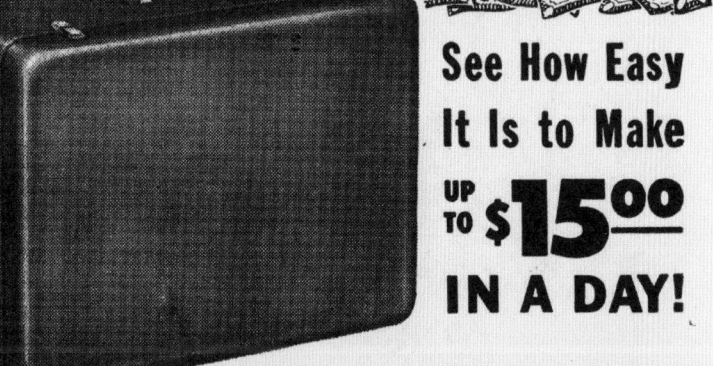

See How Easy It Is to Make UP TO $15.00 IN A DAY!

Do you want to make more money in full or spare time... as much as $15.00 in a day? Then mail the coupon below for this BIG OUTFIT, sent you FREE, containing more than 150 fine quality fabrics, sensational values in made-to-measure suits, topcoats, and overcoats. Take orders from friends, neighbors, fellow-workers. Every man prefers better-fitting, better-looking made-to-measure clothes, and when you show the many beautiful, high quality fabrics—mention the low prices for made-to-measure fit and style—and show our guarantee of satisfaction, you take orders right and left. You collect a big cash profit in advance on every order, and build up fine permanent income for yourself in spare or full time.

YOUR OWN SUITS WITHOUT 1¢ COST!

Our plan makes it easy for you to get your own personal suits, topcoats, and overcoats without paying 1¢—in addition to your big cash earnings. Think of it! Not only do we start you on the road to making big money, but we also make it easy for you to get your own clothes without paying one penny. No wonder thousands of men write enthusiastic letters of thanks.

Just Mail Coupon

You don't invest a penny of your money now or any time. You don't pay money for samples, for outfits, or for your own suit under our remarkable plan. So do as other men have done—mail the coupon now. Don't send a penny. Just send us the coupon.

NO EXPERIENCE NEEDED

It's amazingly easy to take measures, and you don't need any experience to take orders. Everything is simply explained for you to cash in on this wonderful opportunity. Just mail this coupon now and we'll send you this big, valuable outfit filled with more than 150 fine fabrics and everything else you need to start. You'll say this is the greatest way to make money you ever saw. Rush the coupon today!

PROGRESS TAILORING CO., Dept. E-276
500 S. Throop Street, Chicago 7, Illinois

Progress Tailoring Co., Dept. E-276
500 S. Throop St., Chicago 7, Illinois

Dear Sir: I WANT MONEY AND I WANT A SUIT TO WEAR AND SHOW, without paying 1¢ for it. Rush Valuable Suit Coupon and Sample Kit with actual fabrics ABSOLUTELY FREE.

Name_____ Age_____

Address_____

City_____ State_____

Sensational Get-Acquainted Offer to New Friends!

Don't Pay a Penny for these Newest Frocks!

YOU CHOOSE from more than 100 BEAUTIFUL STYLES

and make fine extra money even in your spare hours!

You've never read more exciting news! Think of taking your pick of more than 100 beautiful, colorful, latest-style dresses and making them your very own *without paying even one cent!* All you do now is mail the coupon at the bottom of this page. Don't send any money now or any time. You'll receive *absolutely free* the most thrilling display of gorgeous styles you ever saw ... all the latest fashions ... all the new miracle wonder fabrics like dacron, nylon, orlon ... in convertibles, casuals, mix-and-match, separates—suits, sportswear, and hosiery and lingerie too! Just select the dresses you want for yourself and they're *yours* simply for showing the beautiful styles and sending only a few orders for friends, neighbors, co-workers, or members of your family. That's all! You don't pay one cent for your own dresses—and you can get dress after dress this easy way!

MAKE EXTRA MONEY TOO! The moment folks see the beautiful styles, the vast selection, and the *low, money-saving prices,* they want you to send to famous Harford Frocks for dresses just like them. And for sending us their selections you get your own dresses *without paying a single penny*—and, in addition, you collect and keep a generous cash profit for every order you send. Don't wait! We'll send you everything you need ABSOLUTELY FREE.

Lovely Dresses for CHILDREN of All Ages!

Get them without paying one cent by using our plan! Adorably-styled, long-wearing dresses — including famous Dan River Ginghams ... and also T-shirts, separates, mix-and-match, playwear, nightwear for children.

Women like you write exceptional letters like these

No Longer Buys Dresses! The dresses I used to buy I now get without paying for them! And I make $12.00 to $15.00 in a week spare time besides! DOROTHY HOUGH, Mo.

2 Hours Pays $10.00 My first experience with Harford Frocks netted me $10.00 in about 2 hours. It was fun, and I made new friends. Mrs. S.W. COLE, West Virginia.

FREE! Just Mail Coupon Below!

Send no money! Just write your name, address, and dress size on coupon below (paste it on a postcard) and mail it, and we'll send you the big valuable style display so you can start at once getting your personal dresses without one cent of cost and collecting EXTRA CASH besides. Mail the coupon NOW!

HARFORD FROCKS, INC.
Dept. L-185, Cincinnati 25, Ohio

FREE! *Mail Coupon Now!*

PASTE ON POSTCARD—AND MAIL!
Harford Frocks, Inc., Dept. L-185, Cincinnati 25, Ohio

RUSH ABSOLUTELY FREE the big, valuable Harford Frocks Style Display so I can start quickly getting personal dresses without paying one penny for them, and make extra money in spare time besides.

Name ....
Address ....
City .... State ....
Dress Size .... Age ......

TALES BEYOND BELIEF AND IMAGINATION!
TOMB OF TERROR

Collect all 3 Volumes of Tomb of Terror from PS Artbooks

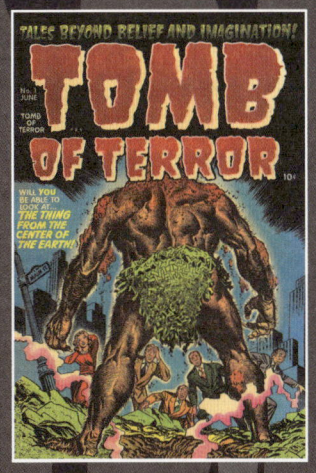

Tomb of Terror
Volume One

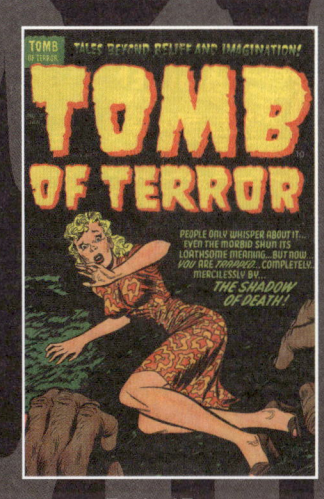

Tomb of Terror
Volume Two

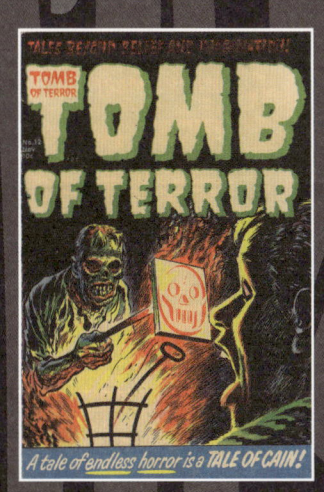

Tomb of Terror
Volume Three

Chamber of Chills
March 1954 - Issue #22

Cover Art - Lee Elias

The Ugly Duckling
Script - Unknown
Pencils - Manny Stallman
Inks - John Giunta

Reincarnation
Script - Unknown
Pencils - Jack Sparling
Inks - Jack Sparling

Lottery
Script - Unknown
Pencils - John Giunta
Inks - Manny Stallman

The Skeptic
Script - Unknown
Pencils - Joe Certa
Inks - Joe Certa

Information Source: Grand Comics Database!
A nonprofit, Internet-based organization of international volunteers dedicated to building a database covering all printed comics throughout the world.
If you believe any of this data to be incorrect or can add valuable additional information, please let us know www.comics.org
All rights to images reserved by the respective copyright holders. All original advertisement features remain the copyright of the respective trading company.

Privacy Policy
All portions of the Grand Comics Database that are subject to copyright are licensed under a Creative Commons Attribution 3.0 Unported License.
This includes but is not necessarily limited to our database schema and data distribution format.
The GCD Web Site code is licensed under the GNU General Public License.

CHAMBER OF CHILLS

TALES OF TERROR AND SUSPENSE!

MAGAZINE

...IS DEATH THE END?

START A FINE BUSINESS IN SPARE TIME!

RUN THE BEST "SHOE STORE BUSINESS" IN YOUR TOWN!

FREE! SELLING OUTFIT

TOP MEN MAKE $5 TO $10 IN AN HOUR!... YOU DON'T INVEST A CENT... MAKE BIG PROFITS... NO STORE OVERHEAD... EXCLUSIVE SALES FEATURES BUILD YOUR REPEAT BUSINESS!

QUICK-START SELLING OUTFIT FREE! YOU DON'T INVEST A CENT!

Now you can have a profitable "Shoe Store Business" right in your hands! None of the expenses of rent, light, fixtures, etc. of the ordinary shoe store. You just make money—up to $84 a week *extra* on just 3 easy sales a day! You're independent, with an opportunity to make a handsome income as long as you care to take orders in a business with a never-ending demand, because EVERYBODY WEARS SHOES.

Just rush the coupon—I'll send you my Quick-Start shoe outfit right away, ABSOLUTELY FREE. Start by selling to friends, relatives, neighbors, to people where you work. Valuable actual samples, and demonstrators of calf skin leather are furnished free of cost to qualified men.

My Professional Selling Outfit contains cut-away demonstrator so your customers can actually *feel* the restful Velvet-eez Air Cushion innersole. Special measuring device—National Advertising reprints—door opener kits—polishing cloths—actual shoes—everything you need to build a profitable repeat business. Here's your chance to join me and get into the BIG MONEY shoe business now!

OVER 160 FAST-SELLING STYLES FOR MEN & WOMEN!

Satisfy the needs and tastes of almost every person in your community. Sell air-cooled Nylon Mesh shoes with Velvet-eezair cushion innersoles—horsehide, kid, kangaroo leather shoes, slip-resistant Gro-Cork soles, oil-resistant Neoprene soles—every good type of dress, sport and work footwear—over 160 styles for men and women! Your customers will be amazed at the comfort they get from walking on 10,000 tiny air bubbles in Velvet-eez shoes. Also special steel shanks. You're way ahead of competition—you draw on our huge stock of over 200,000 pairs—thus your customers get the EXACT style, size and width they order! Your service ends tiresome shopping from store to store trying to find a shoe that fits in a style the customer wants. Special features make it *extra* easy to sell gas station men, factory workers, waiters, etc. Because Mason Shoes are *not* sold in stores, people must buy from YOU and KEEP buying from you!

Start Right NOW!

Just mail the coupon... I'll rush your FREE Starting Outfit that includes EVERYTHING you need to start making exciting cash profits *right away!*

MASON SHOE MFG. CO.
DEPT. MA-306 CHIPPEWA FALLS, WISC.

Get Exciting EXTRA Awards This Year!

This year we are celebrating our "Golden Anniversary"... 50 years of bringing top quality shoes to the men and women of America. Mason Shoe Counselors will share in thousands of dollars of EXTRA prizes... including valuable *free* merchandise awards and bonus checks! Right NOW is the perfect time to start in this profitable business!

NATIONAL ADVERTISING CREATES HUGE DEMAND FOR VELVET-EEZ SHOES!

Due to our National Advertising, millions have seen Mason Velvet-eez Shoes in magazines and on Television. Now we need more good men to satisfy that demand and make plenty of extra cash for themselves. Just show the wonderful exclusive Velvet-eez Air Cushion that brings such comfort to men and women who stand on their feet all day. The Velvet-eez demonstrator you'll get free will make easy sales for you, as it has for others. The famed Good Housekeeping Guarantee Seal is another Mason 'extra' that keeps steady profits rolling in!

Guaranteed by Good Housekeeping

DON'T DELAY

SEND FOR FREE OUTFIT!

MR. NED MASON, DEPT. MA-306
MASON SHOE MFG. CO.
CHIPPEWA FALLS, WISCONSIN

Please rush me your FREE Quick Start Shoe Selling Outfit featuring Air Cushion shoes, other fast sellers, *everything* I need to go into this profitable business, and start making immediate cash profits!

Name_____ Age_____
Address_____
Town_____ State_____

CHAMBER OF CHILLS MAGAZINE, MARCH, 1954, Vol. 1, No. 22, IS PUBLISHED BI-MONTHLY by WITCHES TALES, INC., 1860 Broadway, New York 23, N.Y. Entered as second class matter at the Post Office at New York, N.Y. under the Act of March 3, 1879. Single copies 10c. Subscription rates, 10 issues for $1.00 in the U.S. and possessions, elsewhere $1.50. All names in this periodical are entirely fictitious and no identification with actual persons is intended. Contents copyrighted, 1954, by Witches Tales, Inc., New York City. Printed in the U.S.A. Title Registered in U.S. Patent Office.

THE INNER CIRCLE

The four greatest weird books, in announcing a new policy, have pulled one of the most terrifying coup d'etats in the sanctified realm of horror.

For, CHAMBER OF CHILLS, WITCHES TALES, TOMB OF TERROR, and BLACK CAT MYSTERY have joined together in a four-power horror pact.

And this package of unbeatable shock will come to you in a cyclical pattern of doom, with four distinctive terror books getting to you during a two-month period. Thus, a mag belonging to this group will appear on your newsstands every two weeks -- each one a king of shock.

Just look at this shock king's domain...

BLACK CAT MYSTERY will offer you a package of real-life horror, where man meets man in a mad clash of reality...

WITCHES TALES is designed to tickle your funny bone and chill your spine, the strangest and most different terror mag ever created.

TOMB OF TERROR will consist of stories told out of this world, an unmistakeable unit of horror ripped from the many unexplored voids...

CHAMBER OF CHILLS will carry you to the incredible sphere of the supernatural whose teller is as weird as his stories!

Look for them!

CHAMBER OF CHILLS CONTENTS MAR. No. 22

REINCARNATION

DOWN THROUGH THIS ALLEYWAY-- THOSE NO-GOOD COPPERS WON'T --TRAP ME HERE!

the UGLY DUCKLING

LOTTERY

THEY HAD NO IDEA WHAT THE PRIZE WOULD BE WHEN THEY WON THE...

THE SKEPTIC!

SHOCK LOOMS FROM A SHADOW OF A DOUBT IN...

THAT'S THE HOUSE WE HAVE TO TAKE! WE'LL USE IT FOR OUR LOOKOUT BASE!

$AVE $100.00

Quickly and Easily with this Automatic DATE & AMOUNT BANK

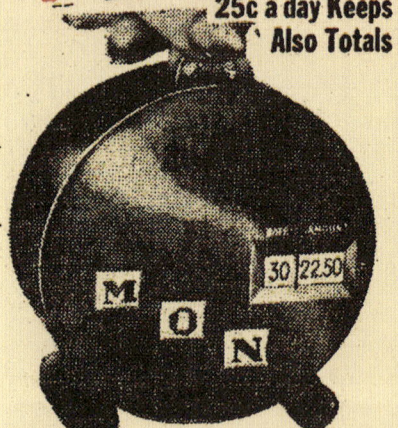

25¢ a day Keeps Calendar Up-to-date Also Totals Amount Saved!

How would you like to save almost $100.00 a year in quarters without ever missing them? Would you like to have money for Christmas or birthday gifts, appliances, clothes, vacations, children's education, or just for a rainy day? Most people never get around to saving, but now, with the new miracle Banclok Date and Amount Bank, it's fun to save a quarter *every* day — and how it mounts up!

What's more, Banclok also totals the amount you save. Can be used year after year.

HERE'S HOW IT WORKS: Banclok *forces* you to save because it is not just an ordinary bank — it's a *perpetual* calendar, too. Every time you put in a quarter the automatic calendar changes the date.

SEND NO MONEY
Just mail coupon today. Your Bancloks will be sent C.O.D. for 10-day trial. Guaranteed to show you a profit in only 8 days or Money Back.

FREE 10-Day Trial "On Approval" Mail Order Today for Prompt Delivery

Reg. $3.50 Mail Order Special **1.98** PPD.

Personalize with initials 25¢ per Letter

LEECRAFT 15th Floor
1860 Broadway, New York 23, N.Y.
Rush me ...... Banclok Date and Amount Banks for 10-day trial. I'll pay postman $1.98 each plus C.O.D. postage (Money-Back Guarantee).
Include Initials............(25¢ per letter)
Print Name ....
Address ....
City............Zone....State....
☐ SAVE C.O.D. and POSTAGE CHARGES
Check here if enclosing full payment with this coupon. Then we pay all shipping charges for you. (Same 10-day trial and Money-Back Guarantee.)

Turn Spare Hours into CASH!

Few Hours Evenings and Week Ends Can Pay up to $16.50 A DAY AND MORE!

Every Car Owner Wants Sensational "Wipe-to-Clean" Plastic **AUTO SEAT COVERS**

EXTRA! Get Your Own Seat Covers as a Bonus!

Earn Big Money Full Time or Spare Hours!

If you want extra money, this is the opportunity you've been waiting for! Start taking orders from car owners everywhere for exciting new Key expertly tailored auto seat covers EXCLUSIVE NEW MATERIALS and PATTERNS to fit every make and model car right up to date. Even one single order a day can pay up to $16.50 for a few minutes pleasant work.

Key's sensationally low prices are just a fraction of what your customer expects to pay. You shove those profit dollars into your pockets plenty fast from the first moment you begin showing the FREE Key Sales Outfit so handy and convenient it fits into your side pocket, yet packed with generous swatches of all our exciting materials. Take this outfit with you wherever you go! EXTRA BONUS SEAT COVER OFFER puts Key seat covers in your car as our gift to you!

No experience needed. Every car owner your prospect. No investment to make. Rush coupon for FREE Sales Outfit valued at $2 and actual samples. Count on Key for fast action.

KEY PRODUCTS CORP., Dept. 3943 — 800 N. Clark St., Chicago 10, Ill.

RUSH COUPON for FREE OUTFIT!
You Don't Need a Car But If You Have a Car—Tell Us!

KEY PRODUCTS CORP., Dept 3943, 800 N. Clark St., Chicago 10, Illinois
Rush Free Sample Outfit at once. You don't need a car to make money—but, if you own a car, include the following information:

Make..........Year..........Model..........
Name..........................
Address........................
City............Zone......State........

the UGLY DUCKLING

IT WAS ONE OF THOSE ACCIDENTS THE NEWSPAPERS DON'T PRINT. VERY FEW PEOPLE KNEW ABOUT IT--THE GUYS WHO SAW IT...THE DOCTORS...AND, OF COURSE, ME. TO USE THE VERNACULAR, IT WAS A REAL LULU. STILL CAN'T GET USED TO IT. OUT OF THE HOSPITAL SIX MONTHS...AND I STILL FEEL ETHERIZED...LIKE I LEFT SOMETHING BEHIND ON THE OPERATING TABLE...

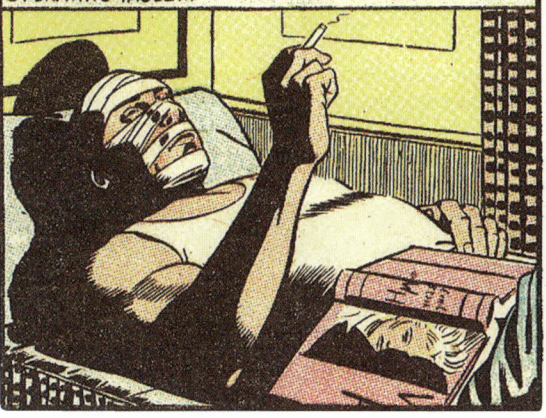

THE DOCTORS SAID THEY DID THE BEST THEY COULD BUT I'D HAVE TO WEAR THOSE BANDAGES FOREVER. ALL THEY COULD DO FOR ME WAS CHANGE THEM WHEN THEY GOT DIRTY...

FEELS ALL RIGHT... LOOKS ALL RIGHT! CHECK...AND DOUBLE-CHECK...!

ONCE I WAS JED BARNES, A GUY WITH A FACE THAT SMILED... BROWN HAIR... WITH A NATURAL WAVE IN IT THAT MADE GIRLS' HEADS TURN! NOW... I'M A CIPHER! A GREAT BIG COVERED-UP WOUND! YEAH, MY ONLY CONSOLATION IS THAT I DON'T HAVE TO SHAVE! HECK, I'M GETTING USED TO THIS FACE!
A...HEM...!
I GUESS IT'S AN ILL WIND... AND ALL THAT JUNK! THAT WAD OF DOUGH I GOT FOR MY ACCIDENT SHOULD LAST FOR A LITTLE WHILE. NICE OF THEM TO GIVE IT TO ME! YEAH, REAL NICE! ANYWAY, I DON'T HAVE TO GO BEGGING. THAT'S THE LAST THING IN THE WORLD I WANT TO DO...
WELL, WHAT'S THE PROGRAM FOR TODAY, MR. MUMMYHEAD? YOU SLEPT AS LATE AS YOU COULD! THE WALLS ARE BEGINNING TO CLOSE IN ON YOU! MIGHT AS WELL GO OUT... AND FACE THE WORLD!
I GRITTED MY TEETH! I HAD TO FACE ANOTHER DAY AND THE FIRST OBSTACLE WAS MY LANDLADY...
MORNING, MRS. LUCAS!
I... I'M SORRY, MR. BARNES, BUT YOU STARTLED ME!
THAT'S QUITE ALL RIGHT, MRS. LUCAS! I GUESS I PAY FOUR TIMES AS MUCH RENT AS ANYBODY ELSE TO EARN THAT PRIVILEGE!
SHE DIDN'T MIND TOO MUCH. A LITTLE SHOCK, MAYBE, BUT A QUICK RECOVERY. I WENT OUT INTO THE STREET AND THE FIRST FLUSH OF DAYLIGHT SMACKED MY BANDAGED FACE. I LIKED IT. IT FELT GOOD, REAL GOOD. I STOOD AT THE DOORWAY, SUCKING IT ALL IN...
NOW... FOR THAT STROLL...
NOBODY WAS AROUND. COULD BE THAT'S WHAT GAVE ME A FALSE SENSE OF SECURITY. SUDDENLY, A PASSER-BY TOOK A QUICK LOOK AT ME... AND WENT ON. THEN ANOTHER... AND ANOTHER... EACH PEEKING AT ME AS THOUGH I WAS SOME SORT OF FREAK. I SQUIRMED, FEELING ROTTEN AND DECAYED INSIDE...
EVERYTHING IN ME SEEMED TO COLLAPSE LIKE A STACK OF DISHES. I HAD TO GET AWAY, BE BY MYSELF... AWAY FROM EVERYBODY. I WALKED A LITTLE FASTER, TURNED A CORNER, AND CRAWLED INTO THE SHADOWS OF AN ELEVATED LINE...
...GOT TO... STOCK UP ON... CONFIDENCE! BOY! DO I NEED IT!
2

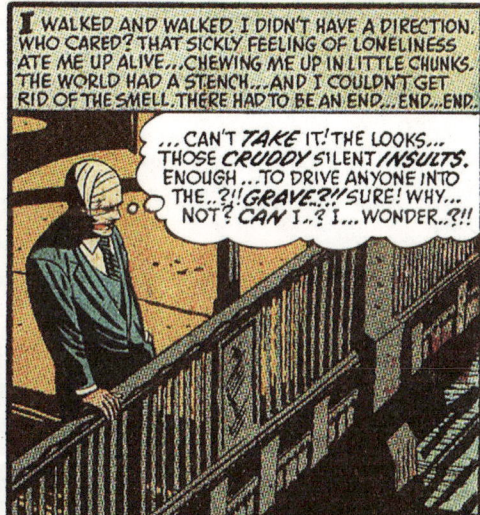

Panel 1: I NEED SOMETHING TO BOLSTER ME...UP! MAYBE A GOOD *MEAL*! THAT'S IT...SOMETHING *SOLID*...!

Panel 2: EVEN A FACE LIKE MINE HAD TO BE FED! I PICKED OUT A QUIET RESTAURANT, A LITTLE NOOK PUSHED BACK IN THE CITY. I WALKED IN, PANGS OF HUNGER GROWLING IN MY STOMACH, AND CAME FACE-TO-FACE WITH THE MAITRE DE. I KNEW WHAT WAS IN HIS MIND...

"LOOK, I'M *HUNGRY*! I'VE GOT *PLENTY* OF *MONEY*! JUST FIND ME A QUIET LITTLE *CORNER* WHERE I *WON'T DISTURB* ANYBODY!"

"I'M *SORRY*, BUT THE *TABLES* ARE...UH... *RESERVED*! THERE IS...NO...ROOM! WILL YOU *PLEASE GO* BEFORE I *CALL* THE *MANAGER*!"

Panel 3: IT WAS BECOMING MESSY SO I TURNED AROUND AND STOMPED OUT. I WENT TO ONE OF THOSE FRANKFURTER STANDS. I DIDN'T HAVE MUCH CHOICE OF A MENU, BUT AT LEAST I ATE.

"NOTHING LIKE A PICNIC IN THE PARK, EH?!! YOU KNOW-- I TURNED DOWN A FILET MIGNON FOR THIS!"

Panel 4: THE TWO DOGS AND A BOTTLE OF SODA POP DIDN'T HELP. I STILL FELT AS CREAKY AS EVER...FELT LOW, DEPRESSED, DOWN IN THE DUMPS, AND AFTERWARDS, IN THE PARK, WHAT I SAW THERE HIT HOME...HIT HOME HARD...STRIKING WITH IMPACT AT MY HEART...

"I *DON'T BELONG* HERE. *THIS* IS FOR THE *LIVING*! NOT...ME! I'M A *GHOST*-- A *SHELL*! I MAKE THEM UNCOMFORTABLE! THEY *PITY* ME...BUT THEY *DON'T* WANT TO *SEE* ME! GOT TO... GET OUT OF... HERE!"

Panel 5: I WALKED AND WALKED. I DIDN'T HAVE A DIRECTION. WHO CARED? THAT SICKLY FEELING OF LONELINESS ATE ME UP ALIVE...CHEWING ME UP IN LITTLE CHUNKS. THE WORLD HAD A STENCH...AND I COULDN'T GET RID OF THE SMELL. THERE HAD TO BE AN END...END...END.

"...CAN'T *TAKE* IT! THE LOOKS... THOSE *CRUDDY* SILENT *INSULTS*. ENOUGH...TO DRIVE ANYONE INTO THE..?!! *GRAVE*?!! SURE! WHY... NOT? *CAN* I..? I...WONDER..?!!"

Panel 6: I WAS ON A BRIDGE. IT WOULDN'T TAKE MUCH. A JUMP... THEN SILENCE....MAYBE BLACKNESS. I LOOKED AT THE WATER, SMOOTH AS GLASS...INVITING, BECKONING. WAS ANYBODY LOOKING? THERE WAS A GIRL....SUDDENLY, I ROCKED. SHE WAS ABOUT TO JUMP...TOO....

"SHOULD SAY SOMETHING... HERE! 'GOODBYE, CRUEL WORLD!' NAW! WHAT... BUSHWAH! STOP *STALLIN'*! HEY! THAT... GIRL! *CLIMBING*...OVER THE...RAIL...!"

Panel 7: I LAUGHED! PROBABLY AN EPIDEMIC! BUT WHAT WAS IT THAT MADE ME RUSH TO HER--THAT MADE ME PULL HER FROM THE PARAPET? SHE STRUGGLED LIKE A WILDCAT, SCREAMING AND FIGHTING. BUT, I WANTED HER TO LIVE... AS I KNEW I WANTED TO LIVE...AS I KNEW ALL PEOPLE SHOULD LIVE...

"*LET ME GO*! DON'T STOP ME! PLEASE...LET ME GO!"

"NO, YOU *DON'T*! YOU'VE GOT *EVERYTHING* IN THE *WORLD* TO *LIVE* FOR! LOOK AT ME! *I SHOULD* ...*KNOW*..!!"

MY ARGUMENTS WORE HER DOWN. AT LAST I WAS ABLE TO GET HER OFF THE BRIDGE...
IT'S THE USUAL STORY. A GIRL FROM THE STICKS... TRIES TO HIT SHOW BUSINESS... MEETS GUYS WITH A GLINT IN THEIR EYES. THE SAME OLD STUFF...! BUT, YOU'RE DIFFERENT. I CAN TELL. SORT OF... WELL... TENDER...!
THANKS! SAME HERE, THOUGH! YOU'RE THE FIRST PERSON THAT TOOK MY FACE... WITHOUT BATTING AN EYE-LASH. MAKES ME FEEL GOOD...!
SURE, I'M CURIOUS... ABOUT THE BANDAGES, I MEAN! BUT, THERE'S MORE TO A HUMAN BEING... TO YOU... THAN A FACE!
I TOOK HER HOME... TO A TINY APARTMENT THAT WAS NEAT... CLEAN... WELL-MANAGED! SHE MADE COFFEE... AND WE CHATTED...
WELL, JED, NOW YOU GOT THE STORY OF MY LIFE... IN DETAIL!
LISTEN, RUTH... AND DON'T GET THE WRONG IDEA. WELL--UH--LET ME HELP YOU OUT! I'VE GOT MONEY. YOU CAN HAVE SOME... BORROW IT, IF YOU LIKE... WITHOUT STRINGS ATTACHED! NO STRINGS!
I FELT REBORN AFTER MEETING RUTH. WE SAW EACH OTHER DAILY FOR A MONTH UNTIL...
RUTH, YOU'RE SURE YOU WANT THIS? I WON'T BE HURT IF YOU BACK DOWN... EVEN NOW! I'LL UNDERSTAND!
DON'T SPOIL OUR WEDDING DAY, JED! I WAS NEVER MORE SURE OF ANYTHING IN MY LIFE!
JUSTICE OF THE PEACE
MARRIAGES PERFORMED
THE NEXT FEW MONTHS WERE THE HAPPIEST IN MY WHOLE LIFE. ONLY ONE THING MARRED IT. RUTH INSISTED I TELL HER ABOUT MY ACCIDENT AND I FINALLY CONSENTED...
IT WON'T MAKE ANY DIFFERENCE, JED! I'VE TOLD YOU A HUNDRED TIMES! DON'T KEEP ANY SECRETS FROM ME!
ALL RIGHT, RUTH, LISTEN THEN! I WAS A MACHINIST! A DARN GOOD ONE... WORKING ON PRECISION CUTTING MACHINES... BIG ONES... WITH SIX ROTARY BLADES...
IT WAS DELICATE WORK. I HAD TO BE CAREFUL! BUT... I DIDN'T SEE THAT OVER-HEAD CRANE... THAT DARNED CRANE. I HAD STEPPED BACK TO ADJUST A LEVER... WHEN IT... THAT CRAZY CRANE... STRUCK ME... KNOCKED ME ONTO THE... CONVEYOR BELT...
I NEVER HAD A CHANCE! I WAS DRAWN INTO THOSE RAZOR SHARP BLADES. HAPPENED SO FAST I COULDN'T EVEN... SCREAM! THEN CAME... NOTHING... NOT EVEN SOUND... JUST A WORLD OF NOTHING. I AWOKE A WEEK LATER... IN THE HOSPITAL...
4

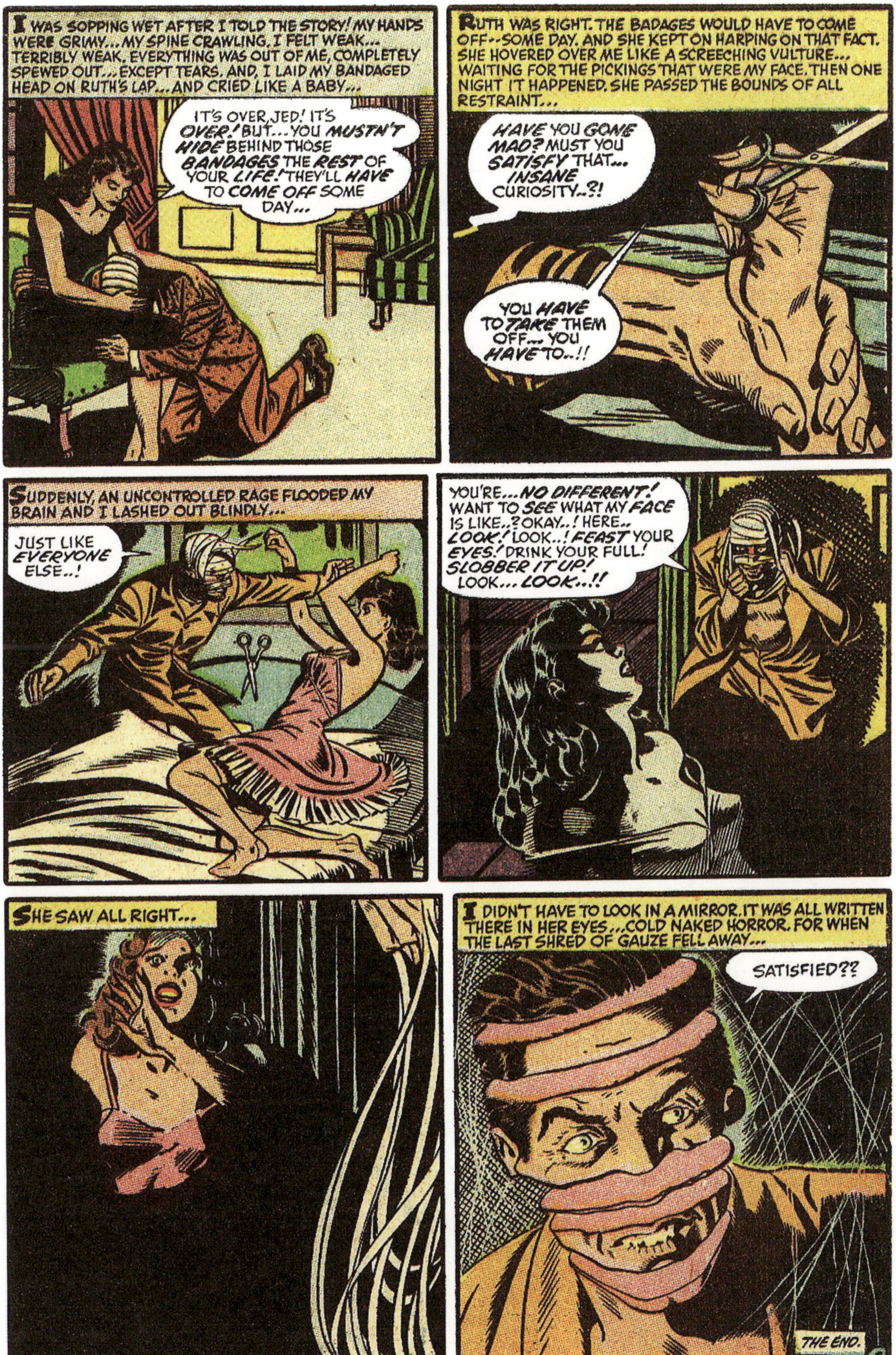

I WAS SOPPING WET AFTER I TOLD THE STORY! MY HANDS WERE GRIMY... MY SPINE CRAWLING. I FELT WEAK... TERRIBLY WEAK. EVERYTHING WAS OUT OF ME, COMPLETELY SPEWED OUT... EXCEPT TEARS. AND, I LAID MY BANDAGED HEAD ON RUTH'S LAP... AND CRIED LIKE A BABY...
IT'S OVER, JED! IT'S OVER! BUT... YOU MUSTN'T HIDE BEHIND THOSE BANDAGES THE REST OF YOUR LIFE! THEY'LL HAVE TO COME OFF SOME DAY...
RUTH WAS RIGHT. THE BADAGES WOULD HAVE TO COME OFF--SOME DAY. AND SHE KEPT ON HARPING ON THAT FACT. SHE HOVERED OVER ME LIKE A SCREECHING VULTURE... WAITING FOR THE PICKINGS THAT WERE MY FACE. THEN ONE NIGHT IT HAPPENED. SHE PASSED THE BOUNDS OF ALL RESTRAINT...
HAVE YOU GONE MAD? MUST YOU SATISFY THAT... INSANE CURIOSITY..?!
YOU HAVE TO TAKE THEM OFF... YOU HAVE TO..!!
SUDDENLY, AN UNCONTROLLED RAGE FLOODED MY BRAIN AND I LASHED OUT BLINDLY...
JUST LIKE EVERYONE ELSE..!
YOU'RE... NO DIFFERENT! WANT TO SEE WHAT MY FACE IS LIKE..? OKAY..! HERE.. LOOK! LOOK..! FEAST YOUR EYES! DRINK YOUR FULL! SLOBBER IT UP! LOOK... LOOK..!!
SHE SAW ALL RIGHT...
I DIDN'T HAVE TO LOOK IN A MIRROR. IT WAS ALL WRITTEN THERE IN HER EYES... COLD NAKED HORROR. FOR WHEN THE LAST SHRED OF GAUZE FELL AWAY...
SATISFIED??
THE END.
5

A Model Girl

Sam Harkness just couldn't believe that his modelling contest would have such a tremendous turnout. Girls from every hamlet, one-horse town, and city entered it — and each one thought she had the stuff to win it. But there was something missing in each of them.

The inter-com on his desk buzzed. He leaned over and flicked it on.

"Miss D'orsay to see you, Mr. Harkness." That was his secretary.

"Oh, yes," he said. "She's an entrant. Send her in."

He snapped shut the inter-com, as if he was mad at it. Plunging into his soft, leather chair, he quickly lit a cigarette, swerved towards the door, and waited. His eyes narrowed to two scrutinizing slits.

Dore D'orsay entered.

Sam jumped. She was majestic, as different from the rest of the girls as night from day, loaded with feminine dynamite and every explosive measure of her liable to go off any second. Anyway, Sam knew, she was pulchritude.

"W — where did you come from?" he asked.

She smiled. "Oh, from somewhere back there," she answered. Her voice was like silk and satin all mixed together.

"That doesn't matter ... now!" Sam ran to her, tenderly led her to a chair and watched her sit down as if she might crack under the strain. "Miss D'orsay, you are the winner of my contest. That is final. Period. Finis. No more said. You are the winner."

"Thank you," Dore D'orsay said, her eyes gleaming, her lips parted in a moon-like crescent. "That's all I want to know." She arose from the chair.

Sam couldn't believe his eyes. Dore D'orsay was leaving.

"Where are you going?" he blurted, trying as best he could to control himself. "Don't go. I'll make you into a star, a shining light in the modelling field. You'll be great."

Dore D'orsay turned.

"Mr. Harkness, I just came here to prove a point. The point has been proven. Nothing else need be said."

"What point? Who knows from points? All I know is that I got in you a winner, a real winner, and you want to run out on me — without an explanation!"

He waited, but Dore D'orsay just smiled. She placed her hand over her head, twisting the fingers in an ugly, gnarled form, and snapped it down.

Sam winced. Something magical happened to Dore D'orsay. She became transformed, metamorphosized. Her smart, black clothes suddenly became a shroud; her hair, once over her head, fell down in stringy silkiness to her shoulders.

Sam fell back in terror.

"I just wanted to prove that all witches ... were not ugly," Dore D'orsay said.

And before Sam was the most beautiful, the most enchanting, the most bewitching witch he ever saw!

STATEMENT OF THE OWNERSHIP, MANAGEMENT AND CIRCULATION REQUIRED BY THE ACT OF CONGRESS OF AUGUST 24, 1912, AS AMENDED BY THE ACTS OF MARCH 3, 1933, AND JULY 2, 1946, OF CHAMBER OF CHILLS MAGAZINE   published   Monthly at   New York, N. Y.   for October 1, 1953.

1. The names and addresses of the publisher, editor, managing editor, and business managers are: Editor: Leon Harvey, 1860 Broadway, N.Y.C.; Managing Editor: Alfred Harvey, 1860 Broadway, N.Y.C.; Business Manager: Robert B. Harvey, 1860 Broadway, N.Y.C. Publisher: Witches Tales, Inc.   1860 Broadway, N.Y.C.

2. The owners are   Witches Tales, Inc.   1860 Broadway, N.Y.C.; Leon Harvey, 1860 Broadway, N.Y.C.; Alfred Harvey, 1860 Broadway, N.Y.C.; Robert B. Harvey, 1860 Broadway, N.Y.C.

3. The known bondholders, mortgagees, and other security holders owning or holding 1 percent or more of total amount of bonds, mortgages, or other securities are: None.

4. Paragraphs 2 and 3 include, in cases where the stockholder or security holder appears upon the books of the company as trustee or in any other fiduciary relation, the name of the person or corporation for whom such trustee is acting; also the statements in the two paragraphs show the affiant's full knowledge and belief as to the circumstances and conditions under which stockholders and security holders who do not appear upon the books of the company as trustees, hold stock and securities in a capacity other than that of a bona fide owner.

(signed) ROBERT B. HARVEY, Business Manager
Sworn and subscribed to before me this 30th day of September, 1953.
MAE J. MASCHERONI (My commission expires March 30th, 1954)

CHILLY
CHAMBER MUSIC
SONGS FROM THE SPOOK BOX!
THEY SAW THREE LITTLE FISHES IN AN ITTY-BITTY POOL!
AND "SWIM?" SAID THE PRETTY GIRL! "SURE -- IF YOU CAN..!"
SO SHE DOVE -- AND HE LAUGHED LIKE A SILLY, GHOULISH FOOL...
HAHA
HA
HA
FOR SHE SWAM -- AND SHE SWAM ALL OVER THE DAM!
CHILLY
CHAMBER MUSIC
SONGS FROM THE SPOOK BOX!
WHEN DAY IS DONE AND SHADOWS FALL...
I DREAM OF YOU!
WHEN DAY IS DONE -- I KISS YOUR LIPS...
AND -- CARESS YOU WITH MY FINGERTIPS!

REINCARNATION
DOWN THROUGH THIS ALLEYWAY-- THOSE NO-GOOD COPPERS WON'T--TRAP ME HERE!
THE MAN RAN FOR HIS LIFE--AS HE HAD ALWAYS BEEN RUNNING ALL HIS LIFE...
ALLEYWAY FORKS HERE...PUFF--PUFF-- I'LL TAKE THE ONE ON MY RIGHT! IT'S MY ONLY CHANCE!
NEXT TIME I CASE A JOINT, I'LL MAKE SURE I HAVE TWO EXITS INSTEAD O' ONE! ALMOST DIDN'T MAKE IT! AND FOR WHAT--? JUST A ROTTEN THREE HUNDRED BUCKS!
1

AND THEN THE MAN LOOKED IN...

WHA---T? CRAZY LIGHTS AND NUTTY NOISES! SOMETHING STRANGE IS GOING ON DOWN THERE!

TWO MORE VOLT INCREASES--AND I'LL KNOW! MUST REMEMBER TO KEEP THE INDUCTION CURRENT NON-FLUCTUATING! THE SLIGHTEST JAR WILL RUIN THE RESULTS!

SQUEAK.. SQUEAK.. SQUEAK..

CURRENT AT ZERO-PEAK EFFICIENCY! VOLTAGE-- 200 MILLION --METABOLIC RATE STEADY... I--I'VE DONE IT! THE GORILLA HAS CHANGED INTO THE MOUSE--THOUGH THE BODY STRUCTURE HAS BEEN MAINTAINED!

THE MOUSE IS DEAD--BUT ITS MIND LIVES ON IN AN ALIEN HOST--THAT OF THE GORILLA'S BODY. THE GORILLA'S MIND HAS BEEN NULLIFIED OR DISPLACED BY THE MOUSE'S PERSONALITY! I'VE CONQUERED DEATH! I'VE DISCOVERED REINCARNATION!

WHILE OUTSIDE...

I--I'M SEEIN' THINGS! I'D SWEAR THIS IS BATTY IF I HADN'T SEEN IT WITH MY OWN EYES! REINCARNATION!

HE PUT ONE MIND INTO THE BODY OF ANOTHER! THAT MEANS ANYONE WHO'S OLD CAN LIVE ON IN ANOTHER PERSON! I GOT TO THINK...THINK!

107

LATER THAT NIGHT, IN A CHEAP HOTEL ROOM, THE MAN THOUGHT...
ESCAPE... ESCAPE...
REINCARNATION
IMMORTALITY
ESCAPE
YEAH--! THAT'S IT! ESCAPE! THE PERFECT SETUP! NO ONE'LL EVER TOUCH ME! WHY DIDN'T I THINK O' IT BEFORE?
SO A FEW DAYS LATER...
--MAYBE YOU'RE RIGHT! MAYBE THIS PLACE DOES NEED CLEANING! IT'S STRANGE THAT THE AGENCY SHOULD SEND ME A JANITOR WHEN I DIDN'T ASK FOR ONE-- BUT I CAN USE YOU! YOU KNOW YOUR DUTIES, OF COURSE?
SURE, DOC... I'LL TAKE CARE O' THIS PLACE LIKE IT WAS MY OWN HOME!
WHICH IS EXACTLY WHAT HE DID! AND DAYS AFTERWARDS...
WHAT ARE YOU DOING HERE? I THOUGHT I TOLD YOU NEVER TO OPEN THIS DOOR!
OH--SORRY, DOC--I JUST...WANTED TO... SCRUB THE FLOORS...!
--AND TO LOOK AT THE MACHINERY, SUCKER!
AND WHILE THE SCIENTIST WORKED COORDINATING AND RE-CHECKING HIS FINDINGS, THE MAN ACTED...
THE BIGGEST HAUL OF MY LIFE! AND NOW ALL I HAVE TO DO IS WALK RIGHT IN WITHOUT EVER WORRYIN' AGAIN--!
THIS IS A STICKUP! I'LL SHOOT TO KILL IF YOU SO MUCH AS MAKE ONE WRONG MOVE! OPEN THE VAULT BEHIND YOU--QUICK!
Y-YOU'RE INSANE! YOU'LL NEVER GET AWAY ALIVE!
3

I'LL TAKE THAT CHANCE! OKAY-- GET GOING! YOU OTHERS-- LINE UP NEAR THE WALL! NO ONE TOUCH THAT BUZZER-- IF YOU STILL LIKE TO KEEP BREATHIN'!
WHAT DO YOU HOPE TO GAIN BY THIS ROBBERY? THE POLICE WILL HAVE YOUR DESCRIPTION. EVEN IF YOU DO ESCAPE!
P-PLEASE LET US GO! WE WON'T TRY TO STOP YOU!
I KNOW YOU WON'T, SISTER--BECAUSE--
--YOU AND YOUR PALS WON'T BE AROUND NO MORE!
SECONDS LATER...
THAT'S RIGHT, SARGE! YEAH.. A 1951 CHEVVIE-- BLUE SEDAN! LICENSE NUMBER 2D 678-L! WE HAVE THE MAN'S DESCRIPTION TOO! WE'LL HAVE HIM TRAPPED IN NO TIME!
BLAM! BLAM!
VRROOM!
BUT THE MAN HAD PLANNED CAREFULLY AND WELL. TWO HOURS LATER, FAR OUT IN A DESERTED SECTION OF COUNTRY...
SAFE AND SOUND! GUESS MY HEIST THREW THE COPPERS OFF FOR AWHILE. THEY'LL BE ON MY TRAIL ANY MOMENT NOW--BUT AT LEAST THE DOUGH'S WHERE I WANT IT!
AND INSIDE THE LABORATORY OF THE SCIENTIST SHORTLY THEREAFTER...
GET OUT! YOU WERE NEVER TO COME IN HERE! YOU'RE FIRED! UH--WHAT...ARE YOU HOLDING IN YOUR HAND?
IT'S A GUN, DOC.. YOU KNOW TO SHOOT PEOPLE WITH!

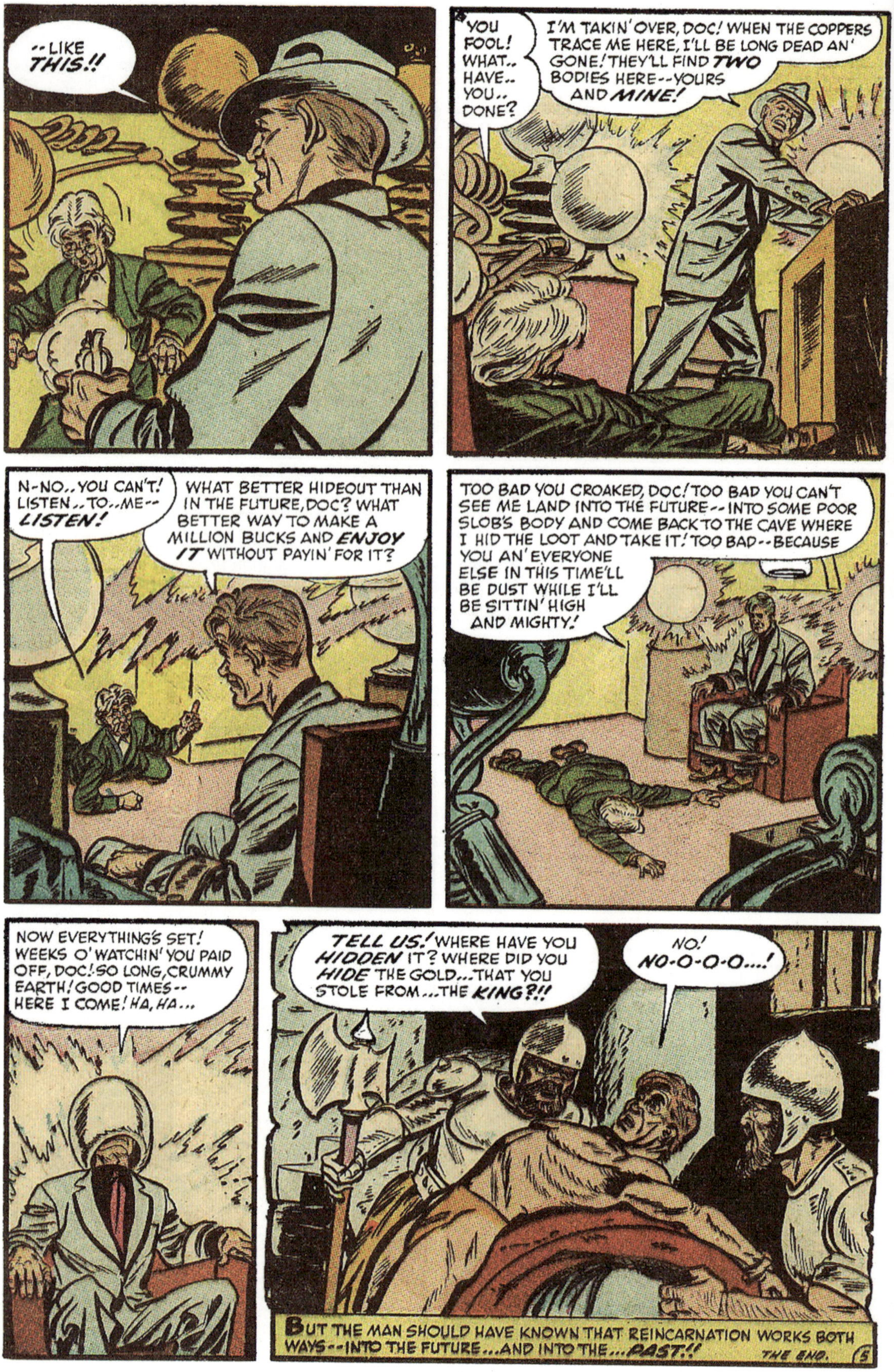
--LIKE THIS!!
YOU FOOL! WHAT.. HAVE.. YOU.. DONE?
I'M TAKIN' OVER, DOC! WHEN THE COPPERS TRACE ME HERE, I'LL BE LONG DEAD AN' GONE! THEY'LL FIND TWO BODIES HERE--YOURS AND MINE!
N-NO.. YOU CAN'T! LISTEN.. TO.. ME-- LISTEN!
WHAT BETTER HIDEOUT THAN IN THE FUTURE, DOC? WHAT BETTER WAY TO MAKE A MILLION BUCKS AND ENJOY IT WITHOUT PAYIN' FOR IT?
TOO BAD YOU CROAKED, DOC! TOO BAD YOU CAN'T SEE ME LAND INTO THE FUTURE--INTO SOME POOR SLOB'S BODY AND COME BACK TO THE CAVE WHERE I HID THE LOOT AND TAKE IT! TOO BAD--BECAUSE YOU AN' EVERYONE ELSE IN THIS TIME'LL BE DUST WHILE I'LL BE SITTIN' HIGH AND MIGHTY!
NOW EVERYTHING'S SET! WEEKS O' WATCHIN' YOU PAID OFF, DOC! SO LONG, CRUMMY EARTH! GOOD TIMES-- HERE I COME! HA, HA...
TELL US! WHERE HAVE YOU HIDDEN IT? WHERE DID YOU HIDE THE GOLD... THAT YOU STOLE FROM... THE KING?!!
NO! NO-O-O-O...!
BUT THE MAN SHOULD HAVE KNOWN THAT REINCARNATION WORKS BOTH WAYS--INTO THE FUTURE... AND INTO THE... PAST!!
THE END.
5

Get PRIZES... make money this Easy Way

WHAT DO YOU WANT MOST FOR A PRIZE? A pretty Wrist Watch — an Archery Outfit — or an Electronic Walkie Talkie? They can be yours, so easily. Many prizes shown here and dozens of others in our Big Prize Book are GIVEN WITHOUT ONE PENNY OF COST for selling just one order of 48 packs of American Vegetable and Flower Seeds at 10¢ a pack.

Most everybody wants American Vegetable and Flower Seeds — they're fresh and ready to grow. You'll sell them quickly to your family, friends and neighbors and get your prize at once. Or, if you want money instead of prizes, keep $1.60 in cash for each 48-pack order you sell.

Thousands of boys and girls, men and women have been earning prizes and extra cash this way for 35 years. You can be a prize winner, too. Just sign and mail the coupon for your order of American Seeds. When sold, send us the money and choose your prize. Isn't that easy? Get busy! Paste coupon on postcard or mail it in envelope today for Big Prize Book and Seeds. Send no money — we trust you.
AMERICAN SEED COMPANY, Dept. 415, Lancaster, Pa.

70 GREAT PRIZES TO CHOOSE FROM

- Basketball Outfit • Cork Gun
- Girls' Shoulder Strap Handbag
- Complete Fishing Outfit
- Dial Typewriter
- Daisy's Red Ryder Air Rifle
- Dick Tracy Camera
- Cinderella Wrist Watch
- Roy Rogers Binoculars
- Ukulele with Arthur Godfrey's famous player
- Boys' Radium Dial Wrist Watch • Woodburning Set
- Movie Projector • Phonograph
- Crystal Radio Kit
- Printing Press • Roller Skates
- Identification Bracelet
- Ready-to-fly Jet Airplane
- Gene Autry Guitar
- Electric Jeep
- Official Size Football

and many more

Here it is... GOLDEN TRUMPET — Heavy gold-plated, over 13" long. Play bugle calls, marches, songs. Case included. Sell only one order.

BOYS', GIRLS' WRIST WATCHES — Dale Evans Bracelet Watch. Sell one order plus $2.75. Roy Rogers Cowboy Watch. Sell one order plus $1.75.

Professional Type Junior Archery Set — Famous Ben Pearson make. Has professional-type 54-inch hardwood bow, 4 feathered arrows, target face, instructions. Sell one order plus 75¢.

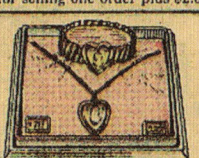

A GREAT FLASH CAMERA OUTFIT — Camera, flash attachment, 4 bulbs, batteries, film. Complete outfit given for selling one order plus $2.00.

CHEMISTRY SET — Famous Chemcraft Set with book of Chemical Magic. Sell one order.

PRETTY TRAVEL CASE — Overnight case with removable tray. Has mirror, lock and key. Sell one order American Seeds plus 75¢.

GOLD-PLATED LOCKET SET — With necklace and expansion bracelet. Each locket holds two photos. Sell only one order plus 75¢.

OFFICIAL SIZE BASKETBALL — Sturdy valve-type ball. For indoor, outdoor use. Sell one order plus 75¢.

WIN a Schwinn BICYCLE
EXTRA $1,500 IN GRAND PRIZE AWARDS
1st Prize $250 • 2nd Prize $150 • 3rd Prize $100
PLUS 20 DELUXE Schwinn BICYCLES
Everyone selling American Seeds is eligible to win GRAND PRIZE AWARDS. Remember, they are in addition to your regular prizes and cash. Coupon brings your first order and complete facts. SEND NO MONEY — we trust you. Paste coupon on postcard or mail in envelope today.

ELECTRONIC WALKIE TALKIE — Remco's complete 2-way talking system. Just string out the wire — start talking. No batteries needed. Sell one order of American Seeds.

A GREAT KNIFE OUTFIT — Big hunting knife plus 4-blade camp knife. Double leather belt sheath. Given for selling one order.

FISHING TACKLE SET — Big 19-piece outfit, including metal carrying case, 46" rod and precision reel. Sell just one order plus 75¢.

COWBOY JR. GUITAR — Complete instructions with song book. Nylon strings. Sell one order plus 75¢.

MAIL COUPON TODAY

AMERICAN SEED CO.
Dept. 416 Lancaster, Pa.

Please send me your Prize Book and one order of 48 packs of American Vegetable and Flower Seeds. I will resell them at 10¢ each, send you the money, and choose my prize.

Name _____
Address _____
City _____
State _____

BE FIRST IN YOUR NEIGHBORHOOD — START TODAY

Read these DIFFERENT MYSTERY MAGAZINES WITH THE EXPERT TOUCH OF MASTER STORY TELLING!

NOW ON SALE

ACCLAIMED THE BEST IN SHOCK MYSTERY, THE BLACK CAT MYSTERY OPENS A TRAIL TO SUSPENSE! DON'T MISS AN ISSUE!

THRILLS AND CHILLS WITH EVER-BUILDING TENSION... YOU'LL GASP AS YOU READ EACH ISSUE OF THE EXCITING CHAMBER OF CHILLS!

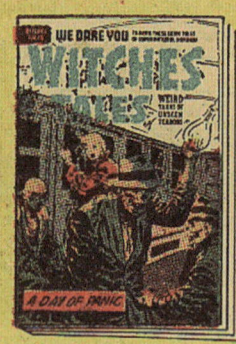

A FLIGHT INTO FANTASTIC FRENZY... EXPLORE THE FORBIDDEN IN EACH ISSUE OF THE WITCHES TALES!

FOR ADVENTURES INTO THE UNKNOWN, FOR INCREDIBLE TREKS TO OTHER WORLDS, READ THE TOMB OF TERROR!

Acclaimed by Millions THE BEST TRUE LOVE STORIES, TORN FROM THE PAGES OF REAL LIFE!

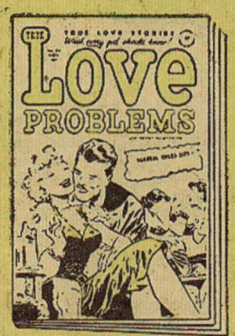

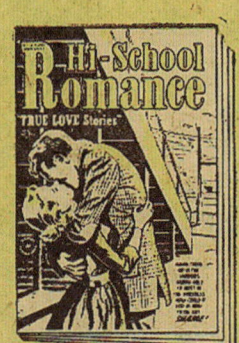

READ EVERY ISSUE! GET YOUR COPIES TODAY!

LOOK HERE! for BIG MONEY MAKING OPPORTUNITIES for MONEY-SAVING GOODS and SERVICES

SALES HELP – AGENTS WANTED

ANYONE CAN SELL famous Hoover Uniforms for beauty shops, waitresses, nurses, doctors, others All popular miracle fabrics nylon, dacron, orlon. Exclusive styles, top quality Big cash income now. real future. Equipment FREE. State your age HOOVER. Dept. A-120, New York 11. N Y

MAKE MONEY! Show friends sensational $1.00 Greeting Card Assortment for birthdays, anniversaries, get-well, etc. A year's supply for average family Also exciting All-in-Fun comic assortment. Samples on approval. Wallace Brown, 225 Fifth Ave. Dept. K-96, New York 10. N Y

FREE! Let me send you (f o b factory) food and household products to test in your home Tell your friends. make money Rush your name and age ZANOL, Dept 6053-A. Richmond St., Cincinnati, Ohio

AMAZING EXTRA MONEY PLAN gives you gorgeous dress without penny cost Rush name today. with dress size HARFORD. Dept L-2180, Cincinnati 25, Ohio

SPARE TIME MONEY plus NEW CAR as encouragement bonus Amazing 60 gauge nylons. 3 pr guaranteed 3 mos Write to WILKNIT, A-7741 Midway, Greenfield, O

STRANGE "DRY" WINDOW CLEANER sells like wild Replaces messy rags. liquids. Simply glide over glass. Samples sent on trial KRISTEE, Dept. 90. Akron, Ohio.

SELL MIRACLE ORLON Embroidered Work Uniforms! Looks, feels, tailors like wool; wears 3 times longer Outwears cotton 5 to 1 Acid-proof. grease-resistant. Washes perfectly pressed. Amazing profits Outfit FREE TOPPS. Dept. 871, Rochester, Indiana.

ADVERTISERS

You're looking at the world's biggest classified advertising buy! SEVENTEEN MILLION circulation at a cost-per-word so low, you'll schedule your advertising here every issue For rates, closing dates, full information write COMIC BOOK CLASSIFIED, 400 Madison Ave., New York 17. N. Y.

HELP WANTED

MAKE MONEY INTRODUCING world's cutest children's dresses. Big selection, adorable styles. Low prices Complete display free HARFORD. Dept. L-2394, Cincinnati, O.

MANUFACTURER—Wants reliable MEN - WOMEN for Profitable Mail Order work. Home. Sparetime. Write LIEBIG INDUSTRIES. Beaver Dam 20, Wis.

GET EXTRA SPENDING MONEY quick and easy. in spare time! Show neighbors gorgeous new greeting card assortments. Year's supply for birthdays, all occasions. at bargain. Everybody buys Pays you big profits. Experience unnecessary FREE Stationery Samples; Assortments on approval STUART GREETINGS, 325 Randolph St., Dept. 607. Chicago 6. Ill.

PHOTO FINISHING

12 JUMBOS 35¢. 8 JUMBOS 25¢, 16 JUMBOS 50¢ from roll or negatives with this ad. C.G. SKRUDLAND, Lake Geneva. Wis.

PERSONAL

BORROWING BY MAIL. Loans $50 to $600 to employed men and women. Easy, quick. Completely confidential. No endorsers. Repay in convenient monthly payments. Details free in plain envelope. Give occupation. State Finance Co., 323 Securities Bldg., Dept. K-74, Omaha 2. Nebraska.

FEMALE HELP WANTED

SEW OUR REDI-CUT HANDY-HANKY aprons at home Easy, Profitable. A & B Enterprises, 2516 N Albert Pike, Ft. Smith, Arkansas.

ADDRESS ADVERTISING Postcards. Must have good handwriting. Lindo, Watertown, Massachusetts.

TRICKS, MAGIC, NOVELTIES

CATALOG OF 3200 NOVELTIES, JOKERS, TRICKS, Funmakers, Magic Gadgets, Timesavers, Hobbies, Models, Guns, Sporting Goods, Jewelry, Cameras, Optical Goods, etc. Send 10¢ to JOHNSON SMITH CO., Dept. 712, Detroit 7. Mich.

INVISIBLE REWEAVING

MAKE BIG MONEY AT HOME! Invisibly reweave damaged garments. Details Free Fabricon, 8332-A S. Prairie, Chicago, Ill.

DISPOSAL UNITS

OUTDOOR TOILETS, CESSPOOLS, SEPTIC TANKS cleaned and deodorized with amazing new product Just mix dry Powder with water; pour into toilet. Safe, no poisons Save digging, pumping costs Postcard brings FREE details. BURSON LABORATORIES, Dept. 0-91, Chicago 22, Illinois.

WHOLESALE CATALOGUE

BE A JOBBER—make big money Draw from our 250,000 stock of toys, novelties, appliances, jewelry, religious goods, nationally-advertised wrist watches—hundreds of others. Get jobber discounts even in small quantities. Profits over 100%! Write for FREE catalog. Modern Merchandise, Dept. CBC, 169 W Madison St., Chicago 2, Ill.

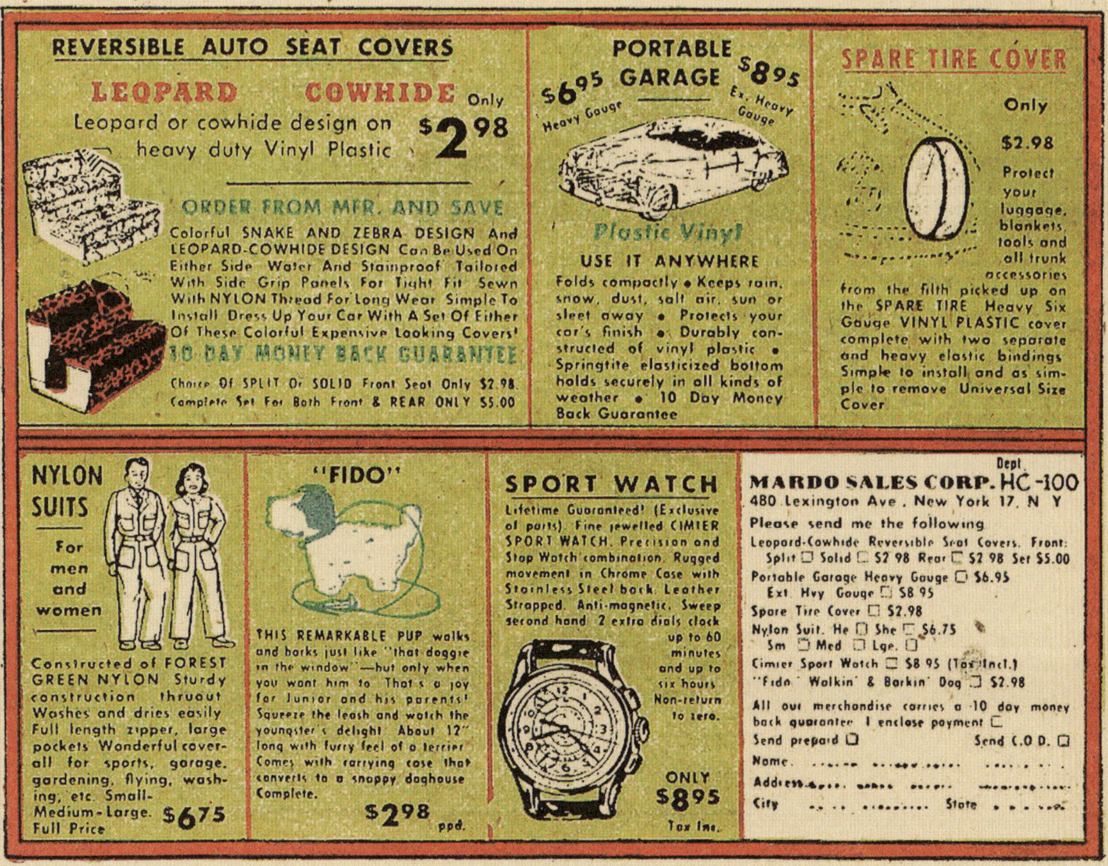

REVERSIBLE AUTO SEAT COVERS
LEOPARD — COWHIDE Only $2.98
Leopard or cowhide design on heavy duty Vinyl Plastic

ORDER FROM MFR. AND SAVE
Colorful SNAKE AND ZEBRA DESIGN And LEOPARD-COWHIDE DESIGN Can Be Used On Either Side Water And Stainproof Tailored With Side Grip Panels For Tight Fit Sewn With NYLON Thread For Long Wear Simple To Install Dress Up Your Car With A Set Of Either Of These Colorful Expensive Looking Covers!
10 DAY MONEY BACK GUARANTEE
Choice OF SPLIT Or SOLID Front Seat Only $2.98
Complete Set For Both Front & REAR ONLY $5.00

PORTABLE GARAGE $6.95 Heavy Gauge $8.95 Ex. Heavy Gauge
Plastic Vinyl
USE IT ANYWHERE
Folds compactly • Keeps rain, snow, dust, salt air, sun or sleet away • Protects your car's finish • Durably constructed of vinyl plastic • Springtite elasticized bottom holds securely in all kinds of weather • 10 Day Money Back Guarantee

SPARE TIRE COVER Only $2.98
Protect your luggage, blankets, tools and all trunk accessories from the filth picked up on the SPARE TIRE Heavy Six Gauge VINYL PLASTIC cover complete with two separate and heavy elastic bindings Simple to install and as simple to remove Universal Size Cover

NYLON SUITS
For men and women
Constructed of FOREST GREEN NYLON Sturdy construction thruout Washes and dries easily Full length zipper, large pockets Wonderful coverall for sports, garage, gardening, flying, washing, etc. Small-Medium-Large. $6.75 Full Price

"FIDO"
THIS REMARKABLE PUP walks and barks just like "that doggie in the window"—but only when you want him to That's a joy for Junior and his parents! Squeeze the leash and watch the youngster's delight About 12" long with furry feel of a terrier Comes with carrying case that converts to a snappy doghouse Complete. $2.98 ppd.

SPORT WATCH
Lifetime Guaranteed! (Exclusive of parts). Fine jewelled CIMIER SPORT WATCH. Precision and Stop Watch combination. Rugged movement in Chrome Case with Stainless Steel back, Leather Strapped, Anti-magnetic, Sweep second hand, 2 extra dials clock up to 60 minutes and up to six hours Non-return to zero.
ONLY $8.95 Tax Inc.

MARDO SALES CORP. Dept. HC-100
480 Lexington Ave., New York 17, N Y
Please send me the following
Leopard-Cowhide Reversible Seat Covers. Front: Split ☐ Solid ☐ $2.98 Rear ☐ $2.98 Set $5.00
Portable Garage Heavy Gauge ☐ $6.95
Ext. Hvy Gauge ☐ $8.95
Spare Tire Cover ☐ $2.98
Nylon Suit. He ☐ She ☐ $6.75
Sm ☐ Med ☐ Lge. ☐
Cimier Sport Watch ☐ $8.95 (Tax Incl.)
"Fido" Walkin & Barkin' Dog ☐ $2.98
All our merchandise carries a 10 day money back guarantee I enclose payment ☐
Send prepaid ☐   Send C.O.D. ☐
Name..........
Address..........
City.......... State..........

They claim this coupon brings you "good luck"

"Six months after mailing the coupon, I had a promotion and a big raise in pay!"

"From the moment I marked the coupon, my luck changed!"

"My break came when I sent the coupon!"

These statements are typical! I.C.S. gets letters like these regularly. Coupon senders report pay raises. Others win important promotions or new, interesting assignments. Still others find happiness, job security, opportunities never dreamed possible.

Is it LUCK? The results are so impressive, so quick in coming, that some say the I.C.S. coupon is "lucky." Of course, that's not true. The real reason for these amazing results is what happens to the person when he or she mails the coupon.

Coupon is first step! Naturally, you want to make good. But you've put off doing something about it. Mailing this coupon is *definite action!* It shows you're fed up with waiting for the breaks. You're determined to make your own breaks! And this determination alone accounts for much of the "luck" you'll start to experience.

You get free guidance! Within a few days you get the helpful and inspiring 36-page book, "How to Succeed." It's crammed with information. For example, it tells you in detail how to plan your career. Also how to prepare for advancement. In addition, you get a free catalog on the I.C.S. course that interests you. With your new-found determination and these two books as your guides, you're ready to cash in on your hidden abilities!

391 I.C.S. courses! You'll find a partial list of courses in the coupon below. Each course is up-to-date, extremely practical, completely success-tested. You study in your spare time. Set your own pace. Correspond directly with instructors. Cost is low. Diplomas are awarded to graduates. I.C.S. training rates high in all fields of business and industry. You won't find another school like it.

Call it being "lucky" or being "smart." Whatever it is, you're one step closer to your goal when you mail this famous coupon!

INTERNATIONAL CORRESPONDENCE SCHOOLS — ICS

BOX 2846, SCRANTON 9, PENNA.

Without cost or obligation, send me "HOW to SUCCEED" and the booklet about the course BEFORE which I have marked X:

ART
- Commercial Art
- Magazine Illustrating
- Fashion Illustrating
- Cartooning
- Sketching and Painting
- Show Card and Sign Lettering

AUTOMOTIVE
- Automobile Mechanic
- Auto Elec. Technician
- Auto Body Rebuilding and Refinishing
- Diesel – Gas Engines

AVIATION
- Aeronautical Engineering Jr
- Aircraft Engine Mechanic
- Airplane Drafting

BUILDING
- Architecture
- Arch Drafting
- Building Contractor
- Estimating
- Carpenter and Mill Work
- Carpenter Foreman
- Reading Blueprints
- House Planning
- Plumbing
- Heating
- Painting Contractor
- Air Conditioning
- Electrician

BUSINESS
- Business Administration
- Certified Public Accountant
- Bookkeeping and Accounting
- Office Management
- Stenography and Typing
- Secretarial
- Federal Tax
- Business Correspondence
- Letter writing Improvement
- Personnel and Labor Relations
- Advertising
- Retail Business Management
- Managing Small Business
- Ocean Navigation
- Sales Management
- Short Story Writing
- Creative Salesmanship
- Traffic Management

CHEMISTRY
- Chemical Engineering
- Chemistry
- Analytical Chemistry
- Petroleum – Nat'l Gas
- Pulp and Paper Making
- Plastics

CIVIL, STRUCTURAL ENGINEERING
- Civil Engineering
- Structural Engineering
- Surveying and Mapping
- Structural Drafting
- Highway Engineering
- Reading Blueprints
- Construction Engineering
- Sanitary Engineering

DRAFTING
- Aircraft Drafting
- Architectural Drafting
- Electrical Drafting
- Mechanical Drafting
- Structural Drafting
- Sheet Metal Drafting
- Ship Drafting
- Mine Surveying and Drafting

ELECTRICAL
- Electrical Engineering
- Electrician
- Electrical Maintenance
- Electrical Drafting
- Electric Power and Light
- Lineman

HIGH SCHOOL
- High School Subjects
- Mathematics
- Commercial
- Good English

MECHANICAL AND SHOP
- Mechanical Engineering
- Industrial Engineering
- Industrial Supervision
- Foremanship
- Mechanical Drafting
- Machine Design-Drafting
- Machine Shop Practice
- Tool Design
- Industrial Instrumentation
- Machine Shop Inspection
- Reading Blueprints
- Toolmaking
- Gas – Electric Welding
- Heat Treatment – Metallurgy
- Sheet Metal Work
- Sheet Metal Pattern Drafting
- Refrigeration

POWER
- Combustion Engineering
- Diesel – Electric
- Electric Light and Power
- Stationary Steam Engineering
- Stationary Fireman

RADIO, TELEVISION COMMUNICATIONS
- Practical Radio – TV Eng'r'ing
- Radio Operating
- Radio and TV Servicing
- Television – Technician
- Electronics
- Telephone Work

RAILROAD
- Locomotive Engineer
- Diesel Locomotive
- Air Brakes   Car Inspector
- Railroad Administration

TEXTILE
- Textile Engineering
- Cotton, Rayon, Woolen Mfg.
- Carding and Spinning
- Warping and Weaving
- Loom Fixing   Throwing
- Finishing and Dyeing
- Textile Designing

Name_____ Age_____ Home Address_____

City_____ Zone_____ State_____ Working Hours_____ A.M. to P.M._____

Occupation_____

☐ Check here for booklet "A" if under 18 years of age

Canadian residents send coupon to International Correspondence Schools Canadian, Ltd., Montreal, Canada. Special tuition rates to members of the U S Armed Forces.

They had no idea what the prize would be when they won the...

LOTTERY

They were explorers of the earth's interior. After finding the Tashkenti Fissure in Northern Gobi, they descended two thousand miles into the bowels of the earth until...

"I TOLD you it was getting BRIGHTER! Look...straight ahead, there's a BIG OPENING there, BRAD!"

"You're right, MANSON! I thought it was another ILLUSION...BUT IT IS LIGHT!"

The last hundred yards to the opening were covered on the dead run, and...

"MANSON! What do you see?"

"Not a BLASTED thing! I'm BLINDED by the LIGHT!"

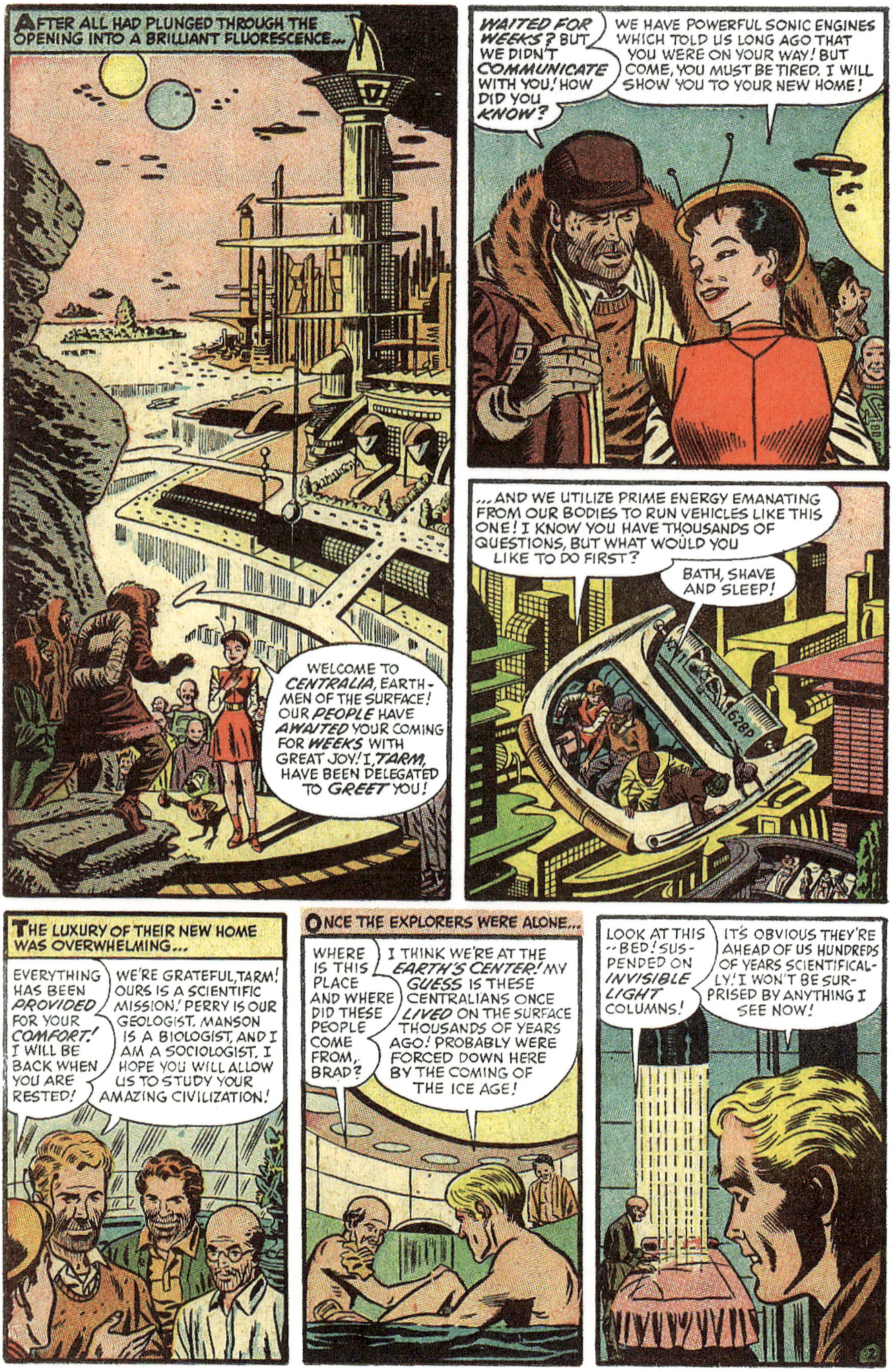
AFTER ALL HAD PLUNGED THROUGH THE OPENING INTO A BRILLIANT FLUORESCENCE...
WELCOME TO CENTRALIA, EARTH-MEN OF THE SURFACE! OUR PEOPLE HAVE AWAITED YOUR COMING FOR WEEKS WITH GREAT JOY! I, TARM, HAVE BEEN DELEGATED TO GREET YOU!
WAITED FOR WEEKS? BUT WE DIDN'T COMMUNICATE WITH YOU! HOW DID YOU KNOW?
WE HAVE POWERFUL SONIC ENGINES WHICH TOLD US LONG AGO THAT YOU WERE ON YOUR WAY! BUT COME, YOU MUST BE TIRED. I WILL SHOW YOU TO YOUR NEW HOME!
...AND WE UTILIZE PRIME ENERGY EMANATING FROM OUR BODIES TO RUN VEHICLES LIKE THIS ONE! I KNOW YOU HAVE THOUSANDS OF QUESTIONS, BUT WHAT WOULD YOU LIKE TO DO FIRST?
BATH, SHAVE AND SLEEP!
THE LUXURY OF THEIR NEW HOME WAS OVERWHELMING...
EVERYTHING HAS BEEN PROVIDED FOR YOUR COMFORT! I WILL BE BACK WHEN YOU ARE RESTED!
WE'RE GRATEFUL, TARM! OURS IS A SCIENTIFIC MISSION! PERRY IS OUR GEOLOGIST. MANSON IS A BIOLOGIST, AND I AM A SOCIOLOGIST. I HOPE YOU WILL ALLOW US TO STUDY YOUR AMAZING CIVILIZATION!
ONCE THE EXPLORERS WERE ALONE...
WHERE IS THIS PLACE AND WHERE DID THESE PEOPLE COME FROM, BRAD?
I THINK WE'RE AT THE EARTH'S CENTER! MY GUESS IS THESE CENTRALIANS ONCE LIVED ON THE SURFACE THOUSANDS OF YEARS AGO! PROBABLY WERE FORCED DOWN HERE BY THE COMING OF THE ICE AGE!
LOOK AT THIS --BED! SUS-PENDED ON INVISIBLE LIGHT COLUMNS!
IT'S OBVIOUS THEY'RE AHEAD OF US HUNDREDS OF YEARS SCIENTIFICAL-LY! I WON'T BE SUR-PRISED BY ANYTHING I SEE NOW!

The next few weeks fulfilled their wildest dreams. They were convinced the lost world they had stumbled upon was indeed a utopia...

"And these tubes FILTER the air, making it STERILE! As a result... there is NO ILLNESS in Centralia!"

"I've noticed the AVERAGE LIFE SPAN is TWO HUNDRED AND TWENTY-FIVE YEARS,... about four times what's normal of Earth!"

"That museum's almost finished, yet it was only started yesterday! I don't see any men working!"

"A hundred years ago MACHINES were BUILT to run MACHINES! They do ALL the work! Centralians are required to report for DUTY once a month... to check and repair the supervisory machines!"

"All your public buildings have no doors and are UNGUARDED! Aren't you afraid of THEFTS?"

"There is NO CRIME in Centralia! The last POLICE force was ABOLISHED three hundred years ago!"

When the Earth scientists had completed their collection of data...

"We have PHOTOGRAPHS... STATISTICS... SAMPLES... and FORMULAS! With this MASS of evidence nobody can dispute the existence of Centralia when we RETURN to Earth!"

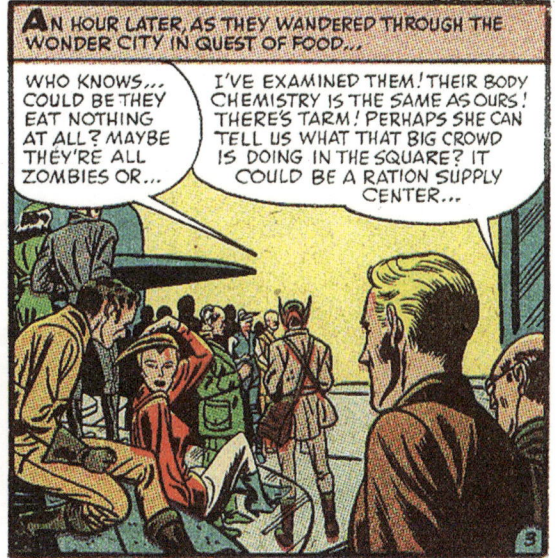

"There's one statistic we've nearly forgotten, Brad! Our FOOD is running low and that's the one thing Tarm hasn't supplied."

"We've been living off our own supplies all these weeks,... but it's awfully embarrassing to ask Tarm for food!"

"Why not? I'm STARVED! Anyhow, we'd NEVER be able to make the long TRIP BACK to the surface! I wonder what the Centralians do eat, anyhow? I've never seen any SIGNS of FOOD around!"

"That's a FACT! I haven't SEEN any LIVE STOCK... or... GRAINS... or ANYTHING! Maybe they do CHEMICAL FARMING?"

"Impossible! They don't have the water supply for that, or the equipment! Synthetics are out also! Their teeth are too good! We'd better find out! This is getting darn serious!"

An hour later, as they wandered through the wonder city in quest of food...

"Who knows,... could be they eat nothing at all! Maybe they're all zombies or..."

"I've examined them! Their body chemistry is the same as ours! There's Tarm! Perhaps she can tell us what that big crowd is doing in the square? It could be a ration supply center..."

3

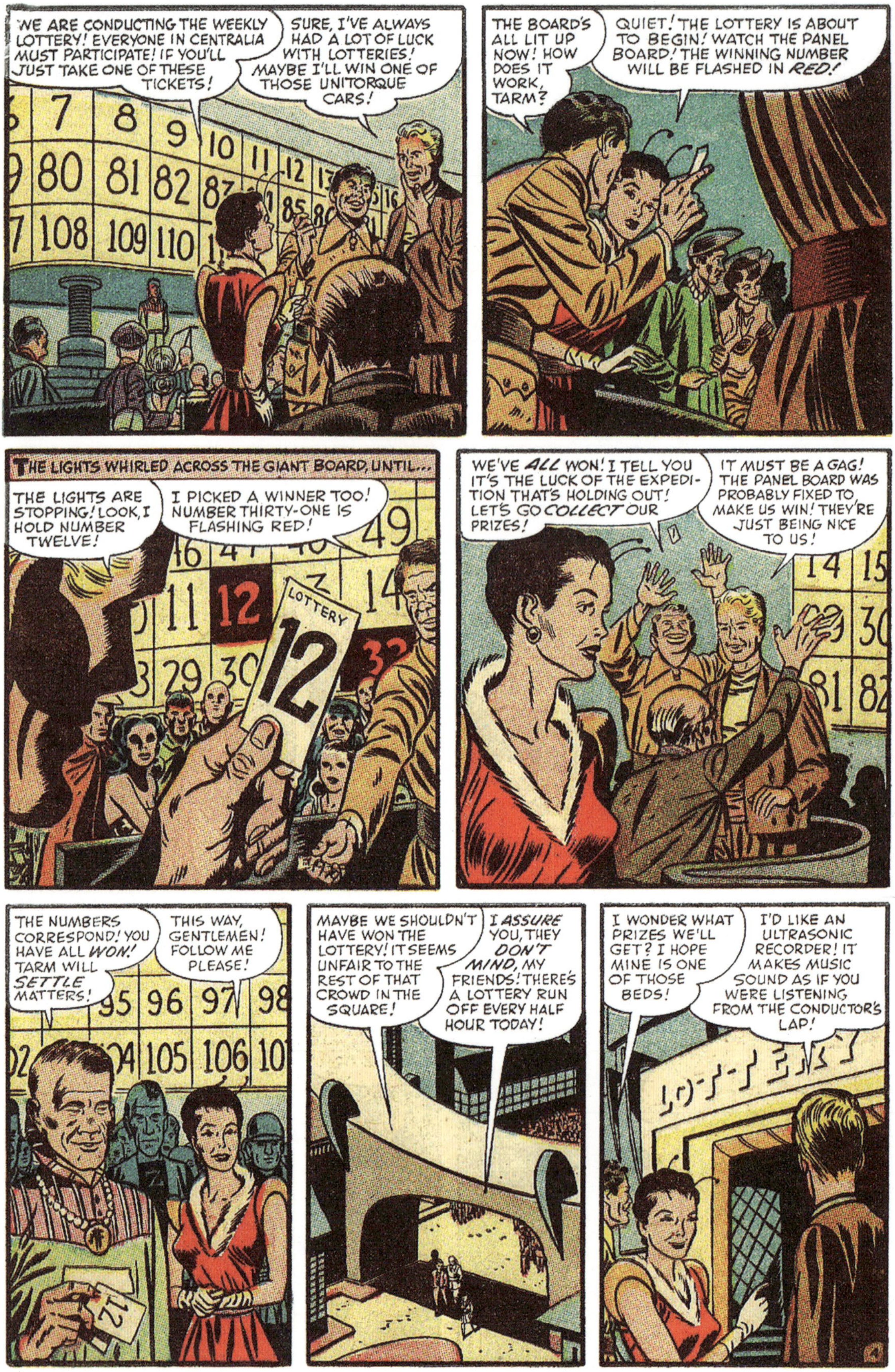

WE ARE CONDUCTING THE WEEKLY LOTTERY! EVERYONE IN CENTRALIA MUST PARTICIPATE! IF YOU'LL JUST TAKE ONE OF THESE TICKETS!
SURE, I'VE ALWAYS HAD A LOT OF LUCK WITH LOTTERIES! MAYBE I'LL WIN ONE OF THOSE UNITORQUE CARS!
THE BOARD'S ALL LIT UP NOW! HOW DOES IT WORK, TARM?
QUIET! THE LOTTERY IS ABOUT TO BEGIN! WATCH THE PANEL BOARD! THE WINNING NUMBER WILL BE FLASHED IN RED!
THE LIGHTS WHIRLED ACROSS THE GIANT BOARD, UNTIL...
THE LIGHTS ARE STOPPING! LOOK, I HOLD NUMBER TWELVE!
I PICKED A WINNER TOO! NUMBER THIRTY-ONE IS FLASHING RED!
LOTTERY
12
WE'VE ALL WON! I TELL YOU IT'S THE LUCK OF THE EXPEDITION THAT'S HOLDING OUT! LET'S GO COLLECT OUR PRIZES!
IT MUST BE A GAG! THE PANEL BOARD WAS PROBABLY FIXED TO MAKE US WIN! THEY'RE JUST BEING NICE TO US!
THE NUMBERS CORRESPOND! YOU HAVE ALL WON! TARM WILL SETTLE MATTERS!
THIS WAY, GENTLEMEN! FOLLOW ME PLEASE!
MAYBE WE SHOULDN'T HAVE WON THE LOTTERY! IT SEEMS UNFAIR TO THE REST OF THAT CROWD IN THE SQUARE!
I ASSURE YOU, THEY DON'T MIND, MY FRIENDS! THERE'S A LOTTERY RUN OFF EVERY HALF HOUR TODAY!
I WONDER WHAT PRIZES WE'LL GET? I HOPE MINE IS ONE OF THOSE BEDS!
I'D LIKE AN ULTRASONIC RECORDER! IT MAKES MUSIC SOUND AS IF YOU WERE LISTENING FROM THE CONDUCTOR'S LAP!
LOTTERY

THIS MOVING WALK WILL TAKE YOU TO YOUR DESTINATION. NOW I MUST SAY GOOD-BYE!
SO LONG, TARM! THANKS FOR EVERYTHING! WE'LL BE SEEING YOU AROUND!
HEY, THIS SURE IS A LONG RIDE! I WONDER WHERE IT LEADS TO?
WE'LL SOON FIND OUT! THAT LOOKS LIKE A PASSAGE ENTRANCE RIGHT AHEAD! YOU KNOW, I'M STILL PUZZLED ABOUT THEIR FOOD SUPPLY! IT'S JUST AS MUCH A MYSTERY TO ME AS IT WAS TWO HOURS AGO!
WELL, HERE GOES! I'M THE FIRST ONE IN!
DON'T HOG THE BEST PRIZES, BRAD! LEAVE SOMETHING FOR US!
SUDDENLY, AS BRAD DISAPPEARED FROM VIEW HIS VOICE CAME BACK IN A TERRIFYING SCREAM...
WHAT THE..?! THAT WAS BRAD'S VOICE!! WHAT HAPPENED, MANSON?
I-I DON'T KNOW! HE MUST HAVE FALLEN OR SOMETHING. I'LL SOON FIND OUT!
AAAAAAAARRRRRRRREE
YEOW! GET ME BACK!!! STOP THE WALK! I KNOW WHAT THEY EAT NOW!! THE LOTTERY TAKES CARE OF IT!!! THESE NICE CIVILIZED PEOPLE ARE...
CANNIBALS! THEY...EAT... EACH OTHER!!! OH...NO...NO!
THE END

CHILLY
CHAMBER MUSIC
SONGS FROM THE SPOOK BOX!
RED SAILS IN THE SUNSET, FAR ACROSS THE SEA...
CARRYING MY LOVER SAFELY BACK TO ME!
?
DARK DAYS ON THE SAILBOAT... AND -- I STAND AGHAST...
FOR THERE'S MY LOVER, SPLOTCHED TO THE MIZZENMAST!
CHILLY
CHAMBER MUSIC
SONGS FROM THE SPOOK BOX!
HEY, JOE! WHERE'D YOU GET THAT NIMBLE GIRLIE?
WHERE'D YOU GET THAT BLONDE-HAIRED SWIRLIE?
LET ME DO THAT DO-ZE-DO!
HEY! WHERE'D YOU GET THAT HURLY-BURLY? HEY, JOE-E-E-E!

THE Satchel

The alleyway was behind me as I came out into Parson Street. I looked down at the street lamp, looked at the man beneath lighting a cigarette, and gripped the handle of the black bag. He was the only one on the block.

I passed him. He exhaled a glob of smoke and took an ordinary look at me.

I rounded the corner and came out on Damon Avenue, a small strip that was shouldered on both sides by ramshackle fences.

I crawled into the shadows and looked back. The man was coming in my direction. He inhaled on his cigarette and I saw his face in its pale glow. It was small but pudgy, with folds rippling through it.

He punched the air with a finger. "Hey, you!" he called.

Stepping back, I quickly sized up Damon Avenue. I gripped the bag tighter and ran. The ground churned beneath me and, for a split second, there was no ground. I landed flush in someone's back yard.

I made out the silhouette of a house before me which ended abruptly and, about eight feet away, I saw the dim outline of another house.

A shaft of light pounded into the darkness, accompanied by the dull rumbling of a window being opened. I looked up. Someone stuck his head out.

"Who's there?"

A voice from behind the fence answered. "It's him," it growled, "the man with the satchel."

I ran towards the blackness between the two houses, turned, and headed down a driveway. Gravel pebbles spilled behind me. The black bag swayed with every step.

Some stiff hedges snapped against my side and I entered them. Thorns cut my face as I came out on the other side. Turning around, I heard the staccotic crunching of gravel, then the sharp retort of the pudgy man's voice. "Stop..!"

Suddenly, something sounding like a siren belted out. It was a woman's scream. She was directly in front of me, and I pushed her aside, running towards the end of the street.

I stopped, and slowly hoisted the satchel protectively in the nestle of my arm. The man with the pudgy face was coming down the street, walking slowly.

"Give me that bag," he said. I backed up, away from him, and wheeled. Again I stopped. Another man was on the other side of me. I looked at the pudgy-faced man again; he was nearer.

"You've got a bomb in that bag," he said. "The radio told us to be on the look-out for you."

Then, I was twisted around, and the second man hit me. I felt dizzy. He hit me again. I tumbled forward, face-downward.

Rolling over, I opened my eyes. The two men had the black bag opened. I managed to smile.

They looked down at me, dropped the bag, and ran. The black bag fell near me and my other head rolled out. I watched it as it halted by the curb.

THIS IS YOUR TICKET TO ANOTHER WORLD!

DON'T MISS THIS THRILLING "BROTHER" MAGAZINE THAT SHOWS YOU THE MEANING OF HORROR IN OTHER WORLDS! READ OF THE MOST AMAZING INVASION THAT *COULD NOT* BE STOPPED... AN INVASION THAT TORE A WORLD APART! YET THE TINIEST POSSIBLE THING WAS ABLE TO BRING AN *END RESULT* THAT WAS A TWIST TO END ALL TWISTS!

YOU WON'T WANT TO MISS *"END RESULT"* JUST ONE OF FOUR GREAT TERROR TALES IN THE LATEST ISSUE OF *TOMB OF TERROR*!

TOMB OF TERROR — Now On Sale

THE SKEPTIC!

Shock looms from a shadow of a doubt in...

THAT'S THE *HOUSE* WE HAVE TO TAKE! WE'LL USE IT FOR OUR LOOKOUT BASE!

IT'S GONNA BE TOUGH, SIR. THERE'S A *SLEW* OF *KRAUT* MG-NESTS BETWEEN *US* AND THAT *JOINT!*

WORLD WAR II -- ON THE EVE OF THE MIGHTIEST BATTLE OF THE WAR, THREE GRIM MEN CAUTIOUSLY MADE THEIR WAY TO THE HIGHLY-STRATEGIC HOUSE ON THE HILL LOCATED IN THE VERY HEART OF ENEMY TERRITORY...

I *DON'T LIKE* THE *LOOKS* OF IT, SARGE, IT SEEMS -- KINDA FUNNY! YOU KNOW -- LIKE IT *DON'T BELONG* THERE AT *ALL!*

LOOK, KID, YOU GOT THE *JITTERS*. NOW *CAN* IT! WE GOT A JOB TO DO!

ALL RIGHT, MEN! LET'S GO! STAY RIGHT ON MY TAIL -- BUT FAN OUT SO'S YOU WON'T BE TAGGED!

OKAY, KID. *THIS IS IT!*

HEADS UP! ENEMY GUN TO OUR RIGHT!

RATATATATA TATATAT

DUCK! I GOT A SPECIAL PRESENT FER THEM!
BARROOOMMM
GET GOING! HURRY--! WE'VE BEEN SPOTTED BY THE OTHERS!
YAAA-A-A-A!
SARGE--GASP...GASP... GET THIS GUY!
BLAM
BANG! BANG!
NEXT TIME, KID-- FIGHT YER OWN BATTLES!
GO AHEAD! WE HAVE NO TIME TO LOSE!
BANG!
BANG BANG
C'MON! GET THE LEAD OUTA YOUR PANTS!
RUN! THEY'RE OPENIN' UP ON US WITH MORTARS!
TWAANGGGEEEE...
MOMENTS LATER, NEAR THE HOUSE...
I DON'T LIKE IT! THEY'RE ALL AROUND THIS HOUSE! AND WE CAN'T STAY OUT HERE EITHER!
WHEN I GIVE THE WORD, KID--MAKE A DASH FOR IT... RIGHT INTO THAT JOINT!
NO! I--CAN'T! SOME-THING'S VERY WRONG ABOUT IT! I--CAN'T!
KLUNK
KLUNK
POKAPOKAPOKPOK!
SEE...YOU... INSIDE...!
C'MON, KID! C'MON, I SAID!
RATATATATATAT

SECONDS AFTERWARDS, INSIDE THE HOUSE...
WOW! I--I ALMOST DIDN'T MAKE IT! SARGE--YOU IN THERE?
YEAH..!
WHAT HAVE WE GOTTEN INTO? I TOLD YOU I DIDN'T LIKE THIS PLACE! IT...GIVES ME THE CREEPS!
THERE YOU GO AGAIN! THAT CRAZY IMAGINATION O' YOURS! CAN IT, I'M TELLING YA! CAN IT!
L-LOOK! WHAT DID I TELL YOU? LOOK AT THOSE COFFINS--AND THOSE DECORATIONS--LIKE THEY WERE V-VAMPIRES--OR--OR GHOULS! THERE AIN'T A SOUND IN THIS HOUSE--NOT A SOUND!
SURE--'CAUSE NO ONE'S BEEN LIVIN' IN IT FER A LONG TIME. YOU'RE DRIVING ME BATTY, KID!
WHEN I WAS A KID, SARGE... I--I USED TO GET STRANGE FEELINGS--LIKE I COULD TALK TO SPIRITS AN' THINGS... YOU GOT TO LISTEN TO ME, SARGE! HEY!! WHERE'S LIEUT. ANDERSON?!! HE'S DISAPPEARED...!
NUTS!
THERE'S GHOSTS IN THIS PLACE! DON'T ASK ME HOW I KNOW! I JUST KNOW IT! THE LOOT'S... DISAPPEARED..!!
WHO KNOWS WHERE HE IS? MAYBE HE'S UPSTAIRS? MAYBE HE WENT DOWN TO THE CELLAR TO LOOK AROUND?!!
I'LL TAKE A LOOK-SEE MYSELF. COVER ME FROM BEHIND, AND WE'LL--
THUD
3

Panel 1: HOLY SMOKE--! KID--IT...IT'S THE LIEUTENANT! HE'S *HAD IT*! HE'S BEEN... HERE ALL THIS TIME!
W-WHA--?!!

Panel 2: I *TOLD* YOU I KNEW *SOMETHIN'* WAS FISHY HERE! GHOSTS-- VAMPIRES--GHOULS...I--I *SEE* THEM! THEY'RE ALL *AROUND*! THEY'RE *LAUGHING*-- HA, HA--HA--
SHADDUP! SHADDUP!

Panel 3: ALL RIGHT SO IT GIVES *ME* THE CREEPS TOO! BUT *THIS* IS *WHERE* WE GOTTA *STAY*, SCOTT. AS *LONG* AS WE *HOLD* THIS PLACE, THE ENEMY CAN'T DO ANYTHING WITHOUT *US* SEEIN' *THEM* FIRST! NOW LET'S SEE WHAT GIVES INSIDE!

Panel 4: CAUTIOUSLY THE TWO MEN TREADED THEIR WAY INTO THE EERIE, FOREBODING INTERIOR...
I--I'M SORRY, SARGE. I JUST LET MYSELF GO, I GUESS. BUT *I SWEAR* THERE'S *GHOSTS* NEAR ME!
JUST WORRY ABOUT KRAUTS, PAL. LET THE GHOSTS TAKE CARE OF THEMSELVES!

Panel 5: W-WHAT'S THAT--? I HEARD SOMETHING! SOMEONE'S BEHIND US, SARGE!
H-HUH?

Panel 6: I'LL *KILL* IT! IT'S NOT ALIVE! IT'S SNEAKIN' UP BEHIND US! *TAKE THAT! AND THAT! AND THAT!*
BANG BANG BANG

Panel 7: I--I KILLED IT, SARGE--I KILLED IT!
CUT IT OUT, KID! IT'S JUST A *STATUE* OF SOME KIND! *STAY HERE!* YOU'RE TOO *JUMPY*. I'M GONNA *SCOUT* AROUND THIS JOINT. KEEP THE GHOSTS COMPANY!

4

SO WHILE THE SERGEANT VANISHED INTO THE BLACKNESS, THE YOUNG G.I. SAT DEATHLY STILL, WAITING--WAITING...
HE THINKS I'M CRAZY. HE THINKS I'M HEARING THINGS--BUT I'M NOT! SOMEONE--SOMETHING IS IN THIS HOUSE WITH ME!
CRUNCH CRUNCH
CRUNCH
CRUNCH CRUNCH CRUNCH CRUNCH CRUNCH
CRUNCH!
CRUNCH
YOU!! I KNEW YOU WERE HERE WITH ME! I KNEW IT WASN'T MY IMAGINATION! GO BACK!
HAVE YOU GONE CRAZY, SCOTT? GET HOLD OF YOURSELF, MAN! OUR LIVES DEPEND ON IT!
B-BUT...Y-YOU'RE DEAD! YOU CAN'T BE ALIVE IN HERE! YOU CAN'T! YOU'RE A GHOST!
SORRY TO DISAPPOINT YOU, SCOTT--BUT I'M VERY MUCH ALIVE--AND I'VE BEEN ALL OVER THIS PLACE. IT'S A PERFECT LOOKOUT POINT! TOO BAD...ABOUT THE SERGEANT...THOUGH!
W-WHAT DO YOU MEAN--TOO BAD? WHAT ARE YOU TALKIN' ABOUT? SARGE--SARGE--HELP! SARGE!!
STOP SHOUTING, SCOTT! THE SERGEANT CAN'T HEAR YOU! HE'S DEAD--DEAD THE FIRST MOMENT HE JUMPED IN AFTER ME! A KRAUT BULLET CAUGHT HIM RIGHT SQUARE IN THE CHEST! THE ONLY GHOSTS ARE IN YOUR IMAGINATION!
THE END

CHARMING BIRD HOUSE AND COMPLETE BIRD CARE STATION

only $1.69

PLUS FREE

PHONOGRAPH RECORD and GIFTS from THE BIRD FRIENDS of AMERICA— Unbreakable Vinyl phonograph record of 18 authentic reproductions of .. Bird Calls and Songs, Bird Picture Book, Bird Food, and Double Throat Bird Call.

Whether you live in country or city, you can get new pleasure and thrills from this amazing complete outfit. Besides you will be performing a needed service for our feathered friends and American wildlife.

Bird House

BIRD FEEDER

BIRD BATH

BIRD CALL RECORD

BIRD BOOK

DOUBLE THROATED BIRD CALLER

Now for the first time ever, you can get this amazing complete outfit. Bird house, bird bath, feeding station, all made of fine rust-proof sheet aluminum embossed and decorated so that the birds will love to use them, plus: • Free bird food • Easy to use bird caller • Bird picture book and • Unbreakable vinylite hi-fidelity record of 18 bird calls and songs — all for the amazing low price of $1.69.

In a few minutes you can set up your outfit on your own window-sill, porch, or tree. Birds will flock to your feeding station, take baths in your bird bath and sing and chirp to your record or your own bird calls. Soon, too, some birds will make their home in your bird house, lay their eggs and start to raise a family. All your friends will envy your wonderful new pets, and your ability to imitate their calls. Parents and teacher will be amazed at how children know and learn to do so many new things.

YOU GET ALL THIS:
- Sheet aluminum bird house, in natural colors
- Simulated leaf bird bath
- Bird feeding station
- Bird food
- Bird call imitator
- Book of 30 bird pictures
- American flag
- Unbreakable vinyl phonograph record with 18 authentic bird calls

10 DAY FREE TRIAL

Just because we know you will love this wonderful bird-care station, we make this offer. Just fill in the coupon below. We will rush your whole outfit by return mail together with the free bird caller, record, bird food, and bird picture book. Set it up and use it for 10 days. If you are not delighted, just return the aluminum house, feeder and bird bath for a refund of the complete purchase price. And keep all the rest as a gift from us. But rush now and be the first in your neighborhood to have this wonderful outfit.

BIRD FRIENDS OF AMERICA, 15TH FLOOR
1860 BROADWAY, NEW YORK 2, N.Y. M

☐ Rush me my complete Bird House, Care Station, Bird Book, Bird Food, Record and Caller for only $1.69. If I am not 100% delighted, I may return the outfit after 10 days free trial, for prompt refund of the full purchase price.

☐ Send C.O.D. I will pay postman $1.69 upon delivery plus a few cents postage.

NAME _____

ADDRESS _____

3 BIG COMIC CARTOON BOOKS

ONLY 98¢

EACH BOOK 128 PAGES
There's a book to please every taste. Remember you get Not just one book for 98¢ but all three books.

The ARMY-NAVY Joke Book—For Everyone The merriest stories, cartoons, jokes about sailors, Waves, soldiers, Wacs, generals and admirals who get theirs in this "pull no punch" gag riot. Illustrated with over 75 of the wildest cartoons.

The Complete GOLF Joke Book—For Dad Surprise Dad—Give him the golfer's laff riot. 128 pages of the funniest golf jokes in all of golfdom. Dad will thank you.

The Complete BASEBALL Joke Book—For You 128 pages of the funniest gags, jokes and stories about our favorite players. Be the first to get Baseball's laugh sensation.

★ **FREE BONUS BOOK** .....
If you buy all three books now and send your payment with the order we will give you the book of the most amazing perfect crimes in America.
• THEY GOT AWAY WITH IT • ALL TRUE
• TEN PERFECT CRIMES

MAIL COUPON NOW...TRY 10 DAYS

STRAVON PUBLISHERS, 113 W. 57 ST., N.Y. 19, Dept. G-161
Rush the three books. I will pay postman 98¢ plus charges. I can enjoy for ten days and return for full refund of purchase price if not satisfied.
☐ Enclosed is 98¢. I will get the 128 page Ten Perfect Crimes book free.
Name_____
Address_____
City_____ Zone____ State____

NOW FLY LIKE A BIRD!

With Wings Made From The Original Sketch of Leonardo Da Vinci's Flying Wings!

Now any adventure loving boy can build Da Vinci's flying wings with just ordinary carpenter's tools.

OFFERED FOR THE FIRST TIME

People said it couldn't be done but Leonardo went right ahead and built the wings and then carted them to a nearby hill and took off. What happened is excitingly told in THE BIRDMAN The Story of Leonardo Da Vinci. See the actual original sketch Leonardo used to build his flying wings with just ordinary tools.

MAIL COUPON NOW!

STRAVON PUBLISHERS Dept. W-691
113 West 57th St., New York 19, N.Y.
I want to try THE BIRDMAN 10-days. I will deposit with postman only 98¢ plus postage. After trying 10-days I may return THE BIRDMAN for a full refund of the purchase price.

NAME_____
ADDRESS_____
CITY_____ ZONE____ STATE____
☐ Check if you enclose 98¢. Stravon pays postage. Same refund.

HOW TO HYPNOTIZE

IT'S EASY TO HYPNOTIZE...
when you know how!

Want the thrill of imposing your will over someone? Of making someone do exactly what you order? Try hypnotism! This amazing technique gives full personal satisfaction. You'll find it entertaining and gratifying. HOW TO HYPNOTIZE shows all you need to know. It is put so simply, anyone can follow it. And there are 24 revealing photographs for your guidance.

SEND NO MONEY

FREE ten days' examination of this system is offered to you if you send the coupon today. We will ship you our copy by return mail, in plain wrapper. If not delighted with results, return it in 10 days and your money will be refunded. Stravon Publishers, Dept. H461 113 West 57th St., New York 19, N.Y.

Mail Coupon Today

STRAVON PUBLISHERS, Dept. H-461
113 West 57th St., N.Y. 19, N.Y.
Send HOW TO HYPNOTIZE in plain wrapper.
☐ Send C.O.D. I will pay postman $1.98 plus postage.
☐ I enclose $1.98. Send postpaid.
If not delighted, I may return it in 10 days and get my money back.

Name_____
Address_____
City_____ Zone____ State____
Canada & Foreign—$2.50 with order

I WILL TRAIN YOU AT HOME FOR GOOD PAY JOBS IN
RADIO-TELEVISION

J. E. SMITH has trained more men for Radio-Television than any other man.

America's Fast Growing Industry Offers You

2 FREE BOOKS SHOW HOW — MAIL COUPON

I TRAINED THESE MEN

LOST JOB, NOW HAS OWN SHOP "Got laid off my machine shop job which I believe was best thing ever happened as I opened a full time Radio Shop. Business is picking up every week."—E. T. Slate, Corsicana, Texas.

GOOD JOB WITH STATION "I am Broadcast Engineer at WLPM. Another technician and I have opened a Radio-TV service shop in our spare time. Big TV sales here ... more work than we can handle."—J. B. Bangley, Suffolk, Va.

$10 TO $15 WEEK SPARE TIME "Four months after enrolling for NRI course, was able to service Radios ... averaged $10 to $15 a week spare time. Now have full time Radio and Television business."—William Weyde, Brooklyn, New York.

AVAILABLE TO VETERANS UNDER G.I. BILLS

WANT YOUR OWN BUSINESS? Let me show you how you can be your own boss. Many NRI trained men start their own business with capital earned in spare time. Joe Travers, a graduate of mine from Asbury Park, N. J., says: "I've come a long way in Radio-Television since graduating. Have my own business on Main Street."

$10 $15 A WEEK EXTRA IN SPARE TIME

Many students make $10, $15 a week and more EXTRA fixing neighbors' Radios in spare time while learning. The day you enroll I start sending you SPECIAL BOOKLETS that show you how. Tester you build with kits I send helps you make extra money servicing sets, gives practical experience on circuits common to Radio and Television. All equipment is yours to keep.

A GOOD PAY JOB

NRI Courses lead to these and many other jobs: Radio and TV service, P.A., Auto Radio, Lab, Factory, and Electronic Controls Technicians, Radio and TV Broadcasting, Police, Ship and Airways Operators and Technicians. Opportunities are increasing. The United States has over 115 million Radios, over 3000 Broadcasting Stations—more expansion is on the way.

A BRIGHT FUTURE

TV now reaches from coast-to-coast. 25 million homes now have Television sets; thousands more are being sold every week. About 200 TV stations are now on the air. Hundreds of others are being built. This means more jobs, good pay jobs with bright futures. More TV operators, installation, service technicians will be needed. Now is the time to get ready for success in TV.

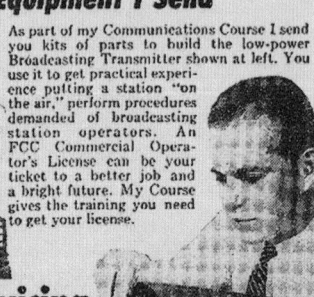

Television Making Good Jobs, Prosperity

Training plus opportunity is the PERFECT COMBINATION for job security, good pay, advancement. In good times, the trained man makes the BETTER PAY, GETS PROMOTED. When jobs are scarce, the trained man enjoys GREATER SECURITY. Radio-TV needs men of action. NRI can provide the training you need for success in Radio-TV for just a few hours of your spare time a week. But you must decide that you want success.

Mail for Actual Lesson and 64-page Book

Without obligating you in any way I'll send an actual lesson to prove that my training is practical, thorough. Also my 64-page book to show good job opportunities for you in Radio-TV. Terms for NRI training are as low as $5 a month. Many graduates make more in two weeks than total cost of training. Mail coupon now. J. E. SMITH, President, National Radio Institute, Dept. ____, Washington 9, D. C. OUR 40TH YEAR.

You Practice Broadcasting with Equipment I Send

As part of my Communications Course I send you kits of parts to build the low-power Broadcasting Transmitter shown at left. You use it to get practical experience putting a station "on the air," perform procedures demanded of broadcasting station operators. An FCC Commercial Operator's License can be your ticket to a better job and a bright future. My Course gives the training you need to get your license.

You Practice Servicing with Equipment I Send

Nothing takes the place of PRACTICAL EXPERIENCE. That's why NRI training is based on LEARNING BY DOING. With my Servicing Course you build the modern Radio shown at right, a Multitester which you use to help fix sets while training. Many students make $10, $15 a week extra fixing neighbors' sets in spare time soon after enrolling. My book shows other equipment you get and keep.

Good for Both — FREE

MR. J. E. SMITH, President, Dept. 4CO2
National Radio Institute, Washington 9, D. C.
Mail me Sample Lesson and 64-page Book, FREE. (No salesman will call. Please write plainly.)

Name _____ Age _____
Address _____
City _____ Zone ____ State _____
VETS write in date of discharge

The ABC's of SERVICING

How to Be a Success in RADIO-TELEVISION

MEN! WOMEN! take orders for famous
NYLONS GUARANTEED 9 MOS.

ONLY YOUR SPARE TIME NEEDED

LOOK AT THESE EXCEPTIONAL
First Week Spare Time Earnings

Space permits mentioning only these few exceptional cases, but they give you an idea of the **Big Money** that is possible in just spare time starting the very first week.

Mr. Richard Peters, Penna. **$63.94** First Week Spare Time	Mrs. W. B. Foss, S. Dak. **$60.47** First Week Spare Time
Mrs. Virgil Hickman, Tenn. **$74.97** First Week Spare Time	Mr. A. E. Lewison, Ga. **$52.26** First Week Spare Time
Mr. Henry O'Rourke, Vermont **$58.89** First Week Spare Time	Mrs. Emery Shoots, Wyo. **$48.69** First Week Spare Time
Mrs. J. A. Sievers, Fla. **$85.14** First Week Spare Time	Mr. J. Hillman Jr., Ohio **$49.72** First Week Spare Time
Mr. Anthony Avrilla, Wash. **$135.00** First Week Spare Time	Mrs. John Gorman, Conn. **$71.54** First Week Spare Time
Mrs. Agnes Michaels, Ind. **$54.18** First Week Spare Time	Mr. W. Riley, Ill. **$72.72** First Week Spare Time
Russell P. Hart, New York **$53.30** First Week Spare Time	Miss Frances Freeman, Texas **$62.73** First Week Spare Time

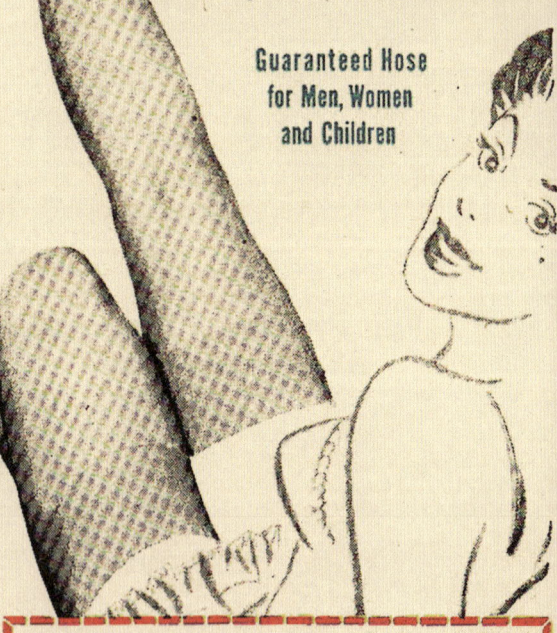

A CAR IN 4 MONTHS—AND UP TO $20 IN A HALF DAY
"I cannot express my thrill upon receiving this beautiful new Chevrolet. I was a bit doubtful at first but now it is a reality and I thank you for making it so. I have earned this car in just four short months and I'm sure others can do the same. Thank you for making it possible for me to earn more money than ever before. I have earned as much as twenty dollars for one half day and my bonus alone for one month was $125.00."—*Mrs. E. A. Conway*

NEW CAR GIVEN OR IF YOU ALREADY HAVE A CAR YOU CAN GET A NEW ONE ON OUR "TRADE-IN" PLAN—
WIL-KNIT actually gives new Fords, Plymouths or Chevrolets to producers as a bonus **in addition to your regular earnings.** It is yours. Or if you now have a car, you can get a new one even quicker under our "trade-in" plan without paying a penny. Get the facts now.

NO HOUSE-TO-HOUSE CANVASSING REQUIRED

Our unusual plan is a sure-fire money maker! Sensational Guarantee is creating a tremendous demand for Wil-knit Nylons! Mrs. Nellie Gail of Iowa started out with me and made $48.89 the very first week in just her spare hours. Mrs. Agnes McCall, of South Carolina, did even better. Her spare time in her very first week brought her earnings of $95.56. Mrs. Walter Simmons of New York turned her spare time into earnings of $92.82 her first week out. THESE EXCEPTIONAL EARNINGS FOR JUST SPARE TIME and in the very first week give you an idea of the possibilities!

GUARANTEED AGAINST Runs, Wear and Even Snags!
Why is it so easy for Wil-knit Salespeople to get orders? I'll tell you—It's because we stand back of Wil-knit Nylons with the most amazing guarantee you have ever heard of. Your customers can wear out their hose. They can develop runs. They can even snag them. No matter what happens to make Wil-knit Nylons unwearable... within 9 months, depending on quantity... **we replace them free of charge under terms of our guarantee.** No wonder women are anxious to buy Wil-knit! And no wonder it is easy to quickly build up a fine and STEADY year around income. Earnings start immediately. Look at these exceptional figures—Lillian A. Bronson of Georgia made $80.60 first week spare time. Ethel Cameron of Michigan, $64.14. Sabine Fisher, New York, reports earnings of $70.10 under our unusual plan just for spare time in her first week. Mrs. Edward Leo of Minn. in writing to thank us for the new Plymouth she received, also reports: "I actually earned $12.00 in fifteen minutes by the clock. I actually couldn't believe I earned that much until I re-checked my figures."

SEND NO MONEY — JUST NAME & HOSE SIZE...

SIMPLY MAIL COUPON. When you send for Selling Outfit, I also send your choice of Nylons or Socks for your personal use. Just rush your name for the facts about the most sensational line of hosiery for men, women and children ever offered. Your friends and neighbors will admire you and this unusual selection of most beautiful hosiery! Just mail coupon or postal card now, and learn at once how you, too, can earn big money in FULL or SPARE TIME and qualify for an *extra bonus* and a New Car over and above your cash earnings. — *L. Lowell Wilkin*

WIL-KNIT HOSIERY CO., Inc., A-8243 Midway, Greenfield, Ohio

Guaranteed Hose for Men, Women and Children

L. Lowell Wilkin, **WIL-KNIT HOSIERY CO., Inc.**
A-8243 Midway, GREENFIELD, OHIO

Be Sure to Send Hose Size

Please rush all facts about your guaranteed hosiery money-making plan and NEW CAR offer. Everything you send me now is FREE.

MY HOSE SIZE IS............ MY AGE IS............ YEARS

NAME ....

ADDRESS ....

CITY .... ZONE ...... STATE ....

EERIE TALES OF SUPERNATURAL HORROR!
WITCHES TALES

Collect all 4 Volumes of Witches Tales from PS Artbooks

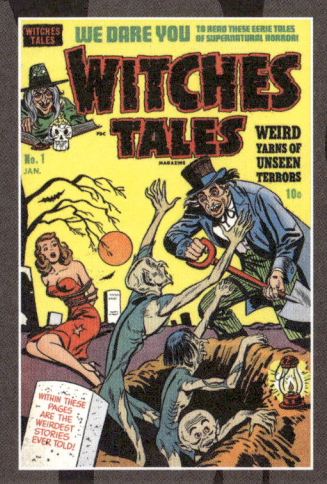

Witches Tales Volume One

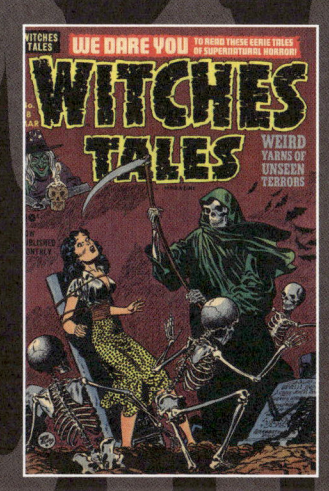

Witches Tales Volume Two

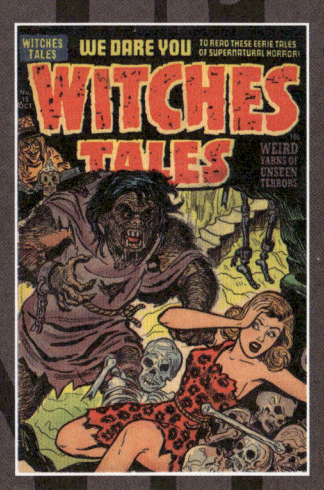

Witches Tales Volume Three

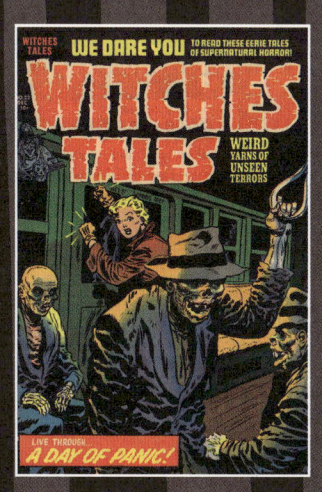

Witches Tales Volume Four

Chamber of Chills
May 1954 - Issue #23

Cover Art - Lee Elias

Heartline
Script - Unknown
Pencils - Manny Stallman
Inks - John Giunta

Invasion
Script - Unknown
Pencils - Jack Sparling
Inks - Jack Sparling

The Museum
Script - Bob Powell
Pencils - Bob Powell
Inks - Bob Powell

Dust Unto Dust
Script - Howard Nostrand
Pencils - Howard Nostrand
Inks - Howard Nostrand

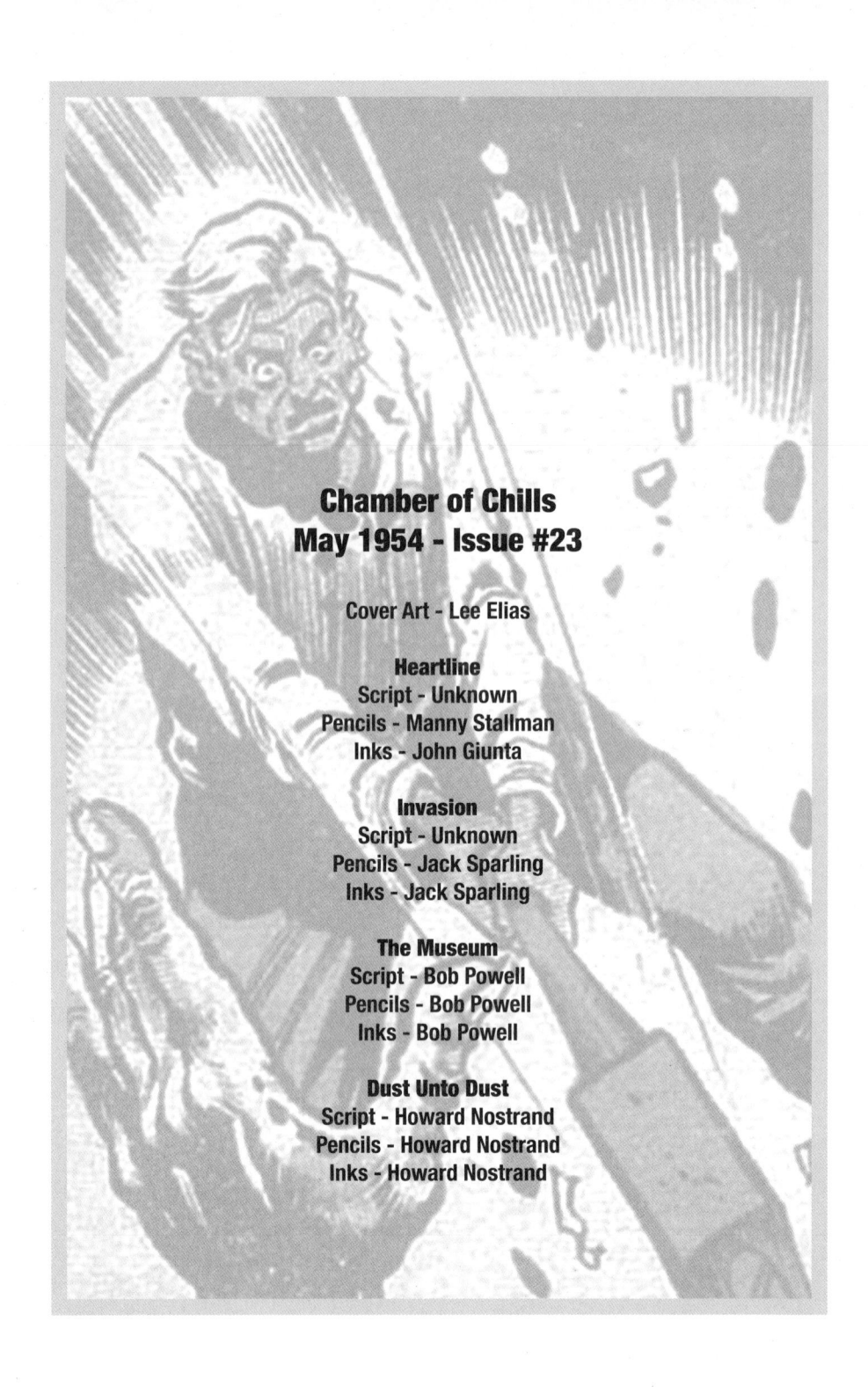

Information Source: Grand Comics Database!
A nonprofit, Internet-based organization of international volunteers dedicated to building a database covering all printed comics throughout the world.
If you believe any of this data to be incorrect or can add valuable additional information, please let us know www.comics.org
All rights to images reserved by the respective copyright holders. All original advertisement features remain the copyright of the respective trading company.

Privacy Policy
All portions of the Grand Comics Database that are subject to copyright are licensed under a Creative Commons Attribution 3.0 Unported License.
This includes but is not necessarily limited to our database schema and data distribution format.
The GCD Web Site code is licensed under the GNU General Public License.

CHAMBER OF CHILLS
TALES OF TERROR AND SUSPENSE!
CHAMBER OF CHILLS
A STRAIGHT LINE TO HORROR IS.... HEARTLINE!

hands tied?

...because you lack a High School diploma?

YOU CAN GET A High School education AT HOME FOR ONLY $6.00 A MONTH!

LOOK at what our former students say!

"The knowledge I gained from the study of your high school course has helped me greatly. Education by correspondence gives one an opportunity to study in privacy. It is particularly suitable for those whose time is limited."
John McHugh
New York, N.Y.

"I wish to express my appreciation to all my instructors for the help and courtesy shown me. I can recommend the American School to anyone who wishes a high school education, but especially to boys and girls living on farms."
Mrs. Thelma Bowers
Livingston, Tenn.

"The thing I liked best about studying by correspondence was the fact that I, being a housewife, could work on my studies when I found time after I had finished my work around the house."
Mrs. Christina Poole
Galesburg, Illinois

"Another thing I liked about the American School is that I was able to suit my payments to my budget. This helped me very much."
Mrs. Eleanor M. Costales
Albuquerque, N. Mex.

Now there's no longer any need for your hands being tied—for your being held back from getting many of the things you want most in life—simply because you don't have that all important high school diploma. It's so simple for you to get a high school education at home, thanks to the world famous American School.

It costs you only $6.00 a month, which includes all books and all instruction. That's only 20 cents a day! Yet it gives you benefits so priceless they cannot be measured in money!

Study at Your Convenience

There are no classes for you to attend. You study in your spare time, in your own home. Yet, wherever you are, you get individual instruction from experienced teachers who take a personal interest in you. Thanks to American School's remarkable home study plan, you progress rapidly... and go ahead as fast as your time and abilities permit. You take up your education where you left off and receive full credit for subjects you have already completed. And you can choose a full high school course or any one of a hundred different academic, commercial and technical subjects.

Want a Better Job, Bigger Pay?

You may find that this high school at home plan will lead to bigger things for you, as it has already done for so many grateful American School graduates. It can do even more than help you earn more money and recapture lost opportunities. It can help you enjoy many of the things you now miss in life... win a more highly respected place in your community... go on to college. American School graduates have been admitted to over 500 different colleges and universities. Many of them testify that the School's training has helped them pass college entrance examinations, make higher grades in college and win scholarships. Its work for over 50 years has been praised by leading educators. Why go on through life any longer with tied hands when you may free yourself and forge ahead by getting a high school education this convenient, low-cost way?

FREE SAMPLE LESSON!

Mail coupon today for an interesting FREE sample lesson that reveals how pleasant and profitable it can be for you to get a high school education at home. Prove to yourself that you, too, may get the priceless benefits it gives, simply by studying at home, at your own convenience. You owe it to yourself to send for this FREE sample lesson TODAY! There is no obligation.

American School
400 MADISON AVE., NEW YORK 17, N.Y.
DEPT. A2

Mail coupon today for FREE sample lesson →

American School, Dept. A2
400 Madison Ave., New York 17, N. Y.

Gentlemen: Please rush me, without cost or obligation, an interesting FREE sample lesson that reveals how pleasant and profitable it can be for me to get a high school education in my spare time at home.

Name_____
Address_____
City_____ Zone___ State___

CHAMBER OF CHILLS MAGAZINE, MAY, 1954, Vol. 1, No. 23, IS PUBLISHED BI-MONTHLY by WITCHES TALES, INC., 1860 Broadway, New York 23, N.Y. Entered as second class matter at the Post Office at New York, N.Y. under the Act of March 3, 1879. Single copies 10c. Subscription rates, 10 issues for $1.00 in the U. S. and possessions, elsewhere $1.50. All names in this periodical are entirely fictitious and no identification with actual persons is intended. Contents copyrighted, 1954, by Witches Tales, Inc., New York City. Printed in the U.S.A. Title Registered in U. S. Patent Office.

THE INNER CIRCLE

WE WANT YOUR LETTERS! All kinds...big ones, fat ones, skinny ones, all sizes and shapes! And... what do we want you to write about?

We want your opinion on that new, terrific, four-power horror pact that CHAMBER OF CHILLS, TOMB OF TERROR, BLACK CAT MYSTERY and WITCHES TALES have entered into... sort of a blood pool! How do you rate this shock king's domain?

Tell us what you like about these four distinctive books that now come to you during a two-month period, a mag appearing on your newsstands every two weeks.

What is the impact of BLACK CAT MYSTERY, where man meets man in a mad clash of reality? How different is the design of WITCHES TALES, the mag that chills your spine and tickles your funny bone? How far are you sent by TOMB OF TERROR, whose stories are ripped from the many unexplored voids? How deep are you in the incredible sphere of the supernatural, which CHAMBER OF CHILLS takes you to?

We want the answers to these questions in your letters. Don't choke up...let us have it, both barrels. All you do is, write to:

WITCHES TALES, INC.
1860 Broadway
New York 23, N.Y.

CHAMBER OF CHILLS — CONTENTS NO. 23

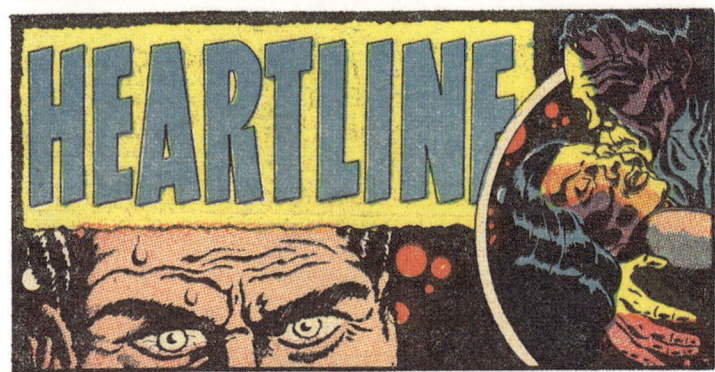

- INVASION
- HEARTLINE
- DUST UNTO DUST
- THE MUSEUM

THE FAMOUS JUELENE SYSTEM GUARANTEE

LOVELIER HAIR IN 7 DAYS OR YOUR MONEY BACK

Give Yourself This Treatment Just Once

That's All We Ask—Just One Trial—You Will Marvel At The Results. You Will Be Absolutely Amazed Or It Doesn't Cost You One Penny. Your Fine Care With Latest JUELENE Formulas May Be The Answer To Your Hair And Scalp Problem.

DON'T WAIT UNTIL IT'S TOO LATE

While there is something new under the sun almost every day, Beauticians, Expert Hairdressers and Dermatologists are all familiar with the use of LANOLIN. In recent years, it has been believed that CHOLESTEROL is the active ingredient of LANOLIN. CHOLESTEROL is an ingredient found in all vegetables, in all animals, and in our own bodies. It is now possible for chemists to produce a synthetic CHOLESTEROL, which makes it possible to use CHOLESTEROL in this Special Hair and Scalp System. Your hair grows from the follicles located in the tissues of your scalp. The condition of your hair depends upon the normal health of your scalp. The LANOLIN Cream Shampoo which you receive with this treatment is to be used as a Shampoo to cleanse the hair and scalp of dust, dried perspiration, grime, etc.

YOU GET EVERYTHING, the JAR of JUELENE SYSTEM (SCALP and HAIR LUBRICANT), the LANOLIN CREAM SHAMPOO, the DH-12 FORMULA containing CHOLESTEROL, PLUS the SPECIAL LANOLIN COMPOUND, ALL A REAL BARGAIN AT $4.60 BUT all YOU PAY is ONLY $2.98, plus postage, FOR EVERYTHING. FOLLOW the JUELENE SYSTEM DIRECTIONS you receive with your package OF THESE 4 FORMULAS, and YOU WILL BLESS THE DAY YOU BEGAN and TRIED THIS PROPER WAY

SEND NO MONEY — MAIL YOUR COUPON NOW
EVERY CENT BACK IF NOT THE BEST YOU EVER USED.

Fine special daily Juelene System care helps PREVENT, DANDRUFFY DULL, DRY, BRITTLE ITCHY SCALP, BURNT HAIR, through lubrication, massage & stimulation.

Being a woman, your hair is in need of either waving, marcelling or pin-curling regularly. Be certain to give your hair and scalp fine special care and to use the special LANOLIN Formula which you get with everything to pin-curl, wave, set your hair. This Formula melts easily, waterproofs the hair, and at the same time helps to hold a setting on styling longer. By resisting perspiration, it not only keeps your hair looking lovelier, more lustrous, but helps to prevent dry, cracking, dandruffy, dull hair conditions.

YOU GET FULL DIRECTIONS ON HOW TO USE EVERYTHING, PLUS A REGULAR $2. LESSON ON HOW TO PIN CURL OVER-NITE, WAVE AND STYLE YOUR HAIR BY JUEL'S HAIR STYLIST.

100% GUARANTEE
MONEY BACK IF NOT SATISFIED!
YOU CAN'T LOSE!

SPECIAL 3 MONTH SIZE TREATMENT

JUEL COMPANY, Dept. A-530
1735 W. 5th Street, Brooklyn 23, N. Y.

I would like to try your special JUELENE SYSTEM of special hair and scalp care. Send me a regular size Jar of JUELENE Formula for daily lubrication, massage, stimulation. A Jar of LANOLIN CREAM SHAMPOO for cleansing the hair. A Jar of DH-12 CHOLESTEROL Formula for use after shampoo. A Jar of Special LANOLIN Compound to use for waving, curling, pin-curling, and to help hold my hair setting longer, more lustrous, and LANOLIN benefits. Send me everything. On delivery, I will pay only $2.98, plus postage. Included will be full JUELENE SYSTEM directions and 100% MONEY BACK GUARANTEE. I must be delighted and pleased in every way or every cent back. I promise that if I am pleased, I will tell my friends about the wonderful JUELENE SYSTEM Formulas and Treatment, and of all of the benefits of fine LANOLIN and CHOLESTEROL. Send everything to

NAME
ADDRESS
CITY   ZONE   STATE

NOTICE: YOU GET ENOUGH OF EVERYTHING TO LAST AT LEAST 3 MONTHS. You get full easy directions on fine daily hair and scalp care, as well as hints and tips on the use of fine LANOLIN and CHOLESTEROL Formulas, in Shampooing and Styling your Hair. A 100% MONEY BACK GUARANTEE will be included in your package, along with full JUELENE SYSTEM directions on Hair and Scalp Care. In use since 1928. The fine JUELENE SYSTEM Formulas have been used by more than one half million women. YOU MUST BE PLEASED OR MONEY BACK.

HEARTLINE
THIS IS THE HEART...
THIS IS THE GIRL...
THESE ARE MY HANDS...

SUSANNE HAS BEEN DEAD FOR THREE MONTHS! YES--THREE MONTHS OF TORTURE AND DOUBT. BUT THAT IS ALL PAST NOW--FOR I KNOW I HAVE SUCCEEDED. ONLY--WHY DOESN'T SHE OPEN HER EYES?
COULD I HAVE MADE AN ERROR?
NO! IT TAKES TIME FOR HER TO BECOME AWARE OF WHAT HAS HAPPENED. I'VE DONE ALL I CAN--AND YET... I'M HELPLESS HERE, WITH NOTHING TO DO!
WAIT--WAIT--TIMELESS WAIT. ALL MY LIFE... I'VE WAITED...
I'LL NEVER FORGET HER--HOW BEAUTIFUL SHE WAS---HOW PATIENT AND UNDERSTANDING AND SWEET. I'LL ALWAYS REMEMBER. THAT DAY, FOR INSTANCE, WHEN WE HELD EACH OTHER CLOSE...
AT LAST, DARLING! AFTER TODAY... I'LL BE RECOGNIZED AS A GREAT SURGEON. AFTER TODAY OUR LIFE BEGINS! WE'UL BE MARRIED!
IT WAS WORTH WAITING FOR, LARRY!
I, LAWRENCE ROMAINE, HAD DISCOVERED A SURGICAL TECHNIQUE THAT COULD ISOLATE AND CUT OUT IN ITS ENTIRETY ANY ORGAN OF THE HUMAN BODY THAT WAS DISEASED--TO BE REPLACED BY ANOTHER ORGAN FROM THE "ORGAN BANK." ONE HOUR LATER...
--AND THERE, GENTLEMEN--IS THE DISEASED ORGAN! THE PATIENT SHALL LIVE. MY PROCESS HAS TAKEN ONLY A FEW MOMENTS--SHORT ENOUGH FOR COMPLETE SURVIVAL!
BRAVO! EXCELLENT! THIS DAY WILL BE LONG REMEMBERED, ROMAINE!
YES- IT WOULD HAVE BEEN WONDERFUL--EXCEPT THAT MY WORLD CAME TO AN END THAT VERY NEXT MORNING. FOR SUSANNE, YOU SEE--DIED OF A HEART ATTACK!
THERE'S NOTHING YOU CAN DO, LARRY. HER DEATH HAS SHOCKED US ALL! BUT YOU HAVE TO LIVE AND CARRY ON. SHE'D HAVE WANTED IT THAT WAY!
SUSANNE... MY SUSANNE...
I'LL NOT BE CHEATED OUT OF OUR LOVE, MY DARLING. I PROMISE YOU, YOU'LL COME BACK! I'LL DEDICATE MY LIFE TO THIS TASK! YOU'LL COME BACK!
2

PERHAPS MY MIND DID CRACK... BUT MY CONVICTIONS WERE NEVER STRONGER OR SANER -- I TOILED FOR DAYS PREPARING THE NECESSARY ARRANGEMENTS. AND THEN -- ONE WEEK AFTERWARDS -- I ACTED!

THIS NEW *CADAVER* HAS ONLY BEEN RECENTLY *BURIED!* IT'S JUST THE *RIGHT BODY* I'M *LOOKING* FOR!

THE *HEART!* STRONG... DURABLE!

DISCOVERIES. GREAT ONES, BUT YET SECRET ONES... DISCOVERIES THAT WOULD MAKE MY PRECIOUS, DEAD SUSANNE RELIVE AGAIN! I DUG HER OUT OF THE COFFIN... PUT HER IN THE CART...

REST WELL INSIDE YOUR *CRATE*, DEAREST. IT WON'T BE LONG NOW!

I SET UP A PRIVATE LABORATORY IN A DESOLATE HOUSE AWAY FROM THE CITY. I TRANSFERRED SUSANNE'S BODY INTO A SPECIALLY-BUILT MORGUE...

YOU'RE NEVER MORE BEAUTIFUL -- NOR MORE DESIRABLE!

NEXT I PUT MY THEORY INTO PRACTICE... *MARCH 24* - AM TRYING HARD TO MASSAGE THE CIRCULATION ROUTES TO THE LEFT VENTRICLE...

NOTHING SEEMS TO BE HAPPENING! BUT I'VE GOT TO KEEP TRYING!

MARCH 25, 27, APRIL 14 --- SAME PROGRESS. SIMPLIFIED TECHNIQUES WITH STILL NO APPARENT RESULTS. PROGNOSIS UNCERTAIN. AM CONTINUING WITH REVIVIFICATION. HEART STOLID AND UNCHANGED...

PERHAPS MORE OXYGEN MAY TURN THE TRICK!

MAY 9 -- HAVE MODIFIED STIMULUS-CHARGES AND HAVE INSTITUTED A NEW VITALIZING PROCESS. THIS MAY PROVE TO BE THE CRUCIAL POINT!

BEGINNING TO *ACT UP!* YES... THERE'S A *DEFINITE* BEAT! THE HEART... IS... ALIVE!

MAY 11-- HAVE SET UP MY APPARATUS AND AM PROCEEDING TO START MY REPLACEMENT TECHNIQUE. HEART IS FRESH AND UNCHANGED. BEAT IS STRONGER AND CARDIOGRAM TEST SHOWS NO ABNORMAL ACTIVITY...
IT SEEMS TO BE... REDDER AND LARGER!
FOR NOW I HAD TAKEN OUT SUSANNES OWN SHATTERED AND DECAYED HEART AND ATTACHED THE MAIN BLOOD ROUTES TO THE CADAVER'S HEART. MAY 14--SUSANNE BREATHES!
HER CHEST...RISING AND FALLING...GOOD!
MAY 21--- HAVE ENLARGED THE BLOOD ROUTES TO INCLUDE ALL THE MINOR ARTERIES AND VEINS. ONLY LYMPH CHANNELS REMAIN UNATTACHED. HEART BEAT SEEMS TO BE INCREASING IN VOLUME--THOUGH IT MUST BE MY IMAGINATION OF COURSE...
CAN'T CONCENTRATE ON MY NOTES. HEARTBEAT LOUDER...
MAY 23--- THERE IS A DEFINITE PARALLEL BETWEEN THE HEART'S COLOR AND SUSANNE'S DEGREE OF REJUVENATION. THE REDDER THE HEART, THE CLOSER SUSANNE WILL BE TO LIFE! AM INCREASING VOLTAGE...
THUMP... THUMP!
IT'S TIME TO PLACE IT INSIDE SUSANNE'S BODY! THIS IS THE MOMENT!
MUST KEEP CALM. QUICKLY NOW--QUICKLY!

NOW I WAIT... WAIT FOR SUSANNE TO COME TO LIFE! AND SUDDENLY... AS I LOOK DOWN ON HER PEACEFUL FACE...
SUSANNE... SUSANNE...
I LOOK INTO HER EYES... THAT SHINE WITH DEATH. HER FACE IS EXPRESSIONLESS... MUTE... AS THOUGH LIFE ITSELF IS A HORROR...
SUSANNE... SPEAK! SAY... SOMETHING!
I BACKED AWAY FROM MY LOVER-CORPSE ...THE BEING WHO RELIVES IN DEATH. SUSANNE'S BEAUTY OVERWHELMED ME... AND I WAITED LONGINGLY... BREATHLESSLY... AS SHE TOOK SOME SLOW SHUFFLES TOWARD ME...
COME, DARLING! OH, COME!
NO... IT WAS NOT TO ME THAT SHE WAS WALKING. IT WAS TO SOMETHING... ELSE. IT WAS A CORPSE... FETID... EARTH-CRACKED... WITH ROTTED RED EYES... TOWARDS A MAN...
NO!
A DEAD CORPSE WITHOUT A HEART ...WHOSE ROTTED HANDS HELD SUSANNE IN A GESTURE OF LOVE...
IT--CAN'T--BE!!
HELPLESS AND HORRIFIED, I SEE TWO DEAD THINGS KISSING... TWO DECAYED THINGS TOUCHING LIPS OF LOVE...
I HEAR A SNAP. IT WAS MY BRAIN. BUT I KNOW WHAT I DID... KNOW WHAT HAPPENED...
SUZANNE... HAS... HIS... HEART.
...AND THE HEART STILL LOVES ITS BODY!
THE END

CHILLY CHAMBER MUSIC
SONGS FROM THE SPOOK BOX!

IN A CANYON, IN A CANYON, EXCAVATING FOR SOME WINE,

LIVED A WINER, A DIRTY WINER, AND HIS DAUGHTER, FRANKENSTEIN.

FED SHE HIM WINE AS THICK AS BATTER, AND ITS TASTE WAS JUST LIKE FIRE!

FOR THE GAL, THOUGH SHE A MONSTER, WAS YET A YOUNG VAMPIRE!

CHILLY CHAMBER MUSIC
SONGS FROM THE SPOOK BOX!

I LOVE YOU, GHOULY, GHOULY, I FEAR.

LIFE WITH ITS HORRORS, LIFE WITH ITS TEARS

FADES INTO NIGHTMARES WHEN I FEEL YOU ARE NEAR!

I LOVE YOU, GHOULY, GHOULY...

"I DO!"

THE STORM

"Dr. Krakow, we've got it!"

"Yes, Storr, it is a fact! We can control nature!"

"Shall I call the commission, sir?"

"Don't be a fool, Storr! *We* have controlled nature... and *we* shall use it!"

"But, sir... it is for mankind! It is not for us..."

"Shut up, fool! What did mankind ever do for you? Send you to rot in a prison? Remember, my amiable assistant, it was I who got you out of that loathesome hole! And I can put you back there if I told your story!"

"I understand fully, Dr. Krakow. What would you have us do?"

"The weather, Storr, can be man's greatest weapon, and we've got it, you and I. We will barrage the city with endless storms—rain, hail, sleet, snow! Lightning will crash on their roofs, thunder will resound through their homes, and just as Noah did, they will have to flee!"

Dr. Krakow's eyes burned a fire of hatred.

"Then we will march into their homes and plunder a life's full! We will be rich... rich... rich!"

At this, Storr's heart took a fiendish leap. The thought kindled his brain and made an inferno of fantastic ideas. Yes, this was indeed a great discovery.

"When do we begin, Dr. Krakow?"

"Aha, Storr! I see you are as eager as I am! I see by your eyes that you have come to my way of thinking!"

"You are quite right, sir. I was a fool to think otherwise."

"Come then, we will set the dynamos in motion!"

The two ascended the long steps of the observatory. Their plans propelled them at a furious speed. Up, up, up to their goal.

"Now, Storr! Spin those marvelous dials!"

ROARRRRRRRR!! BARUUUMMPPHH!!

Round and round it went, gushing electric bolts to the heavens, making a maelstrom in the skies!

Death seemed to take over as clouds smashed into each other and the air exploded with fury. And then doom began to fall...

BLAMMMMM!! CRASHHHHH!!

Hail stones by the billions... rain in loathesome torrents... snow and ice in avalanches!! The sky opened and let out its terror!

"Look at it, Storr! Feast your eyes on their misery!"

"Extraordinary, sir... and we are not even touched!"

"Yes, yes... the skies topple all around, and we are on top of the world!"

CRASHHHHHH! CRANGGGGGG!!

The two gloated together over their new invincible power that would lead them to the kingship of the world! Then suddenly Storr's twisted mind took yet another turn...

"Gaze at your creation, Dr. Krakow! For it will be your last time!"

With that he threw himself upon the scientist, and the two toppled to the floor.

"L-l-let g-g-go, Storrrrrr!"

"Do you think I'm crazy? Why should the two of us rule the world? There is room for just one—and that is I!!"

Storr reached for his knife... and Dr. Krakow gave one last push...

CRASHHHHHH!!!

"You fool, you threw me against the dynamo!"

Dials went berserk! The heavens resounded with the results! And...

BRANNNNNGGGGG! CLAMMMMMM!!

Lighning had struck twice... the observatory went up in all-consuming flames! And two voices were silenced... forever.

Moments later, the skies began to clear.

NOW ON SALE... AT ALL NEWSSTANDS!
AMERICA'S MOST SENSATIONAL COMIC BOOK

TRUE!

FIRST TIME PUBLISHED 10¢

Ripley's Believe It or Not! — FULL LENGTH STORIES IN FULL COLOR

THE MAGAZINE YOU'VE CLAMORED FOR! DON'T MISS IT!

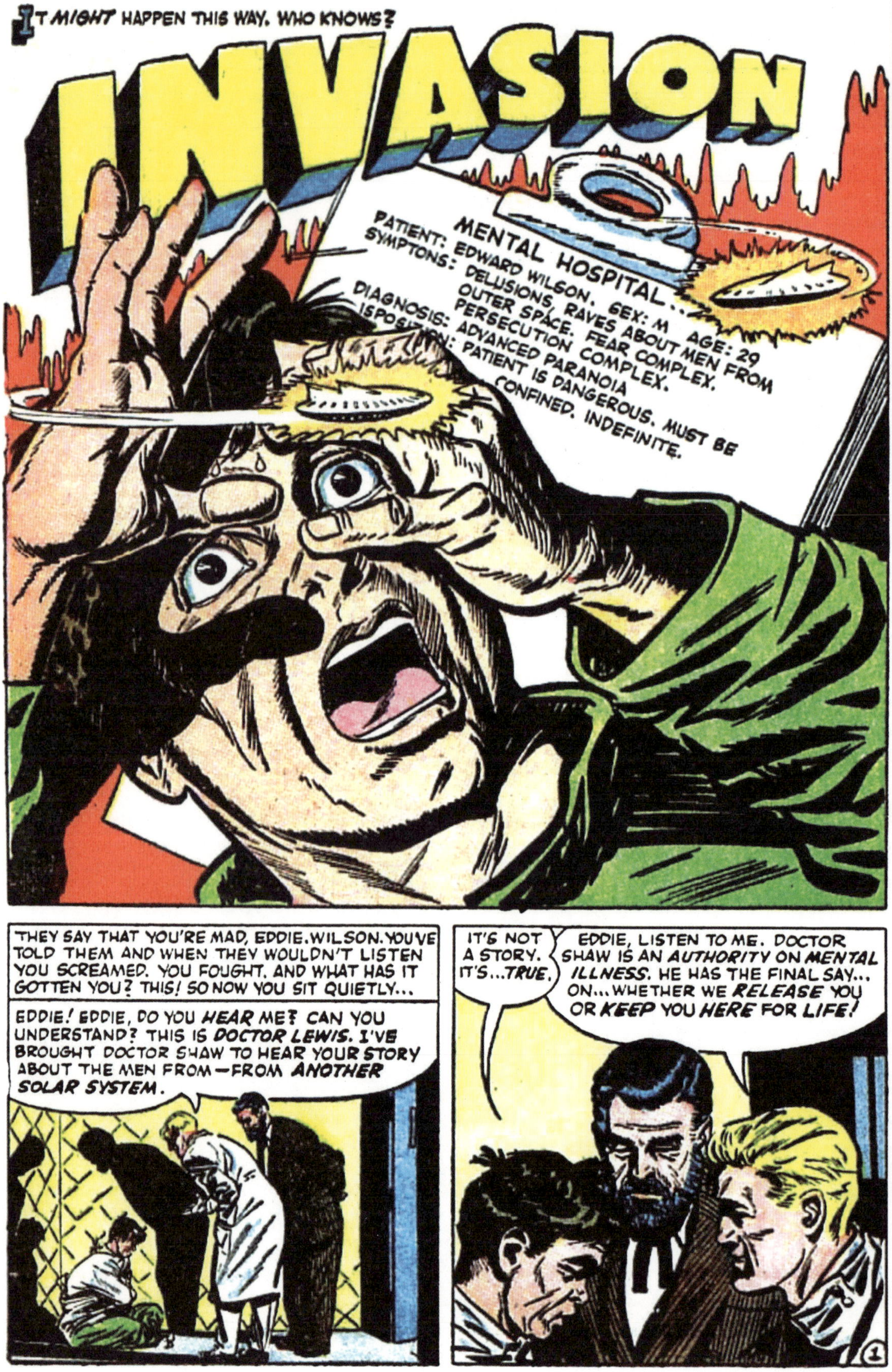
IT MIGHT HAPPEN THIS WAY. WHO KNOWS?
INVASION
MENTAL HOSPITAL...
PATIENT: EDWARD WILSON. SEX: M AGE: 29
SYMPTONS: DELUSIONS, RAVES ABOUT MEN FROM OUTER SPACE. FEAR COMPLEX. PERSECUTION COMPLEX.
DIAGNOSIS: ADVANCED PARANOIA
DISPOSITION: PATIENT IS DANGEROUS. MUST BE CONFINED. INDEFINITE.
THEY SAY THAT YOU'RE MAD, EDDIE.WILSON. YOU'VE TOLD THEM AND WHEN THEY WOULDN'T LISTEN YOU SCREAMED. YOU FOUGHT. AND WHAT HAS IT GOTTEN YOU? THIS! SO NOW YOU SIT QUIETLY...
EDDIE! EDDIE, DO YOU HEAR ME? CAN YOU UNDERSTAND? THIS IS DOCTOR LEWIS. I'VE BROUGHT DOCTOR SHAW TO HEAR YOUR STORY ABOUT THE MEN FROM—FROM ANOTHER SOLAR SYSTEM.
IT'S NOT A STORY. IT'S...TRUE.
EDDIE, LISTEN TO ME. DOCTOR SHAW IS AN AUTHORITY ON MENTAL ILLNESS. HE HAS THE FINAL SAY... ON... WHETHER WE RELEASE YOU OR KEEP YOU HERE FOR LIFE!
1

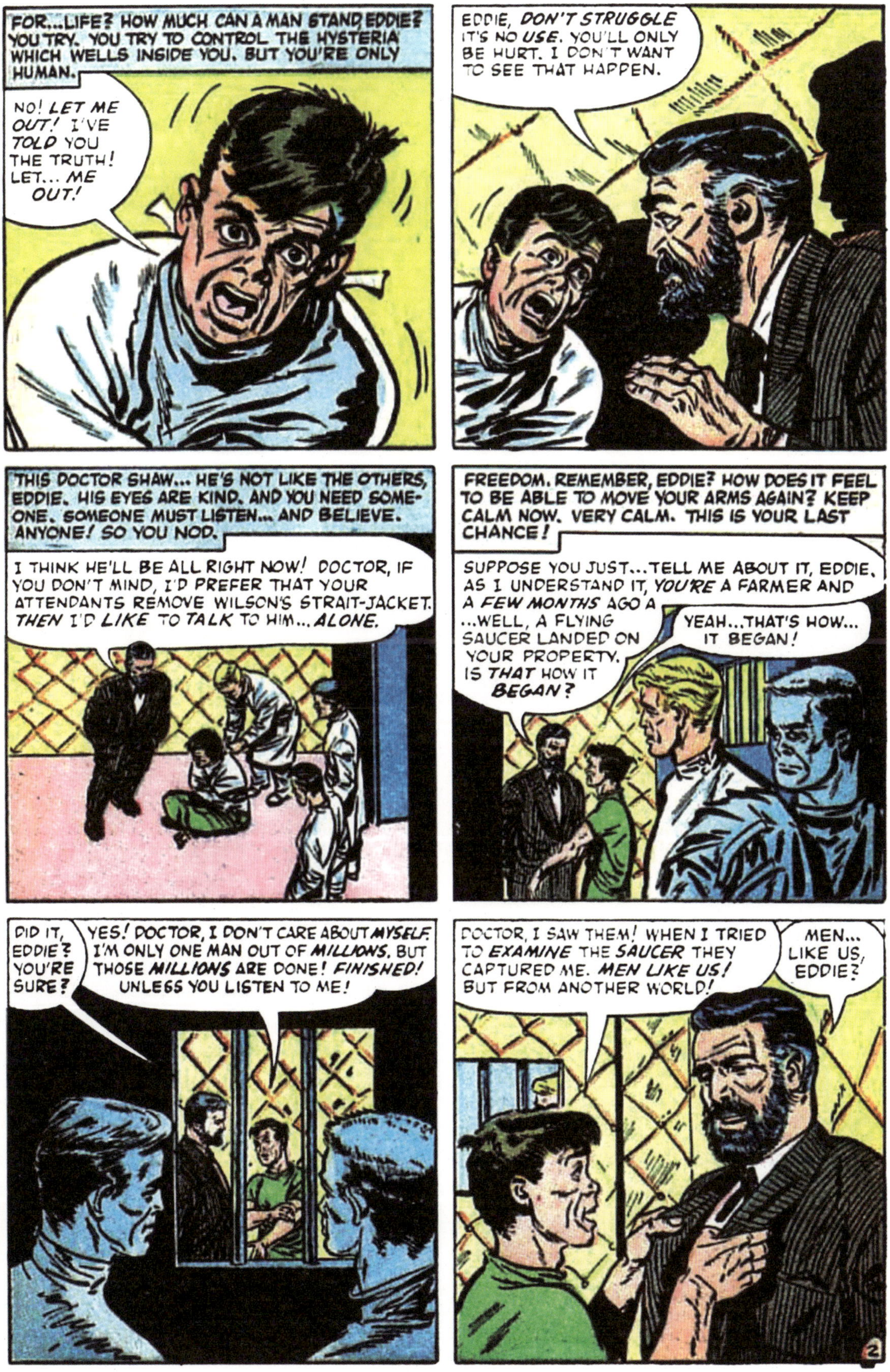
FOR...LIFE? HOW MUCH CAN A MAN STAND, EDDIE? YOU TRY. YOU TRY TO CONTROL THE HYSTERIA WHICH WELLS INSIDE YOU. BUT YOU'RE ONLY HUMAN.
NO! LET ME OUT! I'VE TOLD YOU THE TRUTH! LET... ME OUT!
EDDIE, DON'T STRUGGLE IT'S NO USE. YOU'LL ONLY BE HURT. I DON'T WANT TO SEE THAT HAPPEN.
THIS DOCTOR SHAW... HE'S NOT LIKE THE OTHERS, EDDIE. HIS EYES ARE KIND. AND YOU NEED SOMEONE. SOMEONE MUST LISTEN... AND BELIEVE. ANYONE! SO YOU NOD.
I THINK HE'LL BE ALL RIGHT NOW! DOCTOR, IF YOU DON'T MIND, I'D PREFER THAT YOUR ATTENDANTS REMOVE WILSON'S STRAIT-JACKET. THEN I'D LIKE TO TALK TO HIM... ALONE.
FREEDOM. REMEMBER, EDDIE? HOW DOES IT FEEL TO BE ABLE TO MOVE YOUR ARMS AGAIN? KEEP CALM NOW. VERY CALM. THIS IS YOUR LAST CHANCE!
SUPPOSE YOU JUST...TELL ME ABOUT IT, EDDIE. AS I UNDERSTAND IT, YOU'RE A FARMER AND A FEW MONTHS AGO A ...WELL, A FLYING SAUCER LANDED ON YOUR PROPERTY. IS THAT HOW IT BEGAN?
YEAH...THAT'S HOW... IT BEGAN!
DID IT, EDDIE? YOU'RE SURE?
YES! DOCTOR, I DON'T CARE ABOUT MYSELF. I'M ONLY ONE MAN OUT OF MILLIONS. BUT THOSE MILLIONS ARE DONE! FINISHED! UNLESS YOU LISTEN TO ME!
DOCTOR, I SAW THEM! WHEN I TRIED TO EXAMINE THE SAUCER THEY CAPTURED ME. MEN LIKE US! BUT FROM ANOTHER WORLD!
MEN... LIKE US, EDDIE?
2

YES! LIKE US... AND... NOT LIKE US. WHILE I WAS A PRISONER I HEARD THEM TALKING ABOUT THEIR PLANS! THEY'RE HERE TO TAKE OVER THE EARTH!
I SEE... AND JUST HOW DO THEY INTEND TO... AH... TAKE OVER?
THAT'S JUST IT! NOT WITH GUNS! THEY WON'T USE GUNS. THEY CAN'T! THEY'VE BEEN CONDITIONED... SO THEY CAN'T KILL! THAT'S HOW I GOT AWAY. I... FOUGHT. AND... THEY CAN'T STAND VIOLENCE!
THEY CAN'T STAND VIOLENCE! BUT THEY CAN COME HERE BY TENS AND TWENTIES! THEY CAN FILTER IN. AND THEY'RE WISE! SO MUCH WISER THAN WE ARE. TO THEM WE'RE JUST ...JUST ANIMALS!
DON'T YOU SEE? THEY BECOME JUDGES... POLITICIANS... LITTLE BY LITTLE THEY'LL TAKE OVER ALL THE POWER! THEY'LL LET US LIVE. BUT AS — AS WHAT? CATTLE!
SO TRY HARD, EDDIE. BUT EVEN AS YOU SPEAK YOU'RE WONDERING, AS YOU HAVE SO OFTEN THESE PAST WEEKS, DID IT REALLY HAPPEN? DID IT?
DOCTOR, YOU'VE GOT TO BELIEVE ME! YOU'VE GOT TO! BEFORE IT'S TOO LATE! I KNOW!
I'VE... SEEN THEM. I'VE SEEN THE THINGS THEY CAN DO. THEY'VE MASTERED... SPACE. THEY CAN — MOVE THINGS. BY SHEER WILL-POWER. WITHOUT MACHINERY...
DOCTOR, THEY... THEY CAN EVEN ... WALK THROUGH WALLS!
3

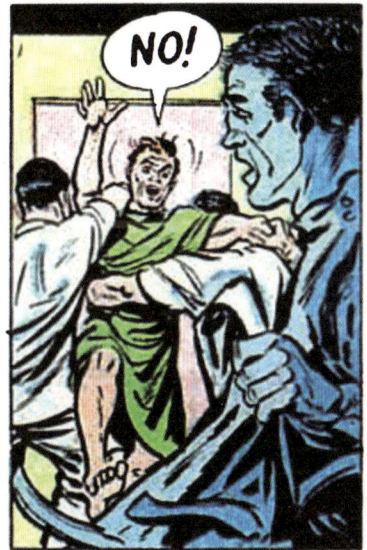

THAT'S WHEN YOU SEE IT, EDDIE. THERE'S MORE THAN KINDNESS IN DOCTOR SHAW'S EYES NOW. THERE'S PITY. AND THE DOUBTS POUND IN YOUR SKULL. DOCTOR, IT... IT *DID* HAPPEN! IT DID ...I'M *NOT INSANE*! TELL ME I'M NOT! TELL ME! LATER, EDDIE. WE'LL TALK *AGAIN*... ANOTHER TIME.	WELL, DOCTOR? PARANOIA? PARANOIA! IN AN ADVANCED STAGE. TOO... BAD...

IF YOU'LL MAKE UP THE NECESSARY COMMITMENT PAPERS, I'LL SIGN THEM— NO...	NO!	BUT THIS TIME, THE STRUGGLE IS DIFFERENT, EDDIE. THIS TIME THE SHADOWS ARE CREEPING INTO YOUR BRAIN EVEN AS YOU FIGHT. BY THE TIME IT'S OVER ... YOU'RE READY TO GIVE UP. WHAT A *PITY!* I *WISH* THERE WERE *SOMETHING* I *COULD* DO FOR HIM. BUT—THERE'S NOTHING!

THE DOOR CLANGS SHUT, AND YOU HUDDLE IN A CORNER OF YOUR CELL, AND WHAT YOU THINK YOU REMEMBER BEGINS TOO FADE. IT GROWS FAINTER...	TRY, EDDIE! TRY! THERE WAS SOMETHING YOU HAD TO DO. A WARNING YOU HAD TO GIVE. TRY! REMEMBER!

147

NO USE, EDDIE? WELL, NO MATTER. NO ONE WOULD BELIEVE YOU, ANYWAY. UNLESS, OF COURSE, THEY HAPPENED TO BE IN THE CORRIDOR LATER...
WELL, GOODBYE, DOCTOR! AND THANK YOU. YOU KNOW YOUR WAY OUT?
YES! GOODBYE.
OFFICE-J.R.LEW
6:10. M-M! THAT LEAVES ME ONLY A LITTLE TIME IN WHICH TO MAKE MY REPORT. I'D BETTER HURRY.
UNLESS THEY HAPPENED TO SEE DOCTOR SHAW PAUSE TO PEER INTENTLY AT THE CORRIDOR WALL, ALMOST AS IF HE COULD SEE THROUGH IT, AS IF HE WERE MAKING CERTAIN THAT--
NOBODY IS ON THE STREET...AND THE CORRIDOR IS EMPTY. GOOD! I CAN SAVE A FEW MOMENTS IF I DON'T WALK ALL THE WAY TO THE FRONT EXIT!
BUT—NO ONE SAW.
SHALL I FILE THIS, DOCTOR? DOCTOR SHAW SIGNED IT BEFORE HE LEFT. IT'S THE COMMITMENT ORDER ON EDWARD WILSON.
YES. I SUPPOSE SO. INFILTRATION FROM SPACE...MEN WHO WALK THROUGH WALLS...POOR DEVIL, HIS CASE WAS HOPELESS. RIGHT FROM THE START.
THE END
5

Safe, New Easy Way STOPS "NAIL BITING" HABIT *INSTANTLY!*

Ends Shame, Pain and Embarrassment of Torn, Ragged, Chewed Fingernails

Doctors agree "nail biting" is a vicious, ugly, unsanitary habit that often leads to serious infections, ugly ingrown nails, pain and embarrassment. Now amazing new medical formula safely stops fingernail biting habit almost instantly. In just days fingernails grow longer, lovelier, healthier with exclusive Elmorene Formula 246. Safe, easy as washing your hands, just rub across fingertips. No sticky lacquers, gloves or trick devices. Formula 246 is invisible on fingers... nobody knows your secret. **ORDER TODAY!**

SEND NO MONEY—7 Day Trial Offer

Send name and address. On arrival pay postman only $2.98 plus C.O.D. charges. Formula 246 must break "nail biting" habit. At end of only 7 days fingernails must be longer, healthier or full refund. Sent in plain package. (Send cash, we pay all postage charges... same guarantee).
FREE of extra cost! Pocket size fingernail brush included on orders from this ad. **WRITE TODAY!**

ELMORENE CO.
290 Madison Ave.
Dept. 82
New York 17, N.Y.

Read these

DIFFERENT MYSTERY MAGAZINES WITH THE EXPERT TOUCH OF MASTER STORY TELLING!

NOW ON SALE

ACCLAIMED THE BEST IN SHOCK MYSTERY, THE BLACK CAT MYSTERY OPENS A TRAIL TO SUSPENSE! DON'T MISS AN ISSUE!

THRILLS AND CHILLS WITH EVER-BUILDING TENSION... YOU'LL GASP AS YOU READ EACH ISSUE OF THE EXCITING CHAMBER OF CHILLS!

A FLIGHT INTO FANTASTIC FRENZY... EXPLORE THE FORBIDDEN IN EACH ISSUE OF THE WITCHES TALES!

FOR ADVENTURES INTO THE UNKNOWN, FOR INCREDIBLE TREKS TO OTHER WORLDS, READ THE TOMB OF TERROR!

Acclaimed by Millions

THE BEST TRUE LOVE STORIES, TORN FROM THE PAGES OF REAL LIFE!

READ EVERY ISSUE! GET YOUR COPIES TODAY!

LOOK HERE! for BIG MONEY MAKING OPPORTUNITIES for MONEY-SAVING OFFERS and SERVICES

SCHOOLS—INSTRUCTION

U. S. GOV'T JOBS! Start high as $316.00 month Men-Women, 18-55. Train for tests NOW! 30,000 jobs open. Get FREE 36-page book showing jobs, salaries, requirements, sample tests. Write Today Franklin Institute, Dept. J-15, Rochester, N Y

SMASH CRIME! Be a Finger-Print Expert, Investigator, for good steady pay. Send for details. Inst. of Applied Science (37 years a Correspondence School). 1920 Sunnyside, Dept. 505, Chicago 40.

VENTRILOQUISM Selftaught—Complete Book 25c. Greenview, Box 61-MA, Whitestone 57, N Y

STAMPS and COINS

COLOSSAL STAMP ZOO FREE—Jungle Beasts, Wildlife, fifteen different including Rhinoceros, Snake, Tiger, Elephant, Zabu, Koalabear, Kookabura, Extraordinary accompanying approvals. Send 10c for handling. Niagara Stamp Co., Niagara-on-the-Lake 538, Canada.

WANTED—1894-S DIME PAY $500.00 Certain 1913 nickel $1,000.00. 1901-S quarter $20.00 to $150.00. Hundreds of others. Know their true value. Complete illustrated catalog 25c. Worthycoin Corporation (D-342), Boston 8, Mass.

COLONIAL COLLECTION Free — Magnicarocious collection, British, French, American and other Colonies. Flowers, Animals, Commemoratives, Triangles, Pictorials. High Values all free "plus" Philatopic Magazine. Send 5c for postage Empire Stamp Co., Dept. HR, Toronto, Canada.

Free Valuable Mystery Gift. Approvals. Raymax, 37-C Maiden Lane, NYC 8.

First U. N set; among World's prettiest. Only 10c. Welles, Box 1246-CG, Church Street Station, NYC 38.

100 BRITISH EMPIRE—All different—plus Valuable Illustrated Book "How To Recognize Rare Stamps." Only 10c! Other Offers Included. Kenmore, XH-305, Milford, N. H.

100 DIFFERENT STAMPS 5c, with approvals. TATHAM STAMP, Springfield 23, Mass.

We purchase Indianhead pennies. Complete allcoin catalog 20c. Magnacoins, Box 61-TT, Whitestone 57, New York.

MONEY MAKING OPPORTUNITIES

EARN EXTRA MONEY weekly mailing circulars for advertisers. Complete instructions—25c. Siwaslian, 4317-C Gleane, Elmhurst 73, N Y

EARN BIG MONEY—INVISIBLY REWEAVE damaged garments at home! Details FREE. FABRICON, 8332 Prairie, Chicago 19.

GROW MUSHROOMS. Cellar, shed, and outdoors. Spare, full time, year round. We pay $3.50 lb. We paid Babbitt $4,165.00 in few weeks. Free Book. Washington Mushroom Ind., Dept. 191, 2954 Admiral Way, Seattle, Wash.

MAKE MONEY Addressing Envelopes! Our information reveals how. Only 30c. Homework, P.O. Box 2224, St. Louis, Mo.

Extra cash. Sparetime. No experience. No investment. Own permanent shoe business. Free outfit. Paragon Shoes, 79X Sudbury, Boston.

MANUFACTURER — Wants reliable MEN-WOMEN for Profitable Mail Order work. Home Sparetime. Write LIEBIG INDUSTRIES, Beaver Dam 20, Wis.

ADDRESS ADVERTISING Postcards. Must have good handwriting. Lindo, Watertown, Massachusetts.

SEW OUR REDI-CUT HANDY-HANKY aprons at home. Easy, Profitable. A & B Enterprises, 2516 N. Albert Pike, Ft. Smith, Arkansas.

OF INTEREST TO WOMEN

WANTED—CHILDREN'S PHOTOS (All Ages-Types) for billboards, calendars, magazines. Up to $200 paid by advertisers. Send small black and white photo for approval (One Only). Print child's full name and parent's name and address on back. Picture returned 30 days. Spotlite Photo Directory, Dept. CC, 5864 Hollywood Blvd., Hollywood 28, California.

BIG DRESS SALE—20 Dresses for only $3.50. Assorted Silk, Wool, Cotton and Rayon. Send only $1.00 deposit and Dress size. Balance C.O.D. Mail Order Mart, 160-G Monroe Street, New York.

TRICKS—MAGIC—NOVELTIES

CATALOG OF 3200 NOVELTIES, JOKERS, TRICKS, Funmakers, Magic Gadgets, Timesavers, Hobbies, Models, Guns, Sporting Goods, Jewelry, Cameras, Optical Goods, etc. Send 10c to JOHNSON SMITH COMPANY, Dept. 712, Detroit 7, Michigan.

FREE CATALOG Magic Tricks, Practical Jokes. TOP HAT MAGIC, Evanston 13, Illinois

INCREDIBLE! Become Mental Superman overnight! Free Booklet! Bijou, Box 1727-O, Hollywood 28, Calif

WHOLESALE NOVELTIES! Forty Samples $1.00 Sebastian, 10934-C Hamlin, North Hollywood, Calif

BE A JOBBER—Make big money. Draw from our 250,000 stock of toys, novelties, appliances, jewelry, religious goods, nationally-advertised wrist watches—hundreds of others. Get jobber discounts even in small quantities. Profits over 100%. Write for FREE catalog. Modern Merchandise, Dept. CBC, 169 W Madison St., Chicago 2, Ill.

MISCELLANEOUS

FREE SEEDS! Grow amazing Cactus plants easily. Send 10c for handling. North Nursery, 1907 Main Street, Niagara Falls, N. Y.

POEMS WANTED for musical setting. Send poems FREE examination. Five Star Music Masters, 392 Beacon Bldg., Boston, Mass.

BORROWING BY MAIL. Loans $50 to $600 to employed men and women. Easy, quick. Completely confidential. No endorsers. Repay in convenient monthly payments. Details free in plain envelope. Give occupation. State Finance Co., 323 Securities Bldg., Dept. K-74, Omaha 2, Nebr.

DISPOSAL UNITS

OUTDOOR TOILETS, CESSPOOLS, Septic Tanks cleaned, deodorized with amazing new safe product. Safe, easy, economical. Saves digging, pumping. Details Free. Burson Laboratories, Dept. O-98, Chicago 22.

START OR ADD TO YOUR COLLECTION WITH FREE 100 Exciting BRITISH EMPIRE STAMPS!

to Make New Friends!

This Entire Valuable Collection YOURS FREE . . . as our gift! GET IT TODAY!

Just imagine . . . a big packet of all different stamps from strange corners of the world . . . guaranteed standard catalog value at least $2.00 . . . yours Free! You'll get stamps from far away British possessions like Pitcairn Islands (where mutineers settled), Falkland Islands (only post office in Antarctic Circle), Tanganyika (land of pygmies and headhunters), Ceylon, Australia, South Africa . . . and many others. This can be the start of a wonderful collection . . . or if you're now collecting stamps, this British Empire group is a prized addition! Best of all, it's yours FREE . . . our gift to you for getting acquainted. Also included FREE is the fascinating and valuable "Stamp Collector's Manual" shown at left. IMPORTANT: Supplies of this remarkable British Empire stamp group are definitely limited—so you MUST ACT AT ONCE. Mail the coupon today. Enclose 10c to help pay postage and handling costs. We'll also include other exceptional values for your inspection. If coupon has been clipped write direct.

KENMORE STAMP CO.
Dept. XM-297
Milford, New Hampshire

Also FREE!
"THE STAMP COLLECTOR'S MANUAL"
Practical, fully illustrated guide to stamp collecting. Valuable information and stories about world's most interesting hobby. Yours FREE if you mail coupon at once!

Mail Coupon Now! SUPPLY LIMITED!

KENMORE STAMP CO., Dept. XM-297
Milford, New Hampshire

Rush me FREE 100 all different British Empire stamps and "The Stamp Collector's Manual". I enclose 10c to help pay postage and handling.

NAME _____

ADDRESS _____

CITY _____ STATE _____

BEAUTIFY YOUR BUST

AND *INSTANTLY* TAKE 2 to 4 INCHES OFF YOUR WAISTLINE

WITH THE FRENCH WAIST SLIMMER BRA

BANISH MIDRIFF "BALLOON TIRE"

Slim your waistline and give graceful uplift to your bust with the new FRENCH WAIST SLIMMER BRA, the amazing 2 in 1 beautifying foundation. Molds your bust and reduces waist at the same time. A special expensive elastic waist belt gives you the tiny waistline the new fashions so require.

NO RISK! TRY YOURS AT OUR EXPENSE.

Try it in your home. Be thrilled —satisfy yourself that the new amazing FRENCH WAIST SLIMMER BRA does all we claim for it—or return it without obligation.

Only $2.98

MAIL COUPON TODAY

10 DAY FREE TRIAL

WARD GREEN CO. Dept. RH
113 West 57th St., New York 19, N. Y.
MY BRA SIZE IS.........
Please rush my FRENCH WAIST SLIMMER BRA in the above size for 10 day FREE TRIAL. If not completely delighted I may return it for full purchase refund.
☐ Please send C.O.D. I will pay postman plus postage.
☐ I enclose $2.98. Ward Green pays postage.

Name..

Address...

City....................Zone.....State.....

THERE WAS NOTHING TO FEAR... FOR THERE WERE ONLY WAX EFFIGIES IN...

THE MUSEUM

JULES MADREAUX WAS THE LAST TO ADMIT THAT HIS WAX MUSEUM WAS A FAILURE, BUT EVEN HE SAW THE HANDWRITING ON THE WALL...

THE *DEVIL* TAKE IT! I *MIGHT* AS WELL PUT THE *SHUTTERS* UP! ONLY SEVENTY-FIVE FRANCS TODAY. NOT *EVEN* ENOUGH FOR A *BOTTLE OF WINE!*

A FACE CAME BY, STRIKING A CHORD OF MEMORY, AND JULES' HOPE ROSE...

WELL, WELL, IF IT ISN'T MY GOOD FRIEND REMMY NOUVELLE, THE FAMOUS JOURNALIST! IT'S BEEN A DOG'S AGE SINCE I SAW YOU LAST!

JULES MADREAUX! YOU HAVEN'T CHANGED A BIT... A LITTLE FATTER AROUND THE JOWLS, BUT STILL THE SAME!

COME IN, REMMY, I WANT TO SHOW YOU MY PLACE, THE GREATEST WAX MUSEUM IN ALL OF EUROPE! FOR OLD TIMES' SAKE, CAN YOU SPARE A FEW MINUTES, EH?
WELL...I HAVE AN ASSIGNMENT FOR THE PAPER, BUT IT CAN WAIT... NOT TOO LONG THOUGH, JULES!
HOW DO YOU LIKE MY LITTLE MUSEUM, REMMY?
STUFFY, DUSTY AND SHABBY, JULES! NO WONDER, NOBODY COMES HERE! AH, WELL, YOU ALWAYS DID LACK IMAGINATION, MY FRIEND! I KNEW THAT WAY BACK AT SCHOOL!
PERHAPS, BUT YOU HAVEN'T SEEN MY DEN OF MURDERERS! THAT IS MY MASTERPIECE!
MORE WAX DUMMIES! IT ISN'T WHAT THE PUBLIC WANTS, JULES! YOU'RE WAY BEHIND THE TIMES! ENTERTAINMENT MUST BE DYNAMIC, ALIVE!
MURDERER'S DEN
YOU CERTAINLY HAVE A GHASTLY LOOKING GANG HERE! I KNOW THAT ONE! DR. ZOUAVE, ISN'T IT?
YES, THE "PRAYING MANTIS" KILLER, WHO HYPNOTIZES HIS VICTIMS BEFORE CUTTING THEIR THROATS. HE'S STILL ALIVE. THE SURETE COULD NEVER TRAP HIM! HAVE YOU EVER SEEN ANYTHING MORE LIFELIKE, REMMY?
THEY LOOK REAL ENOUGH, BUT I DON'T THINK THEY'D FRIGHTEN A CHILD! AFTER ALL, THEY'RE ONLY MADE OF WAX!
YES, BUT I'D WAGER YOU WOULDN'T DARE SPEND A NIGHT IN THIS ROOM ALONE WITH THEM!
NONSENSE, IT WOULDN'T FRIGHTEN ME ONE BIT, BUT NOW I MUST GO! SAY, WHY DO YOU HOLD ME BACK? WHAT IS IT YOU WANT?
FOR OLD TIMES' SAKE, YOU MIGHT HELP ME! IF YOU'D WRITE AN ARTICLE IN YOUR PAPER ON THE MUSEUM, IT WOULD BRING IN BUSINESS! ALL I NEED IS SOME GOOD PUBLICITY, REMMY!
SO THAT'S IT! DO YOU THINK ONE MINUTE I'D LEND MY NAME TO THIS FLEA-BITTEN ENTERPRISE? YOU MAKE ME LAUGH!
FLEA-BITTEN, IS IT? I'LL BET YOU WOULDN'T DARE STAY IN THIS DEN OVERNIGHT! I'D STAKE ALL MY SAVINGS ON THAT!

I OFFER TEN THOUSAND FRANCS IF YOU STAY HERE OVERNIGHT AND THEN WRITE AN ARTICLE ON YOUR EXPERIENCE. I DON'T THINK YOU HAVE THE NERVE!
TEN THOUSAND FRANCS! HMM, EVERY MAN HAS HIS PRICE, JULES! I'LL TAKE YOUR OFFER! JUST BRING ME A BOOK AND A COMFORTABLE CHAIR THAT I CAN SLEEP IN!
THE WAGER WAS SEALED WITH A HANDCLASP. SOON, REMMY WAS LEFT ALONE IN THE SOUNDLESS ROOM, FACING THE FOREMOST MURDERERS OF ALL FRANCE...
BEASTLY LOOKING CREATURE!
REMMY SHIFTED HIS CHAIR TO AVOID ZOUAVE'S RELENTLESS STARE. THE HOURS WENT BY SLOWLY...
BACK OF MY NECK... COLD AND CLAMMY!
HE MOVED! HE... HE TURNED HIS HEAD AND LIFTED THAT RAZOR! I'D SWEAR TO IT!
YOU UGLY BUTCHER, WHY ARE YOU STARING AT ME LIKE THAT? I KNOW YOU'RE MADE OF WAX, BUT YOU'RE HORRIBLE, HORRIBLE!
SUDDENLY, AS THE BOOK SLAMMED TO THE GROUND...
YOU ARE MISTAKEN, M'SIEU NOUVELLE! I AM VERY MUCH ALIVE, AND I RESENT DEEPLY WHAT YOU HAVE SAID ABOUT ME. I'VE BEEN HIDING HERE, WAITING FOR SUCH A VICTIM AS YOU. LOOK AT ME... LOOK INTO MY EYES!
NO, NO! DR. ZOUAVE, YOU ARE MAD... I--I CAN'T MOVE... YOUR EYES ARE DRAINING MY STRENGTH!
NO! NO! AAAARGG!
YOU STUPID PIG! YOU ALWAYS MOCKED ME, ALWAYS INSULTED ME! AND NOW YOU SHALL PAY WITH YOUR BLOOD!
3

REMMY'S SIGHTLESS EYES COULD NOT SEE THE STRANGE TRANSFORMATION...
NOW THE SKEPTIC IS DEAD! A GOOD, QUIET JOB... ALMOST AS WELL AS DR. ZOUAVE HIMSELF! HA HA HA! IF THE MAD DOCTOR COULD ONLY SEE IT!
NOW MY FRIEND, I SHALL REMOVE THE EVIDENCE! IT WILL BE ONE OF THE MANY UNSOLVED CRIMES OF DR. ZOUAVE! I WON'T HAVE TO PAY YOU TEN THOUSAND FRANCS FOR A SMALL ARTICLE! I SHALL HAVE BIG, BLACK HEADLINES AND THEY WILL BRING THE CROWDS TO MY MUSEUM!
BUT AS JULES TURNED FROM GLOATING OVER REMMY'S BODY...
Y!!!!, I-- IT'S DR. ZOUAVE! BUT I HID HIS DUMMY BEHIND THE PLATFORM! HOW... HOW DID HE GET BACK?
M'SIEU MADREAUX, YOU UNDERESTIMATE OUR POWERS! TO YOU, WE ARE MERELY WAX DUMMIES WHO MAKE MONEY FOR YOU! BUT WE HAVE LIVES OF OUR OWN AND FEELINGS WHICH YOU COULD NEVER UNDERSTAND!
NO, NO! I'VE DONE YOU NO HARM! I'VE BEEN GOOD TO YOU... PLEASE DON'T TOUCH ME!
JULES TRIED TO ESCAPE, BUT...
LET ME STRANGLE HIM!
NO, LET ME! I SAW HIM FIRST! HE SHALL BE MY NINTH VICTIM!
I MUST BE MAD! YOU CAN'T ALL BE ALIVE!
LOOK DEEP INTO MY EYES! YOU ARE POWERLESS! ABSOLUTELY POWERLESS! YOUR HEAD IS HEAVY... GOING BACK.. BACK! AH, THAT IS PERFECT!
MY HEAD IS HEAVY... VERY HEAVY!
CLOSER, CLOSER, M'SIEU!
MY HEART... MY HEART!
4

MORNING BROUGHT THE MUSEUM ATTENDANTS WHO STUMBLED ON THE BLOODY TABLEAU...
LOUIS, LOOK, IT IS MADREAUX... DEAD! AND THAT OTHER ONE HAS HIS THROAT CUT!
QUICK, THE... POLICE...!
THE MUSEUM WAS QUICKLY OVERRUN BY GENDARMES...
MADREAUX'S HEART FAILED! I CAN TELL IT WAS WEAK, BUT NOUVELLE'S THROAT WAS CUT BY A RAZOR, LIKE THE ONE THAT DUMMY HOLDS IN HIS HAND.
IT LOOKS LIKE DR. ZOUAVE'S WORK, DOCTOR, BUT THE FINGERPRINTS ON THE RAZOR ARE MADREAUX'S. I FIGURE MADREAUX KILLED HIM, AND THEN FOR SOME UNKNOWN REASON DIED OF FRIGHT!
SOON THE WAX MUSEUM REOPENED, BUT UNDER A NEW MANAGEMENT WHICH UNDERSTOOD THE VALUE OF PUBLICITY...
HURRY, HURRY, SEE THE SENSATIONAL MUSEUM MURDER, EXACTLY AS IT HAPPENED ON THE VERY SPOT IT WAS COMMITTED! ADMISSION ONLY TWENTY FRANCS! HURRY! HURRY!
I WANT TO GO! I WON'T BE AFRAID... THEY'RE ONLY WAX, PAPA!
MURDERER'S MUSEUM
CLEVERLY, THE HORRIBLE MURDER HAD BEEN REPRODUCED IN WAX...
THEY SAY IT WAS DONE ON THIS VERY SPOT. YOU CAN REALLY SEE THE BLOOD!
IT TURNS MY STOMACH! LET'S GET OUT OF HERE!
EEEEE! PAPA, THEY MOVED! I SAW THEM MOVE! I SWEAR THE MURDERERS ARE ALIVE!
JAQUES, HURRY, GET HIM OUT OF HERE! HE'S HYSTERICAL... HE'LL HAVE NIGHTMARES!
IN THAT GHASTLY CHAMBER OF HORRORS WITH ITS DIM FLICKERING LIGHTS, ANYBODY COULD BE MISTAKEN...
THEY MOVED... THEY MOVED!
NONSENSE, JEAN!
THE END

CHILLY CHAMBER MUSIC
SONGS FROM THE SPOOK BOX!

I'VE GOT YOU UNDER MY CHIN...

THE MUSIC PLAYS, THE DANCERS SWAY...

AND I CAN'T WALK AWAY...

CAUSE I'VE GOT YOU UNDER MY CHIN!

CHILLY CHAMBER MUSIC
SONGS FROM THE SPOOK BOX!

SOME FRANTIC EVENING,

YOU WILL MEET A STRANGER, YOU WILL MEET A STRANGER ACROSS A CROWDED TOMB.

THEN SOMEHOW YOU'LL KNOW, YOU'LL KNOW EVEN THEN...

THAT SOMEWHERE YOU'LL MEET HER AGAIN AND AGAIN!

THE MEANING OF DREAMS

Dreams have been responsible for more superstitions, myths, wars and broken lives than anything else in the world. If a dream came true, it was called a portent.

All of us have dreams. We dream when we sleep, and we have day dreams. Our dreams seem to be real; and actual experience after a long time, seems like a dream.

The savage man did not distinguish between dreams and experiences. He believed that when the body slept, the spirit left and went hunting or did whatever he dreamed about.

That is why in Australia aborigines believe the spirit leaves the body when he snores, and the sleeper must not be awakened too suddenly or the spirit would not find the body again. The spirit must be given time to return to the body.

In India, people consider it murder to paint or deface the sleeper because the wandering spirit would not recognize the body to which it belongs. The body would, of course, die.

Portents are easily explained. Let us suppose a ship is about to leave. Relatives and friends gather to see passengers off. Many of the visitors fear an accident or a sinking. Usually nothing happens and they forget what they had dreamed about. But sometimes an accident does happen, and the relative and friend is sure to remember it in full detail. To him, it is the portent.

With things happening all the time, it is no wonder that portents are believed... provided they did happen.

The meaning of dreams was exactly the same to Indians. Algonquins used to put great faith in portents and premonitions. For instance, if an Indian dreamed he was taken captive, he would ask his friends to make a mock attack upon him, capture him, bind him and torture him. He believed that this would fulfill the promise of his dream.

But more often dreams do not come true. The opposite might happen. Thus in Africa, if a Zulu warrior dreamed of death, he knew he would live; if he dreamed of great thirst in the Kalahari Desert, he figured he would find water. The Maoris of New Zealand followed the same line of reasoning.

Meaning of dreams are legion. People are eager to divine their future, and they put much faith in dreams as premonitions of things to come. After all they forget premonitions that did not come true, and they remember the portents that did!

In one case, if a dreamer dreams of a grave —sickness and disappointment are in the cards for him. Unless of course in his dreams, he is rising out of the grave, and in this case, he expects success.

When the maiden dreams she is bedecked with jewels, she will expect a suitable husband. And after marriage, dreams of precious stones promise children.

In many places of the world, people consider it more lucky to dream of receiving than giving away money. To lose money in a dream means bad luck is coming.

Sometimes a woman dreams she lost her wedding ring. According to the book of dreams, that meant her husband would die soon. The explanation of portents holds strongly here. If he survives, she will forget the dream; but if he does die soon, she will talk about her portent for the rest of her life.

Dreams of hens and chickens promise danger. A soaring eagle is an omen of success. Any bird in a dream is the best news to lovers.

Sometimes the actions of animals has a certain significance. For instance, a barking dog in a dream means bad luck; a friendly dog promises the good. A shorn sheep means danger; a fleecy sheep will bring prosperity.

Should a man dream of being hurt by a cat or any vermin, he expects to be overcome by enemies; likewise if in his dreams he killed the cat or vermin, he will triumph over his enemies.

But all books of dreams should be taken with several grains of salt, for dreams are either wishful thinking or dreaded fears.

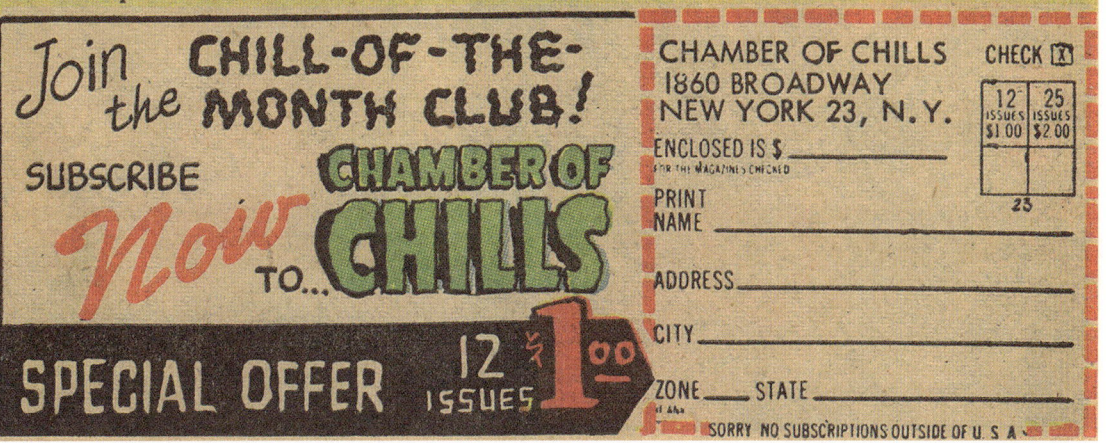

Join the CHILL-OF-THE-MONTH CLUB!
SUBSCRIBE Now TO... CHAMBER OF CHILLS
SPECIAL OFFER 12 ISSUES $1.00

CHAMBER OF CHILLS
1860 BROADWAY
NEW YORK 23, N.Y.

CHECK ☒

| 12 ISSUES $1.00 | 25 ISSUES $2.00 |

ENCLOSED IS $ _____
FOR THE MAGAZINES CHECKED

PRINT NAME _____
ADDRESS _____
CITY _____
ZONE ___ STATE _____

SORRY NO SUBSCRIPTIONS OUTSIDE OF U.S.A.

THE RAIN PELTED DOWN HARD OVER THE GRASS-COVERED EARTH. SUDDENLY FROM UNDERNEATH A WET, GLISTENING TOMBSTONE CAME A HAND...
SIMON LOCKSLEY 1909 1939
IT GROPED AND TWISTED AND CLUTCHED. THEN, AS IF SATISFIED WITH THE VERY RAIN IT HAD MET, MORE OF IT CAME... MORE... AND MORE...
SIMON LOCKSLEY 1909 1939
THE SOFT, BLACK MUD SLIPPED AWAY IN A FALLING OOZE AS THE HIDEOUS HEAD OF A CORPSE BROKE THROUGH IT... LEAVING THE GRAVE BEHIND IT...
SIMON LOCKSLEY 1909
DUST UNTO DUST
SIMON LOCKSLEY 1909 1939

SLOWLY AND TORTUOUSLY, THE CREATURE SHUFFLED FORWARD...THROUGH THE BLACK NIGHT AND RAIN THAT ENGULFED IT LIKE AN ELEMENTAL SHROUD...
IT TURNED, ITS SHUFFLE INCREASED IN TEMPO...SPILLING MUD PUDDLES...
HE'S WAITING... WAITING...
IT TRUDGED THROUGH THE MUD. FOR THE FIRST TIME, IT SMILED...
...WAITING... ALL THESE YEARS...
A TOWN'S LIGHTS TWINKLED THROUGH THE RAIN. THE CREATURE HEADED THERE...
...WAITING... FOR ME!
IN THE TOWN, A MAN SETTLED BACK IN HIS CHAIR. HE WAS A NIGHT-WATCHMAN. A GUN AND HOLSTER HUNG LIMPLY ON THE WALL BY HIS SIDE, LOOKING UNUSED.
MAYBE SOMEDAY I'LL CHANGE THIS JOB...
THE MAN'S ONLY COMPANY IN HIS SHACK WERE THOUGHTS...AND DREAMS... A FEELING OF WARMTH AND SECURITY SPREAD OVER HIM AS HE LISTENED TO THE RAIN OUTSIDE...
TOO LONELY FOR ME! MAYBE--?
SUDDENLY, THE WATCHMAN FROZE, HIS BLOOD STAGNATING WITH FRIGHT. A FIGURE STOOD BEFORE HIM, BROWN, DIRTY DROPS OF RAIN WATER DRIPPING FROM ITS FETID BODY...
WHO'S TH-- SIMON!
2

Y-YOU'RE DEAD! I--I KILLED YOU FIFTEEN YEARS AGO! STAY AWAY FROM ME!
I'VE COME TO TAKE YOU BACK WITH ME, HUGH. OTHERWISE, I'LL NEVER REST IN PEACE!
KEEP AWAY FROM ME! I--I WARN YOU!
COME, HUGH! COME WITH ME! IT'S...TIME!
YOU CAN'T COME BACK... AFTER ALL THESE YEARS! YOU CAN'T!
BLAM
BLAM
BLAM
THE BULLETS PIERCED THE DECAYED BODY WITH THREE SICKENING THUDS--LIKE FIRING INTO A MATTRESS...
IT'S...NO USE, HUGH! I'M DEAD... REMEMBER? COME WITH ME! I BEAR YOU NO GRUDGE!
HUGH BACKED INTO A CORNER, STILL HOLDING THE SMOLDERING FUTILE GUN...THE CREATURE ADVANCED...
HUGH! LISTEN!
NO... NO...
ITS RANK ODOR SUFFOCATED HUGH... ITS STENCH CRAWLING INTO HIS NOSTRILS...NAUSEATING HIM...
HUGH!
GET AWAY...
WITH DESPERATION BORN OF TERROR HUGH TOOK THE FIRE AXE AND SWUNG...
AND SWUNG AGAIN...
AND AGAIN...
3

HUGH BEAT AND HACKED AND HAMMERED AT THE RED PULPY MESS ON THE FLOOR UNTIL HIS ARMS ACHED... UNTIL HE COULDN'T WIELD THE AXE ANY MORE... *IT'S DONE! I'M SAFE...AGAIN!*	**H**UGH LIKED THE SILENCE ABOUT HIM... THE DEATHLY SILENCE THAT SWATHED HIM IN SOFT BILLOWS. HE FORGOT IN IT ...SO EASY TO THINK... LIKE WALKING IN A PERFUMED FOG... *IT'S OVER! I'VE...HEH! HEH! ...WON! CAN'T... TAKE...ME... WON... WON...*	**H**E LOOKED AT THE THING IN FRONT OF HIM UNTIL HE COULDN'T LOOK AT IT ANY LONGER. HE TURNED HIS BACK ON IT AND BURIED HIS FACE IN HIS HANDS...
SUDDENLY A HAND GRABBED HUGH FROM BEHIND...A FOUL, DECAYED, FETID HAND...REEKING PUTRIDNESS...	**H**UGH STRUGGLED AGAINST THE VILE CREATURE... HE STAGGERED... PAWED...SCRATCHED... *GIVE UP, HUGH! YOU CAN'T FIGHT THE THING I'VE BECOME!*	**H**UGH'S STRUGGLING WAS TO NO AVAIL AS THE ROTTING THING DRAGGED HIM AWAY FROM THE SHACK... *NO! NO!*
HUGH HEARD THE SWEET LOLL OF THE WAVES WASHING ON THE SHORE... SMELLED THE ODOR OF DRIFTWOOD AND ROTTING SEAWEED...	**H**E FOUGHT WITH THE ENERGY OF A MAN WHO DOESN'T WANT TO DIE... THRASHING...ROLLING... IN THE COLD WATER... *CAN'T...TAKE... ME...* *UGH!*	**H**E GOT THE UPPER HAND...PUSHING THE CORPSE'S FACE UNDERWATER... PUSHING DEEPER AND DEEPER... *I'LL KILL YOU... AGAIN! YOU WON'T HAUNT ME AGAIN! NEVER...NEVER!*

HUGH LISTENED-THERE WAS NO SOUND. BUT SUDDENLY FROM OUT OF THE MURKY DEPTHS OF THE HARBOR WATER CAME THAT LIVID HAND OF ROTTED DEATH...
THE HAND CLAWED AT HIM...CLUTCHED AND TIGHTENED...GRABBING HIS SHIRT... THE FOG OF FEAR OVERCAME HUGH... ITS SWIRLING DAZE BLACKING HIM OUT...
NO! NO!
WHEN HUGH AWOKE HE FOUND HIMSELF BEING DRAGGED ALONG A DIRT ROAD... DRAGGED BACK...TO THE GRAVEYARD...
WE'RE GOING BACK TOGETHER, HUGH! YOU MUSTN'T BE FRIGHTENED!
WHA...T? PLEASE! OH, PLEASE... SIMON...LET ME GO...
THE CEMETERY CALLED. THE CHIMES RANG OUT. THE GRAVE BECKONED.
LET ME GO, SIMON... I'LL DO ANYTHING!
THERE WAS NO TIME, ONLY MOVEMENT. HUGH SCREAMED AT THE ROTTEN COFFIN BEFORE HIM...
PLEASE...HAVE PITY! OH... HAVE PITY!
COME, MY FRIEND!
HUGH COULD NOT BREAK FREE FROM THE GRASP OF THE PUTRID CORPSE THAT HELD HIM...
DON'T DO THIS TO ME! LET ME BREATHE! LET ME FEEL THE AIR AND THE STIR OF LIFE IN MY LUNGS! PLEASE... PLEASE!
I CAN'T, HUGH. YOU KNOW THAT! SOON THE SUN WILL RISE, AND THEN WE SHALL BOTH FIND HAPPINESS.
NO... NO... NO...
FOR FIFTEEN YEARS YOU'VE LIVED WHILE I'VE ROTTED. AND NOW IT'S TIME TO ADMIT TO YOURSELF THAT YOU TOO...
...HAVE BEEN...
...DEAD!
THE END

COMPLETE TOOL SETS AT THE PRICE OF A SINGLE TOOL!!!

46 Surplus Twist DRILLS $2

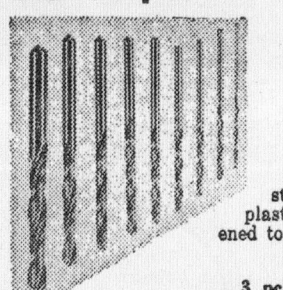

Less than 4½c each. For hand or electric drills. Brand new, genuine hi-grade, hardened carbon tool steel drills. Sell for up to $6 in the stores. You get about 5 each of the most frequently used sizes from 1/16" to ¼". Tempered cutting edges easily bite through steel, aluminum, iron, wood, or plastic. Each drill designed and hardened to give 1800 drillings.

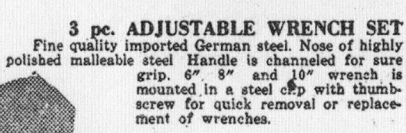

3 pc. ADJUSTABLE WRENCH SET
Fine quality imported German steel. Nose of highly polished malleable steel Handle is channeled for sure grip. 6" 8" and 10" wrench is mounted in a steel clip with thumbscrew for quick removal or replacement of wrenches.

$3.98 complete set postpaid

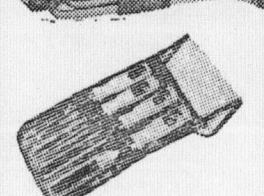

4 pc. CHISEL SET
Tang Chisels, Swedish pattern, drop forged from high quality tool steel, tempered and hardened, beveled and polished blades. Straight hardwood handles, leather tipped. Set contains one each: ¼, ½, ¾, and 1" chisel, in separate transparent compartments of strong plastic kit with yellow binding.

$2.98 complete set postpaid

6 pc. MAGNETIZED SCREW DRIVER SET
Plastic, insulated handles, scientifically designed for non-slip grip. Blades are of highly polished, hardened and tempered quality tool steel.

1—Cabinet, ⅛ x 3⅛"   1—Mechanic, ¼ x 6"
1—Cabinet, 3/16 x 5"   1—Heavy Duty, ⅜ x 8"
1—Stubby, ¼ x 1½"   1—Recess (#2), ¼ x 4"

$2.29 complete set postpaid

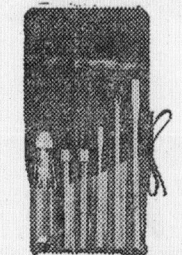

6 pc. INTERCHANGEABLE NUT and SCREW DRIVER SET
Flanged aluminum screw chuck. Faces of all blades cross ground. Handle and blades individually pocketed in heat sealed plastic kit.

1—Cabinet, 3/16 x 4"
1—Mechanic, ¼ x 6"
1—Recess (#2), ¼ x 5½"
1—Nut Driver, ¼ x 3½"
1—Nut Driver, 5/16 x 3½"
1—Amber Handle with Chuck

$1.79 complete set postpaid

5 pc. RATCHET BRACE and BITS
A well constructed ratchet bit brace, designed for heavy duty. Extra heavy chucks will hold bits to 1" Sturdy ratchet and easy turning knobs assure smooth, positive performance. 10" sweep 7/16" stock, highly nickel plated. Alligator spring jaws, hardwood grips. Auger Bits drop forged from high quality tool steel, solid centers, carefully sharpened double cutters, fully polished. Set contains one each of 4, 6, 8, 10, 12/16".

$4.98 complete set postpaid

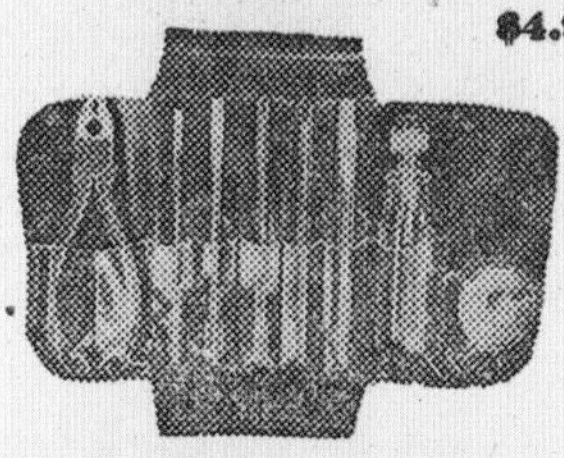

"MY BUDDY" 8 pc. TOOL KIT
Flanged aluminum screw chuck. Fully polished and finished finest tool steel blades. All steel imported roll tape. Each tool in separate pocket of heat sealed plastic case with snap closure.

1—3' Metal Tape   1—Mechanic, ¼ x 3¼"
1—Combination Plier, 4¾" 1—Recess (#1), 3/16 x 3¼"
1—Cabinet, ⅛ x 3¼"   1—Recess (#2), ¼ x 3¼"
1—Cabinet, 3/16 x 3¼"   1—Amber Handle with Chuck

$2.49 complete kit postpaid

INSULATED COMBINATION CUTTING PLIER
Precision made in Germany of hardened and tempered drop forged steel. Handle is serrated and shaped to fit the hand, insulated to withstand 5000 volts. A handy, useful tool with slip joint and side cutter.

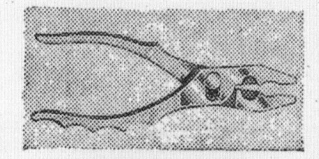

98c postpaid

3 pc. PLIER SET
Finest drop forged imported steel. Ground and polished heads, polished finish, and knurled handles for easier grip. Individually pocketed in heat sealed plastic kit.
1—Linesman Slip Joint, 7"
1—Long Nose, 5⅝"
1—Diagonal, 5⅝"

$2.98 complete set postpaid

MONEY BACK IF YOU DON'T AGREE THESE ARE THE BEST TOOL VALUES EVER!
SEND CHECK, CASH, OR MONEY ORDER AND WE PAY THE POSTAGE . . . IF C.O.D., POSTAGE IS EXTRA!
USE THE ATTACHED COUPON FOR IMMEDIATE DELIVERY!

SCOTT-MITCHELL HOUSE, INC., DEPT. D.G., 400 MADISON AVE., N.Y., N.Y.

Please send me the following items as indicated:

___ 46 DRILLS @ $2.00 per set
___ 3 pc. ADJUSTABLE WRENCH SET @ $3.98 per set
___ INSULATED COMBINATION CUTTING PLIER @ 98c each
___ 6 pc. INTERCHANGEABLE NUT AND SCREW DRIVER SET @ $1.79 per set
___ 5 pc. RATCHET BRACE AND BIT SET @ $4.98 per set
___ 8 pc. "MY BUDDY" TOOL KIT @ $2.49 each
___ 6 pc. MAGNETIZED SCREW DRIVER SET @ $2.29 per set
___ 3 pc. PLIER SET @ $2.98 per set

Enclosed find $_____   ☐ CASH ☐ CHECK ☐ MONEY ORDER
☐ Send C.O.D. PLUS POSTAGE CHARGES

NAME _____ ADDRESS _____
CITY _____ ZONE ____ STATE ____

SCOTT-MITCHELL HOUSE, INC., DEPT. D.G., 400 MADISON AVE., N.Y., N.Y.

HERNIA SUFFERERS!
GET INSTANT BLESSED RELIEF – THE PROVEN WAY

Amazing New... Freedom and Comfort
WITH THE NATIONALLY FAMOUS...

RUPTURE-EASER
A Piper Brace Product

RIGHT OR LEFT SIDE
Pat No 2606551
$3.95

Double **$4.95**

For Men...
For Women
For Children

$3.95 single
$4.95 double

Over **700,000** Grateful USERS!

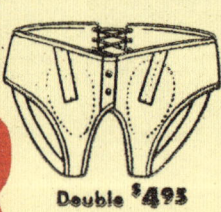

No fitting required!
JUST GIVE SIZE AND SIDE

A strong form fitting washable support designed to give you relief and comfort. Snaps up in front. Adjustable back lacing and adjustable leg strap. Soft flat groin pad — no torturing steel or leather bands. Unexcelled for comfort, invisible under light clothing. Washable and sanitary. Also excellent as an after operation support. Wear it with assurance — get new freedom of action!

NO STEEL OR LEATHER BANDS
You get effective scientific relief without those dreaded steel and leather bands that make hernia affliction such torture to thousands of folks. Rupture-Easer support is firm, gentle, sure — you'll realize a new lease on life with the comfort and assurance Rupture-Easer brings you!

BLESSED RELIEF DAY AND NIGHT
Rupture-Easer is just as comfortable to sleep in, and to bathe in, as it is to wear! Soft scientific pad pressure keeps you safe, awake or asleep. Those who need constant support welcome Rupture-Easer's blessed comfort.

INVISIBLE UNDER LIGHT CLOTHING
Wear Rupture-Easer with new confidence under your lightest clothing. No more visible than any usual undergarment — no revealing bulk to hide. Even worn under girdles and corsets comfortably!

WASHABLE AND SANITARY
Yes, you can wash your Rupture-Easer as easily and safely as your other undergarments. A quick sudsing keeps Rupture-Easer just as fresh as new.

Read What Others Say:
Harley Decoteau, Montpelier, Vt. writes "The last brace you sent me was wonderful. I have been ruptured for 30 years. I am now 36 and in 30 years I have never been more pleased."

Juanita Addison, Twin Falls, Idaho says "I would like to have another Rupture Easer. It really has helped me. I can do practically anything with the Rupture-Easer on."

Mr. George Dorchser, Union City, N.J. says "I am using one of your Rupture Easers now and find it the best I have ever used. I am a truck driver and have tried others that cost 4 and 5 times as much as your hernia support but I get more comfort from your supporter."

there's no substitute for proved **Performance!**

Easy to Order: Just measure around lowest part of abdomen and state right or left side or double.

10 DAY TRIAL OFFER Money back if you don't get blessed relief. Mail orders only

PIPER BRACE CO.
811 Wyandotte, Dept HA-54, Kansas City 6, Mo.

DELAY may be serious!

Use Handy COUPON
...get yours NOW!

PIPER BRACE COMPANY
811 Wyandotte, Dept. HA-54
Kansas City 6, Mo.

Please send my RUPTURE-EASER by return mail.
Right Side ☐ $3.95   Measure around lowest part of
Left Side ☐ $3.95   my abdomen
Double   ☐ $4.95   is _____ INCHES.

(Note: Be sure to give Size and Side when ordering.)
We Prepay Postage except on C.O.D.'s
Enclosed is ☐ Money Order ☐ Check for $_____ ☐ Send C.O.D.

Name _____
Address _____
City and State _____

You Can Be a Bombshell In Any Tough Spot!

NOW... A Rugged Fighting-Man Shows You How To Explode Your Hidden-Powers In Self-Defense

No true American wants to be a tough! But YOU, and every red-blooded man and boy wants to be always ready and able to get out of any tough spot no matter what the odds. You want to have the real know-how of skillfully defending yourself... of fearlessly protecting your property, or your dear ones... against Bullies, Hoodlums, Roughnecks and the like. And, if in service, or going in, you've got to be ready to fight rough and tough, for your very life may depend on it in hand-to-hand combat.

Here's where a rugged, two-fisted fighting man tells you... and shows you... the secrets of using every power-packed trick in the bag. You get it straight from "Barney" Cosneck, in AMERICAN COMBAT JUDO... training-manual for Troopers, Police, Boxers, wrestlers, Commandos, Rangers and Armed Forces. What a man! He's dynamite from head to toes! Twice, he was Big 10 Wrestling Champ, and during World War II was Personal Combat Instructor to the U. S. Coast Guard. "Barney" has devoted most of his life to developing, perfecting, teaching rough, tough fighting tactics. He gives YOU all the angles in easy-to-follow steps. Mastery of his skills and tactics will give even a little guy the blasting-power of a bombshell... to knock the steam out of a bruiser twice his size. "Barney" keeps no secrets in AMERICAN COMBAT JUDO! He tells all... shows all! He gives you the real lowdown on when and how to use each power-packed Blow, Hold, Lock, Jab, Throw and Trip, that will make YOU the "Boss" in any tough spot. You'll be thrilled and amazed when you see what YOU can do with your bare hands... even if you are light and small. For, the real secret of "Barney's" super-tactics is in using the other fellow's muscle and brawn against him... as if it were your own... to make him helpless and defenseless.

200 Dynamic-Action Start-To-Finish photos show you what to do... how to do... the skillful fighting tactics that will make you slippery as an eel... fast as lightning... with striking-power like a panther... with a K.O. punch in both hands. What's more, you'll learn the secrets of using every ounce of your weight... every inch of your size... to give you giant-power... crushing-power... that will keep you on your feet when the other guy's down. Best of all, you'll be surprised how easy it is. Your friends, too, will be surprised when they see your speed, skill and power.

Send for your copy of AMERICAN COMBAT JUDO right now! Keep it for 7 days, and if you don't think it's the best buck you ever spent, return it and get your money back. But, don't wait—you don't know when you may have to do your stuff. ORDER NOW—ONLY $1.00 POSTPAID

SPORTSMAN'S POST   Dept. HC   400 Madison Avenue, New York 17, N. Y.

SEW LEATHER
AND TOUGH TEXTILES
LIKE AN EXPERT

Here's handiest tool you'll ever own! Saves many times its small cost. The SPEEDY STITCHER, automatic awl, sews a lock-stitch like a machine. Even the most unskilled can quickly and expertly repair harness, saddles, tents, awnings, luggage, carpets, auto-tops, sports goods, boots, or anything else made of leather or heavy materials. Also used for livestock cuts. A must for leathercrafters. Get your SPEEDY STITCHER now for heavy-duty sewing jobs in home, shop, on farm. Comes ready for instant use, with reel of strong, waxed thread and set of diamond-pointed, grooved needles in handle, including special needle for shoe tapping. Easy to follow instructions will make you an expert on any tough sewing job. Save money by sending $1.98 cash, check, money order for postpaid delivery. C.O.D. $1.98 plus postal charges. Money back guarantee.

COMPLETE ONLY $1.98 POSTPAID

SPORTSMAN'S POST, Dept. HC, 400 MADISON AVENUE, NEW YORK 17, N. Y.

BOYS, GIRLS, MEN, WOMEN!
The World Is On FIRE
Serve The LORD and You Can Have These Prizes!

CRIME · GRAFT · DOPE · DRINK · WAR

We will send you the wonderful prizes pictured on this page .. or dozens of others, such as jewelry, radium dial wrist watches, tableware, tools, U-Make-It kits, leather kits, sewing kits, electric clocks, pressure cookers, scout equipment, model airplanes, and many others ... all WITHOUT ONE PENNY OF COST. Crime, sin, graft, wars are the greatest they have ever been. Our leaders say a reawakening of Christianity is needed to save us. You can do your share by spreading the gospel into every home in your community. Merely show your friends and neighbors inspiring, beautiful Religious Wall Motto plaques. Many buy six or more to hang in every room. An amazing value, only 35¢ ... sell on sight. Secure big, cash commissions or exciting prizes for selling just **one set** of 24 Mottos. Big Prize catalog sent **Free!** Serve the LORD and earn prizes you want.

YOU CAN MAKE MONEY TOO!

Prizes pictured:
- ROY ROGERS FLASH CAMERA
- VANITY SET
- GABBY HAYES FISHING KIT
- RED RYDER CARBINE
- BOYS' OR GIRLS' BICYCLE
- TEXAN JR. GUITAR
- ROY ROGERS BINOCULARS
- RADIUM DIAL POCKET WATCH
- WRIST WATCHES FOR BOYS AND GIRLS
- ALSO UKELELE WITH ARTHUR GODFREY PLAYER
- RADIO RECEIVING SET FOR SCOUTS
- ELECTRONIC TWO-WAY WALKIE-TALKIE
- WALKING DOLL
- HUNTING KNIFE AND AX
- ARCHERY SET
- FOOTBALL
- JOE DI MAGGIO BASEBALL SET
- TWO-GUN HOLSTER SET
- ROY ROGERS OR DALE EVANS LAMP
- DICK TRACY CAMERA
- CHEMISTRY SET
- REG. SIZE BASKETBALL AND RING
- GIRLS' SHOULDER-STRAP BAG
- WHITE ZIPPER BIBLE
- ROLLER SKATES
- TYPEWRITER
- WOODBURNING SET
- TABLE TENNIS SET

HERE'S HOW YOU GET YOUR PRIZES

Rush your name and address on coupon and we ship AT ONCE PREPAID your first set of 24 big size, 9x11, richly decorated Mottos **On Trust**. When you have sold the 24 Mottos, send the $8.40 you have collected and you can secure your choice of many wonderful prizes. If you prefer to EARN MONEY, send $6.00 and keep $2.40. Hurry, send TODAY for 24 Mottos ON TRUST and big PRIZE CATALOG FREE.

The FUNman, Dept. D-164.
4545 N. Clark St., Chicago 40, Ill.
FREE BIG SIZE CATALOG

Please rush to me on credit 24 Religious Wall Mottos, to sell at 35c each. Also include big Prize Catalog Free. I will remit amount asked within 30 days, select a prize or keep cash commission, as explained under description of prize in BIG PRIZE CATALOG. PRINT BELOW.

NAME _____ AGE _____

STREET or RFD _____

TOWN _____ ZONE ____ STATE _____

Save 1 cent filling in, pasting and mailing this coupon on a 2c postcard today.

FREE! MEMBERSHIP in the FUNman's Fun Club

Just mail coupon below now and we'll send you 24 Religious Mottos ON CREDIT. Easy to sell — you get valuable prizes. EXTRA! If you sell mottos and send payment within 15 days you receive FREE Membership in the FUNman's Fun Club. A membership card, certificate, giant packet of fun materials all yours PLUS extra surprises!

SEND NO MONEY... We Trust You

PS Artbooks

Collect all 4 Volumes of Black Cat Mystery from PS Artbooks

HARVEY HORRORS
COLLECTED WORKS
BLACK CAT MYSTERY
VOLUME ONE

STRANGEST TALES OF FEAR AND TERROR!

BLACK CAT MYSTERY COMICS

No. 30 AUGUST 10¢

GATEWAY TO DEATH! The terrifying truth about the land beyond... and two men who dared enter the forest of horror!

August 1951 - May 1952
Issues 30 - 35

Foreword by
Christopher Fowler

Black Cat Mystery
Volume One

Collect the complete library form PS Publishing
online 24/7 @ www.pspublishing.co.uk

Chamber of Chills
July 1954 - Issue #24

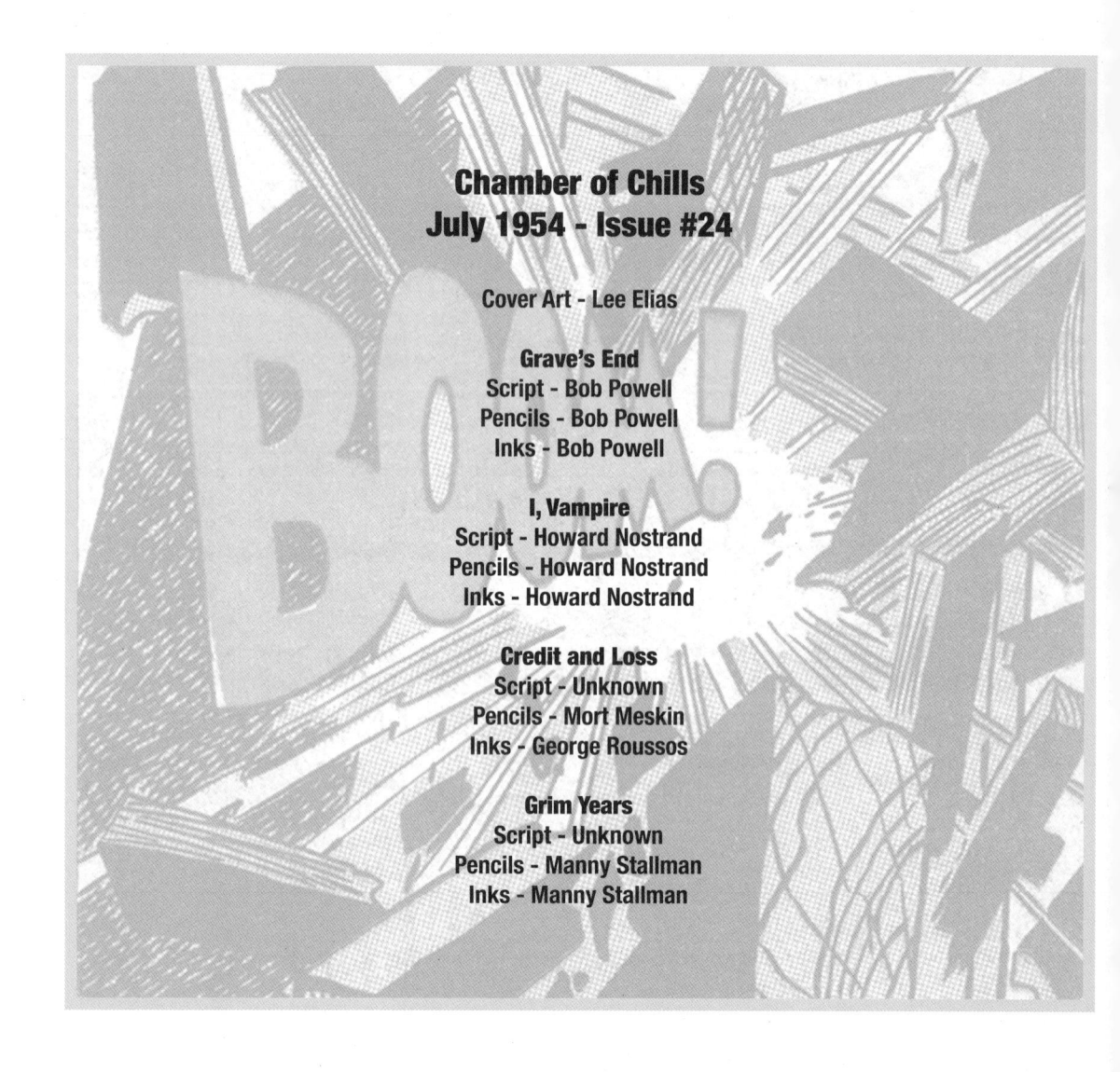

Cover Art - Lee Elias

Grave's End
Script - Bob Powell
Pencils - Bob Powell
Inks - Bob Powell

I, Vampire
Script - Howard Nostrand
Pencils - Howard Nostrand
Inks - Howard Nostrand

Credit and Loss
Script - Unknown
Pencils - Mort Meskin
Inks - George Roussos

Grim Years
Script - Unknown
Pencils - Manny Stallman
Inks - Manny Stallman

Information Source: Grand Comics Database!
A nonprofit, Internet-based organization of international volunteers dedicated to building a database covering all printed comics throughout the world.
If you believe any of this data to be incorrect or can add valuable additional information, please let us know www.comics.org
All rights to images reserved by the respective copyright holders. All original advertisement features remain the copyright of the respective trading company.

Privacy Policy
All portions of the Grand Comics Database that are subject to copyright are licensed under a Creative Commons Attribution 3.0 Unported License.
This includes but is not necessarily limited to our database schema and data distribution format.
The GCD Web Site code is licensed under the GNU General Public License.

CHAMBER OF CHILLS
TALES OF TERROR AND SUSPENSE!
CHAMBER OF CHILLS
MAGAZINE
U WILL BE CAUGHT IN THE CLUTCH OF HORROR IN... GRAVE'S END!

Delicious REDUCING Sweets Taste Like CANDY!

GUARANTEED To Take Off and Keep Off up to
- 5 pounds in 5 DAYS
- 10 pounds in 10 DAYS
- 15 pounds in 15 DAYS
- 25 pounds in 25 DAYS
- 30 pounds in 30 DAYS

... or MONEY BACK!

Date you receive Sweetreets depends on how fast you order, how fast U. S. mails deliver it!

Reach for this sweet instead of fattening foods! A thrilling way to reduce! Delicious new Sweetreets satisfy your craving for high-calorie foods — the No. 1 reason you are overweight! No hungry moments! No hard-to-follow diets! No dangerous drugs! No will power needed!
Guaranteed to taste like candy!

REACH FOR SWEETREETS
Every Time You're Tempted to EAT OR DRINK TOO MUCH!

HERE'S the most joyous news ever released for the overweight! Now you can take off and keep off ugly fat simply by nibbling on delicious-tasting "sweet" every time you're tempted to overeat or drink! In fact, you must take off from 5 to 30 pounds or money back! Do you wonder why everyone was astonished when they proved the most luscious sweet you ever tasted actually takes off and keeps off pound after pound without dangerous drugs, starvation diets, strenuous exercises or other risky, temporary methods?

How Amazing Sweetreets Were Discovered!

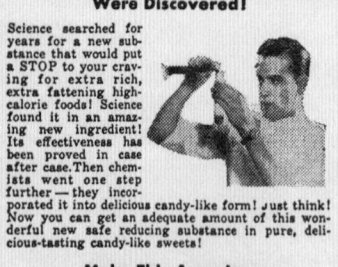

Science searched for years for a new substance that would put a STOP to your craving for extra rich, extra fattening high-calorie foods! Science found it in an amazing new ingredient! Its effectiveness has been proved in case after case. Then chemists went one step further — they incorporated it into delicious candy-like form! Just think! Now you can get an adequate amount of this wonderful new safe reducing substance in pure, delicious-tasting candy-like sweets!

Make This Amazing "Prove-It" Taste Test!

To prove to you there is no difference in the tastiness of your favorite candy and the new Sweetreets reducing candy — WE MAKE THIS DARING OFFER! Place a box of candy along side of a box of Sweetreets. Eat a piece from each box ... slowly. Let your taste buds decide! If you can detect any difference, your full purchase price will be refunded.

How You Get Thin and Stay Thin!

Doctors tell us you are fat because you eat too much EXTRA FATTENING, HIGH-CALORIE FOODS! You have a constant craving for such foods!

You'll have to admit most methods of reducing have failed to do the job! You quickly gain back the few pounds you lost ... here's why. It takes almost superhuman effort to *continue* with most methods of reducing. You count calories, upset your whole family with hard-to-follow diets, endanger your health with drugs! But you will WANT to continue eating Sweetreets! They're so delicious! They're so safe! You'll find yourself eating less high-calorie foods ... taking off from 5 up to 30 pounds ... and you'll keep it off with Sweetreets! This is guaranteed!

Clinically Tested And Proven!

The remarkable appetite-satisfying ingredient in Sweetreets is one of the great reducing discoveries of this generation! Doctors have subjected it to test after test in big hospitals, clinics, laboratories, universities and in private practice. The results have far exceeded expectations! The facts have been published in national magazines, scores of medical journals and medical books — we'll be glad to send your own doctor the medical bibliography.

Do Not Confuse Sweetreets With Anything Else On The Market!

Whatever you do — don't make the mistake of confusing Sweetreets with anything else on the market! Sweetreets are entirely different! Sweetreets contain the amazing new, clinic-tested reducing substance so many doctors prescribe. So don't be fooled by ordinary candy cubes that are no different than the candy you buy at the candy store! Sweetreets are a scientific product of pharmaceutical research — years ahead.

You Don't Cut Down On Foods — You Cut Down On Calories! You Are Always Satisfied — Never, Never Hungry!

When you follow the easy, delightful Sweetreets plan you need never suffer any hunger pangs. You are always satisfied because Sweetreets satisfy your craving for high-calorie foods ... from morning to bedtime! With Sweetreets you don't cut down on

How many times a day are you tempted to eat or drink? Too often, you must admit ... and with disastrous results! You just can't resist! As a result you get fatter and fatter with each extra bite! But now you can control that craving for fattening foods. You can put a STOP to that hard-to-break habit of overeating by simply eating delicious Sweetreets that contain a tasteless, safe ingredient doctors prescribe to help remove your desire to overeat!

the "quantity" of foods ... you just cut down on the high-calorie rich foods! You eat all you want — but your total calorie intake will be LESS! That's the secret.

Don't Die 10, 20, 30 Years Too Soon!

Doctors, health experts, insurance executives have facts and figures that PROVE fat shortens your life! Fat men and women die up to 10, 20 or 30 years earlier than those with normal weight! A fat body leaves you wide open to a long list of diseases — makes it harder for you to survive diabetes, heart trouble, cancer, kidney trouble, pneumonia, high blood pressure — even operations! Play safe — start taking delicious Sweetreets... take off that ugly fat!

SEND NO MONEY!

That's right! You don't have to send any money to *prove* to yourself that Sweetreets can take off 10 pounds in 10 days. Just send for your liberal-sized box of Sweetreets. Try them for 10 days at our risk! Keep a daily record of your weight. If you're not entirely delighted — Sweetreets cost you nothing!

Mail to Sweetreets Div., United Safeway Co., Dept. H M 400 Madison Ave. New York 17, N.Y.

Entire contents copyrighted by United Safeway Co., 1953, N. Y. C.

MAIL NO RISK COUPON TODAY!

SWEETREETS DIV.
UNITED SAFEWAY CO. Dept. H M
400 Madison Ave. New York 17, N.Y.

Yes, rush me a liberal-sized box of Sweetreets. I will pay the postman just the price plus postage and C.O.D. charges. It is understood if I am not absolutely satisfied, entirely delighted, if my scales don't show more loss of weight than I ever thought possible — you will refund my money without question!

☐ $2.98 large size, ☐ 5.98 giant double size

NAME...
ADDRESS...
CITY.......................... ZONE....... STATE.............

SAVE MORE! Send cash, check or money order with coupon and we will pay all postage and C.O.D. charges! SAME MONEY-BACK GUARANTEE!

MONEY BACK GUARANTEE

You MUST lose up to 10 pounds within 10 days — or you pay nothing! So don't delay! Don't risk taking 10, 20 or 30 years off your life with dangerous fat. Get rid of fat with Sweetreets! Hurry — this offer is limited!

CHAMBER OF CHILLS MAGAZINE, JULY, 1954, Vol. 1, No. 24, IS PUBLISHED BI-MONTHLY by WITCHES TALES, INC., 1860 Broadway, New York 23, N.Y. Entered as second class matter at the Post Office at New York, N.Y. under the Act of March 3, 1879. Single copies 10c. Subscription rates, 10 issues for $1.00 in the U. S. and possessions, elsewhere $1.50. All names in this periodical are entirely fictitious and no identification with actual persons is intended. Contents copyrighted, 1954, by Witches Tales, Inc., New York City. Printed in the U.S.A. Title Registered in U. S. Patent Office.

THE INNER CIRCLE

Dig in a messy grave and you'd find terror, wouldn't you? Well, that's what we offer! Crawl through a dark dungeon with time-gnawed walls and you're bound to come out shocked. Right? Well, we give you that feeling ... plus! Look through these stories and you'll find the real thing ... the intangible that makes your blood bubble and your eyes white. This is ... TERROR!!

Every ounce of artificiality has been extracted ... every particle of the synthetic has been subtracted ... and every semblance of the unreal has been protracted. For in these stories, you'll find that distilled element ... the kind that only makes for pure horror.

This is the "distilled element" that makes your reading matter different ... that makes it unique ... that makes it tense ... that makes you come back for more. It's what you want.

And these yelling yarns are the kind that makes the small hours smaller ... and has the chill of doom that only one cold, gray hand could create. These needling narratives have come to you from the nether region, where every step forward takes the reader to an acre that he should stay away from ... but yet is compelled to go. These stories are different. They have the distilled element of fear!

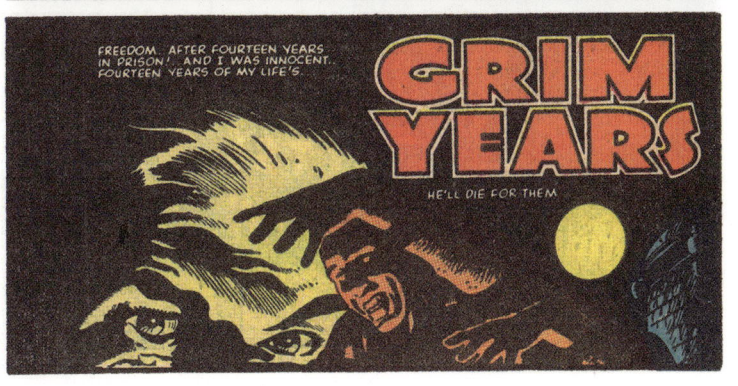

CHAMBER OF CHILLS

CONTENTS NO. 24

CREDIT AND LOSS

I, VAMPIRE

TO YOUR... HA-HA... HEALTH, MY FRIEND!

DOES ALL LIFE STOP AT... GRAVE'S END

GRIM YEARS

FREEDOM. AFTER FOURTEEN YEARS IN PRISON!. AND I WAS INNOCENT. FOURTEEN YEARS OF MY LIFE'S

HE'LL DIE FOR THEM

How do you Measure Up?

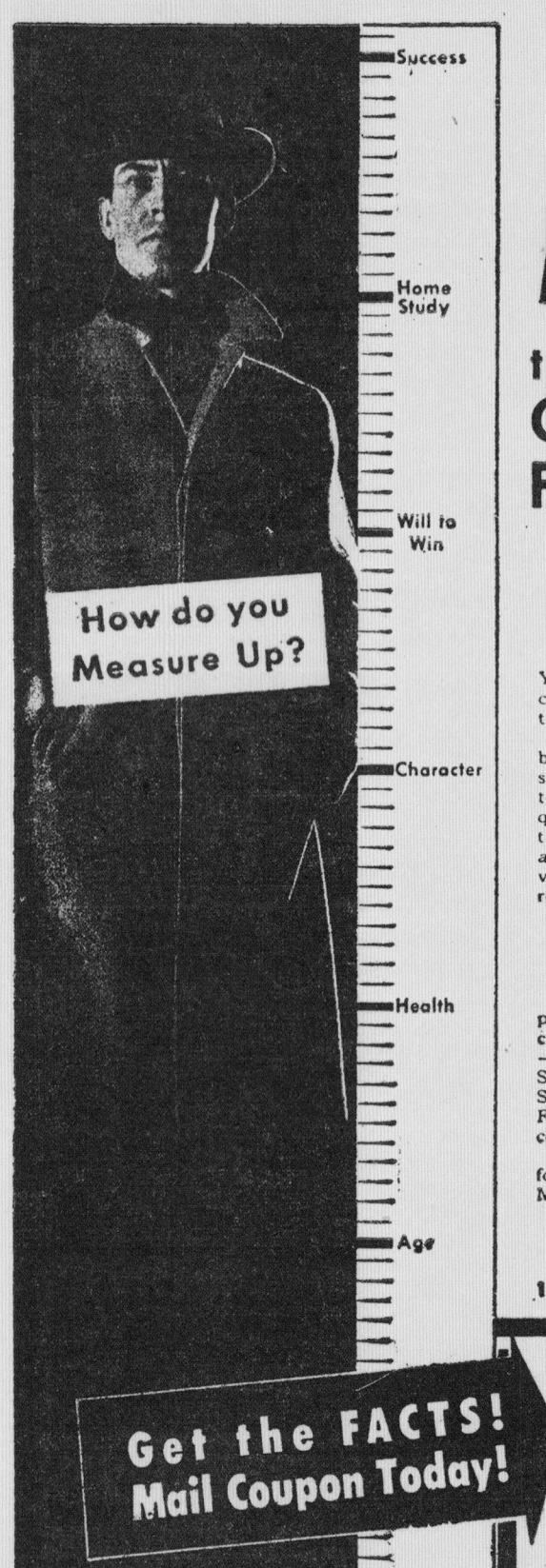

Success · Home Study · Will to Win · Character · Health · Age

Get the FACTS! Mail Coupon Today!

HAVE YOU GOT WHAT IT TAKES?

to become a Criminal Investigator Finger Print Expert?

FIND OUT NOW
at our Expense

You have everything to gain .. nothing to lose! Here's your chance to learn at OUR expense whether you have "what it takes" to become a criminal investigator or finger print expert.

With NO OBLIGATION on your part—mail the coupon below requesting our *qualification* questionnaire. It will be sent to you by return mail. If, in our opinion, your answers to our simple questions indicate that you have the basic qualifications necessary to succeed in scientific crime detection, we will tell you promptly. Then you will also receive *absolutely free* the fascinating "Blue Book of Crime"—a volume showing how modern detectives actually track down real criminals.

Our Graduates Are Key Men in Over 800 Identification Bureaus

So this is your opportunity! We have been teaching finger print and firearms identification, police photography and criminal investigation for over 30 years! OUR GRADUATES —TRAINED THROUGH SIMPLE, INEXPENSIVE, STEP BY STEP, HOME STUDY LESSONS—HOLD RESPONSIBLE POSITIONS IN OVER 800 U. S. IDENTIFICATION BUREAUS! We *know* what is needed to succeed—NOW we want to find out if *you* have it!

Without spending a penny—see how YOU "measure up" for a profitable career in scientific criminal investigation. Mail the coupon today!

INSTITUTE OF APPLIED SCIENCE
(A Correspondence School Since 1916)
1920 Sunnyside Ave., Dept. 1725   Chicago 40, Ill.

INSTITUTE OF APPLIED SCIENCE
1920 Sunnyside Ave., Dept. 1725   Chicago 40, Ill.

Gentlemen: Without obligation or expense on my part, send me your qualification questionnaire. I understand that upon receipt of my answers you will immediately advise me if you think they indicate that I have a chance to succeed in criminal investigation or finger print work. Then I will receive FREE the "Blue Book of Crime," and information on your course and the 800 American Identification Bureaus employing your students or graduates.

Name...

Address...RFD or Zone............

City...State............Age....

Does all life stop at...

GRAVE'S END

"FOOL... AROUND... WITH ANOTHER MAN? EH? NO MORE... ANNA... NO MORE!!!"

LOUIS CONETTI STOOD UP, LOOKING AT ANNA'S LIMP, DEAD BODY. THE RAIN FELL HARD AND CONETTI COULD STILL FEEL HER THROAT IN HIS HANDS. HIS EYES GLEAMED. HE SMILED...

"I HAD TO DO IT! BELIEVE ME, ANNA! MY... PRIDE... WAS HURT!"

THEN, WITH THE SUDDEN HORRIBLE REALIZATION OF WHAT HE DID, CONETTI RAN, LEAVING ANNA'S BODY TO SOAK UP THE MUD AROUND HER...

"GOT... TO... GET AWAY!!!"

"LOUIS— I... UN-N-N-GH-H!"

THE RAIN CONTINUED TO FALL AS CONETTI RAN. HE CUT THROUGH A CEMETERY, CHURNING THE SOFT GROUND BENEATH HIM WITH EVERY STEP. TOMB-STONES, WET AND GLISTENING, STOOD SILENT AND STILL AS HE PASSED THEM...
GOOD SHORT CUT... OUT OF... TOWN...!
GIOVANNI LORENZO 1867 1948
SUDDENLY, CONETTI FELT IT... THE GROUND GIVING-IN... SPLITTING APART... AND HIMSELF FALLING... FALLING...
YAAAAHHHH!
HOW LONG DO YOU THINK SHE'S BEEN DEAD, PAUL?
A SHORT TIME! IT'S HARD TO TELL, THOUGH... IN THIS RAIN!
D... DO YOU KNOW HER?
I'VE SEEN HER ABOUT! HER NAME'S ANNA... ANNA PAPPONI!
WE BETTER NOTIFY THE INSPECTOR!
YES... THE INSPECTOR... AND THE POOR GIRL'S FAMILY!
CONETTI LOOKED UP. DAZED AND SHAKEN, HE MADE OUT A SHAFT OF LIGHT COMING THROUGH A JAGGED HOLE FAR ABOVE HIM. COLD WATER SLUSHED AROUND HIS ANKLES...
WH... WHERE AM I? O... OLD CATACOMB! GOT TO... GET... OUT!
HE FELT THE SOGGY, TIME-EATEN WALLS. HE PULLED OUT A CHUNK OF EARTH... AND STEPPED BACK FROM A GUSH OF WATER COMING THROUGH THE NEWLY-FORMED HOLE...
I... UGH! MORE WATER! UNDERGROUND STREAM... NEARBY...! HAVE TO GET OUT... BEFORE I DROWN!
2

THE RAIN KEPT POURING. FETID WATER SEEPED THROUGH THE HOLE IN THE CATACOMB'S WALL. CONETTI SEEMED TRAPPED...
CAN'T CLIMB...TOO SOFT FOR A FOOT-HOLD! NO OUTLET... NOTHING! W... WHAT AM I TO DO? WHAT..?
HE FELT THE WATER AT HIS KNEE-LEVEL. IT WAS RISING...
I...I CAN'T STAY HERE! I'LL...DIE..!
ANY NEWS OF CONETTI, INSPECTOR?
NONE! HE SEEMS TO HAVE VANISHED!
ARE YOU SURE IT'S HE...WHO DID IT?
REASONABLY SO! WHO ELSE HAD A MOTIVE?
THAT DOG... CAUSING ALL THIS MISERY!
DON'T WORRY! HE'LL BE PUNISHED!
CONETTI WAS LIKE A WILD MAN LOOKING AT DEATH'S FACE. HE CLAWED AT THE SOFT ITALIAN EARTH SURROUNDING HIM...
I'LL DROWN...HERE! I'VE GOT TO GET OUT! GOT...TO... GET...OUT..!
HE TRIED TO PLUG UP THE HOLES, TO STOP THE EVER-INCESSANT FLOW THAT THREATENED TO ENGULF HIM! BUT THE SOFT MUD GAVE WAY...
NO...GOOD..! ROTTEN WATER KEEPS ON COMING...
3

CONETTI KNEW IT... KNEW HE COULDN'T ESCAPE. DEATH WAS ALL AROUND HIM... LIKE THE EVER-RISING WATER...
NO, NO! DON'T WANT TO DIE!
THE WATER WAS UP TO HIS CHEST NOW. IT WAS COLD, DIRTY, MUDDY! CONETTI LOOKED DOWN AT IT, SCREAMING WORDS... PLEADING FOR HELP... CRYING OUT FOR MERCY...
LORD, FORGIVE ME! ANNA... I DIDN'T MEAN IT! ANNA... LET ME LIVE! ANNA..!
MY... POOR... ANNA!
PLEASE... GOD...
PUNISH THE MAN WHO DID THIS TO MY ANNA!
THE WATER ROSE AROUND CONETTI'S CHIN... HIS MOUTH... HIS NOSE. HIS EYES WERE WHITE WITH FEAR ...HIS WHOLE BODY ENCASED IN THIS WATERY SHROUD...
UNTIL IT WAS ALL OVER FOR LOUIS CONETTI...
4

THE RAIN FELL...ON ANNA'S GRAVE, NOW HONORED WITH A FEW FLOWERS...ON HER MOTHER, CRYING AND DRESSED IN BLACK...ON A FEW FRIENDS...

COME...LET US GO..!

THE RAIN CONTINUED TO FALL...AS THE MOURNERS LEFT...

UNTIL IT STOOD ALONE...GLISTENING ...ITS FLOWERS DRENCHED BY THE RAIN...

THEN A PUDDLE OF DIRTY, FETID WATER LOLLED UPON THE GRAVE...

BRINGING WITH IT A FLOATING, ALIEN THING...BRINGING WITH IT A HAND...

BRINGING WITH IT A BODY THAT WASHED UPON ANNA PAPPONI'S GRAVE...

LOUIS CONETTI'S BODY...THAT WAS FLOATED OUT OF THE ABANDONED CATACOMB...NOW FILLED WITH WATER...!

THE END

CHILLY CHAMBER MUSIC
Songs from the SPOOK BOX!

A biscuit, a basket,

A green and yellow casket!

I brought a package to my darling,

But on the way I dropped it!

CHILLY CHAMBER MUSIC
Songs from the SPOOK BOX!

The draining rain sprays the pane...tenderly.

The whistling wind winds round the weeds... tenderly.

And I come to you with arms out wide, and one thought inside of me...

So I take your lips, I take your heart... tenderly!

180

The Intruders

John and Cecelia Worthington didn't know how it happened. They only knew they looked up — he from a magazine, she from her knitting — and saw them.

"My God!" John Worthington gasped.

His wife clung close to him. "Say it isn't true," she said, her words coming in stammers.

But there was no denying it. They were no longer alone in their living room. There were four other people there... people with familiar faces, but people who could never be in their living room.

You see, John's mother and father were there... and they were dead. And Cecelia's Uncle Joshua and Aunt Emily were there, too. And they, too, were dead.

"What are you doing here?" John asked these ivory white creatures that walked about with steps of death.

None of them answered. Instead, they merely marched around the room.

"J-John, what's happening?" Cecelia was beside herself. Sheer horror ruled her emotions.

"Just try and be calm, darling. We'll get to the bottom of this." But John had no idea how he would.

The figures still marched around them. Sometimes they nodded to each other. Sometimes a smile, an ugly, gruesome smile, crossed their faces. But they made no sound.

"Speak! Speak!" Cecelia shouted, looking from one to the other.

John held her back. "Please, Cecelia. Please take it easy."

"How can I take it easy? Our house is filled with the dead! What can we do? What can we do?"

The four figures sat down. Their eyes stared straight ahead.

"Try talking to them, John. Ask them what they want. Ask them why they're here."

John walked over to the creature that once had been his father.

"Dad — uh — sir," he said, not even sure of what to call him. "Why are you here? What do you want of us?"

The creature that had been his father didn't answer. His icy lips parted and let through an eerie smile.

"Force him to talk, John! Hit him! Force him! Hit him!" Cecelia had become hysterical, and the hysteria was wrapping John also.

He shook the creature. He yelled at him. "Tell me! Tell me, do you hear? What do you want from us? Speak! Speak! Speak!"

The creature's eyes suddenly became warm. A glow of sympathy came upon its face. It put a hand on John's shoulder. Then, finally, it spoke...

"John," it said, "you'll understand us very shortly. It's always strange at first. It'll take you a while to see that there's nothing to say when you're dead!"

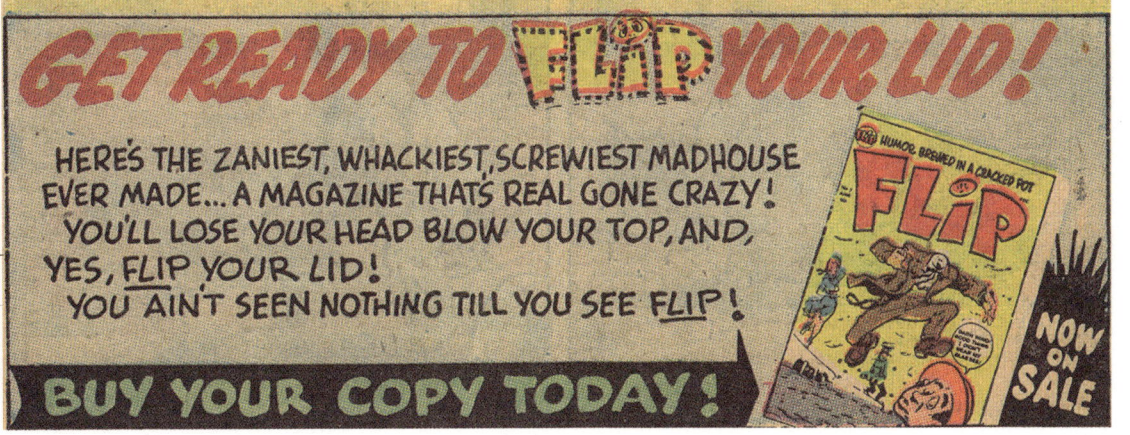

GET READY TO FLIP YOUR LID!

HERE'S THE ZANIEST, WHACKIEST, SCREWIEST MADHOUSE EVER MADE... A MAGAZINE THAT'S REAL GONE CRAZY! YOU'LL LOSE YOUR HEAD BLOW YOUR TOP, AND, YES, FLIP YOUR LID! YOU AIN'T SEEN NOTHING TILL YOU SEE FLIP!

BUY YOUR COPY TODAY!

FLIP — NOW ON SALE

I, VAMPIRE

"TO YOUR... HA-HA... HEALTH, MY FRIEND!"

"GO AHEAD! TAKE A GOOD LOOK AT ME! I *DARE* YOU! HAH! *I* KNOW HOW YOU FEEL!"

"YOU CAN ALMOST SMELL THE EVIL ODOR OF THE GRAVE... THE STENCH OF MY MOULDY COFFIN..! PAH, YOU SAY! I *DON'T WANT* TO LOOK AT YOU! I *DON'T WANT* TO *HEAR* YOUR STORY!"

WELL, LISTEN, ANYHOW! MAYBE... THEN... YOU'LL INVITE ME TO YOUR HOME! AT LEAST... THAT'S WHAT I HOPE...!
"I KNOW WHY YOU HUMANS SHUDDER AND SHAKE WHEN YOU THINK OF US VAMPIRES! YOU PICTURE MY BONY HANDS CLUTCHING AT YOUR HAIR, PULLING YOUR HEAD BACK... BACK... BACK..."
"YOUR NERVES WHINE WITH TERROR AS YOU THINK OF ME AT YOUR THROAT..."
"I CAN UNDERSTAND YOUR POINT OF VIEW. IT'S CERTAINLY NOT A PLEASANT EXPERIENCE. I CAN EVEN SYMPATHIZE WITH YOU FOR HATING US AND FOR HUNTING US DOWN!"
BUT DID YOU EVER THINK OF OUR SIDE OF THE STORY? DID YOU EVER TRY TO UNDERSTAND US... AS I'M TRYING TO UNDERSTAND YOU?
"JUST TRY TO SEE OUR PROBLEM! FIRST OF ALL, THE ONLY TIME WE CAN GO OUT IS AT NIGHT! OFTEN IT'S BITTER COLD! AND OUR SHROUDS ARE WORN THIN! THE WIND CUTS THROUGH OUR SCANT CLOTHING LIKE A KNIFE!"
BRRR! WHAT A NIGHT!
IF ONLY WE DIDN'T HAVE TO GO OUT! AHH... HOW PLEASANT IT WOULD BE TO SPEND THE EVENING IN OUR NICE, WARM COFFINS!
2

"THEN, WE HAVE FEELINGS, TOO! IT HURTS US TO SEE THE EXPRESSIONS ON YOU HUMANS WHEN YOU CATCH A GLIMPSE OF US!"
AAAAAAHHH! VAMPIRES!
"AND DID YOU EVER THINK WHAT IT'S LIKE TO BE CRAMPED ALL DAY IN SUCH A SMALL ROOM... NO WINDOWS... NO VENTILATION... NEVER TO SEE THE SUN..."
"NO! YOU NEVER THINK OF OUR SIDE OF THE STORY! AND YOU THINK WE'RE CRUEL? WELL... HOW ABOUT YOU? I SUPPOSE YOU'RE MERCIFUL WHEN YOU CATCH US!"
A STAKE THROUGH THE HEART! THAT'S THE WAY...
THUDD
CRUUNNCH!
DID YOU EVER TRY TO IMPROVE RELATIONS BETWEEN US? DID YOU? NO! BUT WE ARE GOING TO! WE'LL MAKE THE FIRST STEP TOWARD COOPERATION! JUST WAIT TILL YOU HEAR ABOUT OUR NEW IDEA!
"THAT'S WHAT I WANT TO TELL YOU ABOUT... THAT NEW IDEA! YOU SEE, IN THE PAST WHEN WE LEFT A...ER...A DINING COMPANION... WE NEVER TOOK ANY MONEY!"
WHAT'S THE GOOD OF MONEY TO US!
NO... HEH... HEH... HEH... PLACE TO SPEND IT IN OUR NEIGHBORHOOD!
"THEN ONE NIGHT I GOT THE IDEA! IT WAS DURING THE LAST WAR... AND WE FELT THE STRAIN, TOO! WITH SO MANY WOUNDED AND DEAD, EVEN OUR BLOOD SUPPLY WAS CUT DOWN! WE WERE LOTS MORE ACTIVE, AND HAD TO GO PLACES WE'D NEVER SEEN BEFORE!"
DO YOU SEE IT? IT--- IT'S A WONDERFUL IDEA!
3

"FROM THEN ON WE TOOK ALL THE MONEY WE COULD! OUR SUPPLY GREW... AND GREW... AND GREW!"
FINALLY WE HAD ENOUGH! OF COURSE, WE COULDN'T WORK DIRECTLY OURSELVES ...SO WE HIRED ONE OF YOUR KIND!
YES, SIR! I UNDERSTAND YOU PERFECTLY. A VERY SOUND IDEA. I'LL BE HAPPY TO WORK FOR YOU... AT THE...ER...SALARY YOU STATED!
"YES...OF COURSE IT WAS BLOOD MONEY---"
COME ON, STEP ON IT! AND MAKE SURE YOU GET EVERYTHING DONE ACCORDING TO SPECIFICATIONS!
"AFTER THE BUILDING WAS UP THE PIPES WERE LAID... AND WE WERE JUST ABOUT READY..."
THIS IS THE CRAZIEST JOB I EVER SAW! WHAT ARE YOU...?
NEVER MIND! YOU JUST FOLLOW INSTRUCTIONS. THEY'RE PLAIN ENOUGH!
"YES...IT'S ALL OURS. OUR BANK. YOU MAKE YOUR DEPOSITS... AND YOU GET PAID! A VERY FRIENDLY ARRANGEMENTS!"
I SURE CAN USE THAT DOUGH! AND YOU GUYS CERTAINLY PAY MORE THAN THE OTHER BLOOD BANKS!
I'M GLAD YOU'RE SATISFIED SIR! AND... IT'S IN A GOOD CAUSE... A...ER... AHEM... VERY GOOD CAUSE!
"GET THE IDEA? IT'S SO NICE AND CIVILIZED NOW! PAINLESS... AND NO MORE HARD FEELINGS! SCIENTIFIC, TOO... EXCEPT THAT INSTEAD OF BEING KEPT IN ORDINARY CONTAINERS, THE BLOOD IS STORED IN A HUGE RESERVOIR---"
VAMPIRE STATE BLOOD BANK RESERVOIR
4

"BENEATH THE RESERVOIR ARE THE PIPES---LEADING DOWN --DOWN--DOWN--"
"---AND THE PIPES LEAD TO FAUCETS!"
SCIENCE, PROGRESS! ISN'T IT WONDERFUL? NO MORE SKULKING IN DARK ALLEYS ON COLD NIGHTS---NO MORE SHRIEKS OF TERROR WHEN PEOPLE SEE US!
"OF COURSE, IT HAS MINOR DRAWBACKS. IT ALL COMES SO EASILY, WE HAVE A TENDENCY TO OVER EAT---AND WE STILL DON'T HAVE ENOUGH WILL POWER TO DIET! OUR LITTLE HOUSES ARE GETTING TOO LITTLE FOR US!"
JUST AWFUL, THE WAY WE PUT ON WEIGHT--- BUT WITH SCIENCE TO HELP--WHAT DIFFERENCE? I'M SURE WE CAN EMPLOY CARPENTERS TO MAKE NEW HOMES--WITH WINDOWS --AND MAYBE EVEN FANS! IT'S A WHOLE NEW AGE, AND HAS TREMENDOUS POSSIBILITIES!
YOU SEE... NOW WE CAN BE FRIENDS! WE'RE TRYING SO HARD... WON'T YOU CO-OPERATE? INVITE US TO YOUR HOME... NOT FOR DINNER... OF COURSE... WE CAN ...HEH...HEH... BRING OUR OWN ... JUST A SOCIABLE EVENING... LIKE FRIENDS!
THIS IS A PUBLIC SERVICE LEAFLET, PUT OUT BY THE COMMITTEE TO IMPROVE RELATIONS BETWEEN HUMANS AND VAMPIRES! INVITE A VAMPIRE TO YOUR HOUSE! AFTER ALL, WE ARE BLOOD BROTHERS! PLEASE PASS THIS ON TO A PUBLIC SPIRITED FRIEND WHEN YOU HAVE FINISHED READING IT!

STOP SMOKING

TOBACCO COUGH—TOBACCO HEART—TOBACCO BREATH—TOBACCO NERVES...
NEW, SAFE FORMULA HELPS YOU BREAK HABIT IN JUST 7 DAYS

No matter how long you have been a victim of the expensive, unhealthful nicotine and smoke habit, this amazing scientific (easy to use) 7-day formula will help you to stop smoking—IN JUST SEVEN Days! Countless thousands who have broken the vicious Tobacco Habit now feel better, look better—actually feel healthier because they breath clean, cool fresh air into their lungs instead of the stultifying Tobacco tar, Nicotine, and Benzo Pyrene—all these irritants that come from cigarettes and cigars. You can't lose anything but the Tobacco Habit by trying this amazing, easy method—You Can Stop Smoking!

HOW HARMFUL ARE CIGARETTES AND CIGARS?

Numerous Medical Papers have been written about the evil, harmful effects of Tobacco Breath, Tobacco Heart, Tobacco Lungs, Tobacco Mouth, Tobacco Nervousness... Now, here at last is the amazing easy-to-take scientific discovery that helps destroy your desire to smoke in just 7 Days—or it won't cost you one cent. Mail the coupon today—the only thing you can loose is the offensive, expensive, unhealthful smoking habit!

• YOU CAN STOP

- Tobacco Nerves STOP
- Tobacco Breath STOP
- Tobacco Cough STOP
- Burning Mouth Due To Smoking STOP
- Hot Burning Tongue Due To Smoking STOP
- Poisonous Nicotine Due To Smoking STOP
- Tobacco expense

SEND NO MONEY

Aver. 1½-Pack per Day Smoker Spends $125.90 per Year

Let us prove to you that smoking is nothing more than a repulsive habit that sends unhealthful impurities into your mouth, throat and lungs... a habit that does you no good and may result in harmful physical reactions. Spend those tobacco $$$ on useful, healthgiving benefits for yourself and your loved ones. Send NO Money! Just mail the Coupon on our absolute Money-Back Guarantee that this 7-Day test will help banish your desire for tobacco—not for days or weeks, but FOREVER! Mail the coupon today.

ATTENTION DOCTORS:

Doctor, we can help you, too! Many Doctors are unwilling victims to the repulsive Tobacco Habit. We make the guarantee to you, too, Doctor. (A Guarantee that most Doctors dare not make to their own patients)... If this sensational discovery does not banish your craving for tobacco forever... your money cheerfully refunded.

YOU WILL LOSE THE DESIRE TO SMOKE IN 7 DAYS... OR NO COST TO YOU

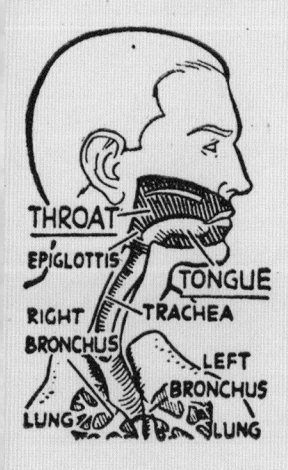

Here's What Happens When You Smoke...

The nicotine laden smoke you inhale becomes deposited on your throat and lungs... (The average Smoker does this 300 times a day!) Nicotine irritates the Mucous Membranes of the respiratory tract and Tobacco Tar injures those membranes. Stop Tobacco Cough, Tobacco Heart, Tobacco Breath... Banish smoking forever, or no cost to you. Mail the coupon now.

Don't be a slave to tobacco.... Enjoy your right to clean, healthful, natural living. Try this amazing discovery for just 7-Days.... Easy to take, pleasant, no after-taste. If you haven't broken the smoking habit forever... return empty carton in 10 Days for prompt refund. Mail the coupon now.

STOP SMOKING—MAIL COUPON NOW!

NO SMOK COMPANY, Dept HNS
400 Madison Ave., N.Y. 17, N.Y.

SENT TO YOU IN PLAIN WRAPPER

On your 10 day Money-back Guarantee, send me No Smok Tobacco Curb. If not entirely satisfied I can return for prompt refund.

☐ Send 7-Day Supply. I will pay Postman $1.00 plus Postage and C.O.D.
☐ Enclosed is $1.00 for 7-Day Supply. You pay postage costs.
☐ Enclosed is $2.00 for 25-Day Supply for myself and a loved one. You pay postage costs.

NAME _____
(Please Print)
ADDRESS _____
TOWN _____ ZONE ____ STATE _____

READ THESE EXCITING MYSTERY MAGAZINES
BLACK CAT
...THE BEST IN SHOCK MYSTERY!
EACH ONE WRITTEN WITH THE EXPERT TOUCH OF MASTER STORY TELLING!
CHAMBER OF CHILLS
GRAVE'S END!
...TALES OF EVER-MOUNTING TENSION!
... STORIES OF FANTASTIC FRENZY!
... EXPLODING INTO THE UNKNOWN!
...HILARIOUS TALES THAT ARE DIFFERENT!
WE DARE YOU
WITCHES TALES
WEIRD YARNS OF UNSEEN TERROR
TALES OF HORROR IN OTHER WORLDS!
TOMB OF TERROR
GOING, GOING, GONE!
HUMOR BREWED IN A CRACKED POT
FLIP
NOW ON SALE AT YOUR FAVORITE NEWSSTAND!

YOU'LL FLIP YOUR LID WITH LAUGHTER AT THIS ZANIEST BOOK OF THE YEAR!
HA-HO
HE-HO
HA-HA
HA-HO
HO-HA
FLIP HUMOR BREWED IN A CRACKED POT
FLIP
HANG AROUND, CHUM---AND YOU'LL FLIP, TOO!
It's crazy man real crazy!
NOW ON SALE!

LIVE TOY CIRCUS
With Performing CHAMELEON -- FREE!

only $1.00

Now, — for the first time ever — you can have a real live circus of your own. Just dozens of fine toys, each wonderful in itself, make up this circus set for the "Greatest Show on Earth." You and your friends can have hours of fun setting up the props for the circus, placing the Ringmaster, clowns, performing animals, and wild animal cages for the many exciting acts. You can even put on a real live trained animal act with the live, performing chameleon who will walk a tight rope, swing on a trapeze and change color right before your eyes from bright green to brown and back again.

Just look at all the things you get for only $1.00. Big Circus Ring, Wild Animal Cages, colorful plastic animals, Kangaroo with baby in pouch, clowns, Ringmaster, Chameleon Leash and Halter, Performing Platform, Tight Rope and Poles, Trapeze, 27 Wonderful pieces in all PLUS — FREE — THE LIVE PERFORMING CHAMELEON, who will not only act in your circus but will make a fine pet too.

Order today at our risk. If you are not satisfied that here is the best toy — the most fun ever — then just return it after 10 days free trial for a full refund of the purchase price — and keep the Chameleon as our gift to you.

ALL THIS INCLUDED FOR ONLY $1.00

15 animals from our wide assortment including Clowns, Bears drinking a bottle of milk, Bunnies, Elephants, Horses, Lions, Tigers, Kangaroos, Monkeys, Deer, Flying Fish, Giraffes, Pelicans and other birds. 10 are made of bright, colorful break-resistant plastic.

- 3 Cages on Wheels
- 1 Tightrope
- 1 Ring Master with Whip
- 15 Circus Animals
- 1 Trapeze
- 1 Circus Ring
- 2 Clowns
- 1 Chameleon Leash and Halter
- 1 Performing Platform
- 1 Set Poles for Tightrope

You get 27 pieces in all, including simple instructions ... AND the LIVE CHAMELEON FREE!

Honor House Products Corp. 15th FLOOR
1860 BROADWAY N.Y. 23, N.Y. DEPT. 34

Rush my Live Toy Circus and FREE Performing Pet Chameleon at once. If I am not 100% delighted I may return it after 10 days free trial for prompt refund of the full purchase price and keep the Chameleon as a gift.

☐ I enclose $1.00 in full payment. The Honor House Products Corp. will pay postage.

☐ Send C.O.D. I will pay postman on delivery plus a few cents postage.

NAME_____
ADDRESS_____

LIVE Performing Chameleon included FREE

Chameleons are real fun. They love to perform. You'll laugh with delight as they run with delicate balance along the tight rope or swing on the trapeze. They are harmless, clean and no trouble at all to keep as pets. Your friends will really gape with surprise when they see him riding on your shoulder. Your parents will be charmed with this small, clean pet. You'll love him. Sold normally for about 75¢, you get this live chameleon FREE with the purchase of your Toy Circus.

Here is our offer. Send us your order for the Live Toy Circus Today. We will send you one of these cute, harmless, performing pet chameleons free with each order. You pay only $1.00 and you must be 100% delighted or your money back.

COMPLETE BAFFLING MAGIC OUTFIT
20 First Class Illusions

BE A MAGICIAN — FOOL AND DELIGHT THEM WITH A FULL 2 HOUR MYSTERY SHOW

Only $1

ROPE TRICK—Cut it in half, yet it is still in one piece and other surprises—yours only with this offer.

GRAVITY—Defy scientific laws. Seeing is believing. You'll fool them plenty when you know how.

MAGIC MIRROR—Spectators will be amazed. With it you read cards, without even looking at them.

FLYING QUARTER—Here's one you can do over and over again and make all the guessers look foolish.

Now the top secrets of 20 professional magic tricks are yours to entertain and amaze your friends and make you popular. With this outfit you get 20 exclusive tricks and the secret knowledge of how to easily perform them all for only $1.00.

You Alone Will Know These Revealing Secrets

Imagine, by just waving your magic wand and shouting a few magic words you will be able to make things disappear and reappear... imagine your friends and mother and dad all being fooled, surprised and amazed. You'll hold them spell-bound. They will just sit open mouthed with wonderment. They'll be delighted, for it's a barrel of fun for everyone. It's so fascinating and thrilling. BUT the hidden secrets will be yours, never to reveal. Follow the simple directions and no one will ever catch on.

No Experience Necessary

The illustrated instructions furnished are so simple you will master all these tricks at once. It's fun practicing too for here you have a short cut to magic learning that starts you doing tricks right away. You can't go wrong... it's as easy as A, B, C's... AND... the set of 20 exclusive tricks is almost a gift at this limited offer price of $1.00.

10 DAYS FREE TRIAL

You'll agree this 20 piece Magic Set is worth much more than our bargain price of $1.00, and it is. We want new friends for our other novelty bargains. We want you to try the set, follow the instructions and if not 100% delighted, return it after 10 days free trial for prompt refund of your dollar. Act at once. Sorry, only three to a customer.

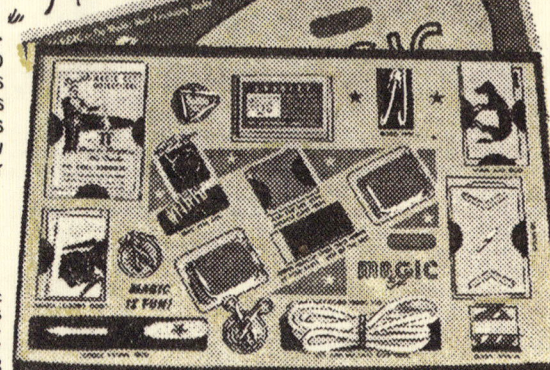

ALL THESE 20 TRICKS INCLUDED
- CUT AND RESTORED ROPE
- FAMOUS PADDLE TRICK
- RING ON STRING
- VIS-ESCAPE
- MAGIC PINS
- RING AND COIL
- GRAVITY DEFYER
- MAGIC MIRROR
- HORSE AND RIDER
- CHINESE LAUNDRY TICKET
- MIRACLE COIN TRICK
- QUESTION MARK
- GRAPPLES
- TWISTER TRICK
- MASTER CARD LOCATION
- PLUS 5 CUT-OUT TRICKS

And special illustrated secret instruction booklet

RUSH COUPON — MONEY BACK GUARANTEE

Honor House Products Corp M-319
351 Wilbur Street, Lynbrook, L. I.
Rush my Baffling Magic Outfit on approval for only $1.00. If I am not completely satisfied I may return it after 10 days free trial for prompt refund of full purchase price.

Name ....
Address ....

☐ Send C.O.D. I will pay postman $1 on delivery plus a few cents postage
☐ I enclose $1 for my MAGIC OUTFIT. The Honor House Products Corp. will pay postage. Same money back guarantee.

NO MATTER HOW YOU JUGGLE THE FIGURES, IT STILL ADDS UP TO...

CREDIT AND LOSS

DEPOSITS	WITHDRAWAL	CREDIT	LOSS
		2.00	
10		.50	
10		1.00	
10			
100			
10			
100			
10			
100			
10			

EVER SEE AN OLD VICTROLA WITH ITS HAND-WINDING JACK AND STEEL FUNNEL? PICTURE YOURSELF A RECORD PLAYING ON IT THAT GETS STUCK IN ITS GROOVE. PICTURE YOURSELF THE END-RESULT. IT LOOKS SOMETHING LIKE THIS...

...I LOVE YOU... LOVE YOU... LOVE YOU... LOVE YOU... LOVE YOU... LOVE YOU... LOVE...

NOW PICTURE YOURSELF ANOTHER FUNNEL... SOMETHING LIKE AN OLD VICTROLA... *DEFINITELY* LIKE A RECORD GETTING STUCK IN ITS GROOVE, TALKING OVER AND OVER AGAIN...

YOU HAVE TO DEPOSIT... TO DEPOSIT... TO DEPOSIT... TO DEPOSIT... TO DEPOSIT...

--AND YOU'LL GET AN IDEA OF WHAT MARTHA PERT SOUNDED LIKE TO HER EVER-SUFFERING SPOUSE, OSCAR PERT!

WHY CAN'T YOU EVER GET IT INTO YOUR THICK-SKULL! MONEY IS MADE TO BE DEPOSITED INTO THE BANK.

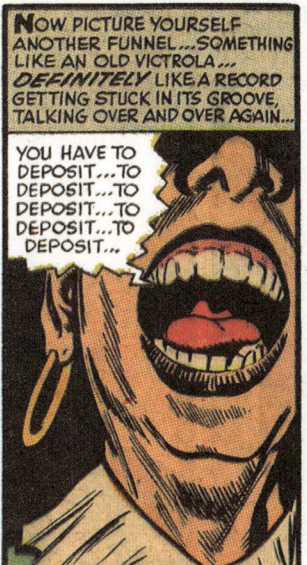

YES, DEAR... YES DEAR..!

DON'T "YES DEAR" ME, STUPID! USE YOUR BRAINS -- IF YOU HAVE ANY! LISTEN TO ME FOR A CHANGE!
Y-YES DEAR...
CRASH!
OH--H! YOU'RE HOPELESS! YOU'RE ABSOLUTELY A WORTHLESS, SHIFTLESS, NO-GOOD, ROTTEN LITTLE FOOL!
YES, DEAR...
BUT BEHIND OSCAR PERT'S MEEK EXTERIOR LURKED A MAN WHO LIKED PEOPLE, HAD AMBITION, AND LOVED HIS JOB. ONLY--THERE CAME A DAY WHEN EVEN THAT WAS TOO LATE...
TOO BAD ABOUT OSCAR PERT. I HEAR THE BOSS IS SET TO FIRE HIM.
YEAH! IT... IT'S HAPPENING ALL OVER!
OSCAR TOOK IT VERY HARD WHEN HE LOST HIS JOB. NOW HE WENT TO WORK AT A FACTORY, BUT WHAT MADE IT EVEN MORE OF A TERRIBLE LOSS WAS HIS GRADUAL LOSS OF FRIENDS...
SORRY, OSCAR... BUT WE... THAT IS -- THE BOYS DON'T FEEL YOU QUALIFY AS A MEMBER OF OUR CLUB. WE HAVE DUES TO PAY, YOU SEE -- AND WELL... YOU NEVER SEEM TO HAVE MONEY. YOU UNDERSTAND?
YES... I SUPPOSE SO, HARRY..!
AND WHY DID ALL THIS COME ABOUT? WELL -- IT COULD HAVE BEEN ANY ONE OF A NUMBER OF THINGS. BUT OSCAR KNEW ONLY TOO WELL THAT IT WAS ALL BECAUSE OF MARTHA!
HMMMPPF! GOOD RIDDANCE TO BAD RUBBISH, I ALWAYS SAY! YOU DON'T NEED THEM AS FRIENDS! FRIENDS ARE COSTLY... EXPENSIVE!
BUT... I NEED FRIENDS! I WANT THEM!
WHAT?!! TALKING BACK... TO ME?!! YOU WORM! HAVING MONEY IS WHAT COUNTS! RIGHT HERE... RIGHT IN THIS BANK-BOOK! DEPOSITING YOUR MONEY IS THE BEST THING THAT CAN HAPPEN TO ANYONE!
YES, DEAR..!

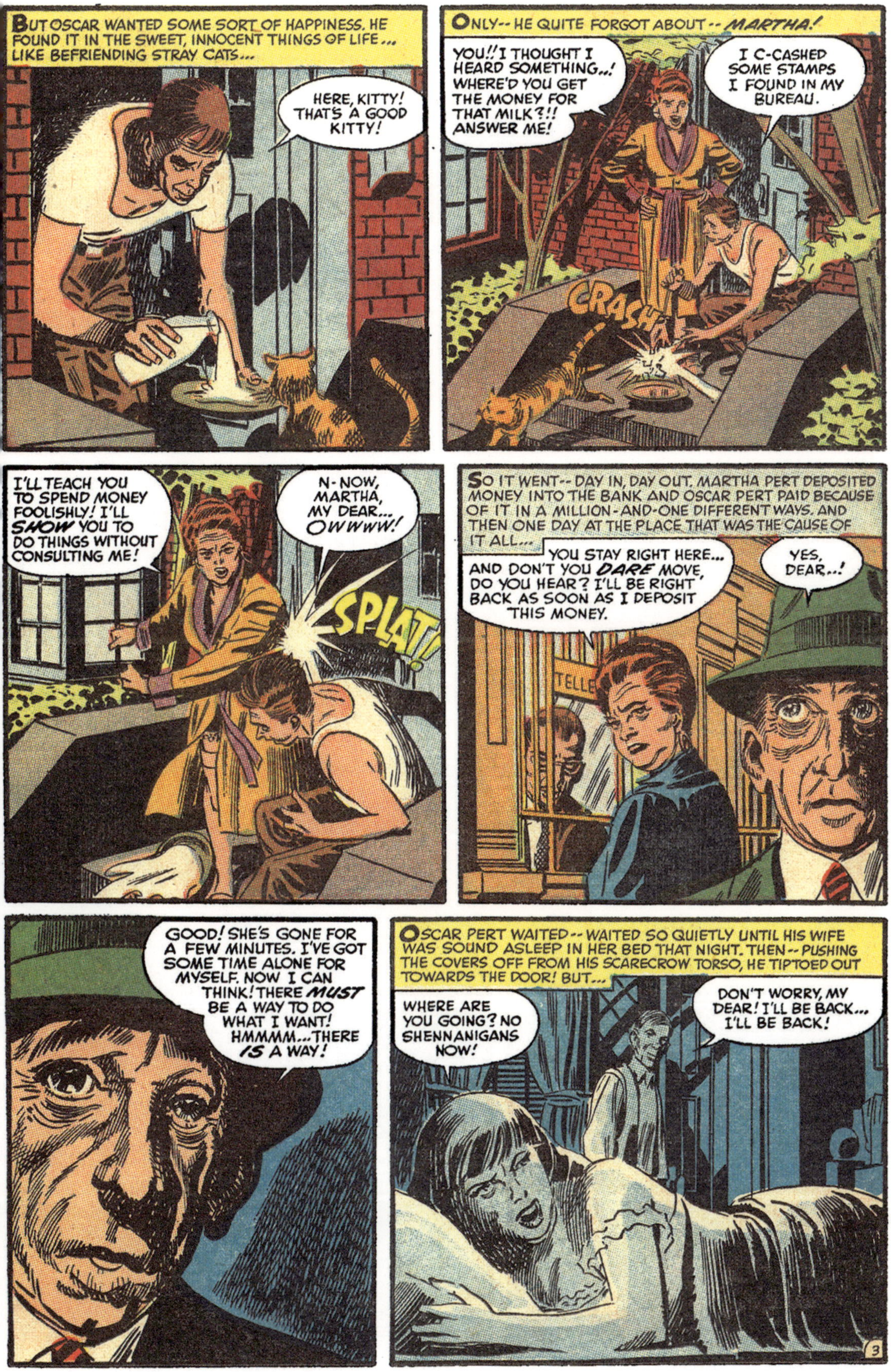

BUT OSCAR WANTED SOME SORT OF HAPPINESS. HE FOUND IT IN THE SWEET, INNOCENT THINGS OF LIFE... LIKE BEFRIENDING STRAY CATS...
HERE, KITTY! THAT'S A GOOD KITTY!
ONLY-- HE QUITE FORGOT ABOUT-- MARTHA!
YOU!! I THOUGHT I HEARD SOMETHING...! WHERE'D YOU GET THE MONEY FOR THAT MILK?!! ANSWER ME!
I C-CASHED SOME STAMPS I FOUND IN MY BUREAU.
CRASH
I'LL TEACH YOU TO SPEND MONEY FOOLISHLY! I'LL SHOW YOU TO DO THINGS WITHOUT CONSULTING ME!
N-NOW, MARTHA, MY DEAR... OWWWW!
SPLAT!
SO IT WENT-- DAY IN, DAY OUT. MARTHA PERT DEPOSITED MONEY INTO THE BANK AND OSCAR PERT PAID BECAUSE OF IT IN A MILLION-AND-ONE DIFFERENT WAYS. AND THEN ONE DAY AT THE PLACE THAT WAS THE CAUSE OF IT ALL...
YOU STAY RIGHT HERE... AND DON'T YOU DARE MOVE, DO YOU HEAR? I'LL BE RIGHT BACK AS SOON AS I DEPOSIT THIS MONEY.
YES, DEAR...!
GOOD! SHE'S GONE FOR A FEW MINUTES. I'VE GOT SOME TIME ALONE FOR MYSELF. NOW I CAN THINK! THERE MUST BE A WAY TO DO WHAT I WANT! HMMMM... THERE IS A WAY!
OSCAR PERT WAITED-- WAITED SO QUIETLY UNTIL HIS WIFE WAS SOUND ASLEEP IN HER BED THAT NIGHT. THEN-- PUSHING THE COVERS OFF FROM HIS SCARECROW TORSO, HE TIPTOED OUT TOWARDS THE DOOR! BUT...
WHERE ARE YOU GOING? NO SHENNANIGANS NOW!
DON'T WORRY, MY DEAR! I'LL BE BACK... I'LL BE BACK!
3

AND WHILE THE MOUNTAIN QUIVERED AND FUMED INSIDE HER ROOM, MAHOMET WORKED IN THE CELLAR EVERY NIGHT FOR A FEW MINUTES, PLANNING HERE, PENCILING THERE...
SHE...DOESN'T SUSPECT. HEH! HEH! ONE TIME...I'M FOOLING HER!
A GRADUAL CHANGE CAME OVER OSCAR DURING THE WEEKS THAT FOLLOWED. HE LOOKED LESS NAG-RIDDEN...LESS HARRIED. EVEN MARTHA BEGAN TO NOTICE IT...
YOU'RE DISGUSTINGLY HEALTHY! WHAT HAVE YOU BEEN UP TO, YOU WORM? IF YOU'VE BEEN SPENDING MONEY, I'LL..!!
TUT, TUT, MY DEAR! YOU TAKE MY PAY-CHECK EVERY WEEK, DON'T YOU? WHAT CAN I DO?
AND EVEN AT THE FACTORY, HIS FELLOW-WORKERS NOTICED THE CHANGE...
LA..LA.. DEE...DA... DUM...
HOLY SMOKE! LOOK'T PERT...WHISTLING? ISN'T THAT SOMETHING?!!
THEN ONE DAY HE CAME HOME TO HIS DEEP, DARK SECRET. BUT IT WASN'T A SECRET ANY LONGER...
IT'S NOT HERE! YOU FOUND OUT! YOU TOOK IT OUT OF MY DESK! YOU TOOK IT WHEN I WASN'T LOOKING! YOU TOOK THE ONE THING I COUNTED ON -- TO GET AHEAD!
OF COURSE!
THAT DRAFTING RULER WAS JUST THE THING I NEEDED FOR MY VACATION. I PAWNED IT...SO I WOULDN'T HAVE TO DRAW FROM THE BANK!
YOU...WHAT?!! PAWNED..?!! YOU...TRADED MY DREAMS...FOR YOUR FAT HIDE! TRADED THEM...SO YOU WOULDN'T HAVE TO DRAW FROM THE BANK! YOU... SELFISH COW!!
MARTHA WENT TO BED THAT NIGHT, CONTENTED. BUT A NOISE AWOKE HER...A STRANGE NOISE...
WHERE IS THAT MOUSEY LITTLE PIPSQUEAK? I'LL FIX HIM FOR INTERRUPTING MY SLEEP!
4

MARTHA PUT ON HER ROBE CLUTCHING IT TO HER AS SHE LUMBERED DOWN THE CELLAR STEPS. SHE CALLED OUT FOR OSCAR... BUT HE WAS NOWHERE TO BE FOUND...
OSCAR! OSCAR! WHERE ARE YOU?!!
TICK TICK! TICK! TICK TICK! TICK
THAT'S STRANGE! HE DOESN'T ANSWER. WHAT'S THAT STUPID BOX DOING THERE?!!
MARTHA LOOKED AT THE BOX. THEN, CURIOUSLY, SHE POKED HER HEAD THROUGH THE BOX'S OPENING...
LET'S SEE... WHAT'S INSIDE...!
BOOM!
LATER, OSCAR PERT WENT TO HIS WIFE'S BANK VAULT, DEPOSITING A WRAPPED PACKAGE. HE KEPT UP THE PROCEDURE UNTIL HE AROUSED THE SUSPICIONS OF THE BANK'S OFFICIALS!
AHEM! EXCUSE ME, MR. PERT... BUT HOW IS MRS. PERT?
YES! WE'VE NOT SEEN HER HERE... LATELY
OH, SHE'S FINE... JUST FINE!
DO YOU KNOW, I'VE LEARNED A GREAT LESSON FROM MRS. PERT! THE LESSON OF FRUGALITY... AND THRIFT! THERE IS NOTHING LIKE A DAILY DEPOSIT!
QUITE RIGHT, MR. PERT!
INDEED, MR. PERT! IT SEEMED AS THOUGH YOUR WIFE BELONGED HERE!
NOW... I'M MAKING A DEPOSIT... OF MRS. PERT! HA HA HA HA HA!
THE END

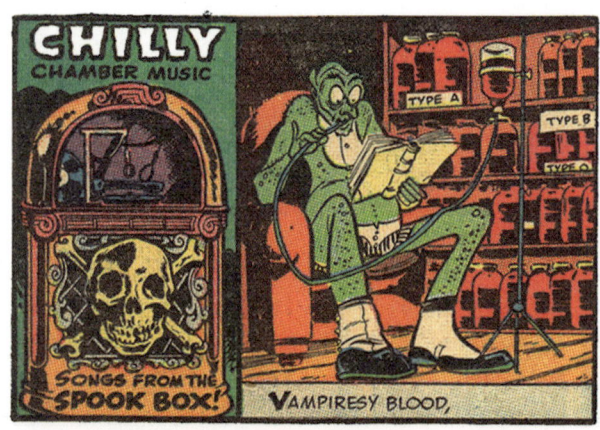

CHILLY CHAMBER MUSIC — SONGS FROM THE SPOOK BOX!

Vampiresy blood,

And ghoulsy blood,

And little ghosts eat ivory!

A mummy'll eat ivory, too, wouldn't you?

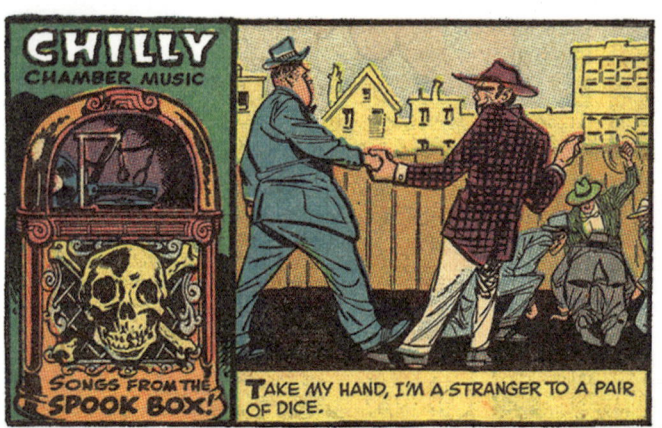

CHILLY CHAMBER MUSIC — SONGS FROM THE SPOOK BOX!

Take my hand, I'm a stranger to a pair of dice.

All lost in a blunderland, a stranger to a pair of dice

So I'll can those dice, I have a pair that are just as nice.

And with them I'll win, 'cause there's a danger to that pair of dice!

196

Investigation

The two little boys stood outside the cottage window, their faces pressed hard against the glass.

"Want to go in?" the one named Michael asked.

"Why not?" his friend Sam answered with a question.

"I-I'd like to," said Michael. "I just wonder what would happen if she caught us."

"Aw, she won't be back for a long time," said Sam. "C'mon, gimme a boost. I'll open the window in a jiffy."

Sam climbed on his friend's shoulders. He made quick work with the window and moments later the two boys were inside the cottage.

"Some miserable layout, huh?" Sam said with a grunt. "Dirty as all get-out."

"D-do . . . do you think it looks like the house of a witch?" Michael almost had to drag out the words.

Sam tried to sound brave. "Never having been in a house of a witch," he said with a smile, "I really wouldn't know."

"No kidding, Sam. Do you think the old lady's a witch?"

"Course not," said Sam. He really wasn't at all sure, but this was a big chance to show a bravery to his slightly timid friend.

"But why do the people keep calling her a witch, Sam? Maybe they know something they haven't told us?"

"I don't know. But we can look this place over and come to our own answers. Let's go, Michael."

The two boys started the investigation. They opened a closet and a broom fell out. It was a different kind of broom to them. It wasn't neat and clean like their mothers'. It had uneven straws that bent to different directions. There was an ugly smell that engulfed the entire broom.

"Do you think? . . ." Michael started.

"Maybe. But we'll have to see more."

Suddenly a rat darted by their path. They fell back. Then they fell back again. A black cat followed the rat.

"What do you think now?" Michael whispered.

Sam didn't answer. His eyes had caught some weird figurines that were standing on the table. He walked over to them. There was one of the devil, one of an ogre, one of the two-headed Janus, many different horrible distorted figures that defied description.

"I think she is a wi—"

BLAMMM!

A sudden gun-shot blasted into Sam's words. The two boys froze for a moment. Then they rushed to the door. They opened it and saw the old woman lying in a pool of blood at their feet. She was dead, dead as any human.

Two townsmen, one carrying a rifle, were at the woman's side.

"I guess we were wrong," said the man with the rifle. "But at least it's a load off our minds!"

Sam smiled to himself as he listened. Then he whispered to Michael: "Let's go back when they're not looking, and get those figurines."

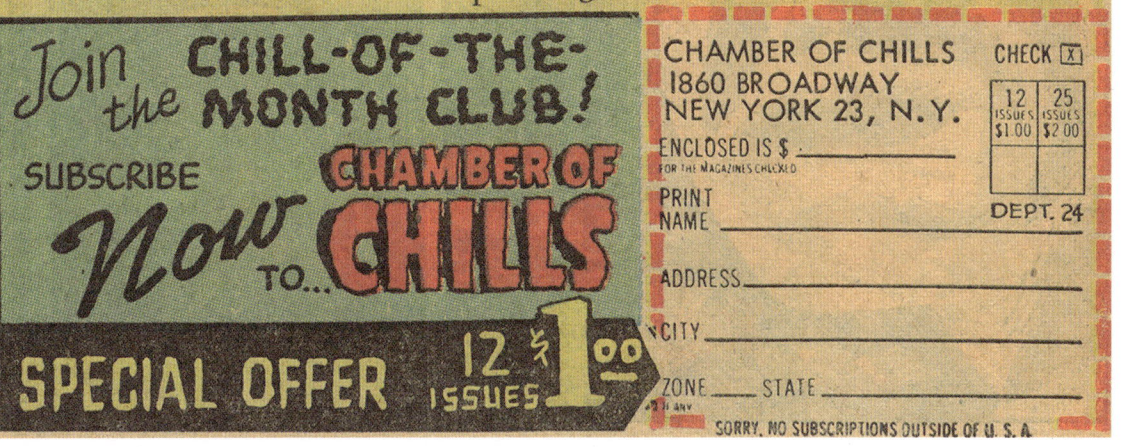

Join the CHILL-OF-THE-MONTH CLUB!
SUBSCRIBE NOW TO... CHAMBER OF CHILLS
SPECIAL OFFER 12 ISSUES $1.00

CHAMBER OF CHILLS
1860 BROADWAY
NEW YORK 23, N.Y.

CHECK [X]

| 12 ISSUES $1.00 | 25 ISSUES $2.00 |

ENCLOSED IS $ _____
FOR THE MAGAZINES CHECKED

PRINT NAME _____
DEPT. 24
ADDRESS _____
CITY _____
ZONE _____ STATE _____

SORRY, NO SUBSCRIPTIONS OUTSIDE OF U.S.A.

GRIM YEARS

HE'LL DIE FOR THEM..

FREEDOM.. AFTER FOURTEEN YEARS IN PRISON!.. AND I WAS INNOCENT.. FOURTEEN YEARS OF MY LIFE'S...

THE HIGH GREY WALLS WERE BEHIND HIM NOW. THE GUARDS WOULD NEVER LOOK IN HIS DIRECTION AGAIN. HE WOULD NO LONGER SEE THE SEARCHLIGHTS. THE FOURTEEN-YEAR TERM IN PRISON WAS OVER. YES, THE ORDEAL WAS FINISHED...

FOURTEEN YEARS! HE'LL PAY FOR EVERY SECOND OF THEM!

THINK BACK TO THE NIGHT OF THE FIRE...
IT'S NO USE! THE PLACE IS GOING TO CAVE IN! STAND CLEAR EVERYONE!
NO! IT CAN'T! NO!
DOWN IT CAME--DOWN WITH A GLARING RED THUNDEROUS ROAR, AND AFTERWARDS--WHEN THE SEARCH PARTY SIFTED THROUGH THE SMOKE AND ASHES, YOU SAW THE CHARRED REMAINS...
THIS BODY WAS DEAD BEFORE THE FIRE! TWO BULLETS IN THE CHEST! RECOGNIZE IT?
BILL! BILL THOMAS--MY PARTNER!
THEY ACCUSED YOU THEN, GRILLED YOU, QUESTIONED YOU, TORTURED YOU IN A DOZEN WAYS. WHY--HOW--WHEN--WHERE--WHY--WHY--WHY--DID YOU KILL HIM? YOU SCREAMED YOUR INNOCENCE IN THE COURT-ROOM LATER, FIGHTING BACK...
I HAVE NO RECOURSE BUT TO SENTENCE YOU TO LIFE-IMPRISONMENT FOR THE MURDER OF YOUR BUSINESS PARTNER!
I DIDN'T DO IT!
PRISON! YEARS AND YEARS AND YEARS. YOUR ATTORNEY WORKING VALIANTLY TO GET A RE-TRIAL. FINALLY--SUCCESS AND RELEASE. FOURTEEN YEARS GONE OUT OF YOUR LIFE. AND NOW YOU'RE BACK FOR--REVENGE!
TELL ME EXACTLY WHERE HE WAS THAT DAY. I'LL PAY YOU WELL!
WELL--HE HAD A DRINK AND THEN HE LEFT.
DAYS OF SEARCH--OF FRUITLESS PURSUIT--WEEKS OF FOLLOWING LEADS, CLUES--MONTHS OF TRACING DOWN THE FACTS. AND FINALLY ONE AFTERNOON, THE JIGSAW PUZZLE FITS INTO PLACE!
"WEALTHY IMPORTER MAKES SENSATIONAL STOCK KILLING! HARRISON COWLES TO OPEN FIRM USING TACTICS OF DEFUNCT COMPANY." AT...LAST!
YOU THINK ABOUT IT--OVER AND OVER AGAIN--LATER IN YOUR ROOM. YOU WANT TO BE SURE--TO TAKE YOUR TIME. YOU HAVE PLENTY OF TIME NOW!
THOMAS PLANTED THE BODY OF SOME UNKNOWN BUM IN OUR OFFICE...SET FIRE TO THE BUILDING...AND VANISHED WITH ALL THE FUNDS. HE LEFT ME HOLDING THE BAG FROM BOTH ENDS--EMBEZZLEMENT AND MURDER! AND--NOW--I'VE FOUND HIM AGAIN.

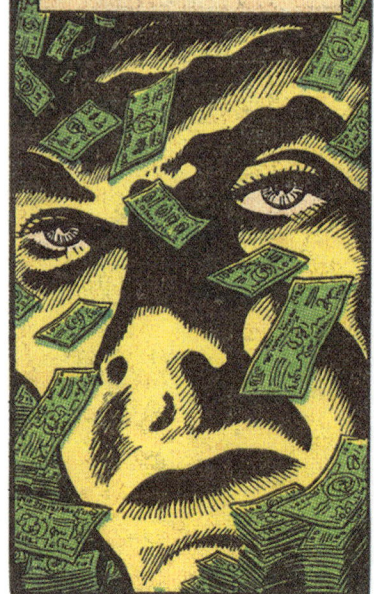

Panel 1: You make your plans. Fourteen years is a long time to pay back a debt, Harrison Cowles! The name mocks you... angers you... *tempts* you into following it--into shadowing him...

He's going home! I'm absolutely certain of it now! Harrison Cowles is-- Bill Thomas!

Panel 2: Then afterwards--in the darkness of protective night--you clinch your suspicions!

There! He's taken off his mask! He's fatter--looking greedier--but still the same Bill Thomas!

Panel 3: Now for your revenge. Now for your slow torture of your enemy. Killing outright is no good, but squeezing him against a wall of fear--IS! And two weeks later, you begin your *revenge*!

I'll cut him out of his business--ruthlessly, cunningly--from all quarters. He'll never know who's doing it. I alone know his methods. And I ALONE will be his judge and executioner!

Panel 4: The months go by. The endless reports and figures and stock quotations of business pile up continuously. Slowly--gradually, you exert a toe-hold into your enemy's business. The toe-hold grows into a firm grip. The firm grip becomes a strangle-hold...

Panel 5: And finally--you have your enemy against a wall of fear! In your new office with your accountant, secretary, typists, assistants about you, you sit back and take stock...

"Your net assets are worth one million dollars, sir. Your stock has a par value of another two million. I should say you're a very rich man!"

"Why-- yes, I am!"

Panel 6: And suddenly the thought comes to you...

I don't WANT Thomas' life anymore! I'm content to let the past die! Strange-- I've worked hard to strangle him-- and I've only become more successful than I could have EVER been!

3

THEN THE *UNEXPECTED* OCCURS! A RUN ON THE MARKET-- SOMEONE HAS CORNERED THE COMMODITY YOU HAVE BEEN SELLING! YOUR PROFITS *MELT* INTO THE GROUND!

STOP! STOP!

YOUR OFFICE BECOMES A JUNGLE OF AGONIZED FEARS! YOUR PANICKY ATTEMPTS TO SELL IN ORDER TO RECOUP YOUR LOSSES LEADS TO-- *DISASTER!*

THE NEWS HAS JUST LEAKED THROUGH, SIR. *WORLD BELMONT* HAS TAKEN OVER CONTROL. IT MONOPOLIZED TRADE *DELIBERATELY!* HARRISON COWLES IS ITS PRESIDENT!

RUINED! AND BY *HARRISON COWLES!*

ONCE IN A LIFETIME CAN BE FORGIVEN-- BUT TWICE DEMANDS *RETRIBUTION!* BILL THOMAS-- ALIAS HARRISON COWLES-- MUST BE *KILLED* LIKE SOME ODIOUS VERMIN. NIGHTS FIND YOU PORING OVER YOUR LAW-BOOKS...

YES... THERE *IS* A WAY! A *FOOLPROOF* WAY!

OPENLY-- YOU VISIT A GUN STORE. OPENLY-- YOU BUY THE GUN WITH THE GREATEST SHOCK-IMPACT VELOCITY SOLD. OPENLY-- YOU MAKE YOUR PLANS...

THOMAS DIES WITHIN A WEEK!

HUH?!!!

CLICK!

IT'S LATE. THE NIGHT IS DARK AND QUIET OUTSIDE THE THOMAS' HOUSE. YOU GRIP THE GUN TIGHTER... AS YOU SEE HIM HUNCHED OVER A DESK, WORKING UNDER A PALE-YELLOW LAMP...

NOW!

201

I'VE WAITED A LONG TIME, BILL! FOURTEEN YEARS, BILL--!
WHAT IS *THIS*? WHAT'S *GOING ON*?!!
BLAM! BLAM! BLAM!
SLOWLY--UNHURRIEDLY, YOU STEP OVER HIS BODY TO PICK UP THE PHONE. OVERHEAD, PANICKY FOOTSTEPS SOUND. THE HOUSE IS WAKENING UP! BUT YOU DIAL, YOUR FINGER FIRM AND UNSWERVING...
THEY SHOULD BE HERE WITHIN MINUTES!
KEEPING THE HOUSEHOLD MEMBERS AT BAY WITH YOUR GUN, YOU CALMLY WAIT UNTIL THE POLICE ARRIVE. THEN--
I KILLED HIM. MY NAME IS WALTER BRAND. HE'S HARRISON COWLES--ALIAS BILL THOMAS. I WAS SENTENCED FOR MURDERING HIM FOURTEEN YEARS AGO. I SERVED MY TIME. AND I CAN'T BE SENTENCED AGAIN FOR KILLING HIM A *SECOND* TIME!
TO PROVE YOUR POINT TO THEM, YOU TUG AT THE DEAD MAN'S FACE FOR THE MASK YOU KNOW HE WEARS. BUT SOMETHING SEEMS TO BE HOLDING IT ON--SOMETHING THAT BRINGS A *CHILL* TO YOUR SPINE!
I...CAN PROVE IT! HE ...WEARS A MASK! LOOK--I..*UGHHH-H*.. IT WON'T COME OFF! HE HAS TO BE HARRISON COWLES ...HE HAS TO BE.!!
WHAT'S HE TALKING ABOUT? WHAT...MASK?!! THIS IS OUR HOUSE!! WE BOUGHT IT!! OH, LORD...THIS MAN'S A...MANIAC! HE KILLED MY HUSBAND...THINKING... THINKING..!! MY GOD! HARRISON COWLES LEFT FOR SOUTH AMERICA...YESTERDAY! DIDN'T HE KNOW THAT?!!
ALL RIGHT! LET'S GO, MISTER!
NO! NO! NO!
YOU HAVE BEEN THE JUDGE, WALTER BRAND. AND YOU THE JUDGE--HAS ALSO BEEN YOUR *EXECUTIONER!*
THE END

400 MOVIE & TV STAR PICTURES
WALLET SIZE — $1.00 POST PAID

A COMPLETE COLLECTION OF ALL YOUR FAVORITES AT A SMALL FRACTION OF WHAT THESE PICTURES WOULD OTHERWISE COST... IF YOU COULD GET THEM! JUST ¼¢ PER PICTURE

Here is a collection of screen favorites that is truly colossal. Large wallet size, beautiful glossy prints perfect for miniature frames, pasting in your album or carrying in your wallet.

Your friends will turn green with envy when they see all these beautiful new photos of filmland's favorites in their latest portraits and informal poses. But this offer is understandably limited to a short time only. Don't delay, fill in the coupon at the bottom of this page and mail it with your $1.00 today. You will receive your 400 star photos by return mail. Remember, this offer is limited — mail your order today!

400 LATEST POSES OF ALL YOUR FAVORITE STARS

FREE BOOKLET
500 Stage and real names of top stars and their birthdays.

Also... 2500 Names and addresses of actors, actresses, and directors, producers, talent scouts.

A real "Who's Who" of Hollywood. This booklet free with each order.

CLIP AND MAIL TODAY
HOLLYWOOD STAR PIX
1860 BROADWAY, NEW YORK 23, N.Y.

Gentlemen: Rush my set of 400 pictures today and also include the free booklet. Send to:

Name _____

Address _____

City _____ Zone ___ State _____

Enclosed is ____ check ____ cash ____ money order.

HOLLYWOOD STAR PIX
1860 BROADWAY, NEW YORK 23, N.Y.

LOOK HERE! for BIG MONEY MAKING OPPORTUNITIES for MONEY-SAVING OFFERS and SERVICES

HELP WANTED

MEN WANTED for jobs on Foreign, Latin America and Far North projects. Truck drivers, $3.55 hour. Electricians, $4.00 hour. Carpenters, $3.70 hour. Laborers, $3.00 hour. Clerks, $3.00 hour. Most all trades wanted. Up to 70 hour week with time and one half for all over 40 hours. Transportation paid. 8 to 24 month contract. Full information of all Firms hiring, living conditions, family accommodation, wages, hours; age, contract requirements, application form, etc, $1.00 Air mail $1.24. Edward O. Burns, 2515 Alden Street, Dept. 37, Dallas 11, Texas.

ANYONE CAN SELL famous Hoover Uniforms for beauty shops, waitresses, nurses, doctors, others. All popular miracle fabrics—nylon, dacron, orlon. Exclusive styles, top quality. Big cash income now, real future. Equipment FREE. State your age. HOOVER, Dept. B-120, New York 11, New York.

AMAZING EXTRA MONEY PLAN gives you gorgeous dress without penny cost Rush name today with dress size. State age HARFORD, Dept. L-6180, Cincinnati 25, Ohio.

EARN EXTRA MONEY Selling Advertising Book Matches. Free sample kit. MATCHCORP, Chicago 32-B, Illinois

ADDRESSING, MAILING Magazines. Samples, 25c. Married, single? PUBLICATIONS. 2272 Hubbard, Memphis 8, Tenn.

BIG Money-making opportunity Exclusive line work uniforms. Jackets, pants. shirts, coveralls Advertising embroidered. Every business prospect Outfit FREE Master Div., 209 Water Ligonier, Ind

MAKE $20-$40 weekly at HOME SPARE TIME MAILERS, 4043 St Clair Ave.. Dept E5. Cleveland, Ohio

BIG MONEY selling waitresses, beauticians, others, guaranteed uniforms $3.98 up Nylons, cottons Sizes 9-52 Free bonus uniform Full, part time Experience unnecessary Free full color catalog. Upland Uniforms 208 East 23rd Dept CB-1 New York

MONEY MAKING OPPORTUNITIES

GROW MUSHROOMS. Cellar, shed, and outdoors. Spare, full time, year round. We pay $3.50 lb. We paid Babbitt $4,165.00 in few weeks. Free Book. Washington Mushroom Ind., Dept. 191, 2954 Admiral Way, Seattle, Wash.

MAKE MONEY INTRODUCING world's cutest children's dresses Big selection, adorable styles. Low prices. Complete display free Rush name. Give age. HARFORD. Dept. L-6394, Cincinnati 25, Ohio.

Sensational New Baby Item Sample 60c Liebig Industries, Beaver Dam 24, Wisconsin

$200 MONTHLY POSSIBLE, raising earthworms! Complete, Illustrated, Instruction Booklet 25c. Ozark Worm Farm-S, Willow Springs, Mo.

EARN BIG MONEY—INVISIBLY REWEAVE damaged garments at home! Details FREE FABRICON, 8332 Prairie, Chicago 19

SCHOOLS—INSTRUCTION

COMPLETE YOUR HIGH SCHOOL AT HOME in spare time with 57-year-old school Texts furnished No classes Diploma Information booklet free American School. Dept X535, Drexel at 58th. Chicago 37, Ill

SIX Algebraic braintwisters solved simply. arithmetically—25c D-20, 6123 Orchard, Dearborn, Mich

SECRETS OF VENTRILOQUISM now revealed! Easy to learn in 60 to 90 days with our Home Study Course Results guaranteed Make Money! Be Popular! Have Fun! Big Opportunity! Radio! Television! Stage Appearances! For FREE Information regarding price and terms. WRITE You must state your age Dummy Catalog 25c FRED MAHER SCHOOL OF VENTRILOQUISM, Box 36, Studio C, Kensington Station, Detroit 24, Mich

PERSONAL

FIND YOURSELF! Take psychological tests at home Receive individualized analysis of your personality, aptitudes abilities Low-cost confidential Details FREE Psychologic Testing Institute Dept 50. 400 N Rush Chicago Illinois

STAMPS and COINS

ALL UNITED STATES STAMPS including those over 100 years old and all foreign including Roosevelts available "On Approval." Send for trial selection. Include 10c for 50 different United States Bargain. GLOBUS, 268 Fourth Ave., New York 10, N. Y., Dept. 609.

We purchase Indianhead pennies. Complete all-coin catalogue 20c. Magnacoins, Box 61-TW, Whitestone 57, New York.

Free Valuable Mystery Gift. Approvals. Raymax, 37-C Maiden Lane, NYC 8.

First U N set. Among World's prettiest. Only 10c. Welles, Box 1246-CG, Church St. Sta.; NYC 38.

107 Iron Curtain Stamps — all different — plus Valuable Illustrated book "How to Recognize Rare Stamps" Only 25c! Other offers included. Kenmore, Milford OH-307, N. H.

Free Surprise Packet with approvals. Fahsing, Dept C, Atascadero, Calif

COLOSSAL STAMP ZOO FREE—Jungle Beasts, Wildlife, fifteen different including Rhinoceros, Snake, Tiger Elephant, Zabu, Koalabear, Kookabura. Extraordinary accompanying approvals. Send 10c for handling Niagara Stamp Co., Niagara-on-the-Lake 538, Canada.

TRICKS—MAGIC—NOVELTIES

PIN-UPS—BIG GLOSSY PRINTS 240 Different Hollywood Models Only $2.00—PIX—Dept. 2-E. Box 1533 Los Angeles 36, Calif.

FREE Catalog Best Magic, Practical Jokes. Top Hat Magic, Evanston 13, Illinois.

MOVIE-TV STAR PICTURES—400 (all different) only $1.00. PIX—Dept 1-E. Box 8635. Hollywood 36, Calif

FOR THIN PEOPLE

DON'T BE SKINNY! New kind of pleasant homogenized liquid super rich in calories. Puts firm flesh on cheeks, bustline, chest, arms, all over body Gains of 20 lbs in 6 weeks reported. Full pint $3.00. If C.O.D. postage extra. Money back guarantee WATE-ON CO., Dept. 116 E, 230 N Michigan. Chicago 1.

HOW TO HYPNOTIZE

IT'S EASY TO HYPNOTIZE...
when you know how!

Want the thrill of imposing your will over someone? Of making someone do exactly what you order? Try hypnotism! This amazing technique gives full personal satisfaction. You'll find it entertaining and gratifying. **HOW TO HYPNOTIZE** shows all you need to know. It is put so simply, anyone can follow it. And there are 24 revealing photographs for your guidance.

SEND NO MONEY

FREE ten days' examination of this system is offered to you if you send the coupon today. We will ship you our copy by return mail, in plain wrapper. If not delighted with results, return it in 10 days and your money will be refunded. Stravon Publishers, **DEPT. H-547** 113 West 57th St., New York 19, N. Y.

Mail Coupon Today

STRAVON PUBLISHERS, Dept. H-547
113 West 57th St., N. Y. 19, N. Y.

Send **HOW TO HYPNOTIZE** in plain wrapper.
☐ Send C.O.D. I will pay postman $1.98 plus postage.
☐ I enclose $1.98. Send postpaid.
If not delighted, I may return it in 10 days and get my money back.

Name ....
Address ....
City .... Zone ...... State ....
Canada & Foreign—$2.50 with order

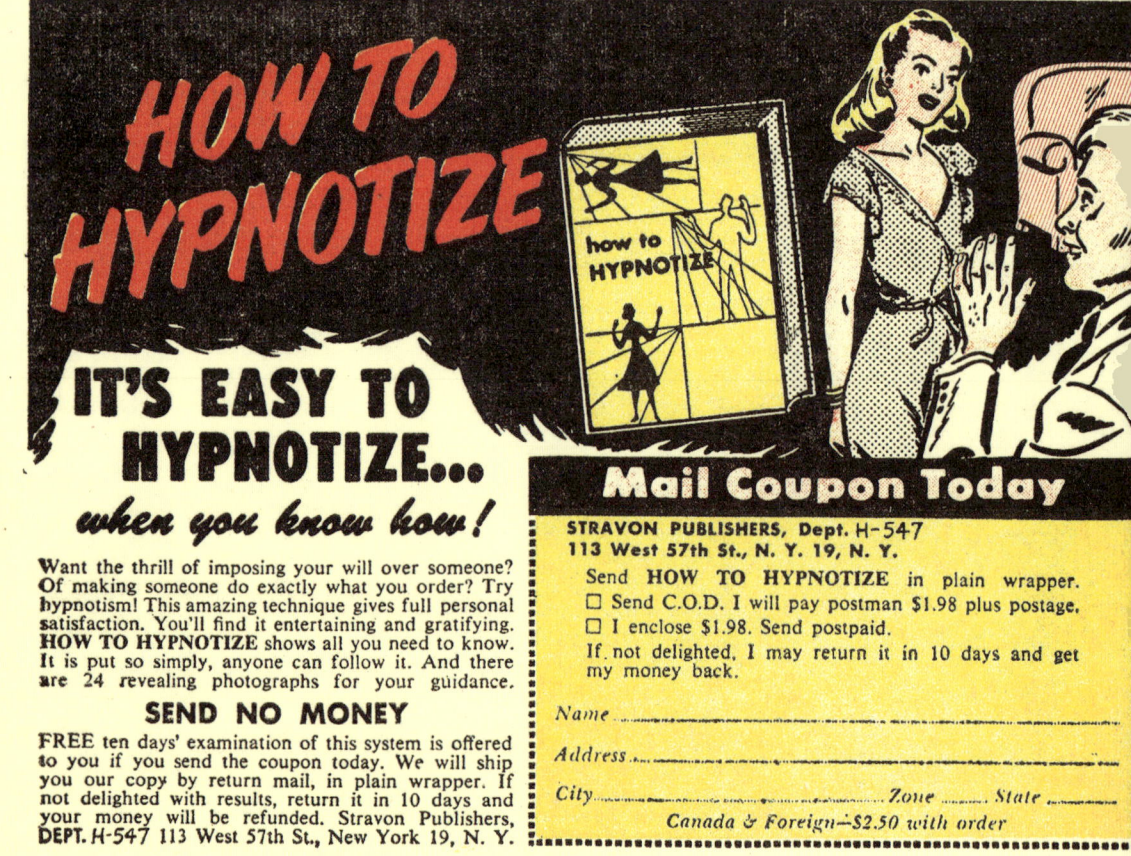

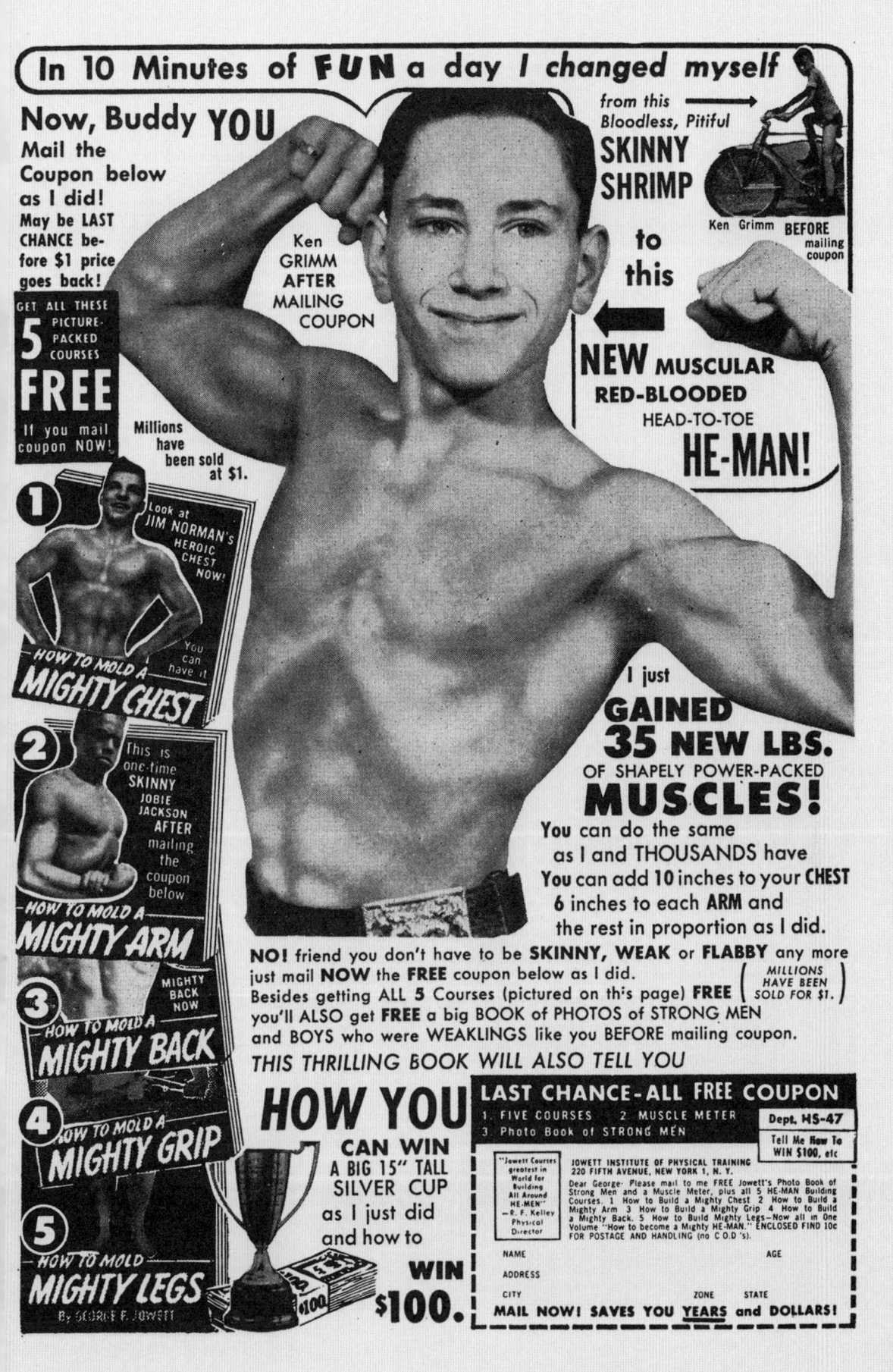

In 10 Minutes of FUN a day I changed myself from this Bloodless, Pitiful **SKINNY SHRIMP** to this **NEW MUSCULAR RED-BLOODED HEAD-TO-TOE HE-MAN!**

Ken Grimm BEFORE mailing coupon

Ken GRIMM AFTER MAILING COUPON

Now, Buddy YOU Mail the Coupon below as I did! May be LAST CHANCE before $1 price goes back!

GET ALL THESE 5 PICTURE-PACKED COURSES FREE if you mail coupon NOW!

Millions have been sold at $1.

1 Look at JIM NORMAN'S HEROIC CHEST NOW! You can have it — HOW TO MOLD A **MIGHTY CHEST**

2 This is one-time SKINNY JOBIE JACKSON AFTER mailing the coupon below — HOW TO MOLD A **MIGHTY ARM**

3 MIGHTY BACK NOW — HOW TO MOLD A **MIGHTY BACK**

4 HOW TO MOLD A **MIGHTY GRIP**

5 HOW TO MOLD **MIGHTY LEGS** By GEORGE F. JOWETT

I just **GAINED 35 NEW LBS.** OF SHAPELY POWER-PACKED **MUSCLES!** You can do the same as I and THOUSANDS have. You can add 10 inches to your CHEST 6 inches to each ARM and the rest in proportion as I did.

NO! friend you don't have to be **SKINNY, WEAK** or **FLABBY** any more just mail **NOW** the **FREE** coupon below as I did. Besides getting ALL **5** Courses (pictured on this page) **FREE** you'll ALSO get **FREE** a big BOOK of PHOTOS of STRONG MEN and BOYS who were WEAKLINGS like you BEFORE mailing coupon. *(MILLIONS HAVE BEEN SOLD FOR $1.)*

THIS THRILLING BOOK WILL ALSO TELL YOU

HOW YOU CAN WIN A BIG 15" TALL SILVER CUP as I just did and how to **WIN $100.**

LAST CHANCE — ALL FREE COUPON
1. FIVE COURSES 2. MUSCLE METER
3. Photo Book of STRONG MEN

Dept. HS-47
Tell Me How To WIN $100, etc

"Jowett Courses greatest in World for Building All Around HE-MEN" — R. F. Kelley Physical Director

JOWETT INSTITUTE OF PHYSICAL TRAINING
220 FIFTH AVENUE, NEW YORK 1, N. Y.

Dear George: Please mail to me FREE Jowett's Photo Book of Strong Men and a Muscle Meter, plus all 5 HE-MAN Building Courses. 1. How to Build a Mighty Chest 2. How to Build a Mighty Arm 3. How to Build a Mighty Grip 4. How to Build a Mighty Back. 5. How to Build Mighty Legs—Now all in One Volume "How to become a Mighty HE-MAN." ENCLOSED FIND 10c FOR POSTAGE AND HANDLING (no C O D 's).

NAME _____ AGE _____
ADDRESS _____
CITY _____ ZONE ____ STATE _____

MAIL NOW! SAVES YOU YEARS and DOLLARS!

I really couldn't blame The Other Girl

It was my own ugly skin that chased him away — but it was a Doctor's Formula that won him back

"Every time I looked in the mirror, I cried a little. I'd see my own awful skin blemishes and then I'd imagine Garth out with her. If only I could have smoother, clearer . . . yes, kissable . . . skin. How I wished I could win Garth back. Then my best friend told me her secret of Dr. Parrish's Double Jar Treatment. A Doctor's Secret, Juel's Be-Gone was such a quick, easy way. Ugly skin goes . . . in its place a new Loveliness . . . a new Life . . . at least that's what it meant for me. Now the skin he was ashamed of is the skin he loves to touch. Garth was mine again . . . completely."

The secret is in the 2 Doctor's Formulas that you, too, can use. Skin specialists agree that externally caused SKIN BLEMISHES CAN BE AVOIDED. They know the formulas and the method. The Doctor's 2 Jar formula was first prescribed in the Doctor's private practice. It worked such wonderful results that the Doctor's patients told their friends. They spread the good word. Now, all you do is follow the Doctor's directions and use these 2 formulas. The entire treatment takes only 3 minutes a day.

1. After you wash your face, you use Juel's Be-Gone Concentrated Special Cleansing Jelly. Your face, like your digestive tract, needs a thorough daily cleansing. Then this wonderful Jelly dissolves dry perspiration, pore clogging dirt, dust, grime. GIVES YOUR PORES A DEEP-CLEANING CONDITIONING.
2. Next . . . apply Juel's Be-Gone Fortified Skin Cream. Your skin needs the DAILY CARE to dry up pimple-causing blackhead plugs and speed healing. This Skin Combination prescribed by the Doctor gives abused neglected skin the special medicated care it needs. Help clean—condition—speed healing. Do this for 7 days. Then LOOK IN YOUR MIRROR. "Mirror, mirror on the wall — who is the fairest one of all?"

You can try Juel's Be-Gone Double Jar Treatment in your own home for a 10 day FREE TRIAL, and see the results on your own face. Imagine, Juel Be-Gone Double Jar Treatment is a formula prescribed by a Doctor, yet you get up to 25 *treatments for only* $2. Send no money, just send your name and address to JUEL COMPANY, DEPT. B, 1735 *West 5th Street, Brooklyn* 23, *N. Y.* NOW. When your Double Jar Treatment with the Doctor's simple, easy Directions is delivered, pay only $2. plus postage and handling charge. (or send $2 cash and you save C.O.D. and handling charges). You must be delighted or you may return it within 10 days and get every penny back — it's absolutely guaranteed. Remember, send your name and address to JUEL COMPANY, DEPT B, 1735 *West 5th Street, Brooklyn* 23, *N. Y.* Act quickly — so you can start sooner. Write Now. While your parcel is on the way to you, be sure to cleanse your face with warm water and rinse it with cold water as often as you can, as soon as you get your two jars — use them and prevent future miseries of bad skin.

* *Another story from the files of Dr. Edward Parrish, M.D., former New York State Health Officer, now consultant on all Juel Products.*

PS Artbooks

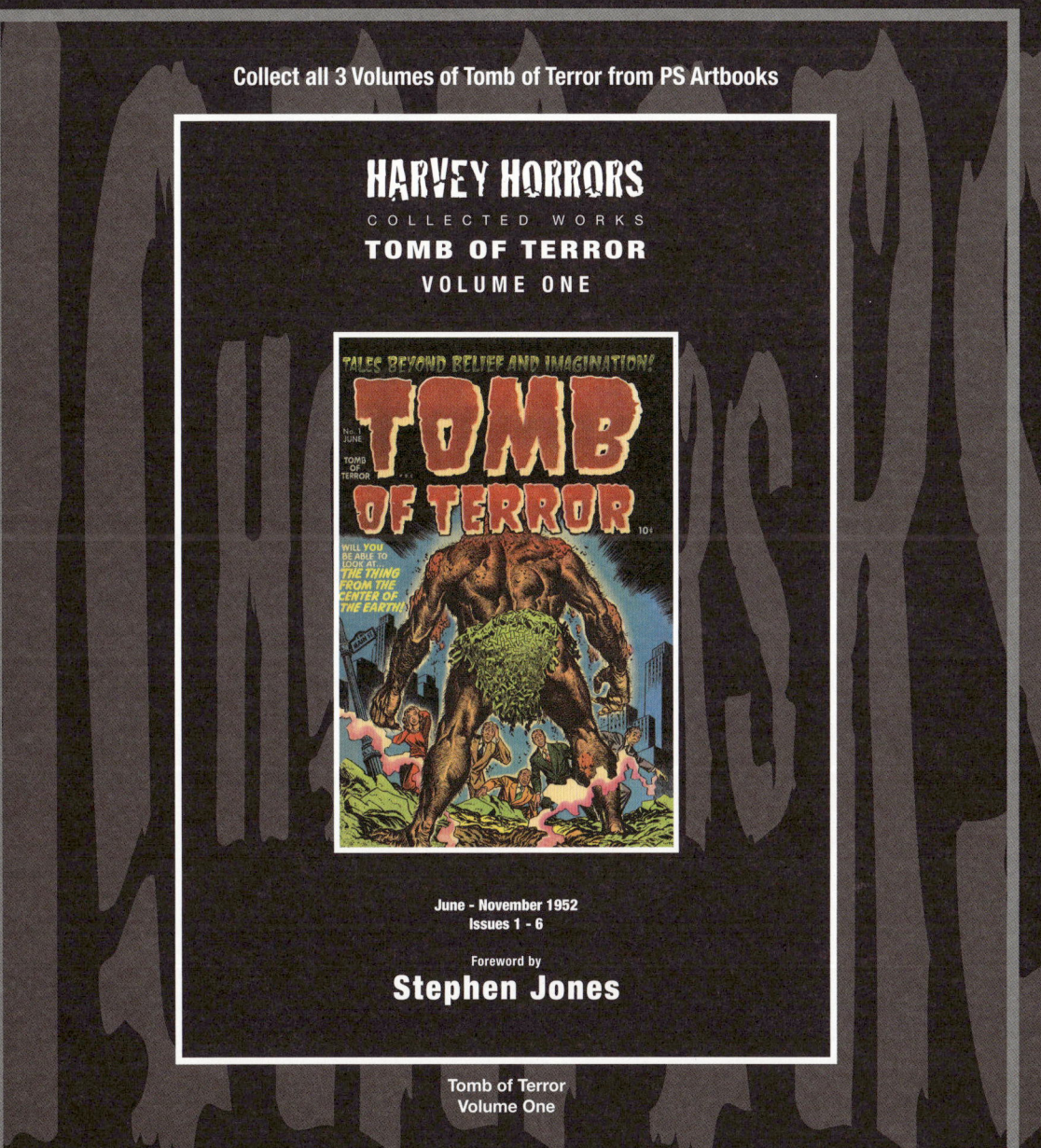

Collect all 3 Volumes of Tomb of Terror from PS Artbooks

HARVEY HORRORS
COLLECTED WORKS
TOMB OF TERROR
VOLUME ONE

June - November 1952
Issues 1 - 6

Foreword by
Stephen Jones

Tomb of Terror
Volume One

Collect the complete library form PS Publishing online 24/7 @ www.pspublishing.co.uk

Chamber of Chills
October 1954 - Issue #25

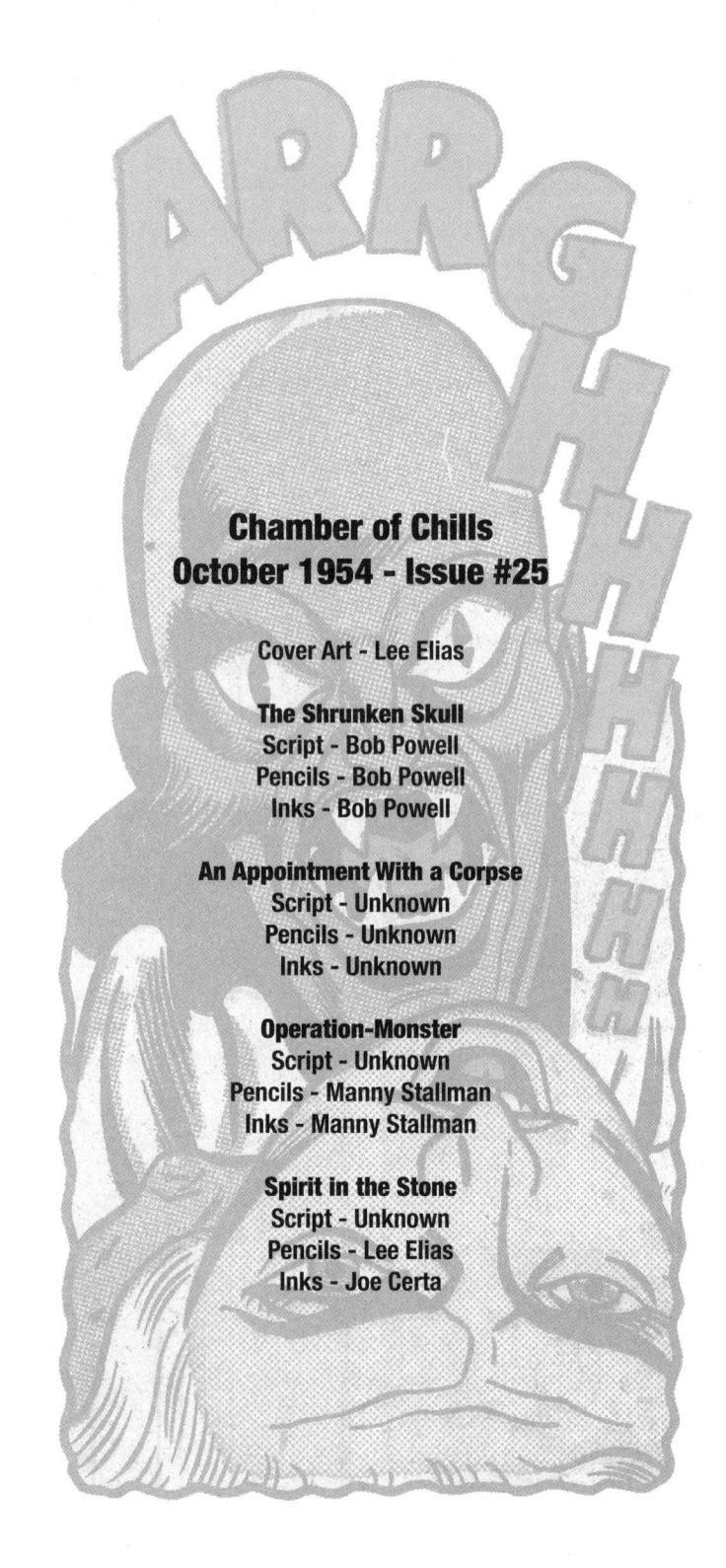

Cover Art - Lee Elias

The Shrunken Skull
Script - Bob Powell
Pencils - Bob Powell
Inks - Bob Powell

An Appointment With a Corpse
Script - Unknown
Pencils - Unknown
Inks - Unknown

Operation-Monster
Script - Unknown
Pencils - Manny Stallman
Inks - Manny Stallman

Spirit in the Stone
Script - Unknown
Pencils - Lee Elias
Inks - Joe Certa

Information Source: Grand Comics Database!
A nonprofit, Internet-based organization of international volunteers dedicated to building a database covering all printed comics throughout the world. If you believe any of this data to be incorrect or can add valuable additional information, please let us know www.comics.org
All rights to images reserved by the respective copyright holders. All original advertisement features remain the copyright of the respective trading company.

Privacy Policy
All portions of the Grand Comics Database that are subject to copyright are licensed under a Creative Commons Attribution 3.0 Unported License.
This includes but is not necessarily limited to our database schema and data distribution format.
The GCD Web Site code is licensed under the GNU General Public License.

BER OF
LLS
TALES OF CHILLS AND SUSPENSE!
No. 25
CHAMBER OF
CHILLS
PDC

Come on, Buddy, Quit being A BAG-of-BONES Weakling like I was

IN 10 MINUTES OF FUN A DAY YOU Can do ALL I did!

I gained **25** Terrific LBS. of **HANDSOME POWER-PACKED MUSCLES** all over!
I improved my **HE-MAN LOOKS 1000%**
I won **NEW STRENGTH** for money-making work! for WINNING at all SPORTS!
I won **NEW POPULARITY** Won NEW FRIENDS, BOYS & GIRLS NEW CHANCES for BUSINESS SUCCESS

BEFORE

Hi Pal! Win $100 as I just did!

"I'm PROUD to be seen with Jim NOW! Everybody admires his build," says Nellie. "Jim can lift the front of a 2700 lb. car. He amazes his friends!"

You'll be A Real ATHLETE in ALL SPORTS Soon after YOU mail Coupon.
Jim is a WINNER in ALL SPORTS NOW. YOU will be, too, soon.

How did I do ALL This? I mailed the Coupon and got These **5** PICTURE-PACKED HE-MAN COURSES
Which YOU can NOW get FREE
BEFORE $1 PRICE GOES BACK
Millions Sold for $1

GET ALL 5 FREE

"I gained 60 lbs. of muscles," says John Sill.
HOW TO MOLD A **MIGHTY CHEST** By GEORGE F. JOWETT ①

"I added 7 inches to my CHEST 3 inches to each ARM," says Jobie Jackson
HOW TO MOLD A **MIGHTY ARM** By GEORGE F. JOWETT ②

HOW TO MOLD A **MIGHTY BACK** By GEORGE F. JOWETT ③

HOW TO MOLD A **MIGHTY GRIP** By GEORGE F. JOWETT ④

HOW TO MOLD **MIGHTY LEGS** By GEORGE F. JOWETT ⑤

YOU CAN WIN a BIG 15" SILVER CUP as I just did! with YOUR NAME engraved on it!

JIM NORMAN AFTER He Mailed Coupon
Below is Cleveland **BEFORE** He Mailed Coupon
90 lb. Skeleton He says, I gained 70 lbs. of mighty muscle

"Congratulations, John! At last you mailed the coupon as EVERY MAN should. Soon You'll be as big and strong as I am," says Jim Norman to John Luckus

COME ON, PAL, NOW YOU give me **10** PLEASANT MINUTES A DAY IN YOUR OWN HOME like Jim did and I'll give YOU A NEW HE-MAN BODY for your OLD SKELETON FRAME

NO! I don't care how skinny or flabby you are I'll make you OVER by the SAME method I turned myself from a wreck to the strongest of the strong. Why can't I do for you what I did for MANY THOUSANDS of skinny fellows like You?

Develop YOUR 520 MUSCLES Gain Pounds, INCHES FAST!

YES! You'll see INCHES of MIGHTY MUSCLE added to your ARMS and CHEST. Your BACK and SHOULDERS broadened. From head to heels you'll gain SIZE, POWER, SPEED. You'll be A WINNER in EVERYTHING you tackle.

Mail the "ALL FREE" coupon get this "AMAZING SECRETS" Photo Book
You'll LOOK, FEEL, ACT, like A Real HE-MAN! Win Women and Men Friends. Win in Sports! Win Promotion, Praise, Popularity.

LAST CHANCE - ALL FREE COUPON

1. FIVE COURSES 2. MUSCLE METER 3. Photo Book of STRONG MEN

Dept. **HS49** Tell Me How To WIN $100, etc.

"Jowett Courses greatest in World for Building All-Around HE-MEN" R. F. Kelley Physical Director

JOWETT INSTITUTE OF PHYSICAL TRAINING
220 FIFTH AVENUE, NEW YORK 1, N.Y.

Dear George: Please mail to me FREE Jowett's Photo Book of Strong Men and a Muscle Meter, plus all 5 HE-MAN Building Courses: 1. How to Build a Mighty Chest. 2. How to Build a Mighty Arm. 3. How to Build a Mighty Grip. 4. How to Build a Mighty Back. 5. How to Build Mighty Legs Now all in One Volume "How to become a Mighty HE-MAN". ENCLOSED FIND 10c FOR POSTAGE AND HANDLING (no C.O.D.'s).

NAME _____ AGE ____
ADDRESS _____
CITY _____ ZONE ___ STATE _____

SAVES you YEARS and DOLLARS!!!

This BOOK will also show You HOW YOU CAN WIN $100.00 and a BIG 15" tall SILVER TROPHY (Your Name On It)

Mail Coupon in Time for FREE offer and PRIZES!

CHAMBER OF CHILLS MAGAZINE, OCTOBER, 1954, Vol. 1, No. 25, IS PUBLISHED BI-MONTHLY by WITCHES TALES, INC., 1860 Broadway, New York 23, N.Y. Entered as second class matter at the Post Office at New York, N.Y. under the Act of March 3, 1879. Single copies 10c. Subscription rates, 10 issues for $1.00 in the U.S. and possessions, elsewhere $1.50. All names in this periodical are entirely fictitious and no identification with actual persons is intended. Contents copyrighted, 1954, by Witches Tales, Inc., New York City. Printed in the U.S.A. Title Registered in U. S. Patent Office.

THE INNER CIRCLE

CHAMBER OF CHILLS
OCT. No. 25

The flames of the fantastic leaps high in the brimstone pit. Again the fuels of suspense and mystery have been fed them. Again, CHAMBER OF CHILLS takes form.

Once again, it is time to take the road of high adventure and travel into the realms of the supernatural.

And it is a strange and exciting road you travel this month, different from anything you have faced before.

You will face the fury of the jungle in the strangest shape it's ever taken in THE SHRUNKEN SKULL!

You will stand high on the top of the tottering trapeze to fulfill APPOINTMENT WITH A CORPSE!

You will go into the inner confines of a weird hospital room and watch with amazement OPERATION MONSTER!

And you will travel to the most occult of caves to witness the reincarnation of the SPIRIT IN THE STONE!

All this and more awaits you now in the eerie route that has been mapped out through the CHAMBER OF CHILLS!

TERRIFIC VALUE!

BE THE FIRST IN YOUR CROWD TO GET THIS SENSATIONAL COLLECTION OF AIRPLANES

AMAZING get acquainted offer! **GIANT COLLECTION** of 40 assorted pieces all yours for only **98¢** TREMENDOUS BARGAIN

Wings away with the new toy sensation. Contains 40 colorful plastic Airplanes. Different styles—Jets, Bombers, DC4's, etc. Ideal for any age group. Full of play value and inexpensive.

LUCKY PRODUCTS   DEPT. H-M9
1860 BROADWAY, NEW YORK 23, N.Y.

Please send me the following. If not delighted my money will be cheerfully refunded.

☐ 40 assorted airplanes. I enclose 98¢.

NAME_____

ADDRESS_____

CITY_____ ZONE_____ STATE_____

Through the *crawling jungle beat* the *drums* of the *living dead*, *ancient rites* are performed by *fetid corpses* guided by a *warped mind* enclosed in...

The SHRUNKEN SKULL

"Twenty five dollars! Going! Going! Gone!! Sold to the man for twenty five dollars. I hope the *mystery box* contains something very valuable, sir..."

Into his apartment, Michael Stearns carried the small box, little knowing the *unearthly horror* of its contents! Slowly he unwrapped it...

"Twenty-five dollars! When will I stop being a sucker for these get-rich-quick schemes of mine?"

213

AAAAH!! IT... IT'S A HEAD! A SHRUNKEN CANNIBAL HEAD!!
MICHAEL CAST THE PUTRID, ONCE HUMAN MASS UPON THE TABLE AND AS HE LOOKED AT IT, IN FEARFUL FASCINATION, THE HORRID FORM SEEMED TO PULSATE WITH LIFE...
THE... THE HAIR! IT... IT'S GROWING! AND THE EYES ARE BLINKING!! OH, NO!! I MUST BE DREAMING...
SLOWLY, THE GROTESQUE MOUTH BEGAN TO OPEN AND SIGH, LIKE THE FLAPPING OF A MILLION PETULANT BAT WINGS IN THE FARTHEST CORNER OF HELL! THEN...
MICHAEL STEARNS--- COME CLOSER AND LISTEN TO MY STORY...
NO!! NO!! I... I MUST BE GOING MAD!
MANY MOONS AGO I WAS A PRIESTESS IN THE SUGALI TRIBE OF THE ORINOCO HEAD-HUNTERS. BUT I WAS IN LEAGUE WITH THE DEVIL-GOD. I HAD POWERS OF EVIL WHICH MADE MY TRIBESMEN FEAR ME...
MICHAEL'S HYPNOTIZED MIND WAS FORCED ACROSS THE SEA AND INTO THE TEEMING JUNGLES TO WITNESS THE SATANIC POWERS OF THE PRIESTESS...
NO! STOP HER!!! SHE IS TURNING MY SON INTO A MONSTER!
SERVANT OF THE DEVIL!! I WILL KILL YOU!!
IT IS DONE! HEHEHE!!! NOW I SHALL RULE WITH MY EVIL POWER... ALL SHALL BOW DOWN TO ME!!
SEIZE HER!!
BRING HER TO THE EXECUTION BLOCK...

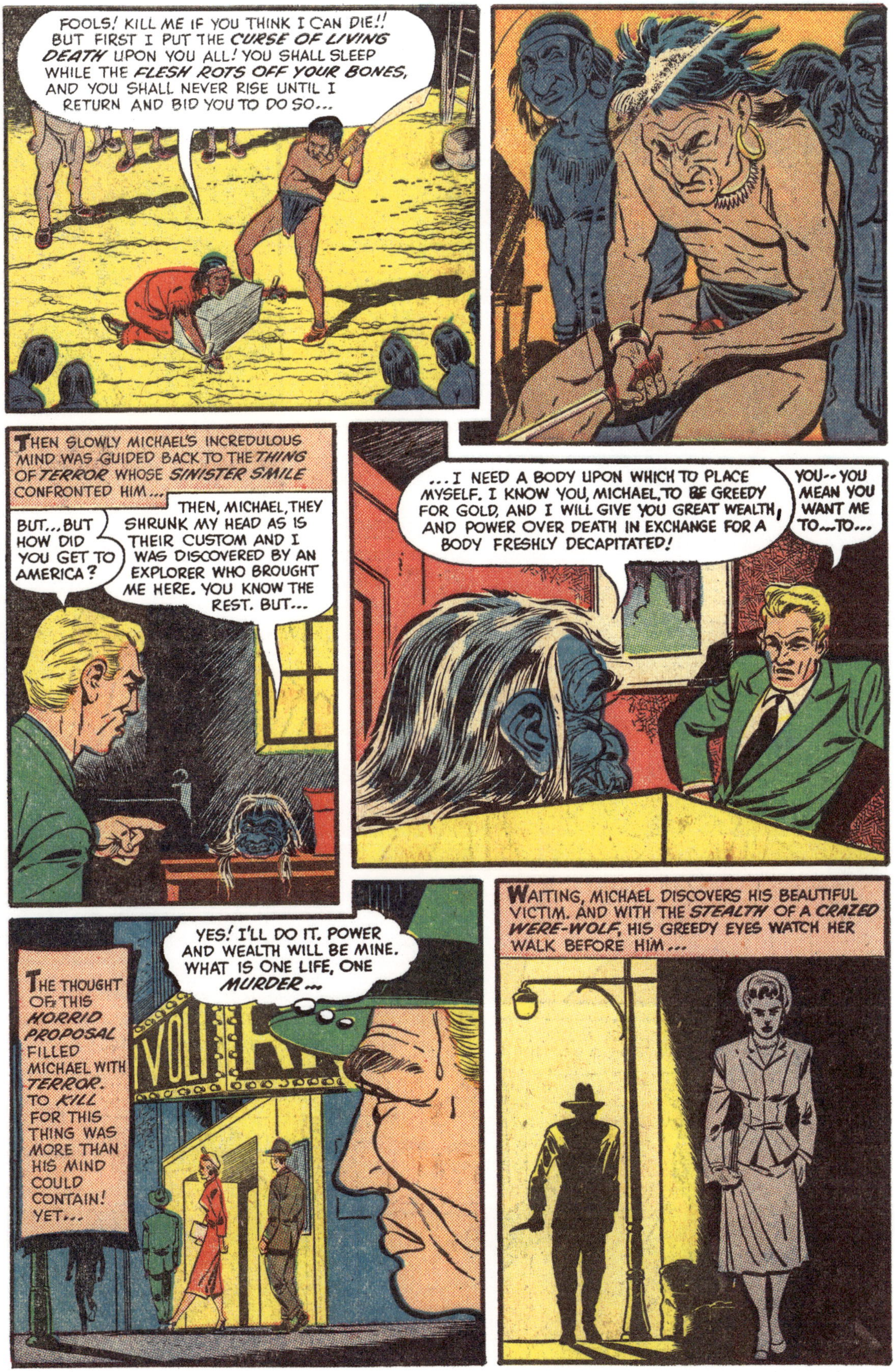
FOOLS! KILL ME IF YOU THINK I CAN DIE!! BUT FIRST I PUT THE CURSE OF LIVING DEATH UPON YOU ALL! YOU SHALL SLEEP WHILE THE FLESH ROTS OFF YOUR BONES, AND YOU SHALL NEVER RISE UNTIL I RETURN AND BID YOU TO DO SO...
THEN SLOWLY MICHAEL'S INCREDULOUS MIND WAS GUIDED BACK TO THE THING OF TERROR WHOSE SINISTER SMILE CONFRONTED HIM...
BUT...BUT HOW DID YOU GET TO AMERICA?
THEN, MICHAEL, THEY SHRUNK MY HEAD AS IS THEIR CUSTOM AND I WAS DISCOVERED BY AN EXPLORER WHO BROUGHT ME HERE. YOU KNOW THE REST. BUT...
...I NEED A BODY UPON WHICH TO PLACE MYSELF. I KNOW YOU, MICHAEL, TO BE GREEDY FOR GOLD, AND I WILL GIVE YOU GREAT WEALTH, AND POWER OVER DEATH IN EXCHANGE FOR A BODY FRESHLY DECAPITATED!
YOU--YOU MEAN YOU WANT ME TO...TO...
THE THOUGHT OF THIS HORRID PROPOSAL FILLED MICHAEL WITH TERROR. TO KILL FOR THIS THING WAS MORE THAN HIS MIND COULD CONTAIN! YET...
YES! I'LL DO IT. POWER AND WEALTH WILL BE MINE. WHAT IS ONE LIFE, ONE MURDER...
VOLI
WAITING, MICHAEL DISCOVERS HIS BEAUTIFUL VICTIM. AND WITH THE STEALTH OF A CRAZED WERE-WOLF, HIS GREEDY EYES WATCH HER WALK BEFORE HIM...

THE UGLY KNIFE DOES ITS BRUTAL WORK...
THAT'S OVER! NOW I MUST GET BACK WITHOUT BEING SEEN...
YOU HAVE DONE WELL!! NOW FOLLOW MY DIRECTION. FIRST YOU MUST PLACE MY HEAD ON THE BODY.
AS THE FOUL HEAD WAS PLACED UPON THE LOVELY BODY, A STRANGE AND WEIRD MOAN WAS HEARD, LIKE A DEMON HOWLING AT THE MOON..THEN...
NOMO OS DIAKETI TIMA!!
EXITIR ACA DIMI!! YA MIYOGURT!!
PUFFF
WHEN THE BLINDING LIGHT DIMMED MICHAEL BEHELD THE GHASTLY APPARITION WHICH HE HAD MURDEROUSLY HELPED TO CREATE...
AIEEEEE!! I...I'VE N-NEVER SEEN ANYTHING SO HORRIBLE!!
OUR WORK HAS JUST BEGUN. WE MUST SAIL FOR MY VILLAGE WHERE I SHALL EXERCISE THE POWERS WHICH ARE MINE BY OCCULT KNOWLEDGE! YOU SHALL MAKE THE ARRANGEMENTS, MICHAEL...

SHE HAS A PRETTY FIGURE ...I WONDER WHAT'S WRONG WITH HER FACE?
SHE'S PROBABLY SOME CELEBRITY AND DOESN'T WANT TO HAVE THE CROWD ANNOY HER. THE STEWARD SAYS SHE'S GOING TO TAKE ALL HER MEALS IN HER CABIN...
PASSENGER
EVERY TIME THAT VEILED WOMAN PASSES I GET A COLD CHILL. IT'S AS THOUGH SOME INVISIBLE FIEND IS RUBBING AGAINST ME...
DO YOU FEEL THAT WAY, TOO? I THOUGHT I WAS IMAGINING THINGS...
AH! AT LAST THE PORT. I CAN FEEL THE EVIL POWERS SURGING WITHIN ME!!! SOON REVENGE AND POWER SHALL BE MINE...
MUST... MUST I GO WITH YOU?
FAR UP THE UNEXPLORED RIVER, FETID WITH THE VENOMOUS, CRAWLING CREATURES OF THE DANK FORESTS, THE TINY BOAT SLITHERED...
THAT POINT UP AHEAD! THAT IS WHERE WE LEAVE THE BOAT!!! OUR JOURNEY IS NEARING ITS END!
I CAN'T WAIT TO LEAVE THIS RIVER. THE LAND CAN'T BE AS BAD AS THIS!!
AAAHHH!!! L--LOOK!! THOSE THINGS!! L--LET'S GET OUT OF HERE!
DO NOT FEAR THEM. THEY ARE CREATURES OF EVIL AND MY FRIENDS! AS LONG AS YOU ARE WITH ME NO HARM WILL COME TO YOU!! ALONE, YOU WOULD HAVE BEEN DEVOURED THE MOMENT YOU SET FOOT IN THE JUNGLE...
MY VILLAGE! AFTER ALL THIS TIME I HAVE RETURNED AS I PROMISED. NOW I SHALL RULE, AND YOU, MICHAEL, SHALL BE REWARDED...
BUT...BUT IT'S DESERTED! THERE'S NOT A LIVING SOUL ANYWHERE NEAR HERE...

BUT THE VILLAGE WAS NOT DESERTED. CAVERNOUS EYES WATCHED WITHOUT SEEING-SKULLS IN A DEATH-LIKE SLEEP OCCUPIED EVERY FILTHY HOVEL...
MY CURSE! IT WORKED!
SKELETONS!! EVERY-WHERE! A WHOLE VILLAGE FULL OF THEM...
NOW TO MAKE THE DEAD RISE!! AID ME YOU EVIL SPIRITS AND CREATURES OF THE FOREST... ARRA BIANITES!! SARTORIS ARTISBY MAKAW LEEY!!
DOSID MAGYOSBAT!!
CLICK
CLACK
RATTLE
AND THEN, ON THAT UNHALLOWED SPOT, APPEARED A SIGHT MORE HORRIBLE THAN DEMON HAD EVER DEVISED...
OH!! HOW HORRID!!! I MUST GET AWAY. NO POWER OR WEALTH IS WORTH THIS...
ACCURSED RACE!!! NOW DO MY BIDDING. DANCE!!!! DANCE THE DANCE OF THE LIVING DEAD!
DANCE, FOOLS!! HEHEHEHEHEHE!!!!!
BOOM!
BOOM
THE MAD, WILD DANCE OF THE LIVING DEAD CONTINUED THRU THE NIGHT, AND THE MANIACAL THROBBING OF THE DRUMS CARRIED TO EVERY CORNER OF THE JUNGLE...
BOOM
BOOM
BOOM

...AND REACHED THE EARS OF HORRIFIED NATIVES MILES AWAY...
DRUMS COME FROM VILLAGE OF UNHOLY DEATH!! EVIL SPIRITS ARE LOOSE TONIGHT...
WE MUST SACRIFICE TO GODS!! THEY ARE IN ANGER!!!
HEHEHEHE!!! DANCE AND BOW BEFORE ME, SLAVES!! BOW, I SAY!! HEHEHE!!!
I CAN'T STAND THIS... I... I MUST DO SOMETHING...
THE MADNESS OF THE DANCE SNAPPED THE DELICATE TISSUES OF MICHAEL'S BRAIN, AND IN SHEER PANIC...
I... I'LL KILL HER... THEN MAYBE THE DANCING WILL STOP!! I--I MUST STOP IT...
NO! NO!! DON'T! I'VE OFFERED YOU RICHES AND POWER! DON'T BE A FOOL...
I CAN'T STAND IT... YOU... YOU'RE THE INCARNATION OF EVIL!!
NOOooo!! ARRGHH!!
THERE!! TAKE THAT...

THEY...THEY'RE COMING TO HER DEFENSE! NO! STOP!! I'M YOUR FRIEND...SHE WAS EVIL!!! NO!!!
AIEEEEEE!!! L--LET ME GO, YOU FOOL!!!
ARRRGHHHH!!
TIME, WHICH PICKS BONES CLEAN, CLAIMS ANOTHER VICTIM IN THE VILLAGE OF DEATH. AND, AS THE LAST BIT OF TISSUE FALLS AWAY, A FAINT SMILE SEEMS TO PLAY ABOUT THE MOUTH OF THE SHRUNKEN HEAD WHICH LIES NEAR THE ROTTING CORPSE...
AND THE DAYS PASSED AS THE MURKY DEPTHS OF THE JUNGLE TRIED TO CONCEAL THE HIDEOUS SCENE OF TERROR AND HORROR...
THE SILENCE OF THE EVIL VILLAGE REMAINS UNBROKEN UNTIL...
LOOK, SMITH, A VILLAGE...
SEEMS TO BE ONE OF THE SUGALI TRIBES! THIS PROMISES TO BE INTERESTING...

"COULD HAVE BEEN A PLAGUE... SO MANY OF THEM!"

"EASY TO SEE IT WASN'T WAR. THEY'VE ALL GOT THEIR HEADS!"

"WE OUGHT TO FIND SOMETHING OF VALUE HERE, ANYWAY..."

Then, as if planned, the evil skull was found!!

"LOOK! A SHRUNKEN HEAD; THESE ARE VALUABLE. WHAT LUCK!!"

Again the SHRUNKEN SKULL of the PRIESTESS of the DEVIL returns to seek new PREY for her WARPED LOVE of POWER and VENGEANCE...

"WELL, SMITH — HOME AGAIN! AND WE DO HAVE GOOD CURIOS TO MARKET, DON'T WE?"

"YES — BUT YOU KNOW, EVER SINCE WE PICKED UP THAT HEAD IN THE DESERTED VILLAGE I'VE FELT UNEASY! I'LL BE GLAD WHEN WE'RE RID OF IT!!"

"FIFTEEN DOLLARS ONCE! FIFTEEN DOLLARS TWICE!! SOLD TO THE GENTLEMAN!!! I'M SURE YOU WON'T BE DISAPPOINTED, SIR!"

And another unsuspecting VICTIM of the SPIRITS of EVIL is tempted by fate toward power and occult knowledge...

"I CAN HARDLY WAIT TO GET HOME TO SEE WHAT I BOUGHT..."

THE END

221

WHEN JACK MALLOY CLIMBED TO THE TOP OF THE BIG TOP TO PERFORM HIS DEATH DEFYING FEATS ON THE HIGH TRAPEZE, HE DIDN'T KNOW THAT HE HAD...
AN APPOINTMENT WITH A CORPSE!
OH! HE MISSED THE TRAPEZE!
I...I CAN'T WATCH IT!
NO... NO!!
JACK!! JAAAAAAA...!
AS THE FALLING MAN HITS THE FLOOR WITH A SICKENING THUD, THE CROWD DOESN'T SEE THE MAN WHO STANDS ABOVE THEM GRINNING EVILLY...
NO ONE WILL EVER KNOW THIS WAS NOT AN ACCIDENT! NOW I WILL GET ALL THE HEADLINES INSTEAD OF JUST BEING ALONZO'S ASSISTANT!
HE...HE'S STILL ALIVE! BUT HOW COULD HE...? I MEAN, MAYBE HE STILL HAS A CHANCE!!
JACK, HOW DID IT HAPPEN!? ALONZO HAS BEEN A TOP PERFORMER FOR TEN YEARS AND HE'S NEVER HAD AN ACCIDENT!

SO ALL DID NOT GO ACCORDING TO THE PLAN IN THE MURDEROUS MIND OF JACK MALLOY! ALONZO STILL LIVED...
HIS...HIS TIMING WAS JUST A FRACTION OFF, AND YOU KNOW, IN OUR BUSINESS, THAT MEANS DEATH!!
POOR GUY- AND YOU MUST FEEL AWFUL, BEING HIS PARTNER FOR THREE YEARS! COME ON, LET'S GET DOWN TO THE HOSPITAL...
I'LL JUST SNEAK IN A FEW MOMENTS BEFORE THE OTHERS... I'VE GOT TO SEE IF HE KNOWS ANYTHING...
YOU! I...I'VE BEEN WAITING FOR YOU, JACK! YOU VIPER- THE MAN WHO I THOUGHT WAS... MY FRIEND! (COUGH-COUGH)
SO YOU DO KNOW I DID IT! WELL, I'M GLAD! I WAS TIRED OF BEING YOUR ASSISTANT!
YOU FOOL...I..I TAUGHT YOU EVERYTHING! MY...MY CURSE IS ON YOU, JACK MALLOY...MY CURSE!! AAAAAAARGHGGHH... THE PAIN...THE PAIN!!!
DIE, ALONZO... DIE! THIS TIME I'LL MAKE SURE...! OH, NURSE... UH, YOU'D BETTER HURRY. HE'S VERY BAD...
...HELP... HELP...
HOW DID YOU GET IN HERE? THERE AREN'T SUPPOSED TO BE ANY VISITORS!
ONLY THE NURSE'S ENTRANCE KEPT THE MANIACAL HANDS FROM TEARING AT ALONZO'S THROAT!! THE VENOM OF JEALOUSY STILL POISONED JACK'S BRAIN...
HOW WAS HE, JACK?
WELL, HE--
EMERGENCY...DOCTOR BRADY...ROOM 13, PLEASE ...EMERGENCY!!!
13
JACK, I'VE THOUGHT IT OVER AND THE SHOW MUST GO ON! FROM NOW ON I'M GOING TO BILL YOU AS OUR GREAT TRAPEZE STAR! WILL YOU GO ON ALONE, TONIGHT?
OF COURSE I WILL... OH, HELLO, JO-JO!
HI, BOSS... HI, JACK! ANY WORD ABOUT ALONZO?
ALONZO The Great!

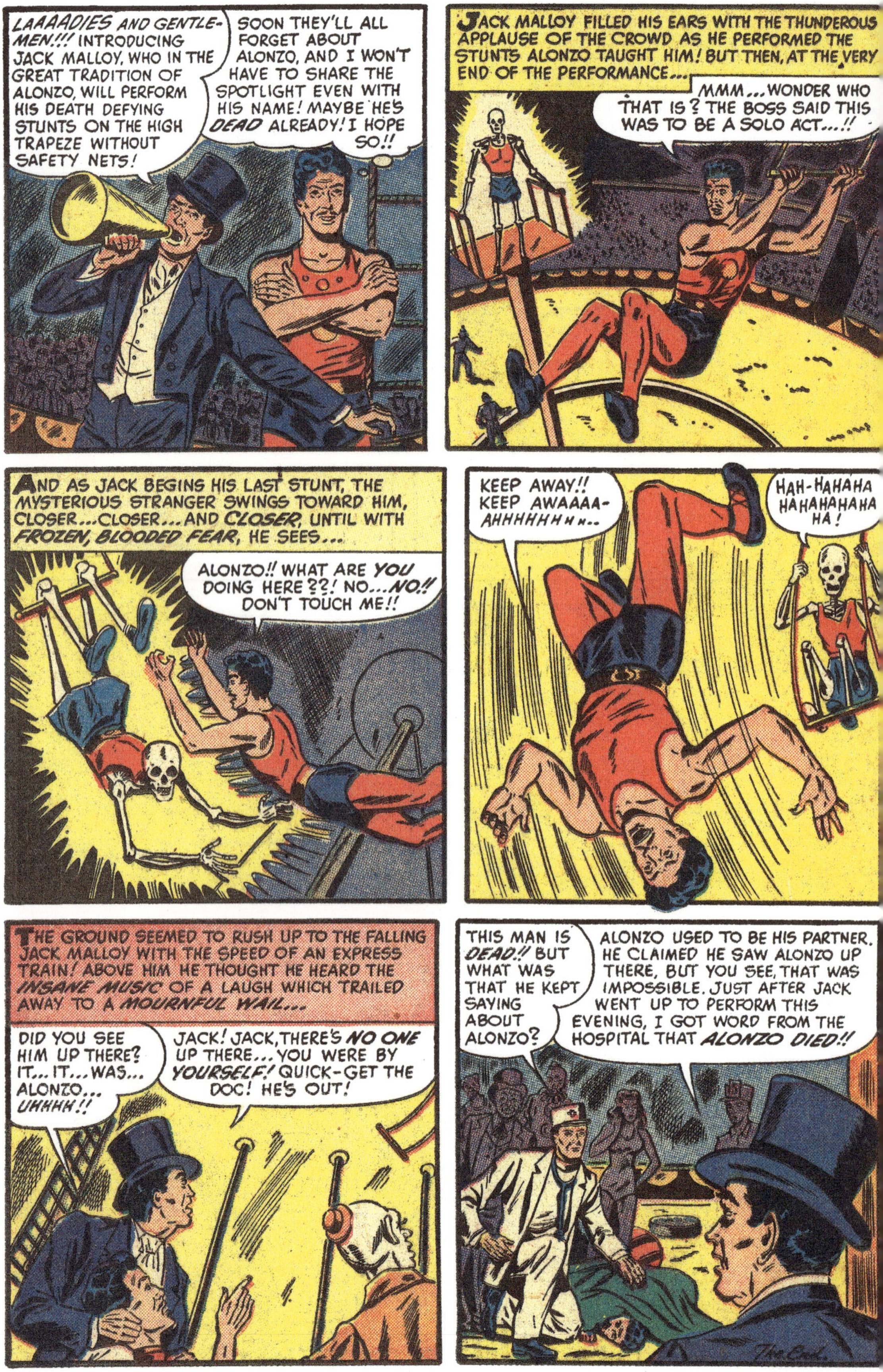
LAAAADIES AND GENTLE-MEN!!! INTRODUCING JACK MALLOY, WHO IN THE GREAT TRADITION OF ALONZO, WILL PERFORM HIS DEATH DEFYING STUNTS ON THE HIGH TRAPEZE WITHOUT SAFETY NETS!
SOON THEY'LL ALL FORGET ABOUT ALONZO, AND I WON'T HAVE TO SHARE THE SPOTLIGHT EVEN WITH HIS NAME! MAYBE HE'S DEAD ALREADY! I HOPE SO!!
JACK MALLOY FILLED HIS EARS WITH THE THUNDEROUS APPLAUSE OF THE CROWD AS HE PERFORMED THE STUNTS ALONZO TAUGHT HIM! BUT THEN, AT THE VERY END OF THE PERFORMANCE...
MMM... WONDER WHO THAT IS? THE BOSS SAID THIS WAS TO BE A SOLO ACT...!!
AND AS JACK BEGINS HIS LAST STUNT, THE MYSTERIOUS STRANGER SWINGS TOWARD HIM, CLOSER... CLOSER... AND CLOSER, UNTIL WITH FROZEN, BLOODED FEAR, HE SEES...
ALONZO!! WHAT ARE YOU DOING HERE??! NO... NO!! DON'T TOUCH ME!!
KEEP AWAY!! KEEP AWAAAA-AHHHHHHhh...
HAH-HAHAHA HAHAHAHAHA HA!
THE GROUND SEEMED TO RUSH UP TO THE FALLING JACK MALLOY WITH THE SPEED OF AN EXPRESS TRAIN! ABOVE HIM HE THOUGHT HE HEARD THE INSANE MUSIC OF A LAUGH WHICH TRAILED AWAY TO A MOURNFUL WAIL...
DID YOU SEE HIM UP THERE? IT... IT... WAS... ALONZO... UHHHH!!
JACK! JACK, THERE'S NO ONE UP THERE... YOU WERE BY YOURSELF! QUICK-GET THE DOC! HE'S OUT!
THIS MAN IS DEAD!! BUT WHAT WAS THAT HE KEPT SAYING ABOUT ALONZO?
ALONZO USED TO BE HIS PARTNER. HE CLAIMED HE SAW ALONZO UP THERE, BUT YOU SEE, THAT WAS IMPOSSIBLE. JUST AFTER JACK WENT UP TO PERFORM THIS EVENING, I GOT WORD FROM THE HOSPITAL THAT ALONZO DIED!!
The End

LOOK HERE! for BIG MONEY MAKING OPPORTUNITIES for MONEY-SAVING OFFERS and SERVICES

SALES HELP — AGENTS WANTED

MAKE $50—$100—MORE! Sell unusual Christmas cards, novelties. Big profits. Amazing bonus reward. Write for Feature assortments on approval, free samples Personal Christmas Cards, free color Catalog. New England Art Publishers, North Abington 1133, Mass.

POSTCARD PUTS YOU IN A FINE BUSINESS! Complete line. Leather jackets, 160 shoe styles. Big Commissions. No investment. Send postcard for Free Outfit. Mason Shoe, Dept. MA-432, Chippewa Falls, Wis.

AMAZING Extra-Money plan gives you gorgeous dress without penny cost. Rush name today with dress size. HARFORD, Dept. M-3180, Cincinnati 25, Ohio.

28 DIFFERENT Christmas Cards FREE plus Box Assortments on approval you can sell for cash. Send no money. Rush name today to General Card Co., Dept. 178-M, 1300 W Jackson, Chicago 7.

FREE HOSIERY! Earn to $3 hour spare time introducing sensational hosiery by giving every man and woman free trial pair! Amazing nylon stockings guaranteed against runs-snags. New miracle one size nylon stretch socks. Fit any size foot. Never sag. Guaranteed one year. Mail postcard for free samples, money-making outfits. State age. Kendex, Babylon 119, N. Y.

NEED EXTRA CASH? Get it selling Blair's unusual line of household and food products. Every housewife a prospect. Products sent on FREE Trial. Write BLAIR, Dept. 84MS, Lynchburg, Va.

$100-$200 IS YOURS SHOWING EXCLUSIVE W/S personalized Christmas Cards—as low as 50 for $1.50 up. FREE SAMPLES, 32 page 4-color catalog Wetmore & Sugden, 90 Monroe Avenue, Rochester 2, New York.

CHEMISTRY

AMAZING NEW Science Book. Experiments, Formulas, Science Catalogue. Only 25c. NATIONAL SCIENTIFIC CO., Dept. CG, 2204 North Ave., Chicago 47.

MONEY MAKING OPPORTUNITIES

RAISE EARTHWORMS! Terrific! Get important information plus true story, "An Earthworm Turned His Life." Send dime. Earthmaster System, 23D, El Monte, Calif.

"HOW TO MAKE MONEY with Simple Cartoons" A book everyone who likes to draw should have. It is free; no obligation. Simply address CARTOONISTS EXCHANGE, Dept. 849, Pleasant Hill, Ohio.

Sew our Redi-Cut Handy-Hanky aprons at home. Easy, Profitable. A & B ENTERPRISES, Dept. C, 2516 N. Albert Pike, Ft. Smith, Arkansas.

BIGGER PROFITS selling Greeting Cards. Get list of sensational Factory Surplus Bargains. $1.25 boxes for 50c, $1 boxes for 35c—while they last! Big line new 1954 Christmas Cards, Stationery, Gifts. Assortments on approval, Personalized Samples FREE! Midwest Cards, 1113 Washington, Dept. J-142, St. Louis, Mo.

$5 to $20 Sparetime. Sewing and Assembling. Write Liebig Industries, Beaver Dam 8, Wisconsin.

SELL CHRISTMAS CARDS! Samples on approval. Writewell, C-1, Boston 15, Mass.

$20 day! Sell name plates for houses. LINDOPLAN, Watertown, Mass.

BIG CASH—make 100%. PROFIT Sell Empire Christmas Cards. 21-card assortment $1. Name-printed stationery, napkins, child's Christmas books. Costs nothing to try. Write for the catalog, Free Imprint Samples, Boxes on approval: EMPIRE CARD, 455 Fox, Elmira, N. Y.

MAKE MONEY Introducing World's cutest children's dresses. Big selection, adorable styles. Low prices. Complete display free. Rush name. Harford, Dept. M-3394, Cincinnati 25, Ohio.

MILITARY COLLECTIONS

Army, Navy patches, brass badges, ribbons, 33 different $1.00—Foreign Armies' prices, 10c. Hobbyguild, 550 Fifth Ave., New York.

STAMPS

COLOSSAL STAMP ZOO FREE—Jungle Beasts, Wildlife, fifteen different including Rhinoceros, Snake, Tiger, Elephant, Zabu, Koalabear, Kookabura, Extraordinary accompanying approvals. Send 10c for handling. Niagara Stamp Co., Niagara-on-the-Lake 538, Canada.

9999 Different from 16 Stamp Companies Approvals Cash $10.00. King, 32 Alexander, Kamloops, Canada.

BAG OF 1,000 STAMPS, unpicked, unsorted, over 30 countries, postpaid, guaranteed, $1.00. HARRISCO, 554 Transit Building, Boston 17, Mass.

FREE! Twelve United States stamps also big lists. Send 3c to cover mailing. Approvals. Littleton Stamps, Littleton F17, N. H.

MISCELLANEOUS

STARTLING NEW BOOK "Truth About Tobacco". Everybody should read it. Only 50c. A. C. Johnson, Chemist, 2204 North Ave., Chicago 47.

POEMS WANTED. Free examination. McNeil, 510C So. Alexandria, Los Angeles, Calif.

COAL BURNING PROBLEMS SOLVED! Amazing additive makes any coal in any stove or furnace burn cleaner, better, longer. Stops soot, smoke, coal gas. No hard clinkers. Perfect for wood, coke, charcoal too. Details FREE. INFURNO, Dept. CBC, 140 N. Dearborn, Chicago, Illinois.

PERSONAL

PEN PALS Everywhere! Magazine, photos, names, addresses, ALL ages. Air-mailed, $1.00. Give age for special list, those near you. PUBLICATIONS, 2272-C Hubbard, Memphis 8, Tenn.

ADVERTISERS

You're looking at the world's biggest classified advertising buy! TWENTY MILLION circulation at a cost-per-word so low, you'll schedule your advertising here every time. For rates, closing dates, full information write COMIC GROUPS CLASSIFIED, 400 Madison Avenue, New York 17.

REVERSIBLE AUTO SEAT COVERS
MADE OF FLEXTON — SERVICE GAUGE PLASTIC FOR LONG WEAR

Zebra-Snake Design

LEOPARD-COWHIDE DESIGN

● Waterproof. Easy to attach to seats for good fit. Roomy and neat. Elastic shirring and reinforced overlap side grips insure over-all seat coverage. Will dress up your car's interior and give protection to seat upholstery. Whisk off mud, oil, sand, grime with a damp rag for bright as new appearance. Sewn with nylon thread for long wear and durability.

ORDER FROM MANUFACTURER AND SAVE!
Choice of split or front seat styles only **$2.98** each. Complete set for Front & Rear only **$5.00**. Specify make of car and seat style with each order. Save Money and buy a set today.

STYLE #400
Snake-Zebra Design — Printed Plastic can be used on either side. Gives snappy distinctive dress up appearance. Front or Rear Seat only **$2.98**

STYLE #500
Leopard Cowhide design on Printed Flexton Plastic. Leopard on one side, Cowhide on the other. Either side gives beauty to your car's seats. Never gets dirty for it cleans with a whisk of a damp cloth. Front or Rear. **$2.98**

RUSH ORDER TODAY!

5 day Money Back Guarantee!

Terrace Sales Dept. HW-109
EAST ROCKAWAY   NEW YORK
Please send me seat covers I have marked I can try for 10 days and return for refund of purchase price if I am not satisfied
☐ Zebra-Snake Design, Reversible
☐ Leopard Cowhide Design, Reversible
☐ Split Seat $2.98   ☐ Solid Seat $2.98
☐ Set (Front & Rear) $5.00
☐ I enclose payment   ☐ Send C O D

Name _____
Address _____
City _____ Zone ___ State _____

THE ARMY ANTS

The professor looked up from his maps.

"Wonder what all the noise is?" he thought.

Folding his papers into a case, Professor Albert Jonson stepped out of his tent. It seemed as if the whole jungle were trembling.

"From the sound of those cries, it could be a jungle fire which is disturbing the animals. H-m-m, better get to the top of that rise and see if I can find out what's happening."

Jonson holstered his revolver, slung his rifle over his shoulder and ran to a small hill which looked down into a valley. A man who made many trips into the jungle to study animal and plant life was familiar with the moods of the black jungle. Yet, Professor Jonson felt that this was different. The shrill shrieks and booming bellows of the animals were unlike those he had ever heard before.

Then, Jonson stood atop the hill scanning the countryside. He fell back in amazement!

Below him the jungle seemed to be ripping itself apart. Two-ton elephants were stampeding in entire herds and now seemed as some prehistoric monsters, their heads thrown high... their eyes blazing with terror. Huge cats bounded ahead... their mighty bodies gripped by spasms of horror. Lighter game tumbled about, trying to escape. All living jungle life was trying to get away from...IT!

"Good heavens, I've never seen anything like it. They all are running away from that certain patch of jungle to the south. I must go down there. I must find out what is frightening the animals."

Professor Jonson scrambled down the hill. He circled the place from which all the animals were escaping. As he approached it, he heard a strange crackling noise... as if a gigantic fire were burning. But there was no smoke! Then, he heard the horrible screams of animals which had been trapped inside the area. Suddenly, the answer struck Jonson.

"ARMY ANTS!" The words crashed through his mind. Ants the size of a man's finger were marching through the jungle. The same fear that had gripped the minds of the animals surged through the man's mind. He had to run, too.

As Jonson turned to run, his foot caught on a vine. He fell! When he regained consciousness, minutes later, his eyes bulged from his forehead.

All around him was a red blanket...a red blanket of death whose snapping jaws had already begun to eat away his flesh!

THE DEVIL'S BLOOD

The storm lashed the surrounding country. Gaunt trees sagged under the terrible onslaught by nature. Dirt roads were swallowed up in seas of mud. Lightning whipped the purple skies. Through all this, a lone man plodded along his way.

"Wow, what a mess. Hey, a light!"

The man splashed through the mud as fast as he could. Soon, he was standing before a small shack. He knocked.

"Yes?"

"Sorry to bother you, Mac, but my car broke down and I thought I'd telephone for help. May I use your phone?"

"I have no telephone, but come in. You're very wet and you look tired."

"Yeah, thanks, I might as well."

Inside, the stranger removed his dripping coat and sat down beside a roaring fire.

"Well, this is certainly better. Glad I saw your light."

"I am very glad, also, young man!"

Gil Dobbs looked about the shack. There wasn't much furniture...a table...bed...picture...PICTURE!

"Hey, isn't that the picture of the DEVIL?" gasped Dobbs.

The old man smiled.

"Yes, I painted it myself."

"I hope you don't get offended, but it looks a lot like you now that I come to think of it," weakly grinned Gil.

"Oh, thank you...I mean, it's probably coincidence."

"Some coincidence. The long ears...sharp nose piercing eyes...just like you've got. Some coincidence."

"Since you're so interested in that picture and the devil, young man, allow me to add to your knowledge of the devil."

For an hour, Gil Dobbs sat spellbound as he listened to lore about the devil. His mind seemed to be in a trance. Then, he heard the old man say, "And through the veins of the devil runs a blue liquid ..not red blood. Oh...how careless of me."

The old man had cut himself with a knife he had been handling. The poison of horror flooded Gil's stomach as he saw a blue liquid ooze from the man's finger!

SAVAGE AUSTRALIAN BOOMERANG

The SECRET of the WILD BUSHMAN

IT ALWAYS COMES BACK

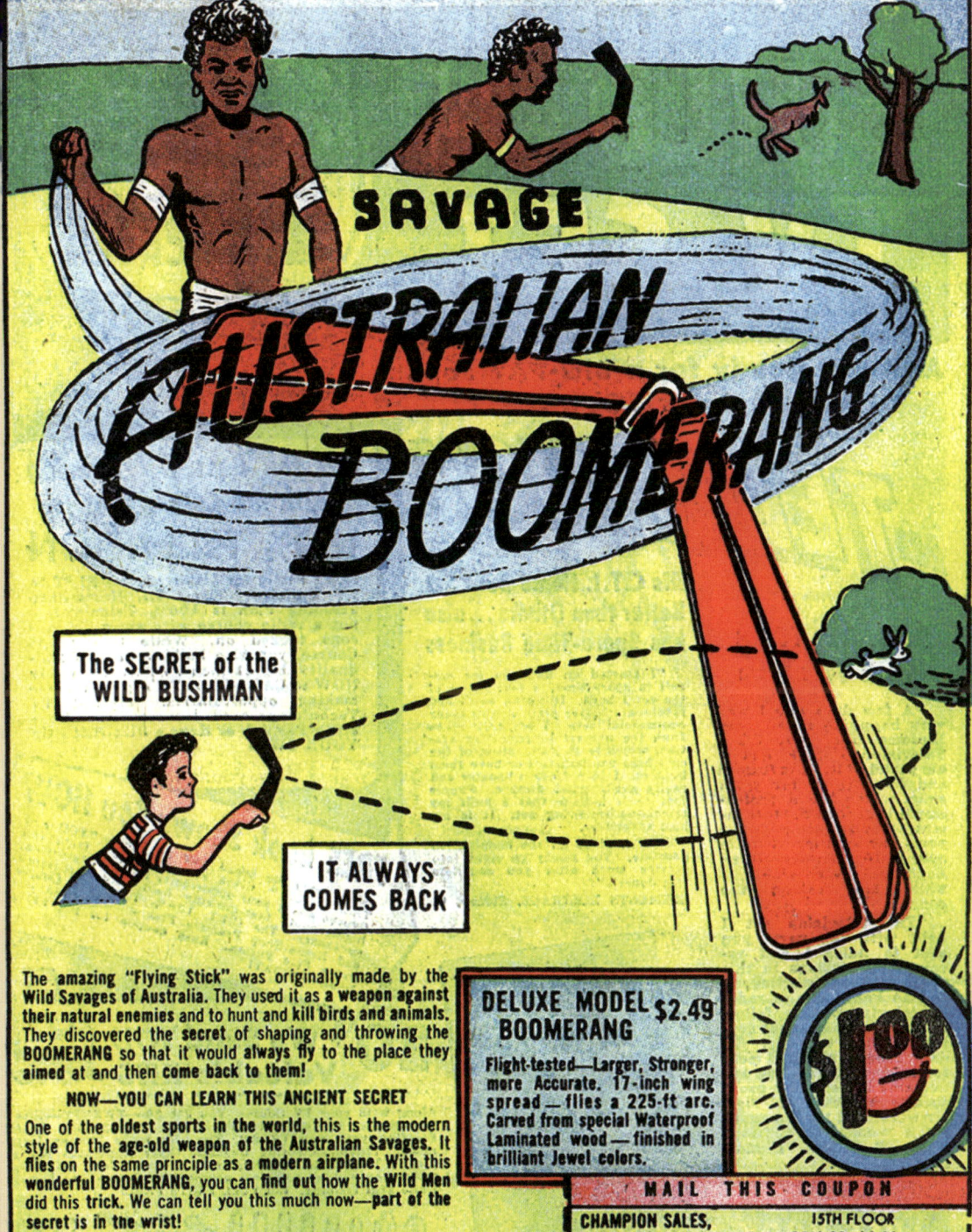

The amazing "Flying Stick" was originally made by the Wild Savages of Australia. They used it as a weapon against their natural enemies and to hunt and kill birds and animals. They discovered the secret of shaping and throwing the BOOMERANG so that it would always fly to the place they aimed at and then come back to them!

NOW—YOU CAN LEARN THIS ANCIENT SECRET

One of the oldest sports in the world, this is the modern style of the age-old weapon of the Australian Savages. It flies on the same principle as a modern airplane. With this wonderful BOOMERANG, you can find out how the Wild Men did this trick. We can tell you this much now—part of the secret is in the wrist!

When you throw the BOOMERANG, it spins out and away in a big circle. It's Amazing! No matter how far or how high or how hard you throw it— it always comes back! Try it in your own backyard or when you go hunting. A little practice gives deadly accuracy.

WONDERFUL FOR HUNTING, TARGET PRACTICE

Almost any object, a rabbit hiding behind a stump or a bird on the wing, is a mark for the flying stick. Or try hitting a balloon floating in the air. If you miss, the BOOMERANG comes back to you like a trained eagle, ready for another flight. Fine as a shotgun target and a new way of teaching your dog to "fetch". Comes with Full Instructions.

CHAMPION SALES,   1860 BROADWAY, NEW YORK 23, N.Y.   15TH FLOOR

DELUXE MODEL BOOMERANG $2.49

Flight-tested—Larger, Stronger, more Accurate. 17-inch wing spread — flies a 225-ft arc. Carved from special Waterproof Laminated wood — finished in brilliant Jewel colors.

$1.00

MAIL THIS COUPON

CHAMPION SALES,   15TH FLOOR
1860 BROADWAY, NEW YORK 23, N.Y.

I ENCLOSE $1.00. Send me the BOOMERANG I have checked below. If not COMPLETELY SATISFIED, I may return in 5 days for full price refund.

☐ Australian Mystery BOOMERANG — $1.00

☐ De Luxe Model BOOMERANG — $2.49. I will pay the balance of $1.49 plus postage on delivery. (SAVE POSTAGE: Enclose $2.50 with this coupon and we pay all postage. Same MONEY-BACK GUARANTEE.)

(PLEASE PRINT)

NAME _____

ADDRESS _____

TOWN _____ STATE _____

BUILD your own TV SET

BIG 21 INCH SCREEN

Also Get Ready for a BIG-PAY Job or a Business of YOUR OWN

in TELEVISION

Get the Best T-V Training with the Course that is 100% TELEVISION

Don't settle for less than the BEST in TV Training. The C.T.I. Home-Shop Training Plan is 100% Television—not a radio course with some TV lessons tacked on. While taking the Course, you also build your own fine-quality, big 21-inch TV Set. Get ready NOW to CASH-IN on TV's great money-making opportunities. Trained TV Technicians needed everywhere. Take a Big-Pay Job or Have a BUSINESS OF YOUR OWN!

Builds Own TV Set Makes $250 Extra

"A few days ago I was very happy to receive my Diploma from your C.T.I. Television Course and I am proud of it. It is framed and hanging in my work shop, which has a professional look with the test instruments I built with the parts you sent me. I made over $250 from spare-time Radio and TV Service jobs while still taking the course.

"The television set I built with the parts you sent is finished and receives all stations in this area. Before starting, I had no knowledge of radio or television. My fellow workers laughed about correspondence training. To date I have repaired sets for most of them. You are welcome to send any prospective students to view my work, and thanks again for a wonderful course."
ERHART BAIER, Elmira, N.Y.

His C.T.I. Home Built Set Better than Others...also has Spare-Time Business

"I started up business for myself in spare-time. I feel proud of the set I built. It works swell and receives a better picture than many commercial sets. I am fifty miles from the nearest broadcasting station, which is Dayton. Most of the sets here use boosters or have them built in. I do not use a booster and really get a good picture. People just can't believe that I built my television receiving set. It is my best advertiser.

"C.T.I. gives all the cooperation possible. You really go right into service work after you complete this course."
CLEMENTS HOLTHAUS, Sidney, O.

FREE book Shows You HOW

Send today for brand new TV Book, "YOU and TELEVISION." Gives you very latest facts and figures about your opportunity in this interesting, highly-paid, fast-growing field. No experience necessary. The C.T.I. 100% Television Course and Home-Shop Practice Plan quickly train you for a Fine Future. Rush coupon for Big FREE Book—TODAY!

20 We Send YOU Valuable KITS

Along with your TV Course, You get 20—TWENTY—Kits of Top-Quality Parts, Tools, Professional Equipment. Besides Building your own TV Set, You also make Testing Instruments, Trouble-Shooting Devices, Other Apparatus you can use on TV Installation, Repair and Service Jobs. Many men more than pay for complete course with Spare-Time Earnings while still training. Get FULL FACTS FREE!

FREE BOOK COUPON

COMMERCIAL TRADES INSTITUTE, 15th Floor
1860 BROADWAY, NEW YORK 23, N.Y.
Send New FREE Book telling how I can Train at Home and make Big Money in Television.

NAME_____

ADDRESS_____

CITY_____STATE_____

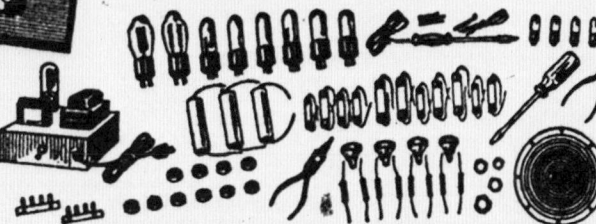

COMMERCIAL TRADES INSTITUTE
1860 BROADWAY, NEW YORK 23, N.Y.   15TH FLOOR

WITHIN THE WHITE WALLS OF A HOSPITAL, DEATH IS A FREQUENT VISITOR PLACING IT'S WET, CLAMMY FINGERS ON MANY A FEVERED BROW... BUT WHO COULD RECKON WITH THE SUDDEN VIOLENCE, THE CRUSHING HORROR THAT WAS CALLED...
OPERATION-MONSTER
GROWRRR!
OH, NO! WHAT DREADFUL MONSTER HAVE WE CREATED?
HELP!! NO!! A-A-A-R-R-GH!!
IN THE OPERATING ROOM OF THE GRAYSON GENERAL HOSPITAL...
SCALPEL, MISS BAXTER--
YES, DOCTOR!
CAREFUL, PHILLIPS, YOU'RE TOO NEAR THE BRAIN!
YOU KNOW IT'S DANGEROUS TO PROBE TOO NEAR THE BRAIN--THE EFFECT ON THE PATIENT---
NONSENSE, DOCTOR! THIS OPERATION CALLS FOR SUCH PROBING!! THE PATIENT IS IN GOOD CONDITION---

--BUT HIS PULSE IS QUICKENING---AND HIS FACE IS ODDLY DISTORTED... I WOULD SUGGEST---
I AM THE SURGEON IN CHARGE OF THIS OPERATION AND I WON'T---
SUDDENLY, THE PATIENT RISES FROM THE TABLE, BUT INSTEAD OF THE HUMAN BEING THAT HAD LAIN THERE, A LOATHESOME HALF-HUMAN APPEARS, A MONSTROUS CREATION OF THE SURGEON'S KNIFE...
DR. PHILLIPS!! L-LOOK!!
YOUR SCALPEL MUST HAVE TOUCHED THE INNERMOST PART OF HIS BRAIN!! HE'S SOMEHOW BEEN TRANSFORMED INTO A--A---BEAST!!!
GROWRRRR
NOBODY CAN LEAVE HERE NOW!! IF OUR HORRIBLE MISTAKE WERE DISCOVERED, THE HOSPITAL WOULD BE RUINED!! WE MUST ALL BE SWORN TO SECRECY--AND HE MUST BE HIDDEN AWAY FOREVER!
WHAT SHALL WE DO? WHERE CAN WE KEEP THIS--MONSTER?
THERE'S AN ABANDONED ROOM ON THE TOP FLOOR--NOBODY GOES THERE!
IN THE DEATHLY QUIET OF THE NIGHT, A STRANGE PROCESSION MOVES, AND EACH WHITE COAT IS A FEARFUL CONTRAST TO THE BLACKNESS OF EVIL IN THE HUMAN HEART!...
HURRY! WE'LL BE SEEN!
HE HAS THE STRENGTH OF TEN MEN!
AAWRR

THERE!! I HAVE THE KEY AND THE LOCK IS SECURE!
BUT HE'S SO STRONG!! ...I'M AFRAID---
THAT EVENING, IN THE DAMAGED BRAIN OF THE CAGED MONSTER, THERE IS NO RECOLLECTION OF HIS FORMER STATE... NOW THERE IS ONLY SMOULDERING RESENTMENT, BRUTAL ANIMAL INSTINCT... AND TERRIBLE STRENGTH!
ROWR-RR!!
WITH HANDS GROWN FIERCE AND POWERFUL, THE BEAST RIPS OPEN THE BARS OF HIS HATED PRISON!!...
...AND FRANTICALLY DESTROYS THE DOOR OF THE ROOM...
UIET
LEASE
CRA SH!
YAAAAAAA
HE'S ESCAPED! I MUST FIND DR. PHILLIPS!!
NURSE! DON'T LEAVE ME HERE!!
3B
HELP!! HELP!!

AS THE DEMONIAC CREATURE CONTINUES TO STAIN THE HALLS OF THE HOSPITAL WITH FRESHLY SPILLED BLOOD, THE POLICE ARRIVE...
CAN'T SOMEBODY STOP HIM?!? HIS STRENGTH IS INHUMAN!
MARCY GENE
HOSPITAL
DISPENSARY
WE'RE THE ONLY ONES LEFT IN THE HOSPITAL!! THE OTHERS ARE EITHER DEAD-- OR THEY'VE RUN FOR THEIR LIVES!
WE CREATED THIS MONSTER, DOCTOR! IT'S OUR DUTY TO DESTROY HIM! MAYBE HE WENT BACK TO HIS ROOM!
EXIT
I CAN'T SEE VERY WELL--BUT THE ROOM SEEMS TO BE EMPTY!
THEN WE'LL GO INSIDE-- AND WAIT FOR HIM TO RETURN!
AS THE MINUTES PASS, TWO FIGURES STAND IN SHADOW, THEIR EYES PIERCING THE DARKNESS FOR A GLIMPSE OF THE TERRIBLE FIEND THEY BROUGHT INTO BEING...
I CAN HEAR THE POLICE BELOW-- SEARCHING FOR HIM!!
WE MUST BE PREPARED TO KILL HIM AT ONCE!! THAT NEEDLE IS OUR LAST...
H-HE'S COMING THROUGH THE WINDOW!!... THAT LOOK IN HIS EYES--HOW HORRIBLE!! I-I CAN'T MOVE MY ARMS...
DOCTOR, THE NEEDLE! ONLY THAT DRUG CAN STOP HIM!!
GRROWRR
RUN, MISS BAXTER! IN MY FRIGHT, I DROPPED THE NEEDLE!
AIEEE!!

LET GO OF ME! YOU CAN'T KILL ME!! I---
ARRGHHHHHHHH
HE'S GOT MISS BAXTER--AND NOW HE WANTS ME!!! BUT WHERE CAN I HIDE?? HE'LL FIND ME ANYWHERE!!
LABORATORY 212
GROARR
IF YOU COME NEAR ME, I'LL CRUSH YOU WITH THIS METAL WEIGHT! THERE IS STRENGTH IN ME, TOO!!
CRACK!
THERE!! WE WILL SEE IF YOUR INJURED BRAIN CAN STAND SUCH A BLOW!!
IN HIS DESPERATE MOVE, PHILLIPS FALLS AGAINST THE TABLE, AND A BEAKER OF SEARING ACID COMES HURTLING DOWN UPON HIM!...
YAA
YAAA

QUICKLY, LIKE A HUNGRY BIRD OF PREY, THE ACID EATS AWAY AT HIS FACE, CAUSING UNSPEAKABLE AGONY--AND A HORRIBLE AND SUDDEN TRANSFORMATION!
MY FACE! WHAT'S HAPPENED TO MY FACE?!?
THERE HE IS!! LET'S GET HIM!!
HE IS A BEAST OF SOME SORT!
I CAN'T SEE!! I CAN'T--
LABORATORY 212
YOU DON'T UNDERSTAND!! I'M A DOCTOR AND I'M RESPONSIBLE FOR THE MONSTER ON THE FLOOR. IT WAS AN ACCIDENT---
NO-AHH!
YOU CAN'T GET AWAY!!
WITH THE VIOLENT BLOW OF THE METAL WEIGHT, THE BRAIN OF THE BEAST IS SUDDENLY RESTORED TO ITS FORMER HUMAN STATE---
MY HEAD!! WH--WHERE AM I??? WHAT'S HAPPENED?
YOU'VE HAD A NARROW ESCAPE, MISTER! ANOTHER MINUTE AND THAT CREATURE WOULD HAVE CRUSHED YOU TO A PULP!!
...AND THE DOCTOR, HIS FACE A MONSTROUS MASK OF HORROR, SPRAWLS LIFELESS ON THE FLOOR...
POOR GUY!! SOMETHING MUST HAVE SNAPPED IN HIS BRAIN!! WE'LL NEVER KNOW THE TRUE STORY NOW!!! BUT AT LEAST WE'VE ENDED THE REIGN OF TERROR BY THIS MONSTER!!
The End

SPIRIT in THE STONE
AFTER THE THING FELL FROM THE SKIES, ONE MAN DREAMED OF GOOD, THE OTHER OF EVIL... BUT NEITHER MAN HAD RECKONED WITH THE CONSEQUENCES OF TINKERING WITH THAT HORRIBLE LIFE FORCE...
WH...YAAAA...THE METEOR'S C-CRACKING APART AND T...THE R-ROCKS! T-THEY'RE COMING AFTER ME! THE ROCKS...T... THEY'RE...ALIVE!
HUNGRY? SURE, I'M HUNGRY! BUT NOT FOR YOUR SO-CALLED COOKING! I'M HUNGRY FOR LIFE, FOR LIVING, FOR ALL THE GOOD THINGS OUTSIDE!
EASY, JACK! YOUR NERVES! REMEMBER, WE'RE SCIENTISTS! WE'RE HERE TO HELP HUMANITY!
HUMANITY? BAH! A LOT ANYONE CARES!
THINK OF OUR WORK, JACK, OUR METEOROLOGICAL OBSERVATIONS! WAIT! THE AUTOMATIC METER ALARM IS RINGING!
BRR-RRNNGGGGG

AN INTERSTELLAR BODY- IT'S PASSING THE EARTH'S ATMOSPHERE! AND THE ALARM'S GETTING LOUDER! THAT MEANS THE BODY'S BIG!
BRR-BRR
I HOPE IT'S BIG ENOUGH TO CRASH THIS ROTTEN PLANET TO ATOMIC DUST! LET IT COME!
G-GOOD GRIEF, IT C-CAN'T BE...! A METEOR... BIG AS THE MOON-AND... IT'S NOT PASSING BY, JACK! IT'S GOING TO CRASH!
WH-WHAMM
J-JACK... OHH!
DOC... YAAAA!
J-JACK! JACK, CAN Y-YOU HEAR ME?
I...I HEAR YOU, DOC! (GASP)...GUESS I'M SHAKEN UP!
I..IT'S UNCANNY... AS...AS IF I SOMEHOW CAUSED IT, WITH MY BLASPHEMY ON SCIENCE!
SKIP IT, JACK! LET'S GO OUTSIDE FOR A LOOK!
MAN, OH MAN, WHAT A BREAK! LOOK AT THE SIZE OF IT! IT'S THE SCIENTIFIC FIND OF THE CENTURY!
IT ALMOST BROKE US, ALL RIGHT! OKAY... I'M COMING!

LOOK HERE! A HOLE, LEADING INTO THE HEART OF THE ASTEROID... IT'S ALMOST LIKE A DOORWAY... INVITING US IN... BUT... HOW...
WHAT'S THE MATTER, DOC? FORGETTING YOUR SCIENTIFIC MANNER? YOU SOUND LIKE YOU BELIEVE IT'S SOME KIND OF MAGIC!
I BELIEVE ONLY IN THE MAGIC OF SCIENCE, JACK! BUT I'VE NEVER HEARD OF... COMING, JACK?
SAY... WHAT'S THIS?
WHERE ARE YOU, JACK?
SHINING... METALLIC... GOLD! A VEIN OF PURE GOLD, RUNNING RIGHT THROUGH THE METEORIC MATTER! WOW!
AND DIAMONDS... AND RUBIES... EMERALDS... TOPAZ! THIS HUNK OF SPACE ROCK'S WORTH MILLIONS... MILLIONS!
IT'LL BE WORTH MORE THAN THAT TO SCIENCE, ONCE I NOTIFY THE UNIVERSITY OF OUR FIND!
I'LL RADIO THEM RIGHT AWAY, AND...
HOLD IT! BACK WHERE YOU ARE! YOU'RE NOT NOTIFYING ANYBODY OF THIS FIND!
YOU CAN'T MEAN IT! IT'S ANOTHER ONE OF YOUR JOKES, JACK! THIS'S THE FIND OF THE CENTURY! WE'VE GOT TO NOTIFY THE UNIVERSITY!
IT'S A FIND, ALL RIGHT– ONLY NOW, IT'S FINDERS KEEPERS! I'M NOT LETTING IT GET AWAY FROM ME!

WE'RE SCIENTISTS... SCIENTISTS, JACK! OUR DUTY IS TO...
YOU STICK TO SCIENCE! I'M THROUGH HELPING HUMANITY! I'M GOING TO BE RICH, AND YOU'RE NOT STOPPING ME!
NO! NO! YOU DON'T KNOW WHAT YOU'RE DOING! YOU'RE...
AAAGGH
I DON'T, EH? I WARNED YOU, DOC!
W...WHAT'S THAT SOUND! IT'S DOC... SCREAMING...IT'S ECHOING AND RE-ECHOING!
AAAAGGGH
OHH! THE VIBRATIONS! MY EARS... S-STOP... STOP IT...AAH!
AAAAGGGH-
THE METEOR...(GASP)...IT'S CRACKING APART! THE VIBRATIONS...AAAH...! MY HEAD... I CAN'T S-STAND THE VIBRATIONS!
CRA-A-ACKK
AAAAGGGH
DOC'S DYING SCREAM...ACTIVATED THE PURE QUARTZ CRYSTALS! (PANT)...HIS SCREAM SET THEM TO VIBRATING...CRACKED THE METEOR APART! RUN...RUN...GOT TO RUN!

BUT WHAT AM I AFRAID OF, NOW? EVEN IF THEY'RE FROM SPACE, THEY'RE ONLY ROCKS! THEY CAN'T HURT ME! BACK... BACK... I'VE GOT TO TURN BACK! ALL THAT GOLD... THOSE DIAMONDS... EEOWW! W... WHAT H-HIT ME!
(GASP)... I... I'M SEEING THINGS! THE R... ROCKS.. T... THEY ARE STARTING TO MOVE! T... THEY'RE..
YEOWW... THEY... THEY ARE! THE ROCKS... THEY'VE GOT A WILL OF THEIR OWN! TH.. THEY'RE ALIVE! THEY'RE COMING AFTER ME!
NO... NO! ROCKS CAN'T BE ALIVE! ROCKS ARE DEAD! ALL THAT GOLD... DIAMONDS... IT'S MINE, MINE! STOP! ST... RAAAA
BAWN-
BANNNG
DIAMONDS... DIA...
The END

RETURN OF THE WEREWOLF!

"Do you think *it* will come, tonight?"

Inspector Wilson looked at the full, blood-red moon. "The time is right!"

"It" was the werewolf!

Both men moved uneasily. They were pressed against a boulder and the cold, harsh wind from the moors cut into their bare faces. The large house that rose before them was black...bleak.

Assistant Inspector Hawkins thought about this amazing case. Three months ago, strange, horrible murders began happening on the moors. People returning home late at night were set upon by some vicious beast. Those who lived swore it was a wolf.

Then, the superstitions of the moors began to be revived. Ever since they had come to the moors, the Wellington family was suspected of being cursed by some terrible sickness. All of the male members of the family were never allowed to walk about alone at certain times of the month. Then, two weeks ago, evidence was uncovered which showed that the murdering beast used the Wellington house as its lair. It took but a few days before the werewolf curse became alive on whispering lips.

So, the two police officers had decided to watch the house and see if any strange creature ventured forth from its forboding walls to wreak horrible death.

"Hawkins...Hawkins, can't you hear me? What's the matter with you?" snapped Inspector Wilson.

"Oh, I'm sorry, sir, just thinking about this blasted case. What's up?"

"Didn't you see a light upstairs?"

"No, sir, that house still looks like a tomb to me!"

Hours passed.

The moors looked like some other planet in the white, ghostly moonlight.

The moon was full.

"Hawkins, did you hear something behind us?"

"Yes sir. I'll go back and investigate."

Filmy clouds passed over the moon.

"Aiiieeeeehhhhh..."

"Hawkins...HAWKINS...ANSWER ME."

Inspector Wilson tore himself from his position and plunged in the direction Hawkins had gone.

"Good Lord, no!"

Bending over Hawkins' slashed body was... A WOLF!

"Arrghh...arrghhh..."

"Keep away from me, you monster...keep away..."

BANG! BANG! BANG!

"The bullets can't hurt it. I-I must run...I..."

"ARRGHHH..."

"Aiieeeehhhh..."

The monster melted away in the blackness.

Minutes later, a hairy shape began to climb up one of the walls of the Wellington house. When it reached the second floor, it disappeared through a window and was seen no more.

The moon was sinking rapidly behind the barren mounds of the moors. The twisted trees offered a grotesque welcome to the approaching dawn. The wind moaned over two still warm corpses.

On the second floor of the Wellington house, John Wellington III rolled over on his back as the first rays of dawn flooded the room. As the sun touched him, he seemed to snap out of the stupor of sleep. He quickly got up and looked down at the floor.

The muddy prints of some horrible beast led to his bed!

Then, as if he had been doing it over and over again, he wiped up the mud. Afterwards, he ran some water in the bathtub.

He was going to wash fresh mud from his bare feet!

GIANT ASSORTMENT of OVER 50 DIFFERENT PLAYTHINGS for only $1

A WHOLE TREASURE CHEST of TOYS

Imagine getting a whole big box of toys at one time? You'll put your hand in the box and you'll start taking out — a Harmonica, a Toy Flute, a Mouth Whistle and a Warbler Bird Call... a Magnet Game, a Water Pistol and a Blow-Ball... over 100 super Decalcomanias and real looking jewelry, a beaded Necklace and a Bracelet... a Sheriff's Badge, a Rubber Knife, a Compass, a fearsome Mask... and many more things to PLAY ALONE with. There are GAMES to Play-with-Friends, among them — a Baseball Game, a Fishing Game, a Battle Game, Paper Checkerboard and Men, Hare and Hounds Game, Donkey Game, Paper Dominoes Game and many more. There are MAGIC TRICKS & ILLUSIONS — such as the amazing Water-Into-Wine Trick, a set of 4 Wire Puzzles, the Magic Sea Shell which blooms when put into water, the Finger Trap, the great Fly Illusion, the Trick Fan, the Card Trix, etc. to mystify your friends and family. There is much, much more — Coloring Games, A Manikin for Drawing, Mazes, Puzzle Games — the big box is just CRAMMED FULL with over 50 of the most wonderful Toys, Games, Magic Tricks and Playthings you've ever seen!

ALL THIS AND MUCH MORE INCLUDED IN THIS ASSORTMENT

T Puzzle • Balloons • Puzzles • Whistles • Spinners • Cowboy • Animals • GAMES • MAGNETS • Party Blowers • Checker Board and Men • TOPS • Fox and Hare Game • Soldiers • Play Money • Pencil Games • MAGIC • Decalcomanias

Only $1

Enough toys to keep a boy or girl happy and busy for days and days. Enough toys to make the youngster feel as rich as a king! A variety and quantity to satisfy every need — Play-Alone, Play-with-Friends, Party-Toys, Indoor-and-Outdoor Toys, Educational Toys — an avalanche of Toys!

Just fill out and mail the convenient coupon. Enclose only $1.00 for each Giant Assortment of Toys. Your order will be mailed immediately, postage paid. Money Back Guarantee if not Satisfied. Send your order now.

RUSH THIS COUPON NOW!

For a child's Birthday Party, this will provide a wonderful selection of gifts for the guests and will keep them busy and happy for hours.

A $5.00 Value for only $1.00 to make new customers for our other Toy and Book Values!

GRIFFIN TOYS   15TH FLOOR
1860 BROADWAY, NEW YORK 23, N. Y.

Please send me................Giant Assortments of Toys at $1.00 each. I am enclosing $............ ....in payment. Money back guarantee if not satisfied.

Name...

Address...

City or Town .... Zone...... State......

Note: We pay postage on all orders. Sorry — no c.o.d.'s

GRIFFIN TOYS 1860 Broadway, N.Y. 23, N.Y.   15th Floor

You, Too, Can Be Tough!
GREATEST SELF-DEFENSE OFFER EVER MADE!

LIGHTNING JU-JITSU

Master Ju-Jitsu and you'll be able to overcome any attack—win any fight! This is what this book promises you! *Lightning Ju-Jitsu* will equip you with a powerful defense and counter-attack against any bully, attacker or enemy. It is equally effective and easy to use by any woman or man, boy or girl—and you don't need big muscles or weight to apply. Technique and the know-how does the trick. This book gives you all the secrets, grips, blows, pressures, jabs, tactics, etc. which are so deadly effective in quickly "putting an attacker out of business." Such as: Hitting Where It Hurts—Edge of the Hand Blow—Knuckle Jab—Shoulder Pinch—Teeth Rattler—Boxing the Ears—Elbow Jab—Knee Jab—Coat Grip—Bouncer Grip—Thumbscrew—Strangle Hold—Hip Throw—Shoulder Throw—Chin Throw—Knee Throw—*Breaking* a Wristlock, or Body Grip, or Strangle Hold—*Overcoming* a Hold-up, or Gun Attack, or Knife Attack, or Club Assault, etc. etc.—Just follow the illustrations and easy directions, practice the grips, holds and movements—and you'll fear no man.

If This Should Happen to You

Would You Know This Quick Defense?

only **$1.00**

included **FREE!**

FREE 5 DAY TRIAL

BEE JAY, Dept. HM-78
400 Madison Ave. N.Y. 17, N.Y.

FREE
How to Perform STRONG MAN STUNTS

With every order we will send you ABSOLUTELY FREE this exciting book! It shows you the *secret way* in which YOU will be able to: tear a telephone book in half—hammer a nail into a board with your bare fist—rip a full deck of cards into two parts—crush and shatter a rock with a blow of your hand—and many other stupendous strong man stunts! All this will be easy for you using the confidential, hidden way shown in this amazing book! Don't miss this amazing combined offer—on our FIVE DAY TRIAL! If not delighted with your results, your money back at once.

BEE JAY, Dept. HM-78
400 Madison Ave. N.Y. 17, N.Y.

Please send LIGHTNING JU-JITSU, plus FREE copy of HOW TO PERFORM STRONG MAN STUNTS. If not satisfied I may return both books in 5 days and get my money back.
I enclose $1—Send Postpaid (Sorry, No C.O.D.'s)

Name..
Address..
City.................... Zone...... State..............

$1 Box of 21 New Christmas Cards

Yours FREE!

B. J. Stuart, President Stuart Greetings

I'll Give You This Feature Assortment of 21 New, Lovely Christmas Cards Free To Prove How Easily You Can Earn **$75.00 OR MORE** Showing These Cards In Your Spare Time!

Amazing Get-Acquainted Offer For
MEN! WOMEN! BOYS! GIRLS!

Imagine! This big box of 21 beautiful new Christmas Cards is yours without one penny's cost to you. You won't be asked to return the cards or pay for them, now or ever. We're making this amazing offer to show you how easily you can make as much as $75.00 and more with our exciting new Christmas Cards!

ANYONE CAN MAKE MONEY THIS EASY WAY!

Whether you're 8 or 80 ... a student, housewife or have a full-time job ... you can make big money in your spare time! You don't need any experience. We'll supply you with a big outfit of actual samples ON APPROVAL. Just show these samples to people you know. Our big values sell on sight—and you keep up to half of each dollar as your big cash profit. You can quickly make $75.00 selling only 150 boxes. With our big line of Christmas and All-Occasion Assortments, Name-Imprinted Christmas Cards, Stationery and other fast-sellers, you make still more money!

OFFER LIMITED ... ACT NOW!

Send no money. Just mail coupon for sample outfit ON APPROVAL and Feature Assortment FREE. You must be satisfied that you can make money this easy way, or you may return the samples only. THE $1.00 FEATURE ASSORTMENT IS YOURS TO KEEP, FREE, WHETHER YOU RETURN THE SAMPLE OUTFIT OR NOT! This offer is limited, one to a family, and may never be repeated.

STUART GREETINGS, Dept. FB-118
4436-38 N. Clark St., Chicago 40, Illinois

I am interested in making money with your outfit of sample assortments. Rush it ON APPROVAL. Include $1 Feature Christmas Assortment FREE, per your offer.

Name_____

Address_____

City & Zone_____ State_____

If for fund-raising, give organization's name below

_____

FREE BOX COUPON

Mail coupon for money-making sample outfit ON APPROVAL. Get Feature Assortment as a FREE GIFT for trying our plan.

Mail Now!

SEE WHAT OTHERS DO!

"I make $30 to $40 a week, in my spare time. It's easy. Your cards sell themselves!"
R.B.T., New Mexico

"Customers can't resist these cards. Showing them is a nice way for any student to earn extra money!"
M. K., Wisconsin

STUART GREETINGS, INC.
4436-38 N. Clark St., Dept. FB-118 Chicago 40, Ill.

PS Artbooks

Collect all 4 Volumes of Witches Tales from PS Artbooks

HARVEY HORRORS
COLLECTED WORKS
WITCHES TALES
VOLUME ONE

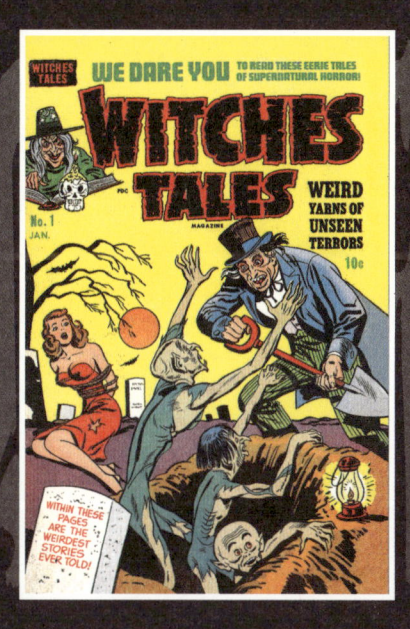

January 1951 - January 1952
Issues 1 - 7

Foreword by
Ramsey Campbell

Witches Tales
Volume One

Collect the complete library form PS Publishing online 24/7 @ www.pspublishing.co.uk

Chamber of Chills
December 1954 - Issue #26

Cover Art - Al Avison

The Eight Hands of Ranu
Script - Unknown
Pencils - Vic Donahue
Inks - Vic Donahue

The Captain's Return
Script - Unknown
Pencils - Vic Donahue
Inks - Rudy Palais

The Ice Horror
Script - Unknown
Pencils - Unknown
Inks - Unknown

Demons of the Night
Script - Unknown
Pencils - Manny Stallman
Inks - Manny Stallman

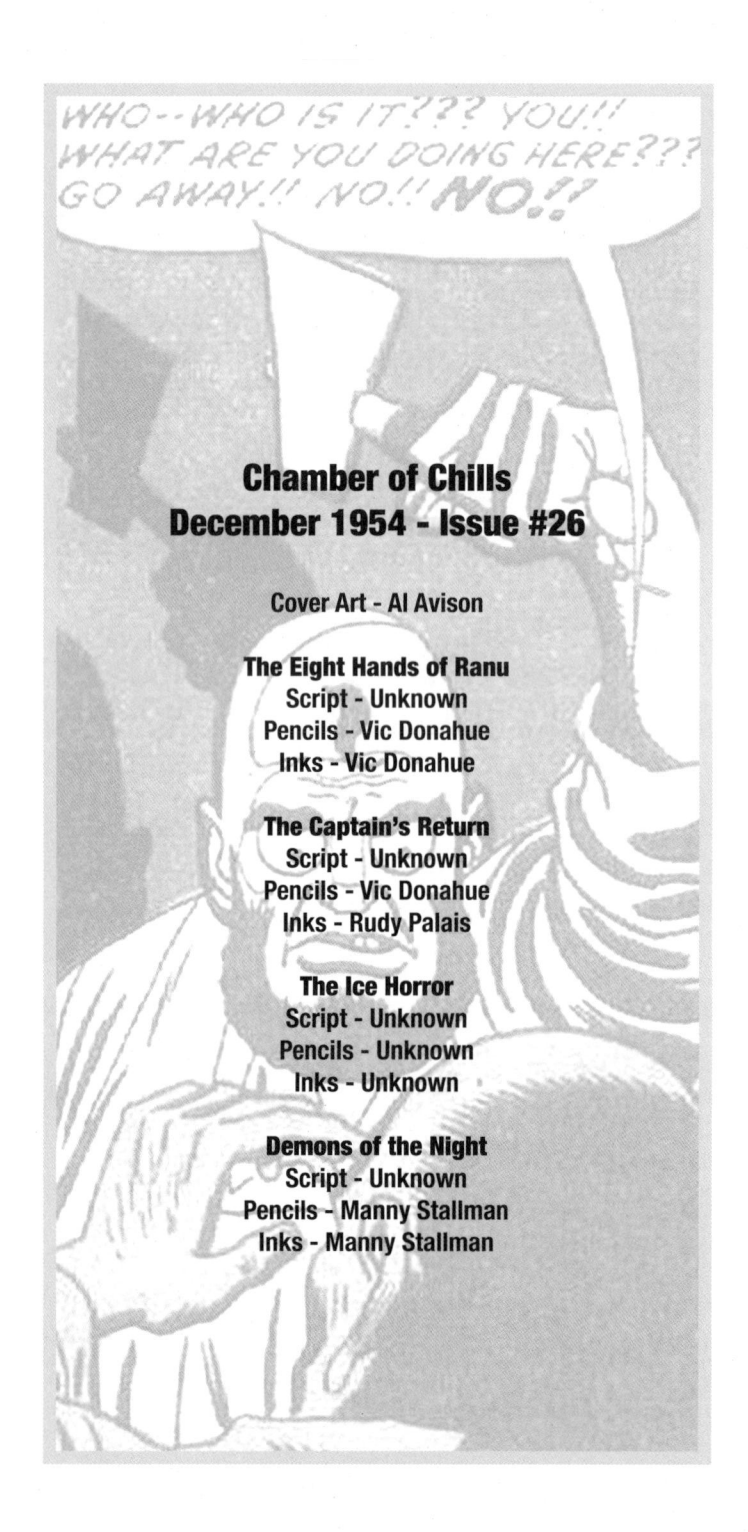

Information Source: Grand Comics Database!
A nonprofit, Internet-based organization of international volunteers dedicated to building a database covering all printed comics throughout the world.
If you believe any of this data to be incorrect or can add valuable additional information, please let us know www.comics.org
All rights to images reserved by the respective copyright holders. All original advertisement features remain the copyright of the respective trading company.

Privacy Policy
All portions of the Grand Comics Database that are subject to copyright are licensed under a Creative Commons Attribution 3.0 Unported License.
This includes but is not necessarily limited to our database schema and data distribution format.
The GCD Web Site code is licensed under the GNU General Public License.

CHAMBER OF CHILLS

TALES OF CHILLS AND SUSPENSE!

MAGAZINE

...Y ONE
...N KNEW
... TRUTH AND
... HAD TO *DIE* TO
... THE SECRET OF THE...
...TAIN'S RETURN!

Success
Home Study
Will to Win
Character
Health
Age

How do you Measure Up?

Get the FACTS! Mail Coupon Today!

HAVE YOU GOT WHAT IT TAKES?

to become a Criminal Investigator Finger Print Expert?

FIND OUT NOW
at our Expense

You have everything to gain — nothing to lose! Here's your chance to learn at OUR expense whether you have "what it takes" to become a criminal investigator or finger print expert. With NO OBLIGATION on your part—mail the coupon below requesting our *qualification* questionnaire. It will be sent to you by return mail. If, in our opinion, your answers to our simple questions indicate that you have the basic qualifications necessary to succeed in scientific crime detection, we will tell you promptly. Then you will also receive *absolutely free* the fascinating "Blue Book of Crime"—a volume showing how modern detectives actually track down real criminals.

Our Graduates Are Key Men in Over 800 Identification Bureaus

So this is your opportunity! We have been teaching finger print and firearms identification, police photography and criminal investigation for over 30 years! OUR GRADUATES —TRAINED THROUGH SIMPLE, INEXPENSIVE, STEP BY STEP HOME STUDY LESSONS—HOLD RESPONSIBLE POSITIONS IN OVER 800 U. S. IDENTIFICATION BUREAUS! We *know* what is needed to succeed—NOW we want to find out if *you* have it!

Without spending a penny—see how YOU "measure up" for a profitable career in scientific criminal investigation. Mail the coupon today!

INSTITUTE OF APPLIED SCIENCE
(A Correspondence School Since 1916)
1920 Sunnyside Ave., Dept. 1746 Chicago 40, Ill.

INSTITUTE OF APPLIED SCIENCE
1920 Sunnyside Ave., Dept. 1746 Chicago 40, Ill.

Gentlemen: Without obligation or expense on my part, send me your qualification questionnaire. I understand that upon receipt of my answers you will immediately advise me if you think they indicate that I have a chance to succeed in criminal investigation or finger print work. Then I will receive FREE the "Blue Book of Crime," and information on your course and the 800 American Identification Bureaus employing your students or graduates.

Name..
Address...RFD or Zone..........
City..........................State...........Age...

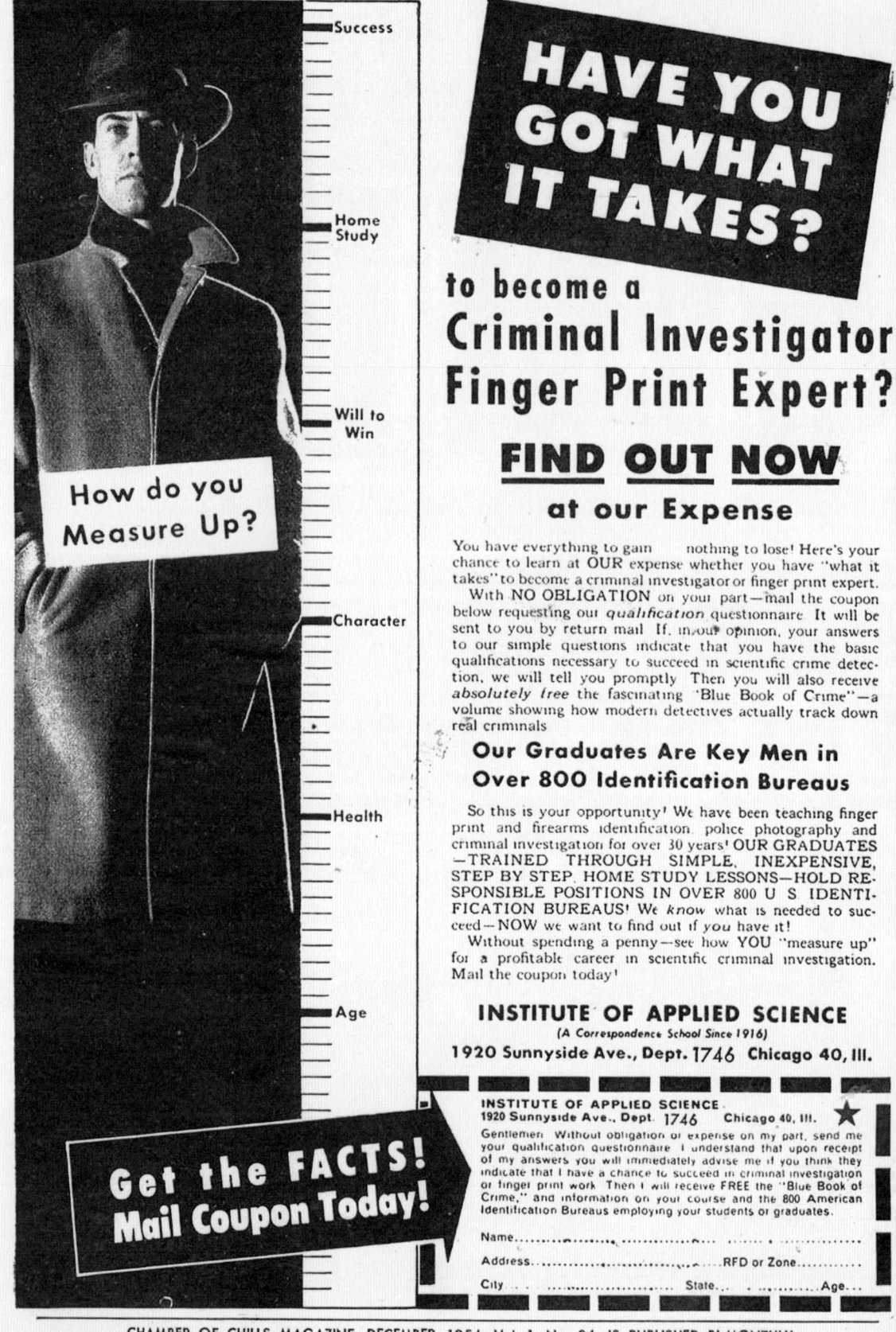

CHAMBER OF CHILLS MAGAZINE, DECEMBER, 1954, Vol. 1, No. 26, IS PUBLISHED BI-MONTHLY by WITCHES TALES, INC., 1860 Broadway, New York 23, N.Y. Entered as second class matter at the Post Office at New York, N.Y. under the Act of March 3, 1879. Single copies 10c. Subscription rates, 10 issues for $1.00 in the U.S. and possessions, elsewhere $1.50. All names in this periodical are entirely fictitious and no identification with actual persons is intended. Contents copyrighted, 1954, by Witches Tales, Inc., New York City. Printed in the U.S.A. Title Registered in U.S. Patent Office.

WELCOME!

The door... you gaze at the door! You cannot take your eyes from the Door of Darkness!

The CHAMBER OF CHILLS lies ready before you, yet you stop as tremors of fear trample through your spine and you tremble in terror!! Why?

Perhaps if you knew the story of the Door of Darkness you would accept its ghastly shape.

Many, many centuries ago when we creatures of the deep occupied and ruled the world above, there was no need for a secret entrance to the CHAMBER OF CHILLS! All was a CHAMBER OF CHILLS!

But when mankind campaigned to erase the horror of the world above, a retreat to the frozen caverns below had to be made. Thus was made the CHAMBER OF CHILLS!

And the door to the vault of terror had to be symbolic of horror supreme. All the monsters, ogres, ghouls, phantoms, zombies, mummies were used for the nefarious task! There could be no mistake. There had to be but one entrance that all could look at and know immediately that it was the Door of Darkness!

Thus its weird and ghastly shape. Thus the hideous and wild gloom that pours from the portal.

So, come now. Hide your eyes if you dare not look at the Door of Darkness. But come now and hasten. The Chamber is ready. It waits with aching arms.

Inside, madness moves about, icy chills are ready to run up and down your spine!

It's time now! Open the Door of Darkness! Now enter....

CHAMBER OF CHILLS

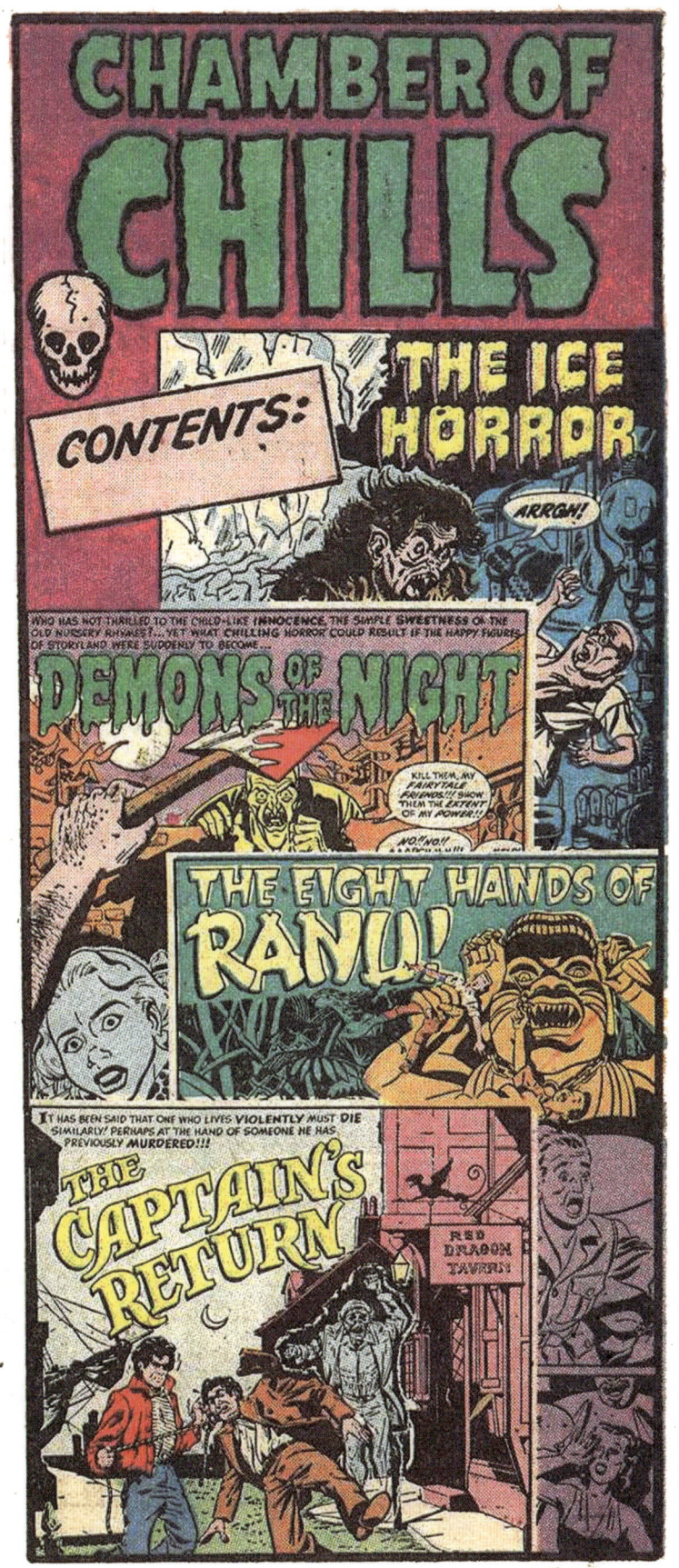

KIDS! BE SURE DAD SEES THIS!

Build a Fine Business... Full or Spare Time!
We Start You FREE—Don't Invest One Cent!

MAKE BIG MONEY
WITH FAST-SELLING WARM
MASON LEATHER JACKETS

SHOE AND LEATHER JACKET ARE BOTH LINED WITH WARM SHEEPSKIN!

Rush Coupon for FREE Selling Outfit!

NOW IT'S EASY to make BIG MONEY in a profit-making, spare-time business! As our man in your community, you feature Mason's fast-selling Horsehide, Capeskin, Suede and other fine leather jackets — nationally known for smart styling, rugged wear, wonderful warmth. Start by selling to friends and fellow workers. Think of all the outdoor workers around your own home who will be delighted to buy these fine jackets direct from you: truck drivers, milkmen, cab drivers, postmen, gas station, construction, and railroad men—hundreds right in your own community! You'll be amazed how quickly business grows. And no wonder!—You offer these splendid jackets at low money-saving prices people can afford! Our top-notch men find it's easy to make up to $10.00 a day EXTRA income!

Be the first to sell men who work outdoors this perfect combination!—Non-scuff, warm Horsehide leather jacket lined with wooly Sheepskin, and new Horsehide work shoe also warmly lined with fleecy Sheepskin and made with oil-resisting soles and leather storm welt!

Even MORE Profits with Special-Feature Shoes

Take orders for Nationally-advertised, Velvet-eez Air-Cushion Shoes in 150 dress, sport, work styles for men and women. Air-Cushion Innersole gives wonderful feeling of "walking on air" all day long. As the Mason man in your town, you actually feature more shoes in a greater range of sizes and widths than the largest store in town! And at low, direct-from-factory prices! It's easy to fit customers in the style they want — they keep re-ordering, too — put dollars and dollars into your pocket! Join the exceptional men who make up to $200 extra a month and get their family's shoes and garments at wholesale prices!

Send for FREE SELLING OUTFIT Today!

Mail the coupon today — I'll rush your powerful Free Jacket and Shoe Selling Outfit including 10-second Air-Cushion Demonstrator, and EVERYTHING you need to start building a steady, BIG MONEY, repeat-order business, as thousands of others have done with Mason!

These Special Features Help You Make Money From First Hour!

Men really go for these warm Mason jackets of long-lasting Pony Horsehide leather, fine Capeskin leather, soft luxurious Suede leather. You can even take orders for Nylon, Gabardine, 100% Wool, Satin-faced Twill jackets, men's raincoats, too! And just look at these EXTRA features that make Mason jackets so easy to sell:

- Warm, cozy linings of real Sheepskin...nature's own protection against cold!
- Quilted and rayon linings!
- Laskin Lamb waterproof, non-matting fur collars!
- Knitted wristlets!
- Especially-treated leathers that do not scuff or peel!
- Zipper Fronts!
- Extra-large pockets!
- Variety of colors for every taste: brown, black, green, grey, tan, blue!

MASON SHOE MFG CO.
Chippewa Falls, Wisc.

SEND FOR FREE OUTFIT!
Dept M-484

Mr. Ned Mason,
MASON SHOE MFG. COMPANY,
Chippewa Falls, Wisconsin

You bet I want to start my own extra-income business! Please rush FREE and postpaid my Powerful Selling Outfit—featuring fast-selling Mason Jackets, Air-Cushion Shoes, other fast-selling specialties—so I can start making BIG MONEY right away!

Name_____ Age_____

Address_____

Town_____ State_____

THE EIGHT HANDS OF RANU!

It is late night and three intruders have found their way into the dread *CONGO ROOM*.. storehouse of weird and grotesque treasures in the home of *JOHN KEYES*, scholar and collector of the grim relics of African black magic...

"HURRY UP, RANCE THIS PLACE IS GIVING ME THE CREEPS!"

"TAKE IT EASY, STEVE. THE STUFF'S WORTH THOUSANDS!"

SUDDENLY...

"WH-WHO'S THERE?"

"GRAB HER, MAC— BEFORE SHE TURNS ON THE LIGHTS!"

TOO BAD YOU GOT A LOOK AT ME, LADY. I GET LIFE IF THE COPS PIN ANOTHER RAP ON ME, AND I HAVE TO MAKE SURE YOU DON'T FINGER MY PICTURE AT HEADQUARTERS.
J-JOHN... H--MMMM!
KLIK!
A GUN WOULD MAKE TOO MUCH NOISE. THIS GADGET OUGHT TO DO THE TRICK.
Sacred Serpent Sword of Sarabi
DON'T WORRY, BOYS! NO ONE'S LAYING THIS JOB AT OUR DOORSTEP. I GOT A PERFECT ALIBI ALL SET UP FOR THE THREE OF US!
EARLY NEXT MORNING, JOHN KEYES MADE A GRISLY DISCOVERY.
MARIA!
REST WELL, MY DEAR. THOSE WHO DID IT ARE DOOMED ALREADY... FOR THE FOOLS USED THE SACRED SERPENT SWORD. YOU WILL BE AVENGED.
SOME DAYS LATER, IN THE OFFICE OF POLICE LIEUTENANT REYNOLDS...
SORRY, KEYES. I HAVEN'T A THING ON YOUR WIFE'S KILLERS. NOT A SHRED OF EVIDENCE.
EVIDENCE WILL NOT BE NECESSARY, LIEUTENANT. YOU HAVE HERE A FILE WITH THE PHOTOGRAPHS OF ALL KNOWN CRIMINALS. I WANT TO LOOK THROUGH THAT FILE.
CAREFULLY, KEYES WENT THROUGH THE PHOTOS, HOLDING THE STRANGE SERPENT SWORD ABOVE EACH...
RANCE COLLINS. HE WAS ONE OF THE KILLERS. THE LEGEND SAYS THAT THIS SWORD BLEEDS WHEN HELD OVER THE LIKENESS OF THE ONE WHO USED IT LAST!
IT--IT'S INCREDIBLE!
2

RANCE COLLINS. STEVE MADROGI. MAC WILKINS. THEY ARE MY WIFE'S MURDERERS.
YOU'D BETTER LEAVE POLICE WORK TO THE POLICE ...AND NOT RELY ON BLACK MAGIC, MR. KEYES. I'VE ALREADY QUESTIONED THOSE THREE, AND THEY HAVE PERFECT ALIBIS.
BESIDES, YOU'D HARDLY EXPECT ANY COURT TO TAKE SUCH SUPERSTITIOUS NON-SENSE AS SERIOUS EVIDENCE.
I TAKE IT SERIOUSLY... AND I'M SURE MY WIFE'S KILLERS WILL, TOO, BEFORE I'M THROUGH WITH THEM. GOOD DAY, LIEUTENANT.
SOME DAYS LATER...
HEY, RANCE...THEY'RE LIKE A TRINKET WE PICKED UP AT KEYES' HOUSE. THINK IT'S A TRAP?
MAYBE...BUT WE HAVE A PERFECT ALIBI...AND WE CAN ALWAYS SAY WE FOUND THIS ONE. LET'S GO!
RARE CONGO AMULETS. WORTH FORTUNE TO OWNER IF HE CONTACTS M. SPERETI... 3 CLAYTON DRIVE
PRESENTLY...
YOU THE GENT THAT SAID ONE OF THESE WAS WORTH A FORTUNE!
YES...BUT I HOPE MY LITTLE AD WASN'T MISLEADING. THAT AMULET IS VALUABLE ONLY BECAUSE IT IS PART OF A CHARM THAT GUARDS RANU AGAINST THE EVIL SPIRITS...A NATIVE CONGO IDOL. HE WHO WEARS IT MAY STEAL RANU WITHOUT HARM!
...AND I AM OFFERING $200,000 IF YOU BRING RANU TO ME. I WILL PAY FOR YOUR PASSAGE, AND ARRANGE TO HAVE SUPPLIES AND INSTRUCTIONS READY WHEN YOU REACH AFRICA.
TWO HUNDRED GRAND FOR A WOODEN STATUE? YOU GOT YOURSELF THREE DELIVERY BOYS, MISTER!
HA-HA! I KNEW THEIR GREED WOULD TRAP THEM! THE AMULET WON'T PROTECT THEM AGAINST RANU! NOTHING WILL PROTECT THEM AGAINST RANU! REST EASILY, MARIA. YOUR MURDERERS ARE SPEEDING TO THEIR DOOM!
3

WEEKS LATER, DEEP IN THE FETID SWAMPLAND BORDERING THE CONGO...
QUIET, RANCE! I SEE RANU--THROUGH THIS CLEARING!
I'LL BE GLAD WHEN THIS TRIP IS OVER. I'D RATHER BE DEAD THAN LIVE IN A MUCK HOLE LIKE THIS!
RANU... BWAMAY... ATTONAH... MY LIFE IS YOUR LIFE, RANU.
ACCORDING TO THE INFO THAT GUY GAVE US, THE WITCH DOCTOR GUARDS RANU WITH HIS LIFE. NO SENSE TANGLING WITH HIM AT CLOSE RANGE!
GOT HIM! FIRE OVER THEIR HEADS AND SCARE THEM AWAY!
CRAK!
SOME PEOPLE MIGHT CALL THIS BABY UGLY... BUT TO ME, HE'S THE PRETTIEST THING I'VE EVER SEEN... 200 GRAND WORTH OF PRETTY!
COME ON, STEVE. THE SOONER I GET OUT OF THIS PLACE, THE BETTER I LIKE IT. WHAT ARE YOU WAITING FOR?
I..I'M SCARED, RANCE. I GOT A LOOK AT ONE OF THOSE NATIVES, AND HE WAS GRIN-NING. WH-WHY SHOULD HE SMILE?
MAYBE THEY DIDN'T LIKE THE WITCH DOCTOR AND ARE GLAD WE BUMPED HIM OFF. WHO CARES? COME ON!
RANU COME BACK.
4

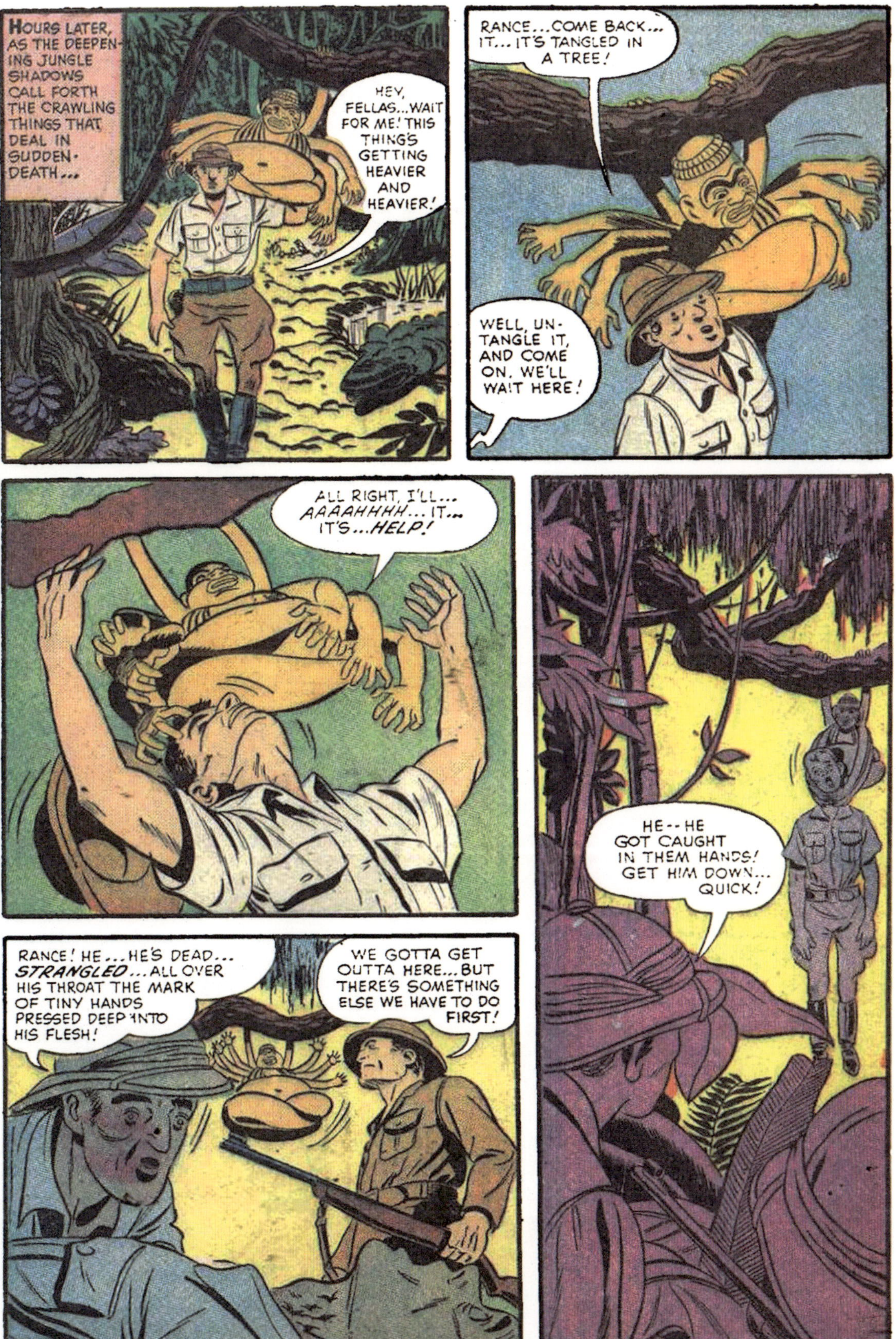
HOURS LATER, AS THE DEEPENING JUNGLE SHADOWS CALL FORTH THE CRAWLING THINGS THAT DEAL IN SUDDEN DEATH...
HEY, FELLAS...WAIT FOR ME! THIS THING'S GETTING HEAVIER AND HEAVIER!
RANCE...COME BACK... IT... IT'S TANGLED IN A TREE!
WELL, UNTANGLE IT, AND COME ON. WE'LL WAIT HERE!
ALL RIGHT, I'LL... AAAAHHHH... IT... IT'S...HELP!
HE--HE GOT CAUGHT IN THEM HANDS! GET HIM DOWN... QUICK!
RANCE! HE...HE'S DEAD... STRANGLED...ALL OVER HIS THROAT THE MARK OF TINY HANDS PRESSED DEEP INTO HIS FLESH!
WE GOTTA GET OUTTA HERE...BUT THERE'S SOMETHING ELSE WE HAVE TO DO FIRST!

WH-WHAT ARE YOU DOING, RANCE?
I'M GONNA ROAST THAT LITTLE WOODEN DEVIL TO ASHES! MAYBE I'M CRAZY BURNING TWO HUNDRED GRAND WORTH OF IDOL, BUT I WANT TO GET OUT OF THIS JUNGLE ALIVE!
ALL RIGHT... LET'S GET MOVING NOW ...FAST!
A LITTLE LATER...
RANCE...DO YOU HEAR IT? SOMETHING CRASHING BEHIND US IN THE BRUSH! DO YOU THINK IT'S...
IT...IT'S AN ANIMAL! IT...IT'S GOTTA BE!
RANCE! I...I CAN'T PULL THE TRIGGER! I'M SCARED!
RANCE ... HELP ME...HELP ME!!
I...I... ARRRGHH!

NO... NO... PLEASE... KILL ME LIKE YOU DID THE OTHERS. ANYTHING... ONLY... NOT THAT.
LEAD, RANU. I UNDERSTAND. I FOLLOW. WHEREEVER YOU GO, I WILL FOLLOW.
SOME WEEKS LATER, IN THE HOME OF JOHN KEYES...
I'VE JUST RECEIVED WORD THAT STEVE MADROGI AND MAC WILKINS HAVE BEEN FOUND IN THE JUNGLE... STRANGLED, MR. KEYES. WHEN YOU LEFT MY OFFICE YOU MADE A THREAT...
SO I DID. THE WAYS OF THE JUNGLE ARE STRANGE, LIEUTENANT--
NATURALLY, I CAN'T CHARGE YOU WITH A THING BUT I'M CURIOUS. THE REPORTS MENTIONED SOMETHING ABOUT AN IDOL NAMED RANU, BUT THE FATE OF RANCE IS UNKNOWN. WHAT DO YOU THINK HAPPENED TO HIM?
I CAN ONLY TELL YOU WHAT THE NATIVES BELIEVE - THAT WHEN SOMEONE KILLS THE WITCH DOCTOR WHO GUARDS RANU...
...THE SPIRIT OF THAT WITCH DOCTOR SOON ENTERS THE BODY OF RANU, AND DOESN'T LEAVE UNTIL THE KILLER AGREES TO BECOME THE NEXT GUARDIAN OF RANU - FOR THE REST OF HIS LIFE!
RANU... BWAMAY... ATTONAH ...MY LIFE IS YOUR LIFE, RANU.
THE END

THE ROTTING DEATH!

"It's the plague! At last it's reached us!!"

It was the terrible truth. The cruel tentacles of the horrible plague had wrapped themselves around Boomtown and were squeezing the town to death!

"First it was the Martins, then the Williamses, and Godfreys, and now it is us! Oh, Martha!"

"John—I am gone... But, flee, run from this decaying death!"

"I will go, Martha... but to seek aid. I am going to Scolville. There is a doctor there—and I will force him to come. It is not only you. We must save all we can!"

"Go, my husband, go!"

John Burton looked back at his wife wasting away to the ravenous disease. He ran from the house and into the stable. He saddled his fastest steed and sped through the streets.

Lying in the gutters of Boomtown were the dreadful victims of the plague. Lined on each side of the roads were these dying sacrifices to the whims of pestilence.

John turned his eyes from this horror and pointed them ever forward along the road to Scolville.

Faster and faster went the steed, kicking the decaying dust of Boomtown behind it.

Night drew near as John reached the town of Scolville. The blackness breathed heavily on the scene.

"Up ahead, there's his house!"

The horse was brought to a halt outside the simple cottage. John dismounted quickly and ran toward the door.

"Open, open fast! Doctor, I need you!"

A little old woman came to the door. "Go away, the doctor is sleeping. He can't be disturbed!"

"Sleep??? When the world is rotting away." He rushed past her and into the kitchen.

"Where is the doctor? Where is his room?"

The old woman pointed to a room in the back. "Don't disturb him, sir, I beg you."

John rushed toward the room and pushed open the closed door. And there was the doctor.

"Keep back, my boy—keep away from me!"

The doctor was covered with ghastly sores which were turning his face and body into a picture of agony—and death!

"Yes, my boy, the plague has reached us, too!"

BIRTH OF A MONSTER

The giant lizard looked out from the huge block of ice.

"Think, my friend, if he was alive! Look at him frozen solid in his full form! Yet, who knows, Pleshko, were the ice to melt, this tremendous beast of past ages might emerge in all its power!"

"Professor Lampl, don't think like that! We mustn't tamper with Nature's super power. You must give this to the museum!"

"Quiet, you fool! Do you think that all my time and money spent in my Antarctic mission will go for nil? I sought a creature of the past—and have found it! Shall I give it up? No!!!"

"But, sir, what can you dare try?"

"Were that creature to come to life, I would have unlimited power! That thirty foot block of ice holds a giant of more than twenty feet high! I could rule the world as its master!"

"Professor Lampl, don't try it! I demand that you forget this mad idea!"

"Mad??? No, fool—ingenious! Get the heating machine ready!"

Pleshko didn't move for a minute. Horrible pictures dashed through his brain as he visioned the terror Lampl could bring. Then he decided to follow the scientist's desires—only to stand as a guard should Lampl's loathesome plan be successful.

"I follow your bidding!"

"Good—now get to work."

Slowly, Pleshko rolled the big heating machine toward the block of ice. He placed the great arms of the machine around the ice and pushed one, two, three dials.

The electrical currents went to work sparking bolts into the ice!

"Look! It's moving, Pleshko! It is alive!"

"Stop! No more! No more!"

Pleshko rushed toward the dials of the machine. Lampl hurled himself upon him. The two twisted in mad battle on the floor as the machine continued to melt the ice.

Lampl was now on top of his assistant—clutching at his throat...

"L-look b-e-e-hind, La-a-mpl! S-e-e-e-e your monster!"

Lampl turned and saw his creature amidst the melted ice. But it was only a tiny lizard, no more than a few inches high! Its "great size" had only been the magnification of the ice!

258

IT HAS BEEN SAID THAT ONE WHO LIVES VIOLENTLY MUST DIE SIMILARLY! PERHAPS AT THE HAND OF SOMEONE HE HAS PREVIOUSLY MURDERED!!!
THE CAPTAIN'S RETURN
RED DRAGON TAVERN
THE CREWS THAT MANNED THE SAILING VESSELS IN THE 19TH CENTURY WERE COMPRISED OF A STRANGE ASSORTMENT OF MEN! SOME WERE HONEST AND LAW-ABIDING... OTHERS WEREN'T!
I WARN YOU, LARENT! AS CAPTAIN OF THIS SHIP I ORDER YOU TO GO BELOW! YOU'RE INSANE IF YE BELIEVE I'VE BEEN HOLDING OUT ON YOU!
YOU LIE! MY SHARE FROM THAT CARGO IS TWICE WHAT I GOT! AND IF YOU'RE NOT GIVING IT TO ME, I'LL TAKE MY SHARE AND YOURS!
LARENT...! YOU ...AGGGRRHHAA! ...I ...WILL... BE... BACK...!
HOLD OUT ON JOHN LARENT, WILL YOU!! HA-HA-HA!!

AND NOW ALL THE MONEY WILL BE MINE!! AND THIS SHIP! YOU HAVE DONE WELL, ROPE...! VERY WELL!!
THE FOLLOWING DAY JOHN LARENT INFORMS THE CREW OF THE NEW REGIME --- IN NO UNCERTAIN TERMS!!!
WHERE'S THE CAPTAIN?
YOU'RE LOOKING AT HIM! I, JOHN LARENT, AM YOUR NEW CAPTAIN! AND ANY OBJECTORS WILL JOIN YOUR OLD ONE! HIS GRAVE IS LARGE ENOUGH FOR YOU ALL!
AYE, AYE, SIR!
TIME PASSED, BUT JOHN LARENT'S VIOLENT LUST HADN'T BEEN SATISFIED!!
JOHNSON THIS PORTS SHIPPING IS MINE! AND ONE WHO THINKS DIFFERENTLY HAS TO ANSWER TO ME!!
YOU'RE A FOOL, LARENT! THE PORT IS FREE! AND WHAT I DO HERE IS MY OWN AFFAIR
WHEN JOHNSON LEFT THE TAVERN, HE WAS FOLLOWED BY LARENT WHOSE UBIQUITOUS ROPE AGAIN DID HIS FIEND-ISH BIDDING! UNSEEN... EXCEPT BY A DEAD MAN!
CROSS JOHN LARENT, WILL YOU!!!
AIEEEEE!!!
HA-HA-HA!!! AND NOW YOUR SHIP TOO, JOINS MY FLEET!
AGGRRRHHAAA!!
EXCELLENT, ROPE!! EXCELLENT! TWO MEN HAVE TRIED TO STAND IN MY WAY! BUT YOU HAVE MURDERED THEM BOTH!

BUT LARENT'S MOMENTARY GLEE VANISHES INTO THIN AIR AS THE HORRIFYING VISION OF THE CAPTAIN SEEMS TO APPEAR SIMILARLY!!
WHAT...!NO! NO! IT CAN'T BE!...YOU ARE DEAD! GO AWAY!
LARENT! I'M STILL YOUR CAPTAIN! HA-HA-HA!
NO! I KILLED YOU! THIS CANNOT BE!
BUT IT CAN, LARENT! IT IS I- YOUR CAPTAIN! REMEMBER??? HA-HA-HA-HA!!!
IN ABJECT TERROR, JOHN LARENT RETREATS FRANTICALLY -- TOO HORRIFIED TO TURN AND SEE THAT THE VISION HAS DISAPPEARED!
HE MUSTN'T CATCH ME! HE MUSTN'T! NO!
BUT THE YEARS PASS, AND WITH THEM PASS LARENT'S FEAR OF THE VISION. AND HIS DIABOLICAL GREED AND VIOLENT LUST BRING HIM FABULOUS RICHES!!!
YOUR FLEET OFFERS A SERIOUS THREAT TO MY MONOPOLY, HAWKINS! MOVE IT TO ANOTHER PORT NOW, WHILE I STILL GIVE YOU THE OPPORTUNITY!
SORRY, LARENT! I REFUSE TO BOW TO YOU AS THE OTHERS DID! THAT'S MY FINAL ANSWER!
THEN THIS IS MY ANSWER, HAWKINS! SAY NO TO JOHN LARENT, WILL YOU?!
AGGRRHHHHAAA!!
YOU STILL DO MY BIDDING, ROPE! WE'VE GONE FAR TOGETHER! HA-HA-HA...!
3

RETURNING HOME TO HIS NEWLY ACQUIRED MANSION PURCHASED WITH BLOOD-STAINED MONEY, LARENT REVELS IN HIS POWER AND INFAMY!
MY CASTLE! ALL MINE! I MEAN OURS, ROPE! OURS! HA-HA-HA!
BUT LARENT'S GLORY IS ABRUPTLY SHATTERED AT THE DREAD SIGHT THAT HAS PLAGUED, HAUNTED HIM THROUGH HIS YEARS OF GREED!
NO! NO! IT CAN'T BE!
BUT IT IS, LARENT! REMEMBER ME??? HA-HA-HA!!!
CLENCHED IN THE COLD GRIP OF FEAR, HE WHIRLS AND RETREATS WILDLY DOWN THE LAVISH CORRIDORS.
YOU'LL NEVER GET ME! NEVER!
HA-HA-HA...!
THEN SUDDENLY, OBSESSED WITH VENGEFUL HATE THAT TRANSCENDS HIS FEAR, LARENT RESOLUTELY DECIDES TO TURN THE ROPE ON HIS TORMENTOR!
THE ROPE! YES! THE ROPE! IT WILL STRANGLE HIM AS IT DID THE OTHERS! AGAIN!!
HE'S YOURS, ROPE!! YOURS! AIEEE!!!
AGGRRRHHAAAA...!!
HA HA! HA! HA! HA!
AS LARENT FALLS, ONE END OF THE ROPE CATCHES ON THE BANNISTER AND AN INVISIBLE HAND TWISTS THE OTHER END AROUND HIS THROAT KILLING HIM... JUSTLY!
The End
4

LOOK HERE! for BIG MONEY MAKING OPPORTUNITIES
for MONEY-SAVING OFFERS and SERVICES

SALES HELP — AGENTS WANTED

MAKE $50—$100—MORE! Sell unusual Christmas cards, novelties. Big profits. Amazing bonus reward. Write for Feature assortments on approval, free samples Personal Christmas Cards, free color Catalog. New England Art Publishers, North Abington 1133, Mass.

POSTCARD PUTS YOU IN A FINE BUSINESS! Complete line. Leather jackets, 160 shoe styles Big Commissions No investment Send postcard for Free Outfit. Mason Shoe, Dept. MA-432, Chippewa Falls, Wis.

AMAZING Extra-Money plan gives you gorgeous dress without penny cost Rush name today with dress size. HARFORD, Dept M-3180, Cincinnati 25, Ohio.

28 DIFFERENT Christmas Cards FREE plus Box Assortments on approval you can sell for cash Send no money Rush name today to General Card Co., Dept. 178-M. 1300 W Jackson, Chicago 7

FREE HOSIERY! Earn to $3 hour spare time introducing sensational hosiery by giving every man and woman free trial pair! Amazing nylon stockings guaranteed against runs-snags New miracle one size nylon stretch socks Fit any size foot. Never sag Guaranteed one year Mail postcard for free samples, money-making outfits State age Kendex, Babylon 119, N Y

NEED EXTRA CASH? Get it selling Blair's unusual line of household and food products Every housewife a prospect Products sent on FREE Trial. Write BLAIR, Dept. 84MS, Lynchburg, Va

$100-$200 IS YOURS SHOWING EXCLUSIVE W/S personalized Christmas Cards—as low as 50 for $1.50 up FREE SAMPLES. 32 page 4-color catalog Wetmore & Sugden, 90 Monroe Avenue, Rochester 2, New York

CHEMISTRY

AMAZING NEW Science Book Experiments, Formulas, Science Catalogue Only 25c NATIONAL SCIENTIFIC CO., Dept CG, 2204 North Ave., Chicago 47

MONEY MAKING OPPORTUNITIES

RAISE EARTHWORMS! Terrific! Get important information plus true story, "An Earthworm Turned His Life" Send dime. Earthmaster System, 23D, El Monte, Calif

"HOW TO MAKE MONEY with Simple Cartoons" A book everyone who likes to draw should have It is free, no obligation Simply address CARTOONISTS EXCHANGE, Dept. 849, Pleasant Hill, Ohio.

Sew our Redi-Cut Handy-Hanky aprons at home Easy, Profitable A & B ENTERPRISES, Dept. C, 2516 N Albert Pike, Ft Smith, Arkansas

BIGGER PROFITS selling Greeting Cards Get list of sensational Factory Surplus Bargains $1 25 boxes for 50c, $1 boxes for 35c—while they last! Big line new 1954 Christmas Cards, Stationery, Gifts Assortments on approval, Personalized Samples FREE! Midwest Cards, 1113 Washington, Dept. J-142, St Louis, Mo

$5 to $20 Sparetime Sewing and Assembling. Write Liebig Industries, Beaver Dam 8, Wisconsin.

SELL CHRISTMAS CARDS' Samples on approval Writewell, C-1, Boston 15, Mass.

$20 day' Sell name plates for houses LINDO-PLAN, Watertown, Mass

BIG CASH—make 100% PROFIT Sell Empire Christmas Cards 21-card assortment $1 Name-printed stationery, napkins, child's Christmas books. Costs nothing to try Write for the catalog, Free Imprint Samples, Boxes on approval EMPIRE CARD, 455 Fox, Elmira, N Y

MAKE MONEY Introducing World's cutest children's dresses Big selection, adorable styles Low prices Complete display free. Rush name Harford, Dept M-3394, Cincinnati 25, Ohio

MILITARY COLLECTIONS

Army, Navy patches, brass badges, ribbons, 33 different $1 00—Foreign Armies' prices, 10c Hobbyguild, 550 Fifth Ave., New York.

STAMPS

COLOSSAL STAMP ZOO FREE—Jungle Beasts, Wildlife, fifteen different including Rhinoceros, Snake, Tiger, Elephant, Zabu, Koalabear, Kookabura, Extraordinary accompanying approvals. Send 10c for handling Niagara Stamp Co., Niagara-on-the-Lake 538, Canada.

9999 Different from 16 Stamp Companies Approvals Cash $10.00. King, 32 Alexander, Kamloops, Canada

BAG OF 1,000 STAMPS, unpicked, unsorted, over 30 countries, postpaid, guaranteed, $1.00. HARRISCO, 554 Transit Building, Boston 17, Mass.

FREE! Twelve United States stamps also big lists. Send 3c to cover mailing Approvals. Littleton Stamps, Littleton F17, N. H.

MISCELLANEOUS

STARTLING NEW BOOK "Truth About Tobacco" Everybody should read it. Only 50c A. C. Johnson, Chemist, 2204 North Ave., Chicago 47.

POEMS WANTED. Free examination. McNeil, 510C So. Alexandria, Los Angeles, Calif.

COAL BURNING PROBLEMS SOLVED! Amazing additive makes any coal in any stove or furnace burn cleaner, better, longer. Stops soot, smoke, coal gas. No hard clinkers. Perfect for wood, coke, charcoal too. Details FREE. INFURNO, Dept CBC, 140 N. Dearborn, Chicago, Illinois.

PERSONAL

PEN PALS Everywhere! Magazine, photos, names, addresses, ALL ages. Air-mailed. $1 00. Give age for special list, those near you. PUBLICATIONS, 2272-C Hubbard, Memphis 8, Tenn

ADVERTISERS

You're looking at the world's biggest classified advertising buy! TWENTY MILLION circulation at a cost-per-word so low, you'll schedule your advertising here every time. For rates, closing dates, full information write COMIC GROUPS CLASSIFIED, 400 Madison Avenue, New York 17.

Zebra-Snake Design

REVERSIBLE AUTO SEAT COVERS
MADE OF FLEXTON — SERVICE GAUGE PLASTIC FOR LONG WEAR

● Waterproof. Easy to attach to seats for good fit. Roomy and neat. Elastic shirring and reinforced overlap side grips insure over-all seat coverage. Will dress up your car's interior and give protection to seat upholstery. Whisk off mud, oil, sand, grime with a damp rag for bright as new appearance. Sewn with nylon thread for long wear and durability.

ORDER FROM MANUFACTURER AND SAVE!
Choice of split or front seat styles only **$2.98** each. Complete set for Front & Rear only **$5.00**. Specify make of car and seat style with each order. Save Money and buy a set today.

LEOPARD-COWHIDE DESIGN

STYLE =400
Snake Zebra Design — Printed Plastic can be used on either side. Gives snappy distinctive dress up appearance. Front or Rear Seat only **$2.98**

STYLE =500
Leopard Cowhide design on Printed Flexton Plastic. Leopard on one side, Cowhide on the other. Either side gives beauty to your car's seats. Never gets dirty for it cleans with a whisk of a damp cloth. Front or Rear. **$2.98**

RUSH ORDER TODAY!

5 day Money Back Guarantee!

```
MARDO SALES CORPORATION, DEPT. DS-200
480 Lexington Ave., New York 17, N. Y.
Please send me the seat covers I have
marked I can try for 10 days and return
for refund of purchase price if I am not
satisfied.
☐ Zebra-Snake Design, Reversible
☐ Leopard Cowhide Design, Reversible
☐ Split Seat $2 98    ☐ Solid Seat $2 9?
☐ Set (Front & Rear) $5.00
☐ I enclose payment   ☐ Send C.O.D.
Name
Address
City              Zone       State
```

THE ANNALS OF HORROR

Beginning with this issue, you, the reader, will have the exclusive opportunity to know the complete and unbelievable story of the science of healing from medicine-man to doctor. Much of what you will read will shock you. But, as people, we are entitled to know the amazing stories of how our ancestors battled plagues, superstitions and death. Remember! Read on at your own risk!

Our first chapter ... THE BLACK DEATH!

The Black Death is the bubonic plague which began in Constantine in 1347 and swept over great parts of Europe, leaving untold death and devastation in its wake. Rats are the carriers of the disease.

1665 was the year of the great plague in London. A bill of mortality for the week August 15 to 22, 1665, read 5,568 persons dead, and 4,237 of these deaths were attributed to the plague. The causes of death as recorded were ascertained by old women employed by the parish authorities to inspect the bodies at each death.

Comets, particularly when accompanied by a cloud of swords, daggers, coffins, and men's heads, were considered to be omens of impending plague. Pepys, in his DIARY, mentions the comet of December, 1664, at which King Charles II and his queen looked from the windows of Whitehall (royal residence in London). The comet appeared again in the February following and once more in March. After these preliminaries the plague broke out in June!

Posters were published in 1665 and 1666 to illustrate events of the plague in London. They showed how trenches were dug in the fields to bury the dead. The bodies, a few in coffins, but most in coarse shrouds or naked, were brought from the city in heavily loaded horse-drawn carts. During the plague, also, many bodies were buried together in large graves and when the plague subsided the level of the field was sometimes raised a foot or more above its original height.

During the plague in London, the doors of the houses were marked with red crosses to indicate that there was plague among the inmates, and armed guards stood in the streets to prevent anyone from coming out. Certain people were known as dog-killers and their job was to slaughter every dog they met. Dogs were believed to carry the plague and thousands of them were killed, but no attention was paid to the rats which were responsible for the epidemic.

If a person was suspected of spreading the disease his fate was quick and final. The absurdity of the evidence upon which some accusations were based made little difference; just mere suspicion was sufficient to cause the people to seek revenge. Many people so accused were burned alive at the stakes.

In addition, those people who were thought to be plague spreaders and who were not killed had other terrors to bear. Many hideous torture devices were made to force the person to confess being a plague spreader. Some were strapped down on racks and their bodies torn apart. Others had their bodies mutilated by white hot pincers. It was a form of witch hunting.

The plague doctor was a curious thing of the plague. Unable to do much with his science, he returned to primitive ways of dealing with sickness. He put on strange costumes to frighten evil spirits away. One of these costumes consisted of a long robe and a wooden bird's head. Spices were poured into the snout to purify the air.

Such was the Black Death! Its terror was world wide. Many thousands of people died needlessly and horribly. The age of reason had not come and would not for a long time yet.

In the next issue of *Chamber of Chills*, you will read all about how medieval doctors operated on patients. It's a chapter you won't want to miss!

The TRUE DIARY of BATTLE..
WARFRONT
NOW ON SALE

MEN-WOMEN-BOYS-GIRLS
PRIZES GIVEN
MAKE MONEY TOO!

RADIO

ELECTRONIC TWO-WAY WALKIE-TALKIE

ROY ROGERS FLASH CAMERA

ROY ROGERS OR DALE EVANS LAMP

ROY ROGERS BINOCULARS

TEXAN JR. GUITAR

GABBY HAYES FISHING KIT

WRIST WATCHES FOR BOYS AND GIRLS

RADIUM DIAL POCKET WATCH

GIRLS' SHOULDER-STRAP BAG

ARCHERY SET

SPORTS EQUIPMENT

TWO-GUN HOLSTER SET

TABLE TENNIS SET

VANITY SET

PRESSURE COOKER

ROLLER SKATES

WALKING DOLL

HUNTING KNIFE AND AX

RED RYDER CARBINE

WOODBURNING SET

JET ENGINE PLANE FLIES 500 FEET!

CHEMISTRY SET

TYPEWRITER

WHITE ZIPPER BIBLE

UKELELE WITH ARTHUR GODFREY PLAYER

RADIO RECEIVING SET FOR SCOUTS

SEWING MACHINE

We will send you the wonderful prizes pictured on this page... or dozens of others, such as jewelry; radium dial wrist watches, tableware, tools, U-Make-It kits, leather kits, sewing kits, electric clocks, pressure cookers, scout equipment, model airplanes, movie machines, record players, and many others...all WITHOUT ONE PENNY OF COST. You don't risk or invest a cent—we send you everything you need ON TRUST. Here's how easy it is: Merely show your friends and neighbors inspiring, beautiful Religious Wall Motto plaques. Many buy six or even more to hang in every room. An amazing value, only 35¢...sell on sight. You can secure big, cash commissions or many exciting prizes for selling just one set of 24 Mottos. Write today for Big Prize catalog sent to you FREE!

SEND NO MONEY—We Trust You!

HERE'S HOW YOU GET YOUR PRIZES

Rush your name and address on coupon and we will ship AT ONCE PREPAID your first set of 24 richly decorated Mottos ON TRUST. When you have sold the 24 Mottos, send the $8.40 you have collected and you can secure your choice of many wonderful prizes. If you prefer to EARN MONEY, send $6.00 and keep $2.40. Hurry, send TODAY for 24 Mottos ON TRUST and big PRIZE CATALOG FREE!

FREE!
MEMBERSHIP in the FUNman's Fun Club

EXTRA! Sell mottos and send payment within 15 days, and we'll give you FREE a year's Membership in the FUNman's Fun Club. Membership card, certificate, secret code, giant packet of fun materials all yours—PLUS many extra surprises!

The FUNman, Dept. K-203, 4545 N. Clark St., Chicago 40, Ill. **FREE BIG PRIZE CATALOG**

Please rush to me on credit 24 Religious Wall Mottos, to sell at 35¢ each. Also include big Prize Catalog FREE. I will remit amount required as explained under description of prize in BIG PRIZE CATALOG within 30 days and select the prize I want or keep a cash commission as explained.

NAME.. AGE......

STREET or RFD..............................

TOWN................ Zone.... STATE..........

SEND NO MONEY...We Trust You!

HERNIA SUFFERERS!
GET INSTANT BLESSED RELIEF – THE PROVEN WAY

Amazing New.. **Freedom and Comfort**

WITH THE NATIONALLY FAMOUS...

RUPTURE-EASER
A Piper Brace Product

RIGHT OR LEFT SIDE
Pat No 2606551 **$3.95**

Double **$4.95**

No fitting required!
JUST GIVE SIZE AND SIDE

A strong form fitting washable support designed to give you relief and comfort. Snaps up in front. Adjustable back lacing and adjustable leg strap. Soft flat groin pad — no torturing steel or leather bands. Unexcelled for comfort, invisible under light clothing. Washable and sanitary. Also excellent as an after operation support. Wear it with assurance — get new freedom of action!

NO STEEL OR LEATHER BANDS
You get effective scientific relief without those dreaded steel and leather bands that make hernia affliction such torture to thousands of folks. Rupture-Easer support is firm, gentle, sure—you'll realize a new lease on life with the comfort and assurance Rupture-Easer brings you!

BLESSED RELIEF DAY AND NIGHT
Rupture-Easer is just as comfortable to sleep in, and to bathe in, as it is to wear! Soft scientific pad pressure keeps you safe, awake or asleep. Those who need constant support welcome Rupture-Easer's blessed comfort.

INVISIBLE UNDER LIGHT CLOTHING
Wear Rupture-Easer with new confidence under your lightest clothing. No more visible than any usual undergarment — no revealing bulk to hide. Even worn under girdles and corsets comfortably!

WASHABLE AND SANITARY
Yes, you can wash your Rupture-Easer as easily and safely as your other undergarments. A quick sudsing keeps Rupture-Easer just as fresh as new.

Read What Others Say:
Harley Decoteau, Montpelier, Vt. writes "The last brace you sent me was wonderful. I have been ruptured for 10 years. I am now 36 and in 90 years, I have never been more pleased."

Juanita Addison, Twin Falls, Idaho says "I would like to have another Rupture Easer. It really has helped me. I can do practically anything with the Rupture-Easer on."

Mr. George Dorchser, Union City, N.J. says: "I am using one of your Rupture Easers now and find it the best I have ever used. I am a truck driver and have tried others that cost 4 and 5 times as much as your hernia support but I get more comfort from your supporter."

there's no substitute for proved **Performance!**

For Men...
For Women
For Children

$3.95 single

$4.95 double

Over **700,000** Grateful USERS!

Easy to Order: Just measure around lowest part of abdomen and state right or left side or double.

10 DAY TRIAL OFFER Money back if you don't get blessed relief. Mail orders only.

PIPER BRACE CO.
811 Wyandotte, Dept HA-54, Kansas City 6, Mo.

DELAY may be serious!

Use Handy COUPON
...get yours NOW!

PIPER BRACE COMPANY
811 Wyandotte, Dept. HA-54
Kansas City 6, Mo.

Please send my RUPTURE-EASER by return mail.
Right Side ☐ $3.95   Measure around lowest part of
Left Side ☐ $3.95   my abdomen
Double ☐ $4.95   is .... INCHES.

(Note: Be sure to give Size and Side when ordering.)
We Prepay Postage except on C.O.D.'s
Enclosed is ☐ Money Order ☐ Check for $ _____ ☐ Send C.O.D.

Name _____
Address _____
City and State _____

FROM THE FROZEN WASTES OF ANOTHER WORLD CAME THIS INHUMAN MONSTER TO PREY ON MANKIND AND GLUT ITS APPETITE ON SOFT FLESH. IT WAS...
THE ICE HORROR!
ARRGH!
THREE FIGURES PLODDED WEARILY THROUGH THE WAILING, FURIOUS MAELSTROM IN THE FROZEN WASTES OF DESOLATE ANTARCTICA – A MAELSTROM PORTENDING THE START OF AN EVIL HORROR!!
HOW MUCH FURTHER, HUGH? MARION CAN'T TAKE MUCH MORE OF THIS!
NO...I... I'M ALL RIGHT! KEEP GOING--!
LOOK! THERE ARE THE LAWRENCE MOUNTAINS! WE'RE NEARLY THERE!
YES! BUT WE'RE ALL NEARLY DEAD FROM EXHAUSTION! WE'LL HAVE TO REST A BIT! THAT CLIMB IS GOING TO BE TOUGHER THAN THIS JOURNEY!

WHO WERE THESE THREE COURAGEOUS PEOPLE? TWO OF THEM WERE YOUNG GEORGE RENS AND HIS FIANCÉE, MARION DANIELS, WHOSE FEARLESSNESS HAD MARKED THEM AS MOST CAPABLE RESEARCH ASSISTANTS FOR HUGH NORDSTORM, WORLD-RENOWNED EXPLORER AND SCIENTIST, THE THIRD MEMBER OF THE EXPEDITION...
HOW MUCH FARTHER, HUGH? WE'VE COVERED THREE-QUARTERS OF THIS RANGE ALREADY!
I KNOW! BUT WE HAVE TO KEEP CLIMBING!
THIS IS ALL A SILLY, FANTASTIC GOOSE-CHASE! I STILL THINK THAT WE'LL NEVER FIND THIS--THIS SO-CALLED "MISSING LINK" OF YOURS!
WE HAVEN'T REACHED THE TOP OF THIS MOUNTAIN YET, GEORGE! UNTIL THEN, KEEP QUIET!
HUGH NORDSTORM WAS DRIVEN BY A RELENTLESS AMBITION! HE WAS DETERMINED TO FIND A NEW SPECIES OF NEANDERTHAL MAN--THE PRE-HISTORIC FORERUNNER OF MANKIND WHICH HE HAD BEEN SEARCHING FOR DECADES...
CAREFUL! THIS FOOTHOLD HERE IS SLIPPERY!
HURRY--BEFORE WEIGHT MAKES THIS PATH GIVE WAY!
THEY WERE APPROACHING THE LAST LAP OF THEIR TREK... SUDDENLY, FROM OUT OF THE SNOW-CLOUDED MIST AND FOG, LOOMED A DARK HOLE IN THE MOUNTAIN-SIDE!
IT'S A CAVE! HUGH--DO YOU SUPPOSE--?
YES! I WAS RIGHT! HERE IS THE CAVE OF THE WINDS AS I DECIPHERED IT FROM THOSE RELICS WE UNCOVERED IN FRANCE TWO YEARS AGO! NOW--IS THIS SO FANTASTIC, GEORGE?
THE CAVE OF THE WINDS, LEGENDARY BIRTHPLACE OF THIS YET UNDISCOVERED SPECIES OF HOMO SAPIENS--A LEGEND THE SCIENTIFIC WORLD HAD MOCKED--BUT HUGH NORDSTORM, UNDAUNTLESS, GRIM, SURE--WOULD NOW PROVE TO BE TRUE!
WHY--I--I CAN'T BELIEVE THIS! DRAWINGS, BAS RELIEFS--PAINTINGS OF ANIMALS ALL ALONG THESE WALLS!
WE'VE FOUND A TREASURE OF SCIENTIFIC LORE!
WHAT'S THAT? GREAT SCOTT! THERE'S A HIDDEN PASSAGEWAY HERE! IT GOES DEEPER INTO THE CAVE!
WATCH IT, HUGH! THAT CORRIDOR DOESN'T LOOK TOO STRONG!

TENSE MINUTES OF PRECARIOUS INCHING THROUGH THE ERODED PASSAGEWAY WHERE ONE FALSE STEP COULD PLUNGE THEM INTO INTERMINABLE DEPTHS-- THEN THEY WERE OUT OF IT AND INTO AN ENORMOUS CHAMBER!
THOSE IDOLS MUST BE THOUSANDS OF YEARS OLD! LOOK AT THE DETAILED CARVINGS!
AMAZING! AND I WOULDN'T BELIEVE IT!
GEORGE--MARION-- PLAY YOUR TORCHES ON THAT WALL FOR A MINUTE! YES-- I THINK WE'VE FOUND IT!
YOU MEAN--WE'VE FOUND THIS NEANDERTHAL SPECIMEN? GOOD LORD!!
CASTING THEIR CAUTION TO THE WINDS, THE THREE EXCITED PEOPLE CHOPPED, DUG, AND GOUGED OUT THE COLD, GLISTENING WALL OF ICE WITH THE FRENZY OF DEMONS POSSESSED--
UGH! IT-- --IT'S SOLID AS A ROCK!
USE MORE POWER BEHIND YOUR SWING! FASTER! FASTER!
HUGH! YOU'VE HIT SOMETHING!
I KNEW I COULDN'T BE WRONG! THIS PLACE HAS ALL THE EAR-MARKS OF A HUGE CAVERN THAT HARBORED THIS RACE DURING THE GLACIER AGE ON EARTH-- WE'LL FIND OUR SPECIMEN HERE--IN THIS WALL!
--AND THERE IT IS!
WHAT A HORRIBLE-LOOKING MONSTER! IT--IT MUST BE ABOUT SEVEN-FOOT TALL.
OHHH!
I--I CAN'T GET OVER THE APPEARANCE AND CONDITION OF THIS-- THIS--THING! IT'S BEEN PRESERVED MAGNIFICENTLY! IT ALMOST LOOKS ALIVE!
IT PROBABLY IS, MY DEAR! THE ANCIENT RECORDS I FOUND DIDN'T LIE! ONE OF THEIR RACE HAS SURVIVED THE SPAN OF CENTURIES..!
3

NOW FOLLOWED WEEKS OF DIFFICULT WORK! THE REST OF THE EXPEDITION WAS SUMMONED AND ARRANGEMENTS WERE MADE TO CARRY THE MONSTER-THING OUT OF THE CAVE AND DOWN TO THE GROUND BELOW...

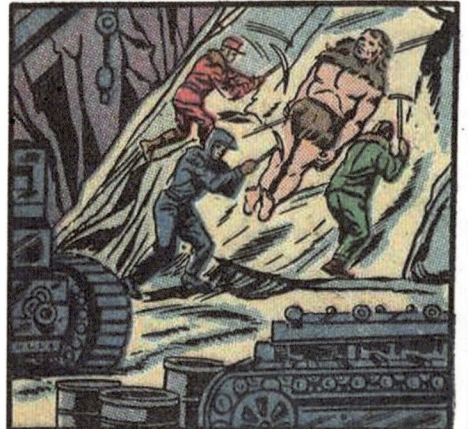

THEN MORE FEROCIOUS WORK! INDEFATIGABLE MEN HEWED OUT A PASSAGE-WAY OF ICE FOR A SLED TO CARRY THE HUGE BLOCK OF FROZEN WATER TO ITS DESTINATION.

AND, FINALLY, MONTHS LATER, A HUGE LINER WAS TAKING IT TO THE UNITED STATES. HUGH NORDSTROM, ALL THIS TIME HAD BECOME INCREASINGLY MOODY AND UNAPPROACHABLE...

WHAT'S COME OVER HIM? IT MAKES ME UNEASY JUST TO LOOK AT HIM!

I DON'T KNOW! THIS DISCOVERY HAS AFFECTED HIM MORE THAN WE UNDERSTAND!

ONCE BACK IN AMERICA, HUGH NORDSTROM DIDN'T PUBLICIZE HIS DISCOVERY AS EXPECTED. INSTEAD, HE SWORE EVERYONE TO SECRECY. AND THREE WEEKS AFTER HIS ARRIVAL, HE SENT FOR GEORGE AND MARION...

COME IN! COME IN! I'VE BEEN WAITING FOR YOU! I'M GOING TO BRING THE MONSTER *BACK TO LIFE!*

SO THAT'S WHY YOU DIDN'T PUBLISH YOUR FINDINGS!

ARE YOU CRAZY? DO YOU EXPECT US TO BELIEVE SUCH POPPY-COCK?

I THINK YOU WILL!

4

HUGH! ARE... ARE YOU INSANE? YOU'VE KNOCKED GEORGE UNCONSCIOUS!
YES MY DEAR-- ALL TO GOOD PURPOSE, AS YOU SHALL SEE! HA-HA!
MINUTES LATER GEORGE RENS CAME OUT OF A SWIRLING BLACKNESS TO FIND MARION AND HIMSELF STRAPPED TO A TABLE, INVOLUNTARILY GIVING BLOOD TO A MONSTER PRE-HISTORIC MAN STILL ENCASED IN ITS BLOCK OF ICE!
PLEASE, HUGH! PLEASE!
HUGH! FOR HEAVENS SAKE! STOP THIS WEIRD THING! YOU'RE TRESPASSING SECRETS NOT MEANT FOR HUMAN KNOWLEDGE!
NO! YOU'LL NOT CHEAT ME OUT OF MY GREATEST EXPERIMENT! IT'S NOT ENOUGH TO JUST REPORT THE DISCOVERY OF A CREATURE SUCH AS THIS! I'M GOING TO BRING IT BACK TO THE WORLD OF MEN AGAIN! MY NAME WILL GO DOWN IN HISTORY!
IT'S OPENING ITS EYES!! EEEEEEE!
SUDDENLY!
ARGGGHH!
W-WHAT HAVE I DONE? STAY BACK!!
AS MARION AND GEORGE STRUGGLE TO FREE THEMSELVES, THE ICE HORROR CLAIMS ITS SHRIEKING VICTIM...
GEORGE! IT'S COMING FOR US!!
DON'T LOOK, MARION! THIS IS THE END!
ARRGGH
CLOSER AND CLOSER IT APPROACHED THEM, ITS BLOOD-RED EYES INTENSE WITH THE LUST TO KILL! THEN, AS IT RAISED THOSE POWERFUL ARMS OF DEATH, A STRANGE PAROXYSM OF COUGHING SEIZED IT--AND SUDDENLY IT DISINTEGRATED BEFORE THEIR EYES!!
COUGH
COUGH
TWO TERRIFIED HUMAN BEINGS LOOKED AT THE PILE OF SLIME AND DECAYING FLESH THAT WAS LEFT, THEIR EYES BULGING WITH THE HORROR OF THE TERRIBLE INCIDENT!
OH, GEORGE... W-WHAT HAPPENED?
OUR RAREFIED AIR MUST HAVE SHREDDED ITS FLESH TO PIECES! THE THING WAS DEAD FOR CENTURIES IT COULDN'T HAVE SURVIVED OUR CLIMATE! POOR HUGH DIED FOR NOTHING--FOR THE PAST HAS RECLAIMED ITS OFFSPRING!
THE END 5

WHO HAS NOT THRILLED TO THE CHILD-LIKE INNOCENCE, THE SIMPLE SWEETNESS OF THE OLD NURSERY RHYMES?... YET WHAT CHILLING HORROR COULD RESULT IF THE HAPPY FIGURES OF STORYLAND WERE SUDDENLY TO BECOME...
DEMONS OF THE NIGHT
KILL THEM, MY FAIRYTALE FRIENDS!!! SHOW THEM THE EXTENT OF MY POWER!!
NO!! NO!! AAARGH-H-H!!!
HELP! HELP!! YAAH-H!!!
IN THE SINISTER BLACKNESS OF MIDNIGHT, A REPULSIVE OLD MAN WANDERS THE STREETS IN SEARCH OF EVIL THAT LIES HIDDEN FROM HUMAN EYES!...
WELL, WHAT HAVE WE HERE?? AN OLD BOOK OF NURSERY RHYMES!! HAPPY LITTLE POEMS FOR THOSE WHO HAVE NOT YET SEEN THE DARKNESS THAT LURKS IN THE MIND OF MAN!!
VOTE
RUB-A-DUB-DUB, THREE MEN IN A TUB; AND WHO DO YOU THINK THEY BE? THE BUTCHER, THE BAKER, THE CANDLESTICK-MAKER. THEY ALL JUMPED OUT OF A ROTTEN POTATO--- TURN 'EM OUT, KNAVES ALL THREE!!
1

"THE BUTCHER, THE BAKER AND THE CANDLESTICK-MAKER!" THREE WORTHY GENTLEMEN!! PERHAPS I CAN ARRANGE TO... MEET THEM!!
A DREADFUL IDEA FORMING IN THE OLD MAN'S TWISTED MIND, HE HURRIES TO HIS GRIMY CELLAR TO SET THE FORCES OF DOOM IN MOTION!...
THIS BOOK WILL FURNISH ME WITH THE INCANTATION TO BRING THE RHYME TO LIFE!! IT SHOULD BE MOST INTERESTING TO SEE THE RESULT!!
ANCIENT INCANTATIONS IN EVIL
LET THE THREE "KNAVES" OF THE RHYME COME FROM THE WORLD OF MAKE-BELIEVE TO THE WORLD OF EVIL AND DEATH!! I, ERIC FALDER, CALL TO YOU!! LUAS SIMUBANTA TABOR!!!
AHH!! THEY BEGIN TO TAKE SHAPE!! MY WORDS HAVE PIERCED THE SHELL OF THEIR SECRET WORLD!!
SOON THREE STRANGE FIGURES APPEAR BEFORE OLD FALDER, THE GARMENTS OF THEIR COMMON VOCATIONS IN CONTRAST WITH THE BOLD AND VICIOUS EXPRESSIONS ON THEIR FACES!...
WE HAVE COME TO SERVE YOU AS YOU COMMAND! THE WORLD OF NURSERY RHYMES EXISTS FOR US NO MORE!!!
THEN YOU ARE MY SLAVES!! YOU CAN BRING ME THE MONEY AND THE POWER I HAVE ALWAYS CRAVED!! WITH YOUR WEAPONS I CAN CONQUER THE MIND AND SOUL OF MAN!!!
2

WHAT DO YOU WISH US TO DO?
STRIKE TERROR AT THE HEART OF THE CITY UNTIL THE PEOPLE ARE FORCED TO CALL ME THEIR RULER!! BRING ME THE RICHES OF THE CITY BANKS!!!
WE SHALL OBEY YOU!!
GO THEN!! THERE ARE NOT MANY HOURS BEFORE DAWN!!
THE LONG NIGHT OF HORROR BEGINS, AS THE REPULSIVE CREATIONS OF A MANIACAL MIND BEGIN THEIR RAMPAGE OF PILLAGE AND MURDER!!
AH-H-H!
WHERE DID THESE MONSTERS COME FROM???
NOW WHAT ARE THOSE THREE UP TO??? I'D BETTER TAKE A LOOK!!
BA
LEXING
JUST WHERE DO YOU THINK YOU'RE---
KILL HIM!!!
WITH THE FEROCIOUS STRENGTH OF A MADMAN, THE BUTCHER PLUNGES HIS CLEAVER INTO THE POLICEMAN...
BANK
AARRGH-H!
3

WHAT'S GOING ON HERE?? YOU CAN'T...
GOOD LORD!
AGAIN AN ORDINARY TOOL BECOMES A VICIOUS WEAPON IN THE HANDS OF A DEPRAVED DEMON OF THE NIGHT!!..
NO!!! DON'T!!! YAIE-EE-EE!!
DRAGGING THE SURVIVING GUARD INTO THE BANK, THE FAIRYTALE FIENDS SET ABOUT OBTAINING THE VAST FORTUNE THAT LIES IN THE STONE VAULTS OF THE BANK!
WHAT IS THE COMBINATION??
YAAH-H-H!!! TAKE THE CANDLE AWAY!! I'LL TELL YOU!!
OUR WORK IS NOT YET DONE!! WE MUST DESTROY MANY PEOPLE UNTIL THE CITY IS PARALYZED WITH FEAR!!
WE'LL LEAVE THE MONEY HERE IN THE PARK-- UNTIL LATER!
HEE-HEE-HEE--
THE EARLY MORNING SILENCE IS BROKEN BY SHRILL SCREAMS OF AGONY AND TERROR AS THE TRIO OF DEATH LEAVE A PATH THROUGH THE CITY THAT IS STREAKED WITH BLOOD!...
OUR MASTER'S WORK WILL BE DONE!
NO! NO! (GASP)
AIEEE!
4

THE SCOURGE OF HORROR CONTINUES UNTIL A SKY STAINED RED ANNOUNCES THE COMING OF DAWN!
SUBW 8TH AV
HELP!
GOOD HEAVENS!
THEY'RE DEMONS!
PANIC STRIKES IN THEATRES... RESTAURANTS, HOMES...
LET ME OUT! HELP! HELP!
--NIGHTCLUBS. WHEREVER GROUPS OF PEOPLE ARE TO BE FOUND!
HELP! POLICE! I'M ON FIRE! HE--AIEEE!
CALL THE FIREMEN!
IT'S GETTING LIGHT! WE MUST RETURN TO OUR MASTER!!
WELL DONE, MY FRIENDS!! I SEE YOU HAVE BEEN SUCCESSFUL!! THE STREETS ARE EMPTY AND EVEN THE AIR SHUDDERS WITH FRIGHT!
5

YOUR WORK IS NOW OVER!! TOMORROW YOU WILL RETURN TO THE WORLD FROM WHICH YOU CAME!! YOU WILL BE NOTHING BUT FIGURES IN A NURSERY RHYME ONCE AGAIN!!
WHEN FALDER HAS LEFT, THE CREATIONS OF HIS DECAYING MIND CROUCH TOGETHER IN THEIR PRISON, THEIR FACES DISTORTED WITH ANGER AND CORRUPTION!...
HE GIVES US LIFE AND WHEN HE IS DONE WITH US, TAKES THAT LIFE AWAY!!
I HAVE NO WISH TO RETURN TO THE WORLD OF CHILDREN'S FANCY!!!
THERE IS ONE THING WE CAN DO! AND IT MUST BE DONE AT ONCE!! HE MUST BE DESTROYED!!!
USING THE BRUTE STRENGTH OF THEIR ANIMAL NATURES, THE DEMONS CRASH THROUGH THE CELLAR DOOR, BENT ON A MISSION OF VIOLENCE!...
HE MUST BE ASLEEP UPSTAIRS!
WE CAN KILL HIM BEFORE HE AWAKES! HURRY!!
SEE HOW HE SMILES--SO PLEASED WITH OUR WORK!!! AND YET HE MEANS TO CRUSH US INTO NOTHINGNESS!! THAT WILL NEVER BE!!
WHO--WHO IS IT??? YOU!! WHAT ARE YOU DOING HERE?? GO AWAY!! NO!! NO!!
6

ONCE MORE THE SHARP EDGE OF THE BLOOD-STAINED CLEAVER RIPS INTO THE FLESH OF A VICTIM --A VICTIM WHO HAD BROUGHT HIS MURDERER INTO BEING!
AWRRRRRRRR
WE CAN BURY HIM HERE IN THE CELLAR-- AND THEN LEAVE THIS PLACE FOREVER!!
WAIT--THE FURNACE!! WHAT AN EXCELLENT OPPORTUNITY TO PLY MY TRADE!! LET ME HAVE THE BODY!!
HIS FACE LIT BY A FIENDISH SMILE, THE BAKER PROCEEDS TO PLACE FALDER'S BODY IN THE ROARING FLAMES OF THE FURNACE--A MONSTER PREPARING HIS WARES AS AN OFFERING TO THE DEVIL!!...
SEE HOW EASILY HE BURNS!! THE FIRE BLAZES AT ITS HIGHEST PITCH!! WE HAVE--
BUT I HAVE DONE NOTHING YET!! THE FLAMES MUST LEAP HIGHER---AND HIGHER!!!
NO! DON'T!! THE PRESSURE IS TOO GREAT!! THE FURNACE WILL--
--AND SUDDENLY THE FURNACE EXPLODES VIOLENTLY, WREAKING DESTRUCTION ON EVERYTHING---AND EVERYONE---IN SIGHT!!...
VROOOOOM!
AND AS THE FLAMES ENGULF THE ROTTING HOUSE OF FALDER, A HARMLESS BOOK OF NURSERY RHYMES BEGINS TO BURN, TAKING WITH IT INTO OBLIVION THE TERRIBLE SECRET OF THE DEMONS OF THE NIGHT!!...
RUB-A-DUB-DUB
THREE MEN IN A TUB
D WHO DO YOU THINK
THEY BE?
E BUTCHER, THE
ANDLESTICK
KER
THE END.
7

PRICES DOWN!
WE MUST CLEAR OUR SHELVES—regardless of cost! Take advantage of this unusual offer while it lasts. You must use the SPECIAL SALES COUPON below in order to get these SPECIAL PRICES!
FLASH!
INDOORS! OUTDOORS! BLACK & WHITE! FULL COLOR! PARTIES! NEWS SHOTS!
"PRESS ACTION" #620 FLASH
An AMAZING Camera. Takes pictures DAY or NIGHT, indoors or outdoors. Sharp BLACK and WHITE snapshots or FULL COLOR photos, using Kodacolor film. 12 Big pictures on 1 Roll of film. Flash attachment snaps on or off in seconds. Catch valuable news photos Win admiration at parties, dances. NOW $4.95
CHECK FOR FILM Special #620 Orthochromatic, 3 ROLLS for.................. $1.00
6.98 NOW 4.95
8.50 NOW 6.98
8.99 6.99
PERFECT for active women and girls. Fine JEWELLED movement in dainty case. GILT hands and numbers. Smart Link Expansion Bracelet NOW $6.98
BEST for active men and boys. SHOCK-RESISTANT and ANTI-MAGNETIC! Luminous Dial! Jewelled Movement! Red Sweep-Second! Expansion Bracelet. NOW $6.99
10.00 7.99
10.50 NOW 8.64
HANDSOME new style in rich GOLD finish case. Smart Midnight Dial is set with 12 Flashing imitation DIAMONDS and RUBIES. Fine Jewelled movement. Luminous Dial, Sweep-Second hand. Gilt Bracelet. NOW $7.99
Ladies' JEWELLED Watch in exquisite little case. GOLDEN SUNBURST style gleams and sparkles in rich beauty. Gilt hands and numbers on two-tone shaded dial. Raised Rock Crystal. Dainty Expansion Bracelet. NOW $8.64
11.00 NOW 8.99
12.00 NOW 9.74
MAGNIFICENT! Two-Tone Dial in contrasting Jet and Pearl-Gray set with 12 Sparkling imitation DIAMONDS and RUBIES. Rich Gilt case. Jewelled movement. Luminous Dial. Sweep-Second hand. Fine Suede Strap. NOW $8.99
DAZZLING! Tiny GOLD finish case in gorgeous design. 12 Flashing imitation DIAMONDS and RUBIES set on rich dial with contrasting Ivory and Jet colors. Superb Jewelled movement. Fine Suede Strap. NOW $9.74
AUTOMATIC DATE INDICATOR
$10.00
TELLS • TIME • DATE • SPEED • DISTANCE
$8.95
SPORTSMAN'S WATCH. Ideal for outdoor use. Measures speed, distance. Luminous Dial, Unbreakable Crystal, fine Jewelled movement. With Expansion Bracelet. $8.95
7 JEWELS
9.95 12.95
Rich BRILLIANT Watch you'll be real proud of! Fine Guaranteed 7 JEWEL Movement. Sparkling Dial set with 11 Flashing imitation DIAMONDS and RUBIES. In GOLD finish case, Dome Crystal. Basketweave Bracelet. NOW $9.95
SPECIAL — This same fine Watch with choice 15 JEWEL MOVEMENT. $12.98
BIRTHMONTH FLOWER WATCH
11.98 15.00
IN 3 JEWEL COLORS
SO BEAUTIFUL! This watch has an exquisitely Flower-Shaped case styled in gleaming GOLD finish, topped by a Petal-face in your own BIRTH-MONTH color. Raised Rock Crystal with rich Gold-figured dial. Fine Jewelled movement. Smart Suede Strap in matching color. NOW $11.98
GENUINE ZIRCON Bridal Set has real ½-CARAT ZIRCON & 7 Sparkling imitation Diamonds. In Genuine 10K GOLD Filled mountings. NOW $4.98
DIAMOND RING for Men. 14K R.G.P. REAL DIAMOND CHIP on Gen. MOTHER-OF-PEARL face. 2 RUBY color side SPARKLERS. NOW $4.98
NO-RISK HOME TRIAL
If not delighted, return for FULL PRICE REFUND. Every article we sell is GUARANTEED! Order from this famous company and be convinced.
IDEAL CO.
BOX 232, MAD. SQ STA., N.Y. 10, N.Y.
GUARANTEED SAVINGS
ROMANCE SET
3.74 4.98
Real Sparkling, Shining BEAUTY! Engagement Ring has 4 Flashing Brilliants and a BEAUTIFUL imitation DIAMOND SOLITAIRE. 7 Twinkling Brilliants in the Wedding Ring 12K GOLD Filled. Both rings NOW $3.74
INITIAL RING
3.79 4.95
A Handsome, Masculine Ring with your own INITIAL set in Raised GOLD effect on a BRILLIANT RUBY-RED color stone. With 2 SPARKLING imitation DIAMONDS on the sides. Rich 14K R G P. NOW $3.79
10K BIRTHMONTH RING
5.98 3.98
Fine BIRTHMONTH RING with your own PERSONAL BIRTHMONTH STONE set in a real GENUINE 10K GOLD Mounting on Solid Sterling Silver shank. Beautifully engraved. Choose Ruby, Emerald or Sapphire colors. NOW $3.98
MAIL THIS COUPON
IDEAL CO., Dept. CS-2T
Box 232 Mad. Sq. Sta., New York 10, N.Y.
SEND NO MONEY! Just cut out pictures of articles desired and attach to this coupon. Pay postman plus few cents postage and excise tax on delivery. THEN EXAMINE IN YOUR OWN HOME. SATISFACTION IS GUARANTEED OR YOUR MONEY BACK.
PLEASE PRINT
NAME
ADDRESS
TOWN STATE
Send RING SIZES, INITIAL WANTED, and your BIRTHMONTH. If you need more room, attach a sheet of paper

You, Too, Can Be Tough!
GREATEST SELF-DEFENSE OFFER EVER MADE!

LIGHTNING JU-JITSU

Master Ju-Jitsu and you'll be able to overcome any attack—win any fight! This is what this book promises you! *Lightning Ju-Jitsu* will equip you with a powerful defense and counter-attack against any bully, attacker or enemy. It is equally effective and easy to use by any woman or man, boy or girl—and you don't need big muscles or weight to apply. Technique and the know-how does the trick. This book gives you all the secrets, grips, blows, pressures, jabs, tactics, etc. which are so deadly effective in quickly "putting an attacker out of business." Such as: Hitting Where It Hurts—Edge of the Hand Blow—Knuckle Jab—Shoulder Pinch—Teeth Rattler—Boxing the Ears—Elbow Jab—Knee Jab—Coat Grip—Bouncer Grip—Thumbscrew—Strangle Hold—Hip Throw—Shoulder Throw—Chin Throw—Knee Throw—*Breaking* a Wristlock, or Body Grip, or Strangle Hold—*Overcoming* a Hold-up, or Gun Attack, or Knife Attack, or Club Assault, etc. etc.—Just follow the illustrations and easy directions, practice the grips, holds and movements—and you'll fear no man.

If This Should Happen to You

Would You Know This Quick Defense?

FREE
How to Perform STRONG MAN STUNTS

With every order we will send you ABSOLUTELY FREE this exciting book! It shows you the *secret way* in which YOU will be able to: tear a telephone book in half—hammer a nail into a board with your bare fist—rip a full deck of cards into two parts—crush and shatter a rock with a blow of your hand—and many other stupendous strong man stunts! All this will be easy for you using the confidential, hidden way shown in this amazing book! Don't miss this amazing combined offer—on our FIVE DAY TRIAL! If not delighted with your results, your money back at once.

only $1.00

HOW TO PERFORM STRONG MAN STUNTS

included FREE!

FREE 5 DAY TRIAL

BEE JAY, Dept. **Dept. HM-IOG**
400 Madison Ave. N.Y. 17, N.Y.

BEE JAY, **Dept. HM-IOG**
400 Madison Ave. N.Y. 17, N.Y.

Please send LIGHTNING JU-JITSU, plus FREE copy of HOW TO PERFORM STRONG MAN STUNTS. If not satisfied I may return both books in 5 days and get my money back.
I enclose $1—Send Postpaid (Sorry, No C.O.D.'s)

Name...
Address..
City...................... Zone...... State............

START YOUR FUTURE TODAY!

Get the facts on NATIONAL SCHOOLS' famous Shop-Method Home Training!

RADIO-TELEVISION & ELECTRONICS

A BRIGHT FUTURE awaits you in booming Radio-TV industry. More than 100 million radio sets, 20 million TV sets, now in use! Backed by National Schools' famous Shop-Method Training from America's Radio-TV Capital you can command good wages in the opportunity-career of your choice — engineer, service-repair, inspector, designer — in radar, electronics — or your own profitable business! Make that bright future come true... start now!

WE SEND YOU COMPLETE PARTS, INCLUDING HIGH-MU TUBES! Yours to keep. You learn by doing, actually build generators, R-F oscillators, and this big Super-Het receiver!

WE SEND YOU THIS STANDARD PROFESSIONAL MULTITESTER! Locates trouble, adjusts delicate circuits — a valuable profit-earner for you when you become a qualified Radio-TV technician!

LEARN HOW YOU TOO CAN EARN TOP MONEY IN THESE BOOMING INDUSTRIES!

LET NATIONAL SCHOOLS of Los Angeles, California, a Resident Technical Trade School for nearly half a century, train you at home for a high-paying future in these big-future industries.

Earn While You Learn!
Make extra money repairing friends' and neighbors' cars, trucks, radios, TV sets, appliances. Every step fully explained and illustrated in National Schools' famous "Shop-Tested" lessons. Latest equipment and techniques covered. You master all phases — start part-time earnings after a few weeks!

YOU RECEIVE FRIENDLY GUIDANCE, both as a student and graduate. Our special Welfare Department is always at your service, to help you with technical and personal problems. You receive full benefit of our wide industry contacts and experience.

DRAFT AGE? National Schools training helps you get the service branch, and higher pay grade you want

APPROVED FOR G. I. TRAINING

AUTO-MECHANICS & DIESEL

EXPANDING AUTO-DIESEL INDUSTRY needs more and more trained men! 55 million vehicles now operating, 6 million more this year — plus 150,000 new Diesel units! Garages, car dealers, transit lines, defense plants, manufacturers, are desperate for the kind of *trained specialists* produced by National Schools' "Shop-Method Home Training." Start *now* on the road to lifetime security. Mail the coupon today!

WE SEND YOU THE TOOLS OF YOUR TRADE! This fully-equipped, all-metal Tool Kit is yours to keep. We also send you a complete set of precision drawing instruments, and Slide Rule. These professional tools help you learn, then *earn!*

NATIONAL SCHOOLS DEPT. 2F-94
Technical Trade Training Since 1905
LOS ANGELES 37, CALIFORNIA
In Canada: 811 West Hastings Street
Vancouver, B. C.
Both Home Study and Resident Courses Offered

FREE! RADIO-TV BOOK & LESSON!

FREE! AUTO-DIESEL BOOK & LESSON!

MAIL COUPON NOW START YOUR HIGH-PAYING FUTURE TODAY!

GET FACTS FASTEST! MAIL TO OFFICE NEAREST YOU!

(mail in envelope or paste on postal card)
NATIONAL SCHOOLS, Dept. 2F-94

| 4000 S. Figueroa Street | or | 323 West Polk Street |
| Los Angeles 37, Calif. | | Chicago 7, Ill. |

Please rush *Free Book & Sample Lesson* checked below. No obligation, no salesman will call.
☐ "*My Future in Radio-Television & Electronics*"
☐ "*My Future in Automotive-Diesel & Allied Mechanics*"

NAME_____ BIRTHDAY_____19___
ADDRESS_____
CITY_____ZONE____STATE_____
☐ Check if interested ONLY in Resident School Training at Los Angeles.
VETERANS: Give Date of Discharge_____

TALES OF TERROR AND SUSPENSE
CHAMBER OF CHILLS

EERIE TALES OF SUPERNATURAL HORROR!
WITCHES TALES

TALES BEYOND BELIEF AND IMAGINATION!
TOMB OF TERROR

STRANGEST TALES OF FEAR AND TERROR!
BLACK CAT MYSTERY

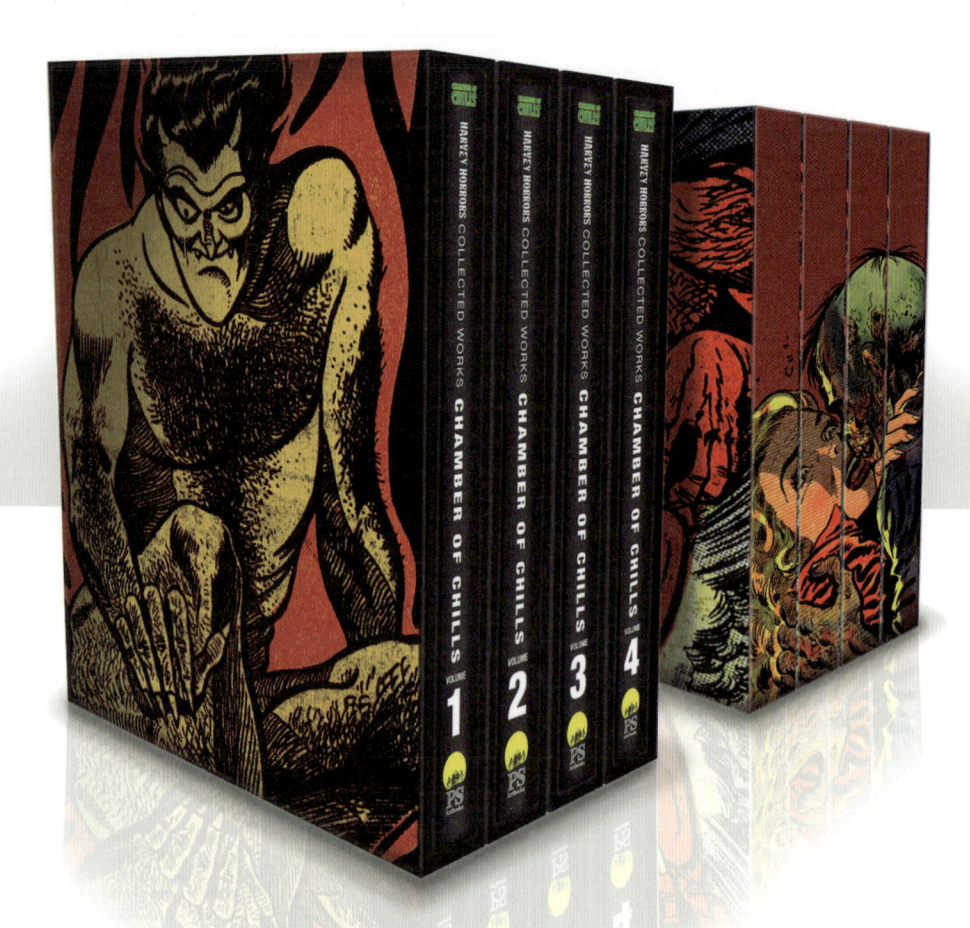

Exclusively for your collection...
300 limited edition slipcased copies.

And you thought we didn't love ya, right? Check these babies out!
Buy the whole run of CHAMBER OF CHILLS slipcased editions and, when all the books
are stacked alongside each other, you'll get this additional neato bigbigbig illustration
of a mouldering corpse trying to get it on with a gorgeous gal —
it's like I've always said . . . these things ain't horror comics: they're romances!
Impress your folks, amaze your friends, astound your analyst and astonish the other guys
in the cellblock. Hey, somebody . . . put on some orchestral muzak and pass me
those tissues — I think I'm gonna cry.

CHAMBER OF CHILLS slipcased and signed edition available from your
favorite comicbooks emporium (so tell 'em, already . . . tell 'em!) or direct from
PS Publishing at http://www.psartbooks.com

But remember, the slipcased signed edition is limited to just 300 copies.

Coming soon . . .
Harvey Horror Softies™

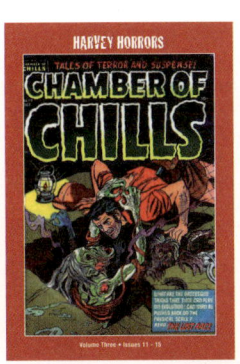

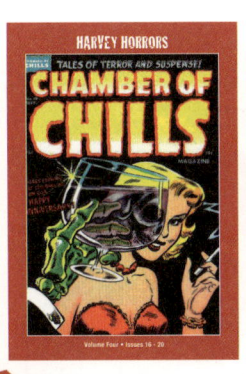

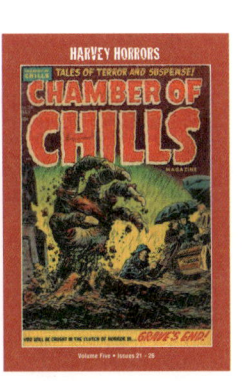

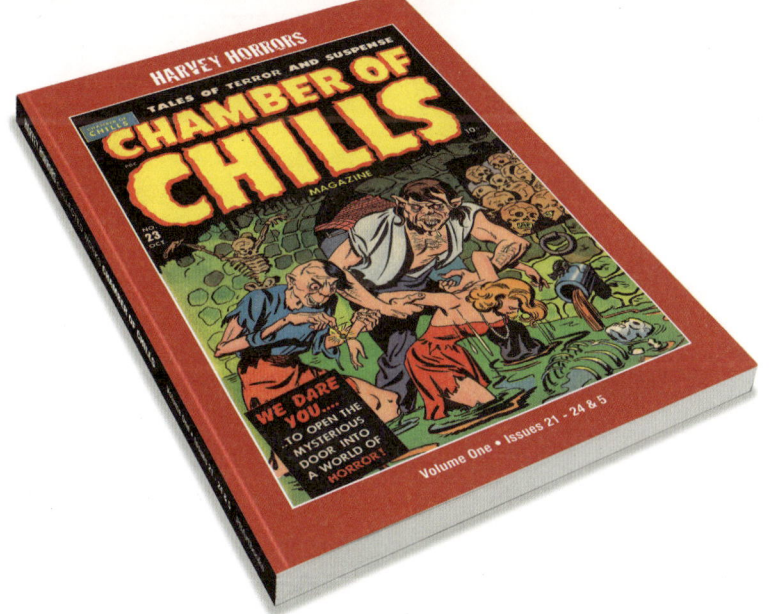

See . . . you talk to us and we listen. What could be easier?
And so it is that, by popular demand, we're making available the whole run of Chamber of Chills
(our very first Harvey Horrors™ title) in a run of sumptuous softcovers, each volume containing
five comicbooks but without the support material featured in the hardbacks.
Harvey Horrors Softies™ . . . the most sensible thing you're going to read about today!

HARVEY HORROR SOFTIES™ available from your local store . . .
but only if you tell 'em! Cover your back and order direct from either
www.psartbooks.com or www.pspublishing.co.uk

COMING SOON FROM PS ARTBOOKS

1949 - 2009
FANTASY & SCIENCE FICTION
60 years of original cover artwork from the magazine

Featuring the profiles of some of the genre's leading artists from it's 60 year history and the chance again to read some of the award winning science fiction that was first published in the magazine.

Look out for this title coming soon from PS Artbooks
for details visit www.pspublishing.co.uk or fantasyandsciencefiction.com

COMING SOON FROM PS ARTBOOKS

THE SOHO DEVIL!

THE · CASEBOOK · OF
BRYANT AND MAY

The critically acclaimed cult detectives Bryant & May are the stars of ten deranged novels that explore London's most arcane mysteries, from its hidden rivers to its secret societies.

And now, thanks to PS Artbooks, they're coming to comics!

Christopher Fowler, a lifelong fan of graphic novels, has teamed with legendary Thunderbirds and Commando artist Keith Page to create a sumptuous, stunningly coloured annual of fun containing a brand-new full-length adventure, a 1960s-set Untold Story, galleries, alternative full-page covers and trivia.
Expect the first volume to become a collectors' item.

You've been warned.

**Look out for this title coming soon from PS Artbooks
for details visit www.psartbooks.com**

ONLY AVAILABLE FROM PS ARTBOOKS

AN ABSOLUTELY ESSENTIAL BOOK ON THE LIFE & ART OF THE SEMINAL CREATOR OF DAN DARE AND THE VERY BEST OF BRITISH COMIC STRIP ILLUSTRATION!

A celebration of the life and art of
Frank Hampson
TOMORROW REVISITED

LIMITED AVAILABILITY

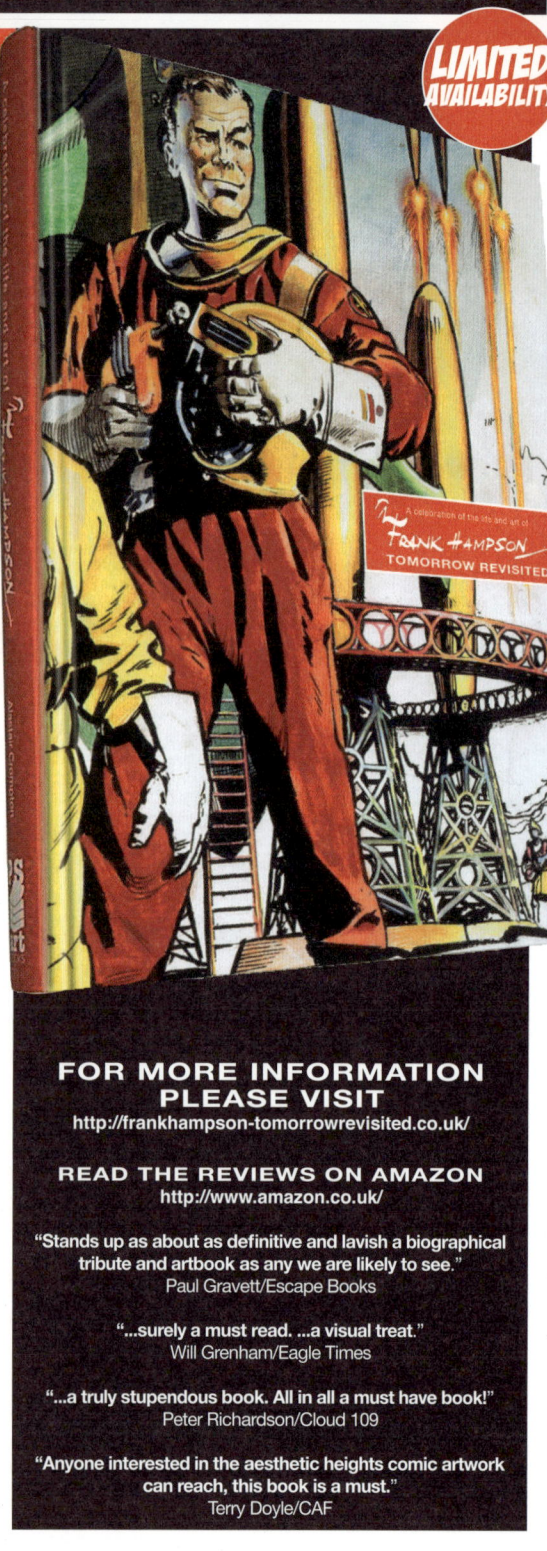

With the best of his original artwork finally printed as it was meant to be seen!

The book is crammed with **superb** examples of **Hampson's best work**, printed in full colour from **original art boards**, so you can see all the **amazing detail** and painstaking backgrounds Hampson was so good at creating. When he had completed **'The Road of Courage'**, Hampson went on to create seven other strip cartoon characters, intended for **Eagle**.
Now these amazing strips are printed for the first time, together with backgrounds and some of the intended story-lines.

Hardcover Bookshop Edition
11" x 8" 208 pages hardback full-colour illustrated biography by Alastair Crompton.
ISBN: 978-1-848631-21-2   RRP **£29.99**

SPECIAL Gold foiled leatherbound Edition in matching gold foiled leatherbound Clamshell Presentation Case
Limited to just 100 signed copies by Alastair Crompton, Peter Hampson, Andrew Skilleter and Don Harley. Complete with a new and unique watercolour/pen & ink illustration by legendary Eagle artist Don Harley.
Plus a limited edition print from the Andrew Skilleter illustration 'HOMAGE Dedicated to the genius of Frank Hampson 1919 - 1985'
ISBN: 978-1-848631-22-9   RRP **£295.00**

FOR MORE INFORMATION PLEASE VISIT
http://frankhampson-tomorrowrevisited.co.uk/

READ THE REVIEWS ON AMAZON
http://www.amazon.co.uk/

"Stands up as about as definitive and lavish a biographical tribute and artbook as any we are likely to see."
Paul Gravett/Escape Books

"...surely a must read. ...a visual treat."
Will Grenham/Eagle Times

"...a truly stupendous book. All in all a must have book!"
Peter Richardson/Cloud 109

"Anyone interested in the aesthetic heights comic artwork can reach, this book is a must."
Terry Doyle/CAF

Order today - only available through PS Artbooks
for details visit www.psartbooks.com or www.frankhampson-tomorrowrevisited.co.uk

AND FINALLY...

Order any **PS Artbooks** title from www.pspublishing.co.uk and receive **10% OFF** and **FREE SHIPPING WORLDWIDE** by entering the code below when you go through the checkout process...

COC004

Offer only valid at www.pspublishing.co.uk

HARVEY